Penny Jordan, one of Harlequin's most popular authors, sadly passed away on December 31st, 2011. She leaves an outstanding legacy, having sold over 100 million books around the world. Penny wrote a total of 187 novels for Harlequin, including the phenomenally successful *A Perfect Family, To Love, Honor and Betray, The Perfect Sinner* and *Power Play*, which hit the *New York Times* bestseller list. Loved for her distinctive voice, she was successful in part because she continually broke boundaries and evolved her writing to keep up with readers' changing tastes. *Publishers Weekly* said about Jordan, "Women everywhere will find pieces of themselves in Jordan's characters." It is perhaps this gift for sympathetic characterization that helps to explain her enduring appeal.

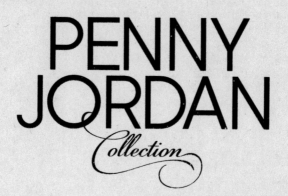

PENNY JORDAN
Collection

CONVENIENTLY HIS

HARLEQUIN®

entertain, enrich, inspire™

ISBN-13: 978-0-373-24961-9

CONVENIENTLY HIS

Copyright © 2012 by Harlequin Books S.A.

The publisher acknowledges the copyright holder of the individual works as follows:

CAPABLE OF FEELING
Copyright © 1986 by Penny Jordan

THE DEMETRIOS VIRGIN
Copyright © 2000 by Penny Jordan

Recycling programs for this product may not exist in your area.

This edition published by arrangement with Harlequin Books S.A.

For questions and comments about the quality of this book, please contact us at CustomerService@Harlequin.com.

® and ™ are trademarks of Harlequin Enterprises Limited or its corporate affiliates. Trademarks indicated with ® are registered in the United States Patent and Trademark Office, the Canadian Trade Marks Office and in other countries.

www.Harlequin.com

Printed in U.S.A.

CONTENTS

CAPABLE OF FEELING 7

THE DEMETRIOS VIRGIN 175

CAPABLE OF FEELING

CHAPTER ONE

'DARLING, I DO HOPE you're going to wear something a little more attractive than that for dinner. You know we've got the Bensons coming and he *is* one of your father's best clients. Chris is back by the way.'

Sophy had only been listening to her mother with half her attention, too overwhelmed by the familiar sense of depression, which inevitably overcame her when she had to spend longer than an hour in the latter's company, to resist the tidal flood of maternal criticism but the moment she heard Chris Benson's name mentioned she tensed.

They were sitting in the garden on the small patio in front of the immaculately manicured lawns and rosebeds. The garden was her father's pride and joy but to Sophie it represented everything about her parents and their life-style that had always heightened for her the differences between them. In her parents' lives everything must be neat and orderly, conforming to a set middle-class pattern of respectability.

She had spent all her childhood and teenage years in this large comfortable house in its West Suffolk village and all that time she had felt like an ungainly cuckoo in the nest of two neat, tiny wrens.

She didn't even look like her parents; her mother was five-foot-three with immaculate, still blonde, hair and plumply corseted figure, her father somewhat taller, but much in the same mould; a country solicitor, who had once been in the army and who still ran his life on the orderly lines he had learned in that institution.

It was not that her parents didn't love her, or weren't kind, genuinely caring people. It was just that she was alien to them and them to her.

Her height, the ungainly length of her legs and arms, the wild mane of her dark, chestnut hair and the high cheekboned, oval face with its slightly tilting gold eyes; these were not things she had inherited from her parents, and she knew that her mother in particular had always privately mourned the fact that her daughter was not like herself, another peaches and cream English rose.

Instead, her physical characteristics had come to her from the half American, half Spanish beauty her great-grandfather had married in South America and brought home. Originally the Marley family had come from Bristol. They had been merchants there for over a century, owning a small fleet of ships and her great-grandfather had been the captain of one of these.

All that had been destroyed by the First World War, which had destroyed so many of the small shipping companies and Sophie knew that her parents felt uneasy by this constant reminder of other times in the shape and physical appearance of their only child.

Her mother had done her best...refusing to see that her tall, ungainly daughter did not look her best in pretty embroidered dresses with frills and bows.

She had disappointed her mother, Sophy knew that. Sybil Rainer had been married at nineteen, a mother at twenty-one and that was a pattern she would have liked to have seen repeated in her daughter. Once too she...

'Of course, Chris is married now...'

Her mind froze, distantly registering the hint of reproach in her mother's voice. 'There was a time when I thought that you and he…' her voice trailed away and Sophy let it, closing her eyes tightly, thinking bitterly that once she too had thought that she and Chris would marry. Chris's father was a wealthy stockbroker and she had known him all through her teens, worshipping his son in the way that teenage girls are wont to do.

She had never dreamed Chris might actually notice her as anything other than the daughter of one of his father's oldest friends. The year he came down from university, when she herself was just finishing her 'A' levels, he had come home.

They had met at the tennis club. Sophy had just been finishing a match. Tennis was one of the few things she excelled at; she had the body and the strength for it and, she realised with wry hindsight, he could hardly have seen her in a more flattering setting.

He had asked her out; she had been overwhelmed with excitement…and so it had started.

Her mouth twisted bitterly. It was not how it had started that she was thinking of now, but how it had finished.

It hadn't taken her long to fall in love—she was literally starving for attention…for someone of her own and she had been all too ridiculously easy a conquest for him. Of course she had demurred when he told her he wanted to make love to her but she had also been thrilled that he could want her so much. Seeing no beauty or desirability in her own appearance, she could not understand how anyone else could either.

She had thought he loved her. She had wanted to believe it. She had thought he intended to marry her. God, how ridiculous and farcical it all seemed now.

Inevitably she had let him make love to her, one hot summer night at the end of August when they were alone in his parents' house...and that night had shattered her rosy dreams completely.

Even now she could remember his acid words of invective when he realised that she was not enjoying his lovemaking, his criticisms of her as a woman, his disgust in her inability to respond to him.

Frightened by the change in him, her body still torn by the pain of his possession she had sought to placate him offering uncertainly, 'But it will get better when we are married...'

'Married!' He had withdrawn completely from her, staring at her with narrowed eyes. 'What the hell are you talking about? I wouldn't marry you if you were the last woman on earth, darling,' he had drawled tauntingly. 'When I get married it will be to a woman who knows what it means to be a woman...not a frigid little girl. You'll never get married, Sophy,' he had told her cruelly. 'No man will ever want to marry a woman like you.'

Looking back, she was lucky to have come out of the escapade with nothing worse than a badly bruised body and ego, Sophy told herself. It could have been so much worse. She could have been pregnant...pregnant and unmarried.

'Darling, you aren't listening to a word I'm saying,' her mother complained a little petulantly, 'and why do you scrape your hair back like that? It's so pretty.'

'It's also heavy, Mother...and today it's very hot.' She said it patiently, forcing a placatory smile.

'I wish you'd have it properly styled, darling...and get some new clothes. Those awful jeans you're wearing...'

Sighing faintly, Sophy put down her book. If only her mother could understand that she could not be what she wanted her to be. If only...

'I've told Brenda to bring Chris and his wife round

to see us. She's a lovely girl,' Brenda was saying. 'An American…they got married last year while we were away on that cruise.' She looked across at her daughter. 'It's time you were thinking of settling down, darling, after all *you* are twenty-six…'

So she was, and wouldn't Chris just crow to know that his cruel prediction all those years ago had proved so correct.

Not that she wanted to get married. She moved restlessly in her deck chair, unwanted images flashing through her mind…pictures of the men she had dated over the years, and the look on their faces when she turned cold and unresponsive in their arms. She had never totally been able to overcome the fears Chris had instilled in her—not of the physical reality of male possession, but of her own inability to respond to him…her own innate sexual coldness. Well it was something no other man was ever going to find out about her. It was her own private burden and she was going to carry it alone.

No male possession meant no children, though. Sighing once again, she opened her eyes and stared unseeingly at her father's neat flower border. Just when she had first felt this fierce need to have children of her own she wasn't quite sure but lately she was rarely unaware of it. She very much wanted children…a family of her own. But she wasn't going to get them, as Chris had so rightly ʌnted her. No man was going to want a woman who was ʌlly incapable of responding to him sexually.

⸱ ring of the telephone bell on the wall outside ⸱ough her despondent thoughts.

⸱ up and hurried into the house via the ⸱. Several seconds later she reappeared, ⸱hy, a frown marring her forehead.

'It's Jonathan,' she told Sophy peevishly. 'Why on earth does he need to ring you at weekends?'

Jonathan Phillips was her boss. Sophy had been working for him for two years. She'd first met him at a party thrown by a mutual acquaintance to which she had gone in a mood of bitter introspection having finally come to the realisation that the happiness and fulfilment of marriage and children would never be hers. She had also been well on her way to getting drunk. She had bumped into him on her way to get herself yet another glass of wine, the totally unexpected impediment of a solidly muscled chest knocking her completely off balance.

Jonathan had grasped her awkwardly round the waist looking at her through his glasses with eyes that registered his discomfort and shock at finding her in his arms.

She had pulled away and he had released her immediately, looking very relieved to do so. She would have walked away and that would have been that if she had not suddenly betrayed her half inebriated state by teetering uncertainly on her high heels.

It was then that Jon had taken charge, dragging her outside into the fresh air, procuring from somewhere a cup of black coffee. Both were acts which, now that she knew him better, were so alien to his normal vague, muddledly hopeless inability to organise anything, that they still had the power to surprise her slightly.

They had talked. She had learned that he was a computer consultant working from an office in Cambridge; that he had his orphaned niece and nephew in his care and tha[t] he was the mildest and most unaggressive man she h[ad] ever come across.

She, in turn, had told him about her languages deg[ree] gained much to the disapproval of her mother, w[ho] believed that a young woman had no need to own living but should simply use her time to find herself a suitable husband—her secretarial abilities, and the dull job she had working in her father's office.

She had eventually sobered up enough to drive home and by the end of the next week she had forgotten Jonathan completely.

His letter to her offering her a job as his assistant had come totally out of the blue but, after discussing it with him, she had realised that here was the chance she needed so desperately to get herself out of the rut her life had become.

It was then that she realised that Jonathan was one of that elite band of graduates who had emerged from Cambridge in the late 'sixties and early 'seventies, fired by enthusiasm for the new computer age about to dawn, and that Jonathan was a world-renowned expert in his field.

Against her mother's wishes she had accepted the job and on the strength of the generous salary he paid her she had found herself a pleasant flat in Cambridge.

She went into the hall and took the receiver from her mother, who moved away but not out of earshot. Her mother disapproved of Jonathan. Tall, and untidy with a shock of dark hair and mild, dark blue eyes which were always hidden behind the glasses he needed to wear, he was not like the bright, socially adept sons of her friends. Jonathan never indulged in social chit-chat—he didn't know how to. He was vague and slightly clumsy, often giving the impression that he lived almost exclusively in a world of his own. Which in many ways he did, Sophy reflected, speaking his name into the receiver.

'Ah, Sophy…thank goodness you're there. It's Louise… the children's nanny. She's left…and I have to fly to Brussels in the morning. Would you…?'

'I'll be there just as soon as I can,' Sophy promised

with alacrity, mentally sending a prayer of thanks up to her guardian angel.

Now she had a valid excuse for missing tonight's dinner party and inevitable conversation about Chris.

'What did he want?' her mother questioned as Sophy replaced the receiver.

'Louise, the nanny, has left. He wants me to look after the children for him, until he comes back from Brussels on Wednesday.'

'But you're his secretary,' her mother expostulated. 'He has no right to ring you here at weekends. You're far too soft with him, Sophy. He's only himself to blame... I've never met a more disorganised man. What he needs isn't a secretary, it's a wife...and what you need is a husband and children of your own,' she added bitterly. 'You're getting far too attached to those children...you know that, don't you?'

Mentally acknowledging that her mother was more astute than she had thought, Sophy gave her a brief smile. 'I like them, yes,' she admitted evenly, 'and Jon is my boss. I can hardly refuse his request you know, Mother.'

'Of course you can. I wish you weren't working for the man. I don't like him. Why on earth doesn't he do something about himself? He ought to tidy himself up a bit, buy some new clothes...'

Sophy hid a smile. 'Because those sort of things aren't important to him, Mother.'

'But they should be important. Appearance *is* important.'

Maybe for more ordinary mortals, Sophy reflected as she went upstairs to re-pack the weekend bag she had brought with her when she had come home, but the rules that governed ordinary people did not apply to near geniuses and that was what Jon was. He was so involved with his computers that she doubted he was aware of anything else.

At thirty-four he epitomised the caricature of a slightly eccentric, confirmed bachelor totally involved in his work and oblivious to anything else.

Except the children. He was very caring and aware where they were concerned.

As she went back downstairs with her case she frowned slightly. Louise would be the third nanny he had lost in the two years she had worked with him and she was at a loss to understand why. The children were a lovable pair. David, ten, and Alexandra, eight, were lively, it was true, but intelligent and very giving. The house Jonathan lived in had been bought by him when his brother and sister-in-law died, and was a comfortable, if somewhat rambling, Victorian building on the outskirts of a small Fen village. It had a large garden, which was rather inadequately cared for by an ancient Fensman and the housework was done by a woman who came in from the village to clean twice a week. Jonathan was not an interfering or difficult man to work for.

'You're going, then!'

Her mother made it sound as though she was leaving for good.

'I'll try and get down the weekend after next,' she promised, aiming a kiss somewhere in the direction of her mother's cheek and jumping into her newly acquired Metro.

Leaving the house behind her was like shedding an unwanted burden, she thought guiltily as she drove through the village and headed in the direction of Cambridge. It wasn't her parents' fault there was this chasm between them, this inability to communicate on all but the most mundane levels. She loved them, of course, and knew that they loved her…but there was no real understanding between them. She felt more at ease and comfortable with Jonathan, more at home in his home than she had ever felt in her own.

Of course it was impossible to imagine anyone not getting on with him. He could be exasperating, it was true, with his vagueness and his inability to live in any sort of order but he had a wry sense of humour…a placid nature…well, at least almost. There had been one or two occasions on which she had thought she had seen a gleam of something unexpected in his eyes. Best of all, he treated her as an equal in all respects. He never enquired into her personal life, although they often spent the evening talking when she was down at his home—which was quite often because, although he had an office in Cambridge, there were times when he was called away unexpectedly and he would summon Sophy to his side to find the papers he was always losing and to generally ensure that he was travelling to his destination with all that he would require.

It was through these visits that she had got to know the children, often staying overnight, and this was not the first time she had received a frantic telephone call from Jonathan informing her of some domestic crisis.

Her mother was right, she thought wryly, what he needed was a wife but she could not see him marrying. Jonathan liked the life he had and he appeared to be one of that rare breed of people who seemed to have no perceptible sexual drive at all. His behavior towards her for instance was totally sexless, as it seemed to be to the whole of her sex—and his own; there was nothing about Jonathan that suggested his sexual inclinations might lie in that direction.

In another century he would have been a philosopher, perhaps.

However much her mother might criticise his shabby clothes and untidy appearance, Sophy liked him. Perhaps because he made no sexual demands of her, she admitted inwardly. Her conviction as a teenager that she was ugly and plain had long been vanquished when she had gone to university and realised there that men found her attractive; that there was something that challenged them about her almost gypsyish looks. A friend had told her she was 'sexy' but if she was, it was only on the surface, and by the time she had left university she was already accepting that sexually there was something wrong. When a man touched her she felt no spark of desire, nothing but a swift sensation of going back in time to Chris's bed and the despair and misery she had experienced there.

Just before she met Jonathan she had been involved with a man she had met through her father—one of his clients, newly divorced with two small children. She had been drawn to him because he was that little bit older... but the moment he touched her it had been the old story and that was when she had decided it was pointless trying any longer. Mentally she might be attracted to the male sex but physically she repulsed them.

When she brought her car to a halt on the gravel drive to Jon's house, the children were waiting for her, David grinning happily. Alexandra at his side.

'Uncle Jon's in his study,' David informed her.

'No, he's not' Alex was looking at the house. 'He's coming now.'

All three of them turned to watch the man approaching them. He was wearing the baggy cord jeans her mother so detested and a woollen shirt despite the heat of the day. His hair was ruffled, his expression faintly harassed.

He was one of the few men she had to look up to, Sophy reflected, tilting her head as he approached. She was five-feet-ten, but Jon was well over six foot with unexpectedly broad shoulders. She frowned, registering that fact for the first time, totally thrown when he said unexpectedly, 'Rugger.'

Her mouth fell slightly open. Previously she had thought him one of the dimmest men she had ever met when it came to following other people's thought patterns and that he should so easily have picked up on hers made her stare at him in dazed disbelief. It really was unfair that any man should have such long, dark lashes, she thought idly...and such beautiful eyes. If Jonathan didn't wear glasses women would fall in love with him by the score for his eyes alone. They were a dense, dark blue somewhere between royal and navy. She had never seen eyes that colour on anyone before.

It wasn't that Jonathan wasn't physically attractive, she mused, suddenly realising that fact. He was! It was just that he carried about him a total air of non-sexuality.

'Louise has gone,' Alexandra told her importantly, tugging on her hand and interrupting her thought train. 'I expect it was because she fell in love with Uncle Jon like the others,' she added innocently.

While Sophy was gaping at her, totally floored by her remark, David remarked sagely, 'No...it was because Uncle Jon wouldn't let her sleep in his bed. I heard him saying so.'

Conscious of a sudden surge of colour crawling up over her skin Sophy stared at Jonathan. He looked as embarrassed as she felt, rubbing his jaw, looking away from her as he cleared his throat and said, 'Uh...I think you two better go inside.'

It couldn't be true. David must have misunderstood, Sophy thought, still trying to take in the mind-boggling implications of the little boy's innocent statement.

She forced herself to look at Jonathan. He was regarding

her with apprehension and…and what…what exactly did that faint glint at the back of his eyes denote? Sophy mentally pictured Louise. Small, petite with black hair and a pixieish expression, the other girl had exuded sexuality and, from the brief conversations Sophy had exchanged with her, she had gained the impression that the other girl had men coming out of her ears.

Jonathan hadn't denied his nephew's innocent revelation, however. She studied him covertly, suddenly and inexplicably granted another mental image. This time it contained Jonathan as well as Louise…a Jonathan somewhat unnervingly different from the one she was used to seeing; his body naked and entwined with that of the other girl's.

Sophy blinked and the vision, thankfully, was gone, Jonathan was restored to his normal self. There was that strange glint in his eyes again though but his voice when he spoke was familiarly hesitant and faintly apologetic.

'I believe she had some strange notion about, er… compelling me to marry her. She wants a rich husband you know.'

Sophy's mind balked a little at taking it all in. That Louise should attempt to seduce Jonathan, of all people, into offering her marriage, seemed impossibly ludicrous. Surely she realised, as Sophy herself had, that he was immune to sexual desire…totally oblivious to it in fact.

Another thought struck her. 'And the other two nannies?' she asked faintly.

'Well, they didn't actually go to Louise's length, but—'

Sophy was too amazed to be tactful. 'But surely they could see that you aren't interested in sex?' she protested.

The dark head bent, and she watched him rub his jaw in his familiar vague fashion, his expression concealed from her as he responded in a faintly strangled voice that betrayed his embarrassment.

'Uh...obviously they didn't have your perception.'

'Well, next time you'll have to employ someone older,' Sophy told him forthrightly. 'Do you want me to get in touch with the agencies while you're away?'

'Er...no. We'll leave it until I get back. Can you stay with them until then?'

'Well, yes...but why delay?'

'Well, I'm thinking about making some other arrangements.'

Other arrangements. What other arrangements? Sophy wondered. As far as she knew, he was the children's only family. Unless——her blood ran cold.

'You're not thinking of abandoning them...of putting them into foster homes?'

'Of course...of course, it's always a possibility.'

Trying to come to terms with her shock, Sophy wondered why she had the feeling that he had set out to say one thing and had ended up saying another...perhaps he was embarrassed to admit the truth to her. 'Surely there must be another way,' she said impulsively. 'Something...'

'Well, there is,' he looked acutely uncomfortable. 'In fact I was going to discuss it with you when I came back from Brussels.'

'Well, why can't you tell me now?'

There were times when his vagueness infuriated her and now was one of them.

'Well...this evening perhaps, when the kids are in bed.'

It was only natural that he wouldn't want them to overhear what he might have to say and so she nodded her head. 'All right, then.'

It was nine o'clock before both children were bathed and in bed. Jonathan's case was packed, his documents

neatly organised and safely bestowed in his briefcase. He
had offered to make them both a mug of coffee while
Sophy finished this final chore and she had urged him to
do so. Up until then he had been hovering like a demented
bloodhound in his study, frantically searching for some all
important piece of paper which had ultimately turned up
under the telephone. Gritting her teeth, Sophy set about
tidying up. Talk about disorganised!

And yet for all his vagueness, Jon could be ruthless
enough when the occasion demanded it, she mused,
pausing for a moment—witness his dismissal of Louise.

She sat down in his desk chair, still half stunned that a
girl as clever and as quick as Louise had honestly thought
she could use her sexual allure to trap Jonathan into
marriage. That must have been what she had thought. No
girl as modern as the children's nanny had been could
possibly have believed that any man would marry her
simply because he had been to bed with her.

Getting up, she made her way to the sitting room most
used by the family. It caught the afternoon sun and she
passed by the deeply sashed Victorian windows staring at
the sunset as she waited for Jonathan.

'Coffee, Sophy.'

For such a large man he moved extremely quietly.
Frowning as she turned round, Sophy was suddenly
struck by the fact that Jonathan was altogether deceptive.
She always thought of him as clumsy and yet when he
was working on his computer he could be surprisingly
deft. She had thought him too obtuse and involved in
his own private thoughts and his work, and yet he was
surprisingly perceptive where the children were concerned
and this afternoon, when he had answered her unspoken
question. He sat down on the ancient, slightly sagging
sofa, the springs groaning slightly as they took his weight.

Standing up he often looked thin and faintly stooping but he wasn't thin, she realised in sudden surprise as he took off his glasses and, putting them down on the coffee table, stretched his body tiredly so that she could see the way his muscles moved beneath his shirt, and they *were* muscles, too...

Still standing by the window she continued to watch him, faintly shocked to realise that in profile his features were attractively irregular and very masculine. Without his glasses he looked different from the normally aesthetic man he appeared to be. He ceased stretching and rubbed his eyes.

'What have you got planned for the children, Jon?'

She sounded more belligerent than she had intended and she half expected him to jump uneasily in apprehension as he was wont to do when she complained because he had upset her neat filing cabinets. Instead, he smiled at her glintingly.

'You sound like a protective mother hen. Come and sit down. I hate having to look up at you,' he added, smiling again. 'I'm not used to it.'

Knowing that she would not get a scrap more information from him until she did as he asked, Sophy took a chair opposite the settee. Beneath that vague exterior lurked a will of iron, as she already knew, but so far she had only seen it in force where his work was concerned.

Suddenly and quite inexplicably she felt tense and nervous, neither of them feelings she was used to experiencing in Jon's presence. To cover them she said quickly, 'Mother was saying only today that you need a wife, Jon, and I'm beginning to think she's right.'

'So am I.' He started polishing his glasses, something he always did when he was nervous, and yet his nervous

movements were oddly at variance with the tense determination she could almost feel emanating from him.

'But not Louise surely?' she began faintly, only to
realise that it was hardly any of her business. And yet the
thought of the pert, dark-haired young woman as Jon's
wife was oddly distasteful to her. She bit her lip and looked
up. Jon was looking at her and it was hard to analyse the
expression in his eyes. All she did know was that it was
unfamiliar to her.

'Not Louise,' he agreed gravely, suddenly looking away
from her, his voice once again faintly husky and nervous
as he cleared his throat and said, totally out of the blue,
'As a matter of fact, Sophy, I was rather hoping that you…'

Her? Jonathan was trying to say that he wanted to marry
her! Oh no, surely she must be imagining things. She must
have misunderstood. She looked across at him and saw
from the hopeful hesitant look he was giving her that she
had not.

'You want to marry me?' she asked disbelievingly, just
to be sure. 'You think we should get married? But that's
totally out of the question.'

She had expected him to accept her refusal immediately;
even to be faintly embarrassed and perhaps a little relieved
by it. After all, he could have no real desire to be married
to her…but to her dismay he shook his head, and plunged
on quickly.

'No, no…listen to me for a moment. You love the kids.'
He paused and while she said nothing Sophy knew she
could not deny it. She heard him clearing his throat again
and held her breath slightly. 'And, er…well…that is…you
don't seem to have a…er…a boyfriend at the present time.'

'I don't want to get married, Jon,' she broke in firmly.
'Not to you nor to anyone else.'

'But you want children, a family.'

There was no hesitation in his voice this time and once again she was astounded by his perception.

'I need a wife, Sophy,' he continued, 'someone to look after the children and to run my home but not someone to…to share my bed.'

The words sank in slowly.

'You mean a…a marriage of convenience?' Sophy asked him uncertainly. 'Is that legal…is…?'

'Perfectly, since no one will know the truth apart from ourselves.'

'But, Jonathan, it's crazy! Just because Louise… Is that why you want to marry me?' she asked, staring at him. 'To stop—'

'It's amazing the lengths some of your sex will go to, to secure what they consider to be a wealthy husband and I'm afraid I am wealthy, Sophy.'

She knew that, and while it had never particularly concerned her she could see, now that he had mentioned it, that he would be quite a financial catch for a woman wanting to marry only for money. Suddenly she felt quite protective towards him.

'The children need you as well, Sophy,' he told her. 'They love you. With you they would be secure.'

'If I don't agree, what will you do…put them in some sort of institution?'

Her mouth went dry at the thought. It was true, she thought bleakly, feeling the pain invade her heart. She did love them…perhaps all the more so because she knew she would never have any of her own.

She watched Jonathan shrug uncomfortably and get up to pace the room. 'What else can I do?' he asked her. 'You know how much time I spend away. It's not fair to them. They need a settled background. They need you, Sophy. *I* need you.'

'To protect you from the likes of Louise.' Sophy agreed drily, adding teasingly, 'Is the thought of an attractive young woman wanting to seduce you really so very repulsive, Jon?' She knew the moment the words left her lips that they were the wrong ones.

Slow colour crawled up under his skin and he turned away from her saying, in a faintly stifled voice, 'I must confess, I do find such determined women...er...intimidating. I had a very domineering mother,' he added almost apologetically.

Busy drawing the inevitable Freudian conclusions it was several seconds before Sophy observed the faintly risible gleam in his eyes and then it was so brief that she decided she must be imagining it. After all what could Jon be laughing at? It was no laughing matter for a man to have to admit he was frightened of the female sex. After all, didn't she herself hold an almost equal fear of his own, albeit for different reasons. Temptingly the thought slid into her mind that as Jon's wife she would be safe for all time from her own fears about her lack of sexuality. There would be no uncomfortable reminders in her unwed state about her inability to respond to his sex nor any fear that others would discover it and mock her for it as Chris had done.

Chris! No one would ever want to marry her, he had said. She took a deep breath.

'All right, then, Jon. I agree. I'll marry you.'

The moment she heard the words she regretted them. Had she gone mad? She couldn't marry Jon. She couldn't but he was already coming towards her, grasping her wrists and hauling her to her feet.

'You will? Sophy, that's marvellous. I can't thank you enough!' He made no attempt to touch her or to kiss her. Then again, why should he? She wouldn't have wanted him to.

Panic set in. 'Jon...'

'I can't tell you what this means to me, to be able to keep the children.'

The children. They would be her family. Already she loved them and found them a constant source of delight. She would have this house, its vast sprawling garden…a whole new way of life which she knew instinctively would delight her. She was no ardent career woman and it was a fallacy these days that housewives and mothers degenerated into cabbages. She would have the constant stimulation of the children's growing minds.

But to marry Jon of all people. She glanced at his tall, slightly stooping frame. Wasn't Jon the ideal husband for her, though? an inner voice asked. Jon, whose lack of sexuality would always ensure that he never learned of her humiliating secret. With Jon there would be no fear of rejection or contempt. Jon wouldn't care that sexually she was frigid—wasn't that the word—she goaded herself. Wasn't frigid the description of herself she was always shying away from, fighting against facing, but the truth nonetheless?

'I…er, thought we might be married by special licence. Perhaps next weekend?'

Special licence. Sophy came out of her daze to stare at him. 'In such a rush. Is that necessary?'

Jon looked apologetic. 'Well, it would save me having to find a new nanny. You can't stay on here, living here while I'm living here too if we're going to get married, Sophy,' he told her with surprising firmness.

She wanted to laugh. She *was* going to laugh, Sophy thought, on a rising wave of hysteria.

Catching back her nervous giggles she expostulated, 'Jon, this is the nineteen-eighties. You're talking like someone out of the Victorian era.'

'Your mother wouldn't think so.'

His shrewdness left her lost for words for a moment. He was quite right. Her mother would most definitely not approve of her living beneath Jon's roof once she knew they were getting married. Neither, she realised hollowly, would her mother be at all pleased by the fact that they *were* getting married. She closed her eyes, imagining the scenes and recriminations. Jon was not her mother's idea of what she wanted for a son-in-law. She would also want a large wedding with Sophy in traditional white, a June wedding with a marquee and...

Groaning slightly she opened her eyes and said faintly, 'Yes, you're right. A special licence would be best and then we needn't tell anyone until afterwards.'

There was a strange gleam in Jon's eyes and this time she was almost sure it wasn't the sunset, reflecting off his glasses, that caused it.

'I'll, er...make all the arrangements then. Do you want to tell the kids or...?'

'I'll tell them tomorrow when you're gone,' she suggested. 'They're always a bit down after you leave, it will cheer them up a bit.'

Although outwardly well adjusted and cheerful children, Sophy knew that neither of them could have gone through the experience of losing their parents without some scars. They were both passionately attached to Jon and she had thought him equally devoted to them. It had shocked her immensely to hear him talk of sending them away...it didn't equate with what she knew of his character somehow.

'I, er...think I'll have an early night,' she heard him saying. 'My flight's at nine and I'll have to be at the airport for eight.'

'Do you want me to drive you?' Jon did not possess a

car; he could neither drive nor, it seemed, had any desire to do so, although he had hired a small car for Louise's use.

'No. I've ordered a taxi. Don't bother to get up to see me off.'

Picking up their coffee cups, Sophy grimaced slightly to herself. She always saw him off on his journeys because she lived in perpetual dread that if she did not he would lose or forget something of vital importance. She made a mental note to tell the cab driver to check the taxi before Jon got out of it and then, bidding him goodnight, carried their cups to the kitchen.

She was tired herself. It had, after all, been an eventful day. On her way to the room she always had when she stayed over at the house and which was next to the children's room, she had to walk past Jon's room. As she did so, she hesitated, still amazed to think that Louise had actually gone into that room fully intent on making love to its occupant. That earlier and extraordinarily disturbing mental vision she had had of their bodies sensuously entwined she had somehow managed to forget.

CHAPTER TWO

SHE WAS AWAKE at half-past-seven, showering quickly in the bathroom off her bedroom. The room which she occupied was what the estate agent had euphemistically described as 'a guest suite'. Certainly her bedroom was large enough to house much more than the heavy Victorian furniture it did and it did have its own bathroom but after all that it fell rather short of the luxury conjured up by the description bestowed on it.

She dressed quickly in her jeans and a clean T-shirt. Her body, once gawky and ungainly, had filled out when she reached her twenties and now she had a figure she knew many women might have envied; full breasted, narrow waisted, with long, long legs, outwardly perhaps, as her friend had once teased, 'sexy', but inwardly... She was like a cake that was all tempting icing on the outside with nothing but stodge on the inside, she thought wryly, pulling a brush through her hair and grimacing at the crackle of static from it.

There wasn't time to pin it up and she left it curling wildly on to her shoulders, her face completely devoid of make-up and surprisingly young-looking in the hazy sunshine of the summer morning.

As she went past Jon's door she heard the hum of his razor and knew that he was up. Downstairs she checked that the cases she had packed for him the previous night were there in the hall. In the kitchen she ground beans

and started making coffee. Jon was not an early morning
person, preferring to rise late and work, if necessary, all
through the night and despite the fact that she knew he
would do no more than gulp down a cup of stingingly hot
black coffee, she found and poured orange juice and started
to make some toast.

He didn't look surprised to find her in the kitchen, and
she knew from his engrossed expression that he was totally
absorbed in whatever problem was taking him to Brussels.

Jon was the computer industry's equivalent of the oil
world's 'trouble shooter'. She had once heard one of his
colleagues saying admiringly that there was nothing Jon
did not know about a computer. Although she knew that
Jon himself would have been mildly amused by her lack
of logic, she herself would have described his skill as
something approaching a deep empathy with the machines
he worked on.

As far as she was concerned the computer world was a
total mystery but she was a good organiser, an excellent
secretary and Jon found her flair for languages very
useful. He himself seemed to rely entirely on the odd
word, nearly always excruciatingly mispronounced from
what Sophy could discover. But then, who needed words
to communicate with a computer? Logic was what was
needed there...and Jon had plenty of that, she thought
wryly as she poured and passed his coffee. Only a man of
supreme logic would propose to a woman on the strength
of needing her to look after his wards and run his home.
And also to keep other women out of his bed, Sophy
reminded herself.

She didn't ask him if he wanted toast, simply pushing
the buttered golden triangles in front of him. He picked
one up, absently bit into it and then, frowning, put it down.

'You know I don't eat breakfast.'

'Then you should,' she reproved him. 'It's no wonder you're so thin.' But he wasn't, she remembered...recollecting that brief, unexpected glimpse of hard muscles.

She heard the sound of a car approaching over the gravel. So did Jon. He stood up, swallowing the last of his coffee.

'I'll ring you on Wednesday to let you know what time I get back. If anything urgent crops up in the meantime—'

'I know where to get in touch with you,' she assured him. She would have to drive into Cambridge later and leave a message on the office answering service asking callers to ring her here at the house. Her mind raced ahead, busily engaged in sorting out the host of minor problems her being here instead of in Cambridge would cause.

She walked with Jon to the taxi...sighing in faint exasperation as he forgot to pick up his briefcase, handing it to him through the open door and then turning to speak to the driver.

'Ticket...' she intoned automatically, turning back to Jon. 'Passport, money...'

He patted the pocket of his ancient tweed jacket, a faintly harassed look crossing his face.

Registering and interpreting it correctly Sophy instructed. 'Stay there, I'll go and get them.'

She found them in a folder beside his bed, and sighed wryly. She remembered quite distinctly handing them to him yesterday and telling him to put them in his jacket pocket.

She ran downstairs and handed the documents to him, catching the driver's eye as she did so. He was looking faintly impatient.

'I'll see you late Wednesday or early Thursday.' She closed the taxi door and waited until it had turned out of the drive.

Back in the kitchen she munched absently at Jon's toast and drank her coffee. She and Jon were to be married. It was incredible, ridiculous…only strangely it didn't seem that way. Already she felt an oddly comfortable pleasure in the thought, as though some burden of pressure had been released. She *wanted* to marry him, she realised with a start of surprise…or at least…she wanted what marriage to him would give her. She frowned. Didn't that mean that in her way she was just as selfishly grasping as Louise? But, unlike Louise, she did care about Jon. As a person she liked him very much indeed. As a man he was so totally unthreatening to her that she found his company relaxing. Marriage to Jon would be like slipping into a pair of comfortable slippers… But on Saturday? She comforted herself with the thought that it was hardly likely that Jon would be able to organise a special licence so quickly. In fact she doubted he would even remember about it once he got on the plane. No doubt the task of sorting out all the arrangements would fall to her once he came back but she would still prefer not to tell her parents until after the ceremony.

Coward, she mocked herself, hearing sounds from upstairs that meant David and Alex were up and about.

She told them about Jon's proposal after breakfast. All three of them were outside, sitting on the lawn. Their open delight and excitement made tears sting her eyes. David flung his arms round her embracing her exuberantly, Alex hanging on to her arm.

'I'm glad he's marrying you and not that nasty old Louise,' she told Sophy. 'We didn't like her, did we, David?'

'No, and neither did Uncle Jon…otherwise he would have let her sleep in his bed.' A thought seemed to strike him. 'Does that mean you'll be sleeping in his bed, Sophy?'

A strange paralysis seemed to have gripped her. She wasn't sure how much the children knew about adult behaviour. They must have learned something from school but their parents had been dead for three years and she could hardly see Jon satisfactorily explaining the so-called facts of life to them. On the other hand, it was pointless telling them a lie.

'No, I won't, David,' she said at last.

She watched him frown and saw that for some reason her answer had not pleased him.

'That's because both of you are so big, I expect,' intervened Alex, ever practical. 'You wouldn't both get in one bed.'

'They would in Uncle Jon's,' David told her gruffly. 'It's huge.'

It was…king size and Jon normally slept diagonally across it. She knew because she occasionally had to wake him up in the morning when he had an early business appointment and he had been up late the previous night working. She had never needed to do much more than lightly touch his duvet mummy-wrapped body though.

'If you're going to get married, why won't you be sleeping in his bed?' he persisted doggedly.

'Married people don't always share the same bed, David,' she told him, giving him what she hoped was a reassuring smile. 'You know what your uncle's like. He often works very late and I like to go to bed early. He would wake me up and then I wouldn't be able to get back to sleep.'

He looked far from convinced, muttering, 'Ladies always sleep with their husbands,' and betraying a innate chauvinism that made Sophy smile. Already at ten he was very, very sure in his masculinity and of its supremacy which was surely something he didn't get from Jon. He was also, as she had often observed, very protective of his sister...and too, of her. She bent forward and ruffled his dark hair.

'Perhaps Uncle Jon doesn't want her to sleep with him, David,' Alex offered, smiling at him. 'He didn't want Louise to.'

The little girl was more right than she knew, Sophy thought grimly, glad of the distraction of the telephone ringing.

As she had half suspected it was her mother, eager to tell her all about the previous evening's dinner party.

'Chris came too,' she told Sophy, oblivious to her daughter's lack of enthusiasm, 'and he brought his wife. Such a lovely girl...tiny with masses of blonde curls and so obviously in love with him. She's expecting their first baby. He asked after you, and didn't seem at all surprised to hear you weren't married.' There was a hint of reproof in her mother's voice. 'He even laughed about it.'

Sophy realised as she replaced the receiver that she was actually grinding her teeth. So he had laughed, had he? Well, he would soon stop laughing when he heard that she *was* married! She stood motionless by the telephone staring blindly out of the study window for a few seconds picturing the ordeal the dinner party would have been for her had she been there...that future dinner parties would have been if it hadn't been for Jon's extraordinary proposal. Without being aware of it had he had saved her from the most galling humiliation and pain. Now she needn't even see Chris, never mind endure his mocking taunts on her unmarried state.

OVER THE NEXT couple of days, cautiously at first and then with growing confidence, like someone blessedly discovering the cessation of toothache and then cautiously exploring the previously tormented area and finding it blissfully whole again, Sophy allowed herself to acknowledge the totally unexpected happiness unfurling inside her.

The children were a constant, sometimes funny, sometimes exasperating joy and one she had never thought to know. For some women the physical act of giving birth was acutely necessary to motherhood but she, it seemed, was not one of them. She could not take the place of the children's dead mother and did not seek to but it gave her a special delight to know that she would have the joy of mothering them. It was this, probably more than anything else, that convinced her that her decision to marry Jon was the right one. She still didn't know how he could even have thought of relinquishing his responsibility for them but then his mind was so wrapped up in his work, that everything else was obviously secondary to it.

On Tuesday evening it rained and they spent the evening going through some old photograph albums David had found in a bureau drawer.

Once she and Jon were married she would ask him if she was to be allowed a free hand with the house, Sophy mused, glancing round the shabby sitting room, and mentally transforming it with new furnishings. At the present moment in time it wasn't even particularly comfortable. Both the sofa and the chairs had loose springs which dug into vulnerable flesh if sat upon.

'Look, Sophy, there's Daddy and Uncle Jon when they were little.'

Sophy glanced down at the open page of the album, her eyes widening fractionally as she studied the photograph Alex was pointing out.

Two lanky adolescent boys stood side by side, one topping the other by a couple of inches. Both of them had identical shocks of near black hair—both of them had the same regular features, hinting at formidably good looks in adulthood.

'Uncle Jon looks really like Daddy there, doesn't he?' Alex commented, wrinkling her nose. 'He doesn't look anything like Daddy did now though, does he, David?'

Thus applied to, her brother studied the photograph briefly and then said gruffly. 'Yes he does…underneath.'

It was an odd remark for the little boy to make and one, Sophy sensed, made in defence of his uncle against his sister's comment.

'Uncle Jon would look much better without his glasses,' Alex continued cheerfully. 'He should wear contact lenses like our teacher at school.'

'He can't,' David told her loftily. 'They don't suit his eyes, and besides, he doesn't need to wear his glasses all the time anyway.'

This was news to Sophy. She had never seen him without them, apart from one occasion she recalled, remembering watching him remove them here in this very room. Then she had been struck by the very male attractiveness of his profile, she remembered and then shrugged mentally. What did it matter what Jon looked like? It was the kind of man he *was* that was important. She already knew all about the pitfalls encountered in getting involved with handsome men. Chris was good looking.

On the Wednesday morning after she had dropped the children off at school she got back just in time to hear the phone ringing noisily.

Thinking it might be Jon, she rushed inside and picked up the receiver, speaking slightly breathlessly into it, barely registering her sudden spearing disappointment at discovering it wasn't him as she listened to the crisp American tones of the man on the other end of the line.

She explained to him that Jon was due back that day, and slowly read back to him the message he had given her, frowning slightly as she did so.

She knew, of course, that Jon often did work for various governments, but that call had been from the Space Center in Nassau, where apparently they were urgently in need of Jon's expertise.

Would that mean he had to fly straight out to Nassau, before they could get married? She shrugged slightly. It didn't really matter when the ceremony took place, surely?

The next time the phone rang it was Jon, ringing her from the airport in Brussels, to tell her the time of his flight.

'I managed to get through a little earlier than planned,' he told her, adding, 'any messages?'

Quickly Sophy told him about the call from Nassau, giving him the number and asking hesitantly, 'Will that mean that you'll have to fly straight out there?'

There was a pause so long that she thought at one point their connection had been cut and then Jon said slowly, 'I'm not sure.' Having rechecked with him the number of his flight, Sophy said goodbye and replaced the receiver.

She would have to ring Heathrow now and check what time it was due to arrive…her mind ran on, mentally ticking off all that would have to be done. The children would have to be collected from school, fed… Yet all the time at the back of her mind was that same ridiculous sense of apprehension.

Suppose Jon had changed his mind about wanting to marry her? How long would he need to be in Nassau? What if he…?

Stop it! she urged herself firmly, reminding herself that less than a week ago there had been no thought in her mind of marriage to anyone, let alone her boss and now here she was in a mild flurry of panic in case they did not marry.

Since the time needed to get to Heathrow and back to meet Jon's flight interfered with the children's school leaving time, and because she knew of no one she could ask to meet them in her place, Sophy rang the school and asked to speak with the headmistress, quickly explaining the situation and getting permission to collect David and Alex on her way to Heathrow just after lunch.

Neither of them stopped chattering during the drive. Oddly enough, this would be the first time either of them had been to the airport and since Sophy always believed in having a little time in hand once they had parked the car she was able to take them to the viewing gallery to watch the flights taking off and landing.

'Will we see Uncle Jon's plane from up here?' David demanded at one point.

Sophy glanced at her watch. Jon's flight was due in in five minutes.

'Yes,' she told him. 'We'll watch it land and then we'll go down to the arrivals lounge to wait for him.

The flight was on time and the plane landed perfectly, so there was no reason for her to feel that odd choking sensation of fear clutch at her throat, Sophy chided herself, especially when she had already watched half a dozen or so planes come and go without the slightest trace of apprehension.

'Look! Look, Sophy...they're putting the stairs up,' Alex told her excitedly, tugging on her hand. 'Can we wait and see Uncle Jon get off?'

Sophy knew from past experience that Jon was likely to be the last to leave the plane but in the face of the little girl's excitement she could hardly refuse. It would be a bit of a rush down to the arrivals lounge...and she always liked to be on hand just in case Jon ran into any problems. There had been that time he had left his passport on the plane and another when he had lost the keys for his briefcase, and the strange buzzing sound emanating from it had drawn frowns and stern looks from the security authorities. In the end it had simply been the alarm he had forgotten to switch off but…

'All right,' she agreed, 'but then we'll have to rush back down.'

'Look…they're getting off now,' David called out, 'but I can't see Uncle Jon.'

As Sophy had guessed, Jon was the last off the plane, a clutch of dark suited business men in front of him, the whole party impeded by the slow progress of an old lady who was having difficulty walking.

One of them, obviously growing impatient, pushed past her. His companions followed suit, and Sophy felt an impotent cry of warning rise in her throat as she saw the old lady lose her balance.

What happened next was so out of character that for a moment or two she actually doubted the evidence of her own eyes.

Jon who never seemed to be aware of what was going on around him…Jon who could often be so clumsy and awkward, moved forward so quickly that Sophy blinked. He caught the old lady before she could fall, supporting her with one arm while he held on to his briefcase with the other. She had never seen anyone move so quickly, Sophy reflected, nor move with such controlled reflexes, unless it was on the sports field.

'Gosh, did you see the way Uncle Jon saved that lady?' Alex asked, round-eyed. 'It was really fast, wasn't it?'

'That's because of playing rugger,' David informed her loftily. 'He used to play when he was at Cambridge.'

'And he did rowing as well,' Alex chipped in, as Sophy drew them away from the viewing windows and towards the arrivals lounge.

She had known about the rugby but it had never occurred to her to think of Jon as an athletic man. Chris who prided himself on his physical fitness spent at least three evenings per week in the gym, jogged and played amateur football but, as far as she knew, Jon did none of these things. There were of course those totally unexpected muscles shaping his shoulders and chest though. Irritated with herself without knowing why, Sophy tried to redirect her thoughts.

For once, Jon managed to negotiate the hazards of passport control and baggage checks without any mishaps.

As he came through the gate Alex slipped her hand from Sophy's and ran towards him. Watching him field her as easily as any rugby ball and transfer his baggage to his other hand, Sophy was forced to admit that there were obviously still some aspects of her future husband that she was not familiar with. The knowledge was a little unsettling. Up until now she had thought she knew Jon very well indeed and had been quite content with the slightly exasperated toleration which was the normal feeling he aroused within her. Indeed she liked feeling faintly motherly and superior to him, she realised. Thoroughly startled by this sudden discovery about herself, she was the last of the trio to step forward and greet him.

'That was really good how you saved that old lady from falling, Uncle Jon,' David was saying. 'We watched you from the gallery, didn't we, Sophy?'

Over David's head the navy blue eyes fixed rather myopically and vaguely on her own.

Alex piped up, 'Yes, Sophy was so surprised that her mouth was open—like this.' She demonstrated

Sophy's stunned surprise far too well, the latter thought uncomfortably, feeling the slow crawl of embarrassed colour seeping up under her skin as Jon continued to look at her.

Her embarrassment heightened when David asked suddenly, 'Aren't you going to kiss Sophy, Uncle Jon? You can do now that you're going to get married.'

'I don't think I will right now, old son, if you don't mind.' Watching Jon ruffle David's hair and listening to the mild, even tone of his voice as he sidetracked his nephew away from such a potentially embarrassing subject, Sophy knew she should be grateful to Jon for what he had done but for some strange reason, what she was really feeling, if she was honest, was a sense of genuine pique. Jon couldn't have made it more plain that the thought of kissing her held absolutely no appeal for him, she thought irrationally. Was she really so unattractive to him that…? She stopped abruptly, stunned by the train of her own thoughts. Of course Jon did not want to kiss her—her or anyone else… indeed that was the reason she had felt able to agree to marry him. So why…?

It must be something to do with all the reunited couples and families freely embracing around them that had aroused that momentary and totally unnecessary fit of pique inside her. Feeling much better now that she had found a logical explanation for her irrational feelings, Sophy hurried to catch up with the others and led the way to where she had parked the car.

CHAPTER THREE

IT WAS GONE ten o'clock, the silence in the study as they both worked a companionable one and then Jon got up and walked over to the window, his back to her as he stared out into the garden. His hair had grown slightly while he was away, Sophy noticed absently and it looked better, even curling faintly into his nape.

'Will you have to fly out to Nassau immediately?' she asked him suddenly, uneasy with the silence she had found so relaxing only seconds before.

He turned round and smiled mildly. 'No, not straight away. Not until Sunday.'

'So…' All at once her throat was dry. 'So you'll still be here for the wedding, then?' Fool, idiot, she derided herself mentally; without him there wouldn't *be* a wedding and she had made him sound like one of the guests.

'Oh, yes…I've made all the arrangements. Got the special licence organised through someone I know in Brussels.'

'You're not having second thoughts, then'

Good heavens, what was the matter with her? What was she asking him for? She was behaving like a total fool.

'No. Are you?'

It was unusual for Jon to ask such a direct question and in such a crisp tone. She shook her head without looking at him, suddenly too restless to stay in her seat. She got up and paced a few steps.

'There is one thing though.' She tensed. 'When we were discussing the...er...style of our marriage I neglected to mention one point.'

'Yes?' Her mouth felt frozen and stiff, so much so that it was difficult to shape the word.

'We have discussed my reasons for our marriage, Sophy, but I don't think we've fully discussed yours. I know you care deeply for the children,' he went on before she could speak, 'but—and please correct me if I am wrong—you could always have children of your own. No, please,' he stopped her when she would have spoken. 'You are, in addition, a very attractive woman.' He saw her expression and his mouth twisted slightly. 'I assure you, Sophy, that even my shortsightedness is not sufficient to blind me to that fact. A woman whom I am sure very many members of my sex would be only too pleased to marry. Men who would want to share with you a far more intimate relationship than the one I am offering.'

It was ridiculous to feel embarrassed but she was.

'I don't want that kind of relationship,' she managed to say thickly, turning away from him.

'I see. This is, I presume, because of the romantic involvement you once had with someone else. You did tell me some such thing the first time we met,' he reminded her.

Her face flamed. She had had so much to drink that night she could not remember what she had told him, but it embarrassed her now to think that she had probably poured out to him all her maudlin misery over what had once been her love for Chris.

'I take it there is no question of this, er...relationship—'

'None at all,' Sophy managed to interrupt huskily.

'I see. Having suffered the pangs of love once and been

hurt by it you have no wish to risk yourself with such an emotion again, is that it?'

It wasn't because she was frightened of *loving* that she was marrying him, Sophy reflected, but it was much simpler and easier to let him believe that than to tell him the truth.

She lifted her head and looked at him, forcing a cool smile. 'Yes, Jon, that is it. The relationship you are offering me, the chance to take over the role of mother to the children, is exactly what I want.'

'Very well...but I must tell you, Sophy, that, er... that there can be no question of me tolerating a sexual relationship which you might form outside our marriage.'

'You mean you wouldn't want me to take a lover?'

'Yes, that is exactly what I mean.'

It was getting dark and in the dusk she could barely see across the room.

The aura that Jon projected when she was not able to see him clearly was unnervingly at odds with the man she knew him to be. Even his voice seemed to have changed, become slightly silky and somehow subtly menacing.

'You have my word that there will be no question of that, Jon,' she told him quietly and truthfully. Not wanting him to ask any more questions she gave a small shrug and added lightly, 'Perhaps, like yourself, I am one of those humans whose sex drive is so low as to be almost nonexistent.'

She thought for a moment he seemed to tense, as though about to say something and wondered uncertainly if she had perhaps hurt or offended him by being so frank. No man would enjoy hearing himself described as virtually sexless, she thought guiltily.

'And this man...the one you loved, Sophy?'

'He's married now. It would never have worked. He

didn't…' she swallowed and told what was in effect merely a half lie. 'He didn't care in the way that I did.'

Suddenly and inexplicably she felt quite exhausted. 'It's been a long day, Jon,' she told him quietly. 'If you don't mind, I think I'll go to bed.'

She knew it would be a long time before Jon came upstairs and, although he smiled vaguely at her as she went out of the room, she sensed that his mind was already on other things.

It had never occurred to her that he might question her motives in agreeing to marry him and was relieved that he had assumed that it was her non-existent love for Chris that had motivated her. It rather surprised her that he should remember her wine-induced confidences on the night of the party when they first met. She had been feeling particularly down at the time otherwise she would never have said a word.

'SO ARE YOU REALLY and truly married now?'

Sophy nodded her head, and smiled at Alex. She was still quite amazed that Jon had managed to arrange the details without any hitch.

She had also been a little surprised at his insistence on a religious ceremony but had said nothing. In all honesty she had to admit there had been something comforting and right about the familiar Church service that had soothed away a lot of her last minute doubts. Now it was too late. They were married, Jon looking exceedingly uncomfortable in a suit he must surely have had since he came down from university and so heavy that it was totally unsuitable for a hot July day, she thought exasperatedly.

'I'm going to have to do something about your clothes,' she told him wryly. 'They're atrocious.'

'Are they?' He stared vaguely at her, frowningly perplexed, and yet as he turned his head slightly to answer a question David had asked him, Sophy was sure she saw his mouth curl faintly in amusement. What had she said to amuse him? Nothing, surely?

There was no question of a honeymoon of course. Jon was flying to Nassau in the morning and following the early morning wedding ceremony Sophy intended to spend the afternoon checking that everything was in order for his trip. 'I'll have to give my mother a ring and tell her the news,' she murmured, blenching a little at the thought of that ordeal.

'Er, no. I think it would be better if we drove over there now and I told her.'

She stared at Jon unable to believe her ears. Jon was terrified of her mother.

'Jon, there's really no need,' she began.

'I think there's every need.' The cool firmness in his voice silenced her protests and even David and Alex stopped what they were doing to look at him. Probably because they were so unused to hearing their uncle speak in such decisive tones.

'But you don't have time. Your flight—'

'Is all perfectly organised, thanks to my wife. And we have plenty of time. We'll have a quick snack lunch and leave straight away. All of us.'

And so it was that at three o'clock in the afternoon Sophy found herself drawing up outside her parents' front door. Once she had stopped the car Jon clambered out, knocking his head as he did so. The front passenger seat of her car was far too small for him. It was easy to overlook how big a man he really was, Sophy reflected, watching him help the children out.

'You're going to need a larger car.'

'Only when you're travelling in it,' Sophy told him

wryly, leading the way through the garden to the back of her house, knowing that on such a lovely day her parents would be in the garden.

They were, but they weren't alone and Sophy came to an abrupt halt as the ring of her high-heeled sandals on the crazy paving path caused the tall blonde man lazing in a deckchair to turn his head and look at her.

'Sophy...good heavens.'

He hadn't changed, Sophy thought, registering the lazy insolence in his voice, the mockery with which his glance slid over her body, as though reminding her that he knew how lacking in femininity it really was.

'Sophy?' Her mother suddenly appeared through the french windows, carrying a tray of tea things, her mouth rounding in astonishment. 'You didn't say you were coming over this afternoon.' There was just a touch of reproof in her mother's light voice, and Sophy suppressed a faint sigh. Her mother liked everything done by the book, arrangements properly made... She should have thought about that.

'It's my fault, I'm afraid, Mrs Marley.'

For the first time since seeing Chris she became conscious of Jon standing beside her.

'Your... Oh!' There was no mistaking the displeasure in her mother's voice and Sophy felt her guilt turn into quiet despair.

'Where's Father?' she asked, scanning the garden.

'He's showing Felicity, my wife, the new rose arbour he's building,' Chris answered easily. 'I rather think I shall have to watch my wife, Mrs Marley,' he added charmingly to Sophy's mother, 'I do believe she's falling rather hard for your husband.'

Listening to her mother's girlish trill of laughter, Sophy was overwhelmed by a familiar feeling of alienation. She didn't fit in here in this neat overtidy garden…in this peaceful English family scene. Chris was more at home here than she was, she thought bitterly, and her mother more pleased by his company than she ever was by hers.

'Nonsense, you foolish boy,' she chided Chris. 'Anyone can see that Felicity only has eyes for you. She's so much in love with you.'

She could almost see Chris preening himself under her mother's flattery and suddenly Sophy felt the most acute dislike for him. She had fallen out of love with him a long time ago but this dislike was a new and gloriously freeing thing, giving her the courage to say calmly, 'Mother, there's something I—'

'I think I should be the one to break our news to your parents, Sophy.'

The deep and commanding tones of Jon's voice broke through her own, silencing her. She blinked and turned round to study him, wondering at this sudden assumption of masculine authority, half expecting to see someone else standing behind her. But no, it was still Jon, looking thoroughly hot and uncomfortable in his baggy cords and thick woollen shirt, his glasses catching the sunlight and obscuring his eyes from her.

Their voices had obviously carried down the garden, and Sophy watched her father walking towards them accompanied by Chris's wife. She was every bit as pretty as her mother had said but Sophy felt no envy for her, only a certain wry sympathy. Unless he had changed dramatically, Chris did not have it in him to be loyal and loving to one woman, even one as lovely as this. Her pregnancy barely showed, her light summer dress showing off her summer tan.

'Darling, let me introduce you to an old friend of

mine.' Irritatingly it was Chris who took charge of the proceedings, drawing his wife towards him.

'Oh, not another old flame, darling....' The fluttery voice was unexpectedly hard, and instantly Sophy revised her opinion. Chris's wife was not the delicate little flower she looked. On the contrary, she was every bit as hard as Chris himself, she thought inwardly, taking the hand the other girl extended.

'Heavens, aren't you tall!' Innocent blue eyes slid upwards over Sophy's body. 'You must be almost six foot.'

'Five-ten actually.' From somewhere Sophy managed to summon a cool smile. Six foot made her sound like a giantess—a freak almost.

'And this,' Chris was looking past Sophy now to Jon and the children. His mouth curled in a dazzling smile, laughter lighting his eyes as he looked at Jon. 'You can only be Sophy's boss!' His glance swept derisively over Jon's appearance, and Sophy could almost see him comparing it with his own. The immaculate white cotton jeans, the cotton knit jumper in blues and greens banded with white...the elegantly cool casualness of his appearance in comparison to Jon's.

Chris's rudeness did not surprise her, but the blindingly fierce stab of mingled anger and protectiveness she felt, did. She reached out instinctively to take Jon's hand in her own, unaware of the deeply gold glitter in her eyes as she said firmly, 'And my husband. That's what we came to tell you... Jon and I were married this morning.'

'Married!' Her mother looked shocked and disbelieving, and Sophy was furious with her when she cried out, 'Oh, Sophy...no...how could you do this to us?' her eyes dropping immediately to her daughter's tautly flat stomach.

Fury kicked sharply beneath her heart as Sophy realised what her mother was thinking.

'Sophy is not pregnant, Mrs Marley.' She was still holding Jon's hand and the firmness with which he squeezed her fingers was intensely reassuring. She was beginning to feel as though she had strayed into a bad dream. She had known her parents would not be pleased… but that her mother should actually think she was pregnant. She was burning with embarrassment on her parents' behalf. Neither of them had made the slightest attempt to put Jon at ease or to make him feel welcome.

'Then why such a rush?' her mother complained. 'Why didn't you say anything the last time you were here?' She looked suspiciously from her daughter's flushed face to the one of the man behind her. 'I know what it is,' she said shrilly. 'You've married her so that you'll have someone to look after those children. I told you he was making use of you.'

Sophy couldn't endure it. She turned blindly towards Jon saying huskily, 'I think we'd better leave,' but the hard pressure of his hand holding hers held her back.

'You do your daughter a severe injustice, Mrs Marley,' he said very gently. 'I married Sophy quite simply because I love her.'

Even her mother fell silent at that, rallying enough to add huffily, 'Well, I still think you should have told us, Sophy. I can't understand why you should have got married in such a hole-and-corner fashion at all…and in such a rush!'

'Because I want to be with Jon and the children, Mother,' she managed evenly. 'That was why.'

'Well you can't expect your father and me not to be shocked. Not even to tell us about the wedding—'

'I had the most wonderful wedding,' Felicity cut in cattily. 'Five hundred guests and a marquee on the lawn at home. Mummy said it was her dream come true for me.'

'Good old Sophy! Married, eh?' Chris was eyeing her with open mockery. 'I never thought I'd see the day. You know, old boy, I once actually bet Sophy that she'd never find a man to marry her.'

'Well, you see, you were wrong.'

Was she imagining the faint rasp beneath Jon's mild tone? She must be, Sophy thought, her skin suddenly burning with furious anger as she heard Chris saying quite distinctly to his wife, 'Not as wrong as all that.' He turned to Jon and taunted smilingly, 'She told you about our little bet, then, did she?'

'She may have mentioned it.' Jon looked totally vague and disinterested. 'But it was a very long time ago, wasn't it?' He said it so mildly that there seemed to be no outward reason why Chris should colour so hotly until Jon added equally mildly, 'Really I'm surprised you even remember it. Sophy can't have been more than nineteen or so at the time.'

The children were pressing quietly against her side, and Sophy turned to her mother pinning a smile on her face.

'I think we'd better leave now, Mother. Jon has to fly to Nassau in the morning.'

'*Jon* has to...' Chris's eyebrows rose. 'Dear me, how very unromantic but then no doubt as you're both living in the same house you've already had ample opportunity to—'

'Become lovers?' Jon seemed totally oblivious to Chris's malice. 'Oh, about the same opportunity as any other couple of our age and situation in life,' he agreed cheerfully.

'Mummy would never have agreed with me living with Chris before we were married,' Felicity chipped in dulcetly, earning an approving glance from *her* mother, Sophy noted.

'No?' Really, it was quite incredible how Jon's face changed when he removed his glasses. He had been in the act of polishing them when Felicity spoke and there was quite definitely something almost satanic about the way his eyebrow rose and his mouth curled as he looked across at the other girl.

'And we were engaged for twelve months.'

'A wildly passionate romance.'

Sophy couldn't believe her ears. Chris was red to the tips of his ears and an unbecoming tightness had formed round Felicity's bowlike mouth. Sophy was quite sure that Felicity and Chris had been lovers well before the date of their marriage; how could it be otherwise when Chris was such a highly sexed man. She had no doubt that the little act Felicity was putting on was purely for her parents' benefit.

'I think we'd better leave.'

Neither of her parents made any attempt to stop them going but Sophy didn't realise that Jon had misinterpreted the reason for her tiny sigh of relief, as they got in the car and he said in an unusually clipped tone. 'Don't let it bother you, Sophy. The loss is theirs, not yours. Good heavens,' he muttered in a much more Jon-like tone, 'can't they see that you're worth a dozen of that stupid, vain little butterfly?'

Wryly she smiled across at him, and said huskily. 'Thanks...for everything.' She was remembering how he had claimed that he loved her, protecting her from Chris's malice.

ALL FOUR OF THEM were subdued on the way back, although it wasn't until the children were in bed and they were alone that Jon again raised the subject of her parents.

'I hope you weren't too hurt by what happened today, Sophy,' he began uncertainly. 'If I had known…'

'I stopped being hurt by the fact that I'm not the daughter my parents wanted, a long time ago,' she said calmly. 'But I was angry, Jon…angry and embarrassed that they should show such a lack of welcome and politeness to you.'

He shrugged and looked slightly uncomfortable as though the emotion in her voice embarrassed him.

'I don't suppose we'll see that much of them,' he rumbled clearing his throat. 'Er…Benson, I suppose he's the one.'

'Yes,' Sophy agreed tightly. 'Yes, he's the one…but it's all over now, Jon. My life and loyalty lie with you and the children now.'

'Yes…'

Why should she feel that there was a certain wry irony in the way he was looking at her?

SOPHY SPENT THE fortnight Jon was away in Nassau organising her new life. From now on Jon would work mainly from home when he was in England, so she moved some of the files from the office in town to his study. She managed to do some fence building in her relationship with her parents but admitted to herself that it could never be the warm one she had once wanted. As she had firmly told her mother, Jon was now her husband and he and the children came first. Grudgingly this had been accepted, but Sophy doubted that there would be much contact between them in the future.

She also spent time planning how she was going to refurbish the house. Jon had given her permission to do exactly what she wanted and had also told her she need not stint on cost. She had been a little surprised to discover that he had also organised a new bank account for her and had placed into it what seemed to be an impossibly large sum of money.

She had always known that he was a reasonably wealthy man but she had not realised, until now, exactly how wealthy. Perhaps because Jon himself never looked like an even remotely prosperous man, never mind a rich one.

That was something else she would have to do something about, she decided on the Wednesday before he was due back. She would go through his wardrobe, discover what size he was and start restocking it. She still burned with resentment when she thought about the way Chris had looked at him.

If ever she had worried about falling for Chris again she did so no longer. Indeed it amazed her that she could ever have found him the slightest bit attractive. The wounds he had inflicted still hurt but she found the man himself contemptible.

Sophy was familiar enough with the clothes Jon wore not to be too surprised by the collection of hairy suits and worn tweed jackets she discovered in his wardrobe. Rather wryly she wondered what on earth it was about the colour of mud that attracted him so much but other than that, her search was briskly impersonal and she stopped only to check on sizes before closing the wardrobe door and leaving the bedroom. Its furniture, like that in the rest of the house, was of no particular style or beauty. Jon had told her that he had bought it with the house. She planned to get rid of the majority of it, but not until she had decided what was to take its place.

Her decision made, she didn't waste any time. After picking the children up from school she drove briskly towards Cambridge.

'You're going the wrong way,' Alex told her.

Sophy shook her head. 'No, I'm not. I want to do some shopping. Your uncle needs some new clothes.'

The silence from the pair in the back seat confirmed Sophy's view that she was far from the only one to note the lack of appeal about Jon's attire.

He must be boiled alive in those heavy cords he favoured and those woollen shirts, especially during the heatwave they were having at the moment.

She wondered wryly how on earth he was getting on in Nassau. When she had remarked that he was going to be hot he had told her that the temperature in computer operational rooms was always maintained at a set point, no matter what the climate.

It didn't take long to park the car and Sophy knew Cambridge well enough to head straight for a small street which housed half a dozen or so exclusive shops catering for both men and women.

She stopped outside the window of one of them surveying the grey blouson jacket with its royal blue lining and the matching, pleated trousers, also trimmed in blue.

'I don't think Uncle Jon would like that,' David informed her doubtfully.

Sophy grinned. She could just picture Jon's face if she produced something as radically modern as that. No, what she had in mind was something rather more conservative.

'Then we won't go in,' she told David equably, herding the pair instead to a shop two doors down which stocked a range of Jaeger clothes for men.

It took her over an hour to make her final choice, which included two shirts, one in silk and one in cotton in a shade of blue which Alex had informed her was exactly the same as Jon's eyes.

Having chosen those it had proved fairly easy to pick out the basis of a new wardrobe for him based almost entirely on blue and cream—including a softly blue herringbone tweed jacket which she was pleased to see bore no resemblance whatsoever to the ones already in his wardrobe.

Having paid the bill and escorted the children outside she remembered that both of them seemed short of casual T-shirts and that she could do with some inexpensive casual wear herself. The heatwave which had begun in the early part of the month was still persisting with no let-up forecast and her wardrobe was not really geared to such hot weather.

It only took them a few minutes to walk to Marks & Spencer, where she gave in to Alex's entirely feminine whim to be kitted out in a range of separates in pretty pinks. Even David allowed himself to be persuaded into a pair of brushed denim jeans in a soft olive colour to which Sophy added several T-shirts and thin cotton jumpers.

'Look over there. Uncle Jon would look nice in that, Sophy,' Alex informed her, having by now thoroughly entered into the spirit of things.

On the display she had indicated, Sophy could see a range of men's casual separates in a soft, pale sand colour.

She went over to inspect them, trying in her mind's eye to imagine Jon dressed in the well-cut brushed denim jeans and matching bush shirt, the toning grey and sand jumper draped casually over the model's shoulders adoring Jon's, and failed miserably. Even so…he *was* short of jeans, and she could always bring them back. Recklessly she bought a full outfit, adding socks and the shoes that the assistant pointed out to her, only remembering on the way out that she hadn't got anything for herself.

A rack of pale green cotton shorts with matching patterned short-sleeved shirts and plain T-shirts caught her eye, and while she was studying them Alex tugged away from her hand, coming back several seconds later proudly clutching a mint and white bikini plus a pair of matching shorts.

'Look at these, Sophy,' she demanded. 'They would look great with those shorts and things. You could sunbathe in the garden in them.'

It was years since she had worn a bikini—four at least. That was how long it had been since she had last been abroad. She no longer felt so ashamed of her body that she could not bring herself to reveal more of it than actually necessary, but even so…a bikini?

'I don't…' she began and then seeing how Alex's face fell, amended her remark quickly, 'I don't see why not! Come on, let's go and pay for all these things, and then as a special treat…'

'Fish and chips?' they both begged together.

Laughing, she gave way.

'Uncle Jon hardly ever lets us have chips,' David complained on the way home. 'He says they aren't good for you.'

'He's quite right,' Sophy agreed, firmly squashing any hopes David might have that she would not. There was a rather neglected vegetable plot in the garden and she had already tentatively wondered about planting it next year. There was obviously some of her father in her after all, she thought wryly. She must make a mental note to get the ground cleared and dug over in the winter, not by the arthritic James who normally did the gardening but by someone younger and stronger. Instead, James could supervise the planting next year.

'I wish we had a swimming pool,' Alex sighed when they reached home. 'A lovely, cool swimming pool.'

'Try a cold shower instead,' Sophy suggested wryly, laughing when both children groaned.

This evening the heat was almost oppressive, but there was no sign of any impending storm.

'What are you going to do with Uncle Jon's new clothes?' Alex asked after supper. 'Keep them as a surprise?'

'No, I think I'll just hang them up in his wardrobe ready for him.'

'But what about his old ones?' Alex demanded. 'Are you going to throw them away?' She posed the question with a certain amount of delighted relish.

'Er...no, I...'

'You could send them all to the cleaners,' David offered practically and knowingly. 'That way he would have to wear the new ones but he wouldn't be able to shout because you'd thrown the others away.'

Slightly startled, Sophy glanced at David's downbent head. She hadn't even thought he was listening to their conversation, but he was obviously far more astute and mature than she had known.

'Uncle Jon never shouts,' Alex protested loyally.

'No, but he does get angry,' David told her calmly, 'Not many people know about it, though, because he just speaks very quietly.'

He was right, Sophy reflected. Jon did go very quiet when he was angry, and somehow that controlled softness in his voice was even more alarming than if he had bellowed at full volume.

'I'm glad Uncle Jon married you and not Louise,' Alex confided happily to Sophy, leaning her head affectionately against the latter's knee.

'Don't be silly,' David told his sister scornfully. 'Uncle Jon would never have married Louise.'

'No, he was frightened of her,' Alex confided naively. 'He always used to go...er...er...a lot more when she was there.'

If it was possible David looked even more scornful. 'That wasn't because he was frightened of her, silly,' he told Alex. 'It was because...' He went bright red and closed his mouth, an expression crossing his face that somehow reminded Sophy of Jon.

'Because what, David?' she pressed, as confused herself as Alex plainly was.

He wouldn't look at her, scuffing the toe of his shoe against the worn carpet, eventually muttering, 'Oh, nothing...'

Wise enough not to press him, Sophy was nevertheless still bewildered. As she got them ready for bed she told herself that it could be nothing more than a little boy's natural desire to protect those closest to him, and David adored his uncle, there was no doubt about that.

CHAPTER FOUR

ON FRIDAY MORNING, after dropping the children off at school, Sophy made her way to Cambridge to do the weekly food shopping. Exhausted by the heat and press of people in the shops she was only too pleased to get back inside her car. The air inside was stifling, and winding down the windows, she drove home.

She was expecting that Jon would ring sometime during the course of the day to tell her what flight he would be on. She had bought smoked salmon for dinner tomorrow because she knew he liked it, and there was a ham in the fridge which she had baked especially the day before. When she got back she would make up his bed...and perhaps pick some flowers for the sitting room.

Abruptly she shook her head. Their marriage was a business relationship, she reminded herself severely. Jon would be understandably embarrassed if he came home to find she had made a lot of special arrangements to welcome him. But even while she acknowledged the sense of her thinking there was a niggling sense of disappointment as though she had been denied some small pleasure she had been anticipating.

Although it was only eleven o'clock, the heat when she stopped the car on the drive, was enervating. Listlessly she ferried the shopping into the kitchen and put it all away. The cotton T-shirt she was wearing was sticking uncomfortably to her skin, and there were grubby marks

on her matching cotton denim skirt where she had touched
it with her hands. The pretty, pale blue outfit, so crisp and
neat when she went out, now looked tired and limp. She
had rolled her hair up into a knot to keep it out of the way
and the back of her neck ached from the weight of it and
the shopping.

Tiredly she made her way upstairs, going first to the
airing cupboard and collecting fresh bedding for Jon's
room.

The door was slightly open and with her arms full she
had to lean against it to open it wider to get in.

'What…?'

She heard the startled exclamation as she stepped into
the room and shocked by the total unexpectedness of it she
stood stock still, her eyes flying wide open as she clutched
the bedding to her.

'Jon?' Her voice sounded rusty and thick, totally
unfamiliar…as unfamiliar to her as the figure standing
beside the bed, she thought wildly, swallowing the lump
of tension which seemed to have invaded her throat, totally
unable to withdraw her stunned gaze from the body of the
man standing in front of her, completely naked apart from
the brief white towel wrapped round his hips.

Perhaps it was the whiteness of the towel that made
Jon's skin look so brown, she thought hazily, silently
observing the healthy sheen on skin that adhered firmly
to male muscles. His hair was wet, which must explain
why in its damp tousled state and the way it clung to his
scalp it should so suddenly make her aware of the faintly
arrogant masculinity of Jon's features. The blue eyes were
narrowed and watchful but curiously brilliant and sharp
for someone who needed such strong glasses, the dark
hair clinging to his head mirrored in colour and texture

by that which ran diagonally and vertically along the male planes of his body.

The most curious sensation was washing over her. She felt so weak that her legs barely seemed able to support her. With a small moan she tottered to the bed, sinking down onto it still clutching the bedding.

'Sophy! Are you all right?'

So it was Jon! No mistaking that pleasantly mild voice.

'No. Yes…it's the heat,' she managed disjointedly, suddenly uncomfortably aware that the heat of which she spoke came from inside her body and not from outside. Anxiously she clutched the linen even closer to her chest, shamingly aware of the sudden tension in her nipples. For goodness' sake, she chided herself mentally, pull yourself together. She had seen men without their shirts on before— without even as much as Jon was wearing. At least, she had seen Chris… But his body had been nothing like Jon's, she realised weakly. Nothing like as tautly masculine. She had never for instance possessed the slightest desire to reach out and touch Chris, to see if his skin felt as silkily warm as it looked.

'What are you doing here?' Her voice sounded breathless and too high. She could see Jon frowning as she managed to drag her bemused gaze from his body to his face. Thank God he was short-sighted, she thought wryly, feeling her face flame for what she might have betrayed to him if he hadn't been.

'I…er…got an earlier flight then I intended. Sorry if I shocked you.'

Shocked her? There was nothing but mild vagueness in his voice; nothing to make her feel that he didn't just mean his apology in the sense of having shocked her by his unexpected arrival, and yet… She glanced at him covertly and told herself she was imagining things in thinking that he was ascribing her shock as being due to his semi-nude state.

'Here, let me take those from you.' He stepped towards her and instantly she was aware of the clean, soapy smell of his body. Instinctively she shrank back, still clutching the bedding, all too uncomfortably aware that her body was still betrayingly aroused by the sight of him but he was already reaching for the linen in her arms and somehow Sophy found herself relinquishing it. As he moved back, his hand brushed against the curve of her breast and immediately Sophy jumped.

'Sorry about that... I can hardly see a damn thing without my glasses.' The words were muffled as he turned away from her.

His back was as brown and well-muscled as his chest, Sophy thought, admiring it and his legs, long and roughened by dark hairs. As she stood up and caught sight of her own reflection in the mirror she decided it was just as well Jon was short-sighted. Where her T-shirt clung to the contours of her breasts it clearly revealed their aroused contours and the firm peaks of her nipples.

'I'll, er... I'll come back and make the bed later,' she managed to say as she hurried out of the room and into the protection of her own.

It was only later when she had managed to restore a little of her normal calm, with a cool shower and a change of clothes that she realised she had said nothing to Jon about the changes she had made in his wardrobe.

She found him downstairs making some coffee, and what was more he was wearing the sand-coloured stonewashed denims she had bought for him in Marks & Spencer.

'Something seems to have happened to my clothes,' he remarked equably when she walked in. 'I don't suppose you happen to know anything about it.'

'Er...they're at the cleaners. I thought...that is we thought...well, with the heatwave continuing, I had to get the children some lighter things and...' Her voice petered out uncomfortably as she realised just exactly what she had done.

'You were thoughtful enough to get some for me at the same time,' Jon concluded gently. 'That was very wifely of you.'

'Well, if you don't like them, you don't have to...that is...' Realising that she was gabbling, Sophy forced herself to stop. What was happening to her? Anyone would think she was frightened of Jon when in actual fact he was the mildest and gentlest man alive.

'I thought those awful hairy suits and ancient cords were too heavy for this weather,' she told him simply, 'but if you don't like what I got for you they can easily be changed.'

'You're not trying to change me into a male model, by any chance?'

A smile lurked at the corner of his mouth and taking heart from it, Sophy shook her head, adding impishly, 'Some hope, you're far too big and muscular.'

She wasn't sure which of them looked the more surprised. A deep mortifying burn of colour spread over her skin but fortunately Jon seemed to be oblivious to it. He had turned away from her to watch the coffee filtering. He was probably as embarrassed as she was herself, she thought wryly, and wondered why she should find that thought so dismal. What did she want? For Jon to do something macho like take her in his arms and let her see how well her description matched reality? Jon wasn't like that. He wasn't interested in her, or any other woman, sexually. She knew that.

'I'm tired... I think I must be suffering from jet lag. I think I'll go out and have a sleep in the garden.'

Did he want to sleep or was he simply wanting to escape from her company? Sophy wondered, watching him wander outside. Well at least now she could go up and make his bed but when she got upstairs she found that he had made it for himself. She shrugged dismissively. Of course Jon was used to looking after himself...or was this a polite way of informing her that he did not expect to find her in his room again?

Moved by some impulse she wasn't ready to define Sophy went into her own room and changed into the bikini Alex had picked out for her. She had already worn it once earlier in the week and that exposure to the sun had turned her skin the colour of clotted cream.

When she got outside Jon was lying sleeping in a deck chair, oblivious to her presence. She tried to settle down; first by stretching her body out on the towel she had brought downstairs with her and then by going back inside to dig out a paperback book to read. It was all useless. A restless nervous energy seemed to possess her body, making it impossible for her to simply lie down and relax. When Jon had been asleep for just over a hour she got up and started on some desultory weeding. The activity helped to soothe her a little but her heartbeat seemed to be much faster than usual, her skin damp with a heat that wasn't entirely due to the sun.

At two o'clock she abandoned her self-imposed task and went back inside, getting out the blender to make lemonade, her hands moving deftly as she did so. Leaving it to cool she used what was left from the jug she had made the previous day to fill two glasses, putting them on a tray and then defiantly carrying it outside to where Jon still slept.

The sun had moved slightly and now slanted across his face, revealing the taut bone structure. The hair flopping on to his forehead looked disarmingly soft and silky. Would it feel like Alex's?

Suddenly aware of what she was doing Sophy snatched back the hand she had extended towards his face and instead placed it firmly on his shoulder, shaking him.

He was awake immediately blinking his eyes slowly as they focused on her. 'I've brought you some lemonade. If you sleep too much now, you won't be able to tonight.' How cross and ungracious she sounded, Sophy thought. What was the matter with her?

Jon reached for his glasses which he had discarded several feet away on the lawn and Sophy bent to retrieve them for him at the same time. It was a small task she had performed more times than she could count but this time, as she handed them to him and watched him put them on, for some reason her body felt as though it were in the grip of a deadly paralysis.

It was impossible for her to move away even when his slightly stunned glance slid over her, taking in the brevity of her bikini. She could almost see him cringing away from her, she thought bitterly, immediately stepping back and retreating to her own towel. Why on earth hadn't she put on something more discreet, covered herself up a little more? If she carried on like this much longer he might begin to think that she was…what? Trying to seduce him?

Prickles of heat ran across her skin, her body tense. What a ridiculous thought…of course she didn't want that. After all, one of the main reasons she had married him had been to escape from any sort of sexual involvement.

Confused and alarmed by both her thoughts and her feelings Sophy got up and rolled up her towel.

'Had enough?' Jon asked mildly, watching her.

'It's almost time to pick up the children.' It was true, after all. 'I've left all your post on your desk if you want to go through it.'

There, that made her feel better—restored their relationship to its proper footing—reminded her that there was nothing between them other than a business relationship and a certain amount of cool friendship, and that was the way she wanted it, she told herself firmly. She had the children to share her love with...

Love! She froze, staring blindly into space. How on earth had that crept into her thoughts?

The sudden touch of Jon's fingers on her bare arm made her jump visibly and swing round. He was standing right behind her, holding his empty lemonade glass, watching her rather uneasily.

'Sorry if I shocked you. I just wanted to say I'll come with you to get the kids.'

'Very well. It won't take me long to shower and get changed.'

For the first time it hit her that she was behaving far from naturally with Jon. She no longer felt completely at ease in his company...far from it.

She was as good as her promise, arriving back downstairs again within half an hour, dressed comfortably in a soft, mint-green cotton skirt and a pastel-toned, patterned shirt.

Jon had his usual battle clambering into the car. 'Next week we get a new car,' he told her wryly as she drove off, adding, 'Is there any make in particular that appeals to you?'

Sophy shook her head.

'I'm told BMW make a good vehicle,' Jon offered. 'How about them?'

'They're very expensive,' Sophy warned him.

Beside her, Jon shrugged. 'That doesn't matter…safety and comfort do.'

'You managed to sort everything out in Nassau, then?' Sophy asked when the silence began pressing painfully on her screaming nerves.

'Yes. Oh, that reminds me…Harry Silver, my contact over there, will be coming to stay in Cambridge soon for a week or so. He and I used to be at university together. I'd like to invite him and his wife over for dinner one night.'

He might just as well be an employer giving his housekeeper her instructions, Sophy thought bitterly, immediately chiding herself for the thought. *She* was the one at fault, she was reacting in a totally unfamiliar and unreasonable way and had been ever since she walked into Jon's room and found him there.

That must be it, she decided, relieved to have hit upon an explanation for her behaviour. It was the shock. The shock of seeing him, a mocking inner voice demanded, or the shock of *how* she had seen him?

'Is anything wrong?'

Sophy bit her lip. So even Jon had noticed her tension. 'No…I think it's just this heat,' she gave him a brief smile. 'Sometimes I find it a bit wearing. Unlike you.'

A strange silence followed her last two words, and for some reason Sophy felt constrained to explain them. 'That is…you've got such a good tan you must enjoy sunbathing.'

'There were times when I had to wait for them to run certain tests. Lillian was kind enough to take pity on me and let me have the use of her patio and pool whilst I was doing so.'

'Lillian?' Sophy asked sharply, taking her eyes off the road for a second to look at him.

'Harry's assistant,' Jon responded vaguely. 'She had a condominium near the Centre, with a communal pool.

It was much more convenient to stay there whilst I was waiting for the results of the tests rather than to go back to my hotel.'

A sensation unlike any other Sophy had experienced in her life was boiling through her; a mixture of anger, resentment and—jealousy—she recognized dully. She was jealous of this unknown Lillian, Jon spoke about so easily. Was that why he didn't want *her* in his room because…? Abruptly she brought her careering thoughts to a halt. Why should Jon have reacted any differently to this Lillian than he did to any other woman? What on earth was the matter with her? She was behaving like a jealous wife suspecting her husband of having an affair.

Fortunately they had reached the school and in the excitement of the children greeting Jon she was able to bring herself under some sort of control.

Tea was a light-hearted meal, although she herself took a back seat in the conversation.

'Uncle Jon looks nice in his new clothes, Sophy,' Alex announced approvingly. 'We got you some in blue because that's the same colour as your eyes,' Alex informed her uncle, dimpling a smile at him, 'and Sophy has sent all your old things to the cleaners.'

THE WEEKEND WAS as hot as the rest of the week had been and they spent most of it in the garden. Sophy was having trouble sleeping. Each day seemed to drain a little more out of her, and yet she was so tensely wound up that she just could not relax. Her whole body was gripped by a peculiar and unfamiliar tension which left her nerves on edge and made her muscles ache. But at least no one else seemed to be aware that anything was wrong with her.

Even worse than her growing inner tension was the compulsion she seemed to have developed to be with Jon, and yet when she was with him, she felt acutely tense, unable to so much as sit down for more than five minutes at a time.

The trouble was, she thought exhaustedly on Sunday afternoon, that while she had suddenly become aware of him as a man, Jon simply did not see her as a woman at all. He would be deeply embarrassed if he knew the reason for the way she occasionally found herself looking at his body. She was embarrassed herself. Embarrassed and annoyed. What was the matter with her? Even with Chris, when she had been deeply in love with him, she had felt no stirring of desire within her to know him as a man.

Perhaps it was simply the fact that Jon was so elusive… so completely disinterested and unaffected by her that was making her behave like this, she decided, turning over onto her stomach and trying to relax. She could feel the heat of the sun seeping into her skin as she tried to come to terms with the reality of such contrary behaviour. Was that it? Subconsciously did she see Jon as a challenge? Was that what was making her behave so oddly? A desire to arouse within him a male reaction to her as a woman? But why? That was totally against everything she had felt when she first married him.

At last, worn out by her thoughts, she fell into a light sleep.

SOMEONE WAS TOUCHING her skin with the lightest of movements, strong fingers moving against her spine. She moved languorously beneath them, enjoying the slow sweet wave of sensuality rippling through her.

Jon…Jon was touching her…caressing her as…

'That's it, Uncle Jon, you've got him now.'

The breathy whisper close to her ear made her tense and wake up properly, quickly rolling over.

Alex was squatting beside her, Jon bending over her holding one palm cupped.

'You were being explored by a caterpillar,' he told Sophy with a smile. 'We were trying to remove him without disturbing you.'

A caterpillar! It was because of a caterpillar that Jon had touched her? Indignation and disappointment merged sharply within her. For some reason she almost wanted to cry.

'Hey, come on, it's nothing to be frightened of. In fact he's very handsome, look.' Jon extended his cupped palm towards her so that she could admire the furry creature and dutifully she managed to summon a thin grimace, her colour changing suddenly as she remembered how her body had slowly arched beneath what she had thought was his caress. Had he realised? She darted a quick glance at his face but it was mildly unreadable, nothing in the blue eyes to tell her what he might or might not have thought, and for the first time she realised how very, very good Jon was at concealing his thoughts and feelings.

After that it became ever harder for her. For one thing it was no longer possible for her to deny to herself that sexually she was attracted to Jon. That more than that she wanted to touch him and be touched by him in return. She tried to tell herself that she was having these odd fantasies simply because she knew they were impossible and that in that way they allowed her to imagine she was sexually responsive without running the risk of Jon discovering she was not, since he would never be her lover.

What made it worse was that she seemed forever to be bumping into Jon in a semi-nude state. He was working at the house and either he was just coming out of the bathroom clad in nothing more than a brief towel, or he was in the garden, sunbathing in a pair of faded denim shorts that fitted him so snugly they might almost be indecent.

And that was not all. Sophy knew she was challenging his sexuality. Knew it and despised herself for it, and yet seemed unable to do anything about it. She wanted him to react to her as a woman. But why? If he did she knew what the outcome would be. As far as she was concerned sex was something that was painful and humiliating. She was thoroughly confused by herself and what she was doing. Thoroughly and completely.

CHAPTER FIVE

'I'VE GOT TO GO into Cambridge today—I don't know when I'll be back, probably later this afternoon.'

They were all having breakfast and Sophy inclined her head in acknowledgement of Jon's remarks. From today she was going to start behaving differently, she told herself. It was pointless trying to attract the attention of a man who had told her that he had no interest in her sex. She had been acting very irresponsibly, and she was lucky that Jon was so completely oblivious to what she had been trying to do, otherwise he would have been very embarrassed.

Jon's taxi was due to arrive while she was taking the children to school, and driving them there she found herself fretting over the fact that she was not at home to see Jon off. That such a small thing should have such a tremendous effect on her, was worrying. She tried to rationalise her behaviour by telling herself she was naturally worried because she knew that Jon was bound to forget some all important something but deep down inside she knew it was not that. She wanted to be there physically, to be with him, she realised on a sudden start of disquiet, not liking the conclusions that went with the realisation.

When she got back, the house felt empty. She performed her normal household chores automatically and then went into the study to check through the morning's post. There was nothing that was particularly urgent but there was a letter with an airmail stamp from Nassau addressed to

Jon and marked 'Private and Confidential'. Was it from his friend? Or was it from the woman who had allowed him to use her apartment and pool? She didn't like the sensations stirring deep inside her. She had no right to be jealous of any friendships Jon might form outside their marriage and besides, what was there to be jealous of? She had known when she married Jon what their marriage would be and she had been happy with that knowledge. She had also believed that Jon was as immune from sexual desire as she felt herself to be. And so he was, she told herself firmly, but somehow she couldn't stop herself from thinking that maybe in Nassau he had discovered a woman who could break through his barrier of indifference. The thought made the unpleasant sensations lodged beneath her breastbone, increase. Tension held her body in a vice-like grip, jealousy tormenting her mind with mental pictures of Jon's tanned body entwined with that of some unknown but lithely desirable woman whose face she could not see.

Telling herself that it was the heat that was making her so on edge and prickly, Sophy went upstairs, stripping off her clothes and standing beneath the shower, letting the cool water slide off her over-heated skin.

Only when it was starting to raise goosebumps did she emerge from the water, towelling herself dry briskly. It was too hot to work indoors, and she was too restless to concentrate on anything. She might as well spend what was left of the morning sunbathing, she thought wryly, hunting through her drawer for her bikini. As she stood up she caught a glimpse of her nude body in the mirror. The sun had turned her skin a soft, golden colour banded by cool white where her bikini had concealed it from the hot rays. The colour suited her, she recognised, her attention caught and held by her own reflection. It was years since she had looked at her body—really looked at it that was, perhaps

not even since that débâcle with Chris. Now she studied
what she saw, with careful eyes, noting the slender strength
of her shoulders, the fullness of her breasts tipped with
deep coral, the flatness of her ribcage and the slight swell
of her stomach. She had a woman's body now, not a girl's,
curved and feminine but those curves and the warm glow
of her skin offered a promise the woman inside could not
fulfill. She might look entirely female and desirable, but
she was not, she reminded herself bitterly, and the desire
she felt to reach out and touch Jon and to be touched by
him in return must surely spring from some contradictory
impulse inside her which knew quite well that it was safe
to torment her in this fashion since there was no question
of that desire ever being fulfilled. No doubt if Jon did
make any attempt to touch her she would recoil from him
as she had done from all the others, fearing his discovery
of the truth about her; that she was just an empty sham
of femininity.

She was supposed to be sunbathing, not standing here
letting herself get morose, she reminded herself, hurriedly
tugging on her bikini and going downstairs.

The garden was slumbrous with heat, bees droning
drunkenly from flower to flower, heavy with pollen.
Above her the sky was a hot blue arc, the grass beneath her
feet was drying out in patches where the sun had burned it.
She really ought to do some weeding, she thought, wryly
glancing at the untidy beds, but she was too tired. Since Jon
came back she hadn't been sleeping very well, something
she had refused to admit to herself until now.

She lay on her stomach, pillowing her head in a cushion,
and then remembering the small white bank of flesh across
her back, reached behind herself and unfastened the ties
of her bikini. It was completely private in the garden and
she was unlikely to be disturbed.

In her sleep she moved, turning on to her side, and curling her body inwards slightly into a position that was automatically defensive.

Someone was touching her, stroking her skin. Jon! A wave of pleasure shivered through her and she stretched beneath his touch like a cat asking to be stroked, opening her eyes and saying his name with sleepy delight.

Only it wasn't Jon, it was Chris, the expression on his face frighteningly resentful as his fingers tightened round her unprotected breast, squeezing painfully...hurting her.

She was instantly and icily cold, shrinking instinctively from him, any thought she had entertained that she might be turning into a sex-starved female ready to welcome any man's caresses dying instantly and completely. The only sensation Chris's touch aroused was one of intense revulsion. Angrily she reached out to push him away, but he was too strong for her, burying his fingers in her hair, and tugging painfully on it as he pushed her back on to the ground.

Somewhere she could hear the sound of a car and struggled harder but all her struggles seemed to do was to inflame him further. She could feel the hot urgency of his breath against her skin, his voice thick and angry as he muttered, 'You bitch...you deserve this!' His mouth was on hers, his teeth savaging her tightly closed lips. She could hear footsteps coming towards them, shaking the sun-baked ground so that she could feel the movements against her ear. She tried to push Chris away thankful that they were about to be interrupted but was unprepared for the suddenness with which he released her and stood up. She turned her head, but the sunlight dazzled her for a moment.

'I think you'd better tidy yourself up a bit, darling, your husband's here.'

What an actor Chris was, pretending that she had welcomed his touch when…Jon…Jon was back! She sat up quickly, struggling with the ties of her bikini.

'Why not let me do that for you?' Chris was actually daring to reach out and touch her.

'Get away from me!' She stood up shakingly, securing the strings, and looked at Jon. He seemed to be studying the progress of a particularly heavy bee.

'Thank heavens you're back. Chris forced himself on me, Jon,' she told him thickly. 'I was asleep and…'

'Oh come on, darling, surely you can do better than that?' Chris was jeering now, but she could see the very real hatred in his eyes, and wondered at the cause of it. Why was Chris doing this to her? And then instinctively she knew. He had never forgiven her for her frigidity and now he wanted to punish her for daring to find sexual happiness with someone else.

'I'm sure your husband is nowhere near as stupid as he looks.' He looked tauntingly at Jon, who returned the look with mild curiosity. Grinning at her, Chris walked away from them. Sophy watched him go in complete silence. Hadn't Jon understood what she was telling him?

She heard a car engine fire and then slowly purr down the drive and bitter resentment flooded through her body. It was wrong and unfair that Chris should be able to walk away like that after physically molesting her and humiliating Jon. She took a deep breath and found that she was shaking…tense with an anger that had to find an outlet.

'Do you realise that if you hadn't come back when you did he would probably have tried to rape me?' she cried emotionally. 'And you let him just walk away. You… for God's sake, Jon, what kind of husband are you?' she demanded thickly.

Had he even heard what she was saying? He appeared to be studying one of the flowers but at last he lifted his head and looked at her in that rather abstracted way of his, glancing away to remove a piece of fluff from his shirt-sleeve before replying.

'The kind who feels that when he discovers his wife in the arms of an old lover, discretion might possibly be the better part of valour,' he told her calmly. 'You must admit that I had no way of knowing whether his embrace was welcome or not, Sophy.'

'But I'm married to *you*,' she pointed out despairingly. God, didn't he even care the smallest bit? Wasn't he the slightest bit jealous or resentful? If she had been the one to walk into that scene…if she had discovered him…

'Our marriage does not give me the right to assume physical chastity on your part.'

'But you said—' She broke off. What was the use? Jon plainly did not care one way or the other, despite his statement before they were married that he would not expect her to take lovers.

'Always logical and calm, that's you, isn't it, Jon?' she demanded bitterly. 'You're just like one of those damned computers you're so fond of—incapable of any human emotional reaction.'

She pushed past him and ran into the house, going straight up to her room, and flinging herself face down on the bed. She badly wanted to cry, in a way she couldn't remember doing in years. Chris's attack had frightened her; her body ached with the tension that fear had brought, and her breast throbbed where he had hurt her but what hurt far more, was Jon's calm indifference. He had stood there and let Chris insult him and her, and he had said nothing—not even when she had told him that Chris had attacked her. He had looked at her with his face wiped clean of all expression—totally emotionless.

She was his *wife* for heaven's sake. She had a right to expect his protection…his…his championship. Chris had hurt and frightened her…and primitive though it was, she acknowledged that she would have liked to have seen Jon hurt and frighten him in return. Had he believed what Chris had said to him? She swallowed suddenly turning over and staring unseeingly up at the ceiling. Surely not? She had been so caught up in her own feelings, in the shock of listening to Chris's lies, that it had never occurred to her that Jon might believe them, that he might take what had happened at face value.

Did he really think she was that sort of woman? The sort who would break the solemn vows of marriage… who would allow herself to be involved with a man who was already married, who had once treated her with such contempt? Didn't Jon know her at all?

Tiredly she got up, but instead of going downstairs and apologising to Jon for her outburst and talking to him about what had happened as she knew she should, she showered again, and dressed slowly, too heart-sick to face him. Her apology would have to wait until she was in a calmer frame of mind. As she went downstairs, she heard sounds from the study and guessed that he was working. Well, that gave her an excuse not to interrupt him.

He was still working when she went to fetch the children back from school. For once their energy and chatter gave her no pleasure. She felt drained and deeply unhappy. This was the time when she needed a mother or a sister to talk to, she thought wearily, someone who would understand what she was feeling.

When they got back, an unfamiliar brand new car was parked outside the house. Mentally admiring the sleek lines of the very expensive BMW, Sophy shepherded the children inside the house. The car probably belonged to one of Jon's clients, many of whom were extremely wealthy men and she paused outside the now silent study, reluctant to disturb a business meeting.

The children it seemed had no such qualms and burst in before she could stop them, Alex shouting out, 'We're back, Uncle Jon!'

Reluctantly she followed them to find that Jon was alone in the study. She glanced round it and then looked at him. 'I thought you had someone with you,' she told him. 'There's a car outside.'

'Yes.' For once he looked neither vague nor embarrassed. 'It's yours… I bought it for you this morning.'

She had to sit down to get over the shock. Jon had bought that car for her! 'But it's so expensive! Jon…'

'You said we needed a larger car and from what I can discover, this one seems to combine all our requirements. Of course, if you would prefer something else?'

She shook her head. 'No…no, of course not.'

'It's ours?' David was wide-eyed with excitement. 'Come on, Alex,' he instructed his sister, 'let's go and have a look at it.'

In the end all four of them went back outside, the children enthusing over the car whilst Sophy admired it in stunned silence. She was pleased to see that it was fitted with rear seat belts for the children. When she got inside she found it both luxurious and well equipped. At David's insistence they went for a short drive although she was not familiar enough with the car's automatic gears and power steering system to take them very far.

'Jon, it's…it's very generous of you,' she said haltingly when they got back. The words seemed to stick in her throat, her earlier accusations lying painfully on her

conscience. She wanted desperately to call back those
earlier ugly words, but found she could not do so in front
of the children, and it still tormented her that Jon might
actually have believed Chris's lies.

Supper was an uncomfortable, silent meal; even the
children, it seemed, were aware of the tension existing
between the two adults. Afterwards, when Sophy was
supervising their baths, she was shocked when Alex asked
her hesitantly, 'Have you and Uncle Jon quarrelled?'

'No, of course not,' she assured the little girl swiftly.
'Whatever gave you that idea?'

'I'm not sure.' She screwed her eyes up and then said
slowly, 'P'haps because at tea time it just felt like you had
quarrelled…all stiff and sharp somehow.'

'Well, I promise you we haven't,' Sophy reassured her
kissing the curly head, feeling guilty because she was the
one responsible for the atmosphere Alex had so accurately
described.

She had to apologise to Jon, she acknowledged mentally
as she tucked both children up in bed, and kissed them
good night. She had been wrong to say the things she had
to him and then to flounce off in a huff. After all why
should she expect him to…to behave like a real husband?

She pressed her fingers to her temples which were
throbbing with tension and pain. What had she been hoping
for when she ran inside like that? That Jon might follow
her…that he might… What?

Telling herself that there was nothing to be achieved by
putting off the evil moment she went back downstairs. Jon
was in the study. She knocked briefly and then went in,
her eyes immediately going to the letter in front of him,
recognising it as the one which had arrived from Nassau
that morning.

'This is from Harry Silver,' he told her. 'Confirming

his visit. He'll be bringing his wife with him. I thought we might have them here to dinner.'

'Jon, I must talk to you.' How stiff and unnatural her voice sounded. She could see Jon frowning and her heartbeat suddenly increased, thudding nervously into her chest wall. 'I'm sorry,' she said miserably, 'and I owe you an apology… I shouldn't have spoken to you the way I did…I was wrong.'

'Yes, you were,' he agreed evenly, standing up and coming round the front of the desk. There was a look in his eyes she found hard to recognise, but instinctively she took a step backwards, only to find that Jon was right in front of her. 'Very wrong,' he murmured softly reaching out and pulling her into his arms. 'I'm not a computer, Sophy…and I *am* capable of feelings. These feelings.'

His mouth moved on hers with unerring instinct, caressing, arousing…seducing her own, she recognised in stunned bewilderment as it parted eagerly responding to the warm exploration of his lips like the thirsty earth soaking up rain. The bruises Chris had inflicted were forgotten, her whole body felt hollow and light, empty of everything but the sensation of Jon's mouth on her own. He was kissing her in a way she had always dreamed of being kissed, she acknowledged hazily, with an expertise and knowledge she had never imagined he would own. Immediately she tensed but Jon wouldn't let her go.

'Oh, no,' he whispered, transferring his mouth from her lips to her ear. 'You don't get out of this so easily, Sophy.' One hand left her body to cup her face, firmly but without the pain Chris had inflicted on her.

He had removed his glasses and this close to, his eyes were an unbelievable blue…not sapphire and not navy but something in between, she thought hazily, unable to tear her own away from them. Jon was still speaking and it took several seconds for her to register the words.

'After all,' he said silkily, 'wasn't it this you wanted when you lashed out at me earlier?'

Instantly she felt sick and shaken. Did he honestly believe that of her; that she had deliberately tried to incite him to…to this?

She shook her head, the bitter denial bursting from her throat before she could silence it.

For a second he said nothing, then she felt his hold slacken slightly, his eyes shuttered as he released her and stepped slightly away. Immediately she shivered, feeling bereft…aching for the warmth of his arms around her once more.

'Forgive me.' His voice was harsher than she had ever known it. 'I obviously mistook anger for frustration.'

Frustration? Slowly his meaning dawned and a scarlet wave of anger scalded its way over her skin. Did he actually think she had deliberately tried to incite him to…to make love to her…because she was suffering from frustration because he had interrupted her with Chris? That she wanted *him* to finish what Chris had started? The thought made her feel acutely sick and for the second time that day she was bitterly angry with him.

Tears stung her eyes but she refused to let them fall.

'You couldn't be more wrong,' she told him thickly. 'I wasn't lying to you when I said Chris attacked me, and as for thinking I wanted you to…to finish what he had started….' She swallowed hard on the nausea clutching her stomach. 'You're doing both of us an injustice. I can't think why you married me, Jon, if that's the sort of woman you think I am. I'm tired, Jon,' she told him listlessly as the surge of anger drained away, leaving her feeling exhausted both emotionally and physically. 'I think it must be this hot weather that's making everyone so on edge. I'm going to bed.'

She hesitated by the door, consumed by a totally crazy desire to turn round and go back, to beg him to take her back in his arms and kiss her again but somehow she found the strength to resist it.

Upstairs she was too tired even to start undressing. She caught a glimpse of her reflection in her mirror and stared at her swollen mouth touching it tentatively with her fingertips. When Jon had kissed her she had experienced sensations so totally alien and yet so totally known that she was still shocked by them. But not as shocked as she had been by Jon's assured experience. When she had thought about him kissing her she had imagined his touch would be hesitant, unsure and perhaps rather clumsy but his mouth had moved on hers with wholly masculine authority, subtly demanding, revealing a wealth of experience she had never expected him to have. For a man who openly expressed a lack of interest in sex, Jon had revealed a totally unexpected degree of expertise. And she wasn't sure she liked it. Where and with whom had he gained that expertise? Had he once perhaps been deeply in love? So deeply in love that it had made him eschew all further emotional or physical involvement? She shivered slightly, faintly disturbed by the discovery than Jon was not what she had thought him to be...that there was obviously much of himself that he kept hidden. But why had he kissed her?

That was a question to which she could not find an answer other than perhaps out of male pride because she had verbally challenged his sexuality.

Yes...she decided finally, that must be it. Yet didn't that explanation too, indicate that Jon was not the totally non-sexual, mild man she had always believed him to be? Had she simply deceived herself or had he deliberately deceived her and if so, why? Why present an image to her that was, at least partially, false? That was something she was too tired to even try and analyse. Tomorrow, she told herself sleepily, as she prepared for bed, she would try to unravel these mysteries tomorrow.

In the morning Sophy overslept slightly and, much to the children's disappointment, opted not to use the new car to take them to school. After explaining that she needed to drive it by herself to get used to it first, she managed to placate them.

She had promised to drive Jon into Cambridge when she had dropped the children off and had decided to combine it with a shopping trip.

'We could meet for lunch.' Jon suggested, as she was parking. 'Unless of course you won't have time.'

Sophy had been dreading being alone with him after what had happened the previous evening but he was his normal mild, calm self, and she had even been able to persuade herself that most of last night's heart searchings had been prompted by nothing more than her own imagination. After all, it was not perhaps surprising that she should enjoy his kiss. She had wanted him to touch her for long enough.

'Er…no. Lunch would be lovely,' she stammered, realising that Jon was waiting for her response.

'Good.'

The smile he gave her made her heart lurch drunkenly and, for some stupid reason, she simply sat in the car and watched him walk away, unable to take her eyes off his lean, lithe body. He was wearing his new clothes as though he had always worn them and watching the way more than one woman turned to observe his long legged progress down the street, Sophy found herself wishing she had left him to his baggy cords and shapeless shirts. She didn't want other women looking at him, she realised with a sharp pang. She didn't want them admiring the masculine lines of his body, the breadth of his shoulders beneath the fine cotton of his shirt…

Like someone moving slowly in a dream, she shook her head, trying to disperse it, forcing herself to get out of the car and lock it.

Her shopping didn't take her long, and she was finished in plenty of time to get to the office where she had arranged to meet Jon. So much time in fact that when she found herself studying an attractive lemon sundress in a shop window, she gave in to the temptation to go inside and try it on.

It fitted her perfectly, enhancing the golden gleam of her skin and bringing out the red highlights in her hair. Tiny shoe-string straps tied on her shoulders in provocative bows, a broad stiffened belt emphasising the narrowness of her waist, before the skirt flared out over a slightly stiffened underskirt.

'It might have been made for you,' the assistant said, truthfully.

'I'll take it…' Sophy took a deep breath, 'and I'll keep it on…'

The other girl's eyes twinkled. 'Mmm…well I certainly think he'll appreciate it, whoever he is.'

'My husband.' The admission was made almost before she was aware of it and angry colour flooded her skin. Of course she wasn't buying this dress for Jon's benefit! She was buying it because it was cool and she was hot… and besides it was time she had some pretty things and…

Impatiently she waited for the girl to take her cheque and put her things into a bag, regretting now her impulsive decision to wear the dress but too embarrassed to do anything about it.

She found Jon waiting for her when she got to the office. He opened the door for her and, as the strong midday sunlight fell on his face, she realised he looked tired. Lines of strain harshened the shape of his mouth and for some reason he looked almost unfamiliar; harder, more male. As though she were seeing him properly for the first time Sophy stared at him, confused. He in turn was studying her, looking at her with such an air of open appraisal that the sundress, so pretty and cool in the shop, now seemed somehow provocative and dangerous.

'It's such a hot day I thought we'd eat at the Mill.'

The restaurant he named was on the river and very popular. Sophy doubted that they would be able to get a table but she was anxious to escape the tense atmosphere of the small office. It seemed to be stifling her. It must be the heat, she thought dizzily as they went outside but even in the fresh air the tension remained.

In the narrow streets the heat was like a thick blanket, clogging her throat when she tried to breathe. Far too acutely conscious of Jon at her side, she started to walk faster, arriving at the car hot and out of breath. In contrast Jon looked cool and lazily at ease. But was he? Some sixth sense made her study him more closely. A tiny pulse flickered unevenly under his skin. This constraint between them was a new thing, and one she did not know how to handle. Almost overnight Jon had turned from a kind, unthreatening man whom she liked very much and was fond of in a sisterly fashion, into a stranger, for whom her feelings were anything but sisterly.

Her face burned as she remembered his laconic accusation the previous evening. She had goaded him deliberately, she recognised that now. She wanted him to react physically to her comments but not because of Chris. All the feelings she had been fighting so hard to suppress flooded through her as she started the car. Why did she have to discover them now, when it was too late? Why had she not realised before their marriage that she was vulnerable to Jon's attraction? Was it because they were married that she was seeing him in this new light?

The questions buzzed in her tired brain like swarming wasps, making her stall the car and have to restart it, whilst Jon sat silently at her side.

To her surprise he had booked a table for them at the Mill. Not outside where everyone else seemed to be eating but in the dim coolness of the mill itself. Once a working flour mill, the building had been enterprisingly converted into a restaurant some years ago. Recently it had been taken over by a young couple with an enthusiasm for wholesome natural food, which was attractively presented.

Sophy ordered unenthusiastically, knowing that she was far too wrought up to enjoy her meal. Her throat seemed to have closed to an aching tightness, her whole body in the grip of an unfamiliar tension. She wanted to be with Jon and yet she didn't. Being alone with him made her feel nervous and on edge. Something she had never experienced in his company before, but a feeling she was familiar with nevertheless. She had experienced it every time she had dated a man she liked and whom she had thought might help her to overcome the stigma that Chris had labelled her with. It was the utmost stupidity to want Jon physically, she told herself despairingly, and it was not even as though he wanted her.

She managed no more than a few bites of both her first and main courses, refusing a sweet, and playing with her cup of coffee whilst Jon buttered biscuits and helped himself to the Stilton.

Why had she ever thought him clumsy? she wondered absently, watching the neat methodical movement of his hands. In moments she was totally absorbed in watching him, in wondering what it would be like to feel those long fingers against her skin...

'Sophy.'

She looked up, confused by the sudden curling ache in the pit of her stomach, her breath catching suddenly, trapped deep in her lungs as she saw the way he was looking at her.

'Jon?'

'Some boxes are better never opened, Pandora,' he said quietly in answer to her unspoken question, 'but it's too late for going back now.'

Sophy moistened her dry lips with the tip of her tongue, dreading what he might be going to say. She had seen in that look they had just exchanged a recognition of the desire he had stirred within her, and was ashamed of her own betrayal.

'What do you mean?' She was playing for time, hoping to stall whatever was to come but Jon did not want to play. She could tell that from the way his jaw tensed, his eyes narrowing faintly as he studied her face.

'Isn't it obvious what I mean?' he asked quietly, carefully pushing aside his plate and looking at her. She wanted to look away but it was impossible, some power beyond her own puny strength refused to allow her to drag her gaze away from his. 'I want you dammit, Sophy,' she heard him saying rawly, the words falling around her, splintering through her self-control and shattering it completely, shocking her with their intensity, stunning her into silence with their totally unexpectedness. 'I want you as a man wants a woman, in my arms...in my bed. Oh, it's all right,

I'm not going to force myself on you. I simply brought you here so that we could discuss this sensibly.'

From somewhere she managed to find her voice, the sound of it raw and husky in her own ears as she stammered helplessly, 'But you don't...you aren't like that.'

His mouth twisted with unfamiliar cynicism, his voice very soft and faintly metallic as he told her, 'You're wrong, Sophy, I do...and I most certainly am, much as it pains me to admit it. Poor Sophy,' his voice mocked her in its irony, 'how shocked you look, and no wonder...but did you really think me so sexless? Oh, I know you don't find me physically appealing but unfortunately a human being's ability to experience desire is not in direct ratio to physical attractiveness. Or is that another truth you find hard to digest? Poor Sophy, indeed. How disconcerting all this must be for you.... You preferred to see me as more machine than man, I'm afraid but you really only have yourself to blame,' he told her harshly. 'I'm not blind despite these...' He touched his glasses, his eyes and mouth hard. 'Whether you're willing to admit it or not, you've been deliberately provoking me recently. Why? Because of Benson?'

Unable to listen to any more, Sophy reacted wholly instinctively and did something she'd never done before in her life. She got up and fled from the room, rushing out to the car before Jon could stop her, quickly starting it and driving off.

It wasn't until she reached home that the full enormity of what she had done actually dawned on her. She had left Jon stranded at the Mill. All because she didn't have the courage to be as open with him as he had been with her and tell him that her recent provocative behaviour had sprung from a mingling of pique and curiosity and had had nothing to do with Chris at all. No, not just pique and curiosity…there was desire as well; the same desire that was curling through her body now as she remembered what he had said to her about wanting her.

Suddenly galvanised into action she ran to the phone and looked up the number of the Mill, quickly dialling it. It seemed an age before anyone answered. Impatiently she asked for Jon and, after what seemed like an endless wait, was told that he had left.

He must have got a taxi, she reflected guiltily. Why had she reacted like that…like a gauche and embarrassed teenager? What on earth could she say to him when he came home?

CHAPTER SIX

ONLY HE DIDN'T come home. At least not immediately, and he wasn't back when she returned from collecting the children from school either. She had dialled the office several times without getting a reply and was now beginning to get seriously alarmed…he had every right to be angry with her but to do this. Where was he?

She had to fib to David and Alex, telling them that he had gone out on business. Fortunately they were too accustomed to his sudden departures and arrivals to question her more closely, because she was sure her anxious expression would not have deceived them for very long if they had.

Supper time came and went and there was still no sign of him. Sophy stayed up until gone midnight, her mind in total panic. Had he walked out on her? Was he so angry with her that he could not bear to come back? Or had he perhaps taken her sudden flight as an indication that she found his revelations totally repellent…that she found *him* totally repellent? Biting her lip anxiously she paced the floor, tension seizing her body as she heard a car coming up the drive.

The taxi driver greeted her appearance with a relieved grimace. 'Passed out cold I think he has,' he informed her bluntly.

At first when she looked into the taxi she thought he was right but Jon was conscious, although undeniably drunk.

Between them she and the driver managed to get him into
the house where he collapsed on to the settee.

The smell of whisky clung to his skin and his breath.

'At least he's not a violent drunk,' the taxi driver comforted her when she went out to pay him. 'Real gentlemanly
he was until he passed out.'

Slowly Sophy went back inside. Jon never drank more
than the odd glass of spirits or wine; she had never ever
seen him like this, nor thought that she would. Had he done
this to himself because he wanted her? She ached to tell
him the truth…that she wanted him too, and wished more
than ever that she had not rushed off in that silly fashion
at lunchtime, but she had been shocked and, yes, angry
too that he could be so blind about her. It was insulting
that he should believe that she could not see beyond his
public façade to what lay behind but until very recently
she could not, she reminded herself…until she had married
him, until David had made that innocent remark about
Louise—in fact, she had never considered him as a sexual
human being at all…so perhaps it was no wonder he had
spoken the way he had.

He moaned and she went across to the sofa, reflecting
grimly that in the morning he would have an outsize
hangover and a stiff neck if she left him where he was…but
how could she move him? She tried and found it impossible
and instead made him as comfortable as she could, relief
invading her now that he was actually back.

'WHY IS UNCLE JON sleeping in the sitting room?' Alex
asked the question innocently at breakfast time.

It was David who replied, eyeing his sister faintly
scornfully, as he said. 'It's because he's been drinking.
He smells just like Daddy did when he and Mummy had
been to a party.'

'Yes, but why does that make him sleep downstairs?' Alex persisted, breaking off as the subject of her question came into the kitchen. The blue eyes looked slightly bloodshot, the brown skin faintly sallow.

'Coffee?' Sophy asked quietly.

Jon nodded and then closed his eyes, moaning faintly as he did so. 'What happened?' he demanded wryly, sitting down beside Alex and taking the coffee Sophy poured for him.

'I don't really know. A taxi driver brought you back.'

'Oh, God, yes…I bumped into some friends I was at Cambridge with. Which reminds me…I think I accepted an invitation to a party for both of us tonight.' He fished in his pocket and produced a scrap of paper with an address scribbled down on it. 'Yes, there it is…'

'You haven't had enough partying?' Sophy asked him drily, taking the paper and smoothing it out.

'Mmm…but we ought to go. It's someone who's just setting up on his own and he needs my help. If you don't fancy it, I could always go alone.'

Instantly Sophy recognised that she did not want that at all. She wanted to be with him…accepted by his friends as his wife.

'No…no. It will be a pleasant change.' She would have to arrange a babysitter, but that should not be too difficult. Helen Saunders at the Post Office had a teenage daughter who was trying to save up to buy her first car. Susan was a pleasant, responsible girl, who Sophy knew she could trust with the children.

'Why don't you go upstairs and go back to sleep?' she suggested to Jon, noting his bleary eyes and haggard appearance.

'Mmm…sounds like a good idea.'

She watched him go, conscious of an urge to rush after

him and go with him to fuss over him as though he were genuinely her husband.

'Poor Uncle Jon, he looks really poorly,' Alex commented sympathetically, finishing her breakfast.

SUSAN SAUNDERS proved willing to babysit, and having arranged to pick her up at eight Sophy went upstairs to study the contents of her wardrobe. She had attended several business cocktail parties with Jon before and knew what to expect. As his secretary she had always worn something businesslike and formal but now she was his wife. In the end she selected a simple cream silk shift-style dress, which had been an impulse buy in London and which had been so hideously expensive she had been too guilty to wear it.

Holding it up against herself she saw how the cream silk emphasised her tan and the silky richness of her hair. The demure front was offset by the deep vee back; the dress would be pleasantly cool on what she suspected was going to be an oppressively hot evening.

Her mind made up, she went back downstairs, not giving in to the temptation to walk into Jon's room and see if he was awake. Sooner or later they were going to have to talk; she was going to have to explain to him that the reason she had fled so abruptly had not been because she was shocked by his disclosures or found them distasteful. Even now she found it hard to grasp that he had made them, that he had told her that he wanted her.

He came downstairs just after lunch, looking worn and tired. 'God, I feel dreadful,' he told her wryly. 'It's a long, long time since I've been in the state I was in last night.' He sat down at the kitchen table and leaned his head back. 'I have the most God-awful headache.'

Silently Sophy produced some Alka Seltzer, watching

the face he pulled as he drank it. 'Filthy stuff,' was his only comment before he closed his eyes again.

'Jon, about yesterday.' It had to be said before she lost her courage but the look in his eyes as he opened them immediately silenced her.

'Not now, Sophy,' he said wearily. 'Just leave it, will you? I think I'd better get some fresh air…'

He didn't want her to go with him, Sophy could tell that. Was he regretting saying to her what he had? Idly her eyes registered his progress to the door, her senses wondering how she could ever have been ignorant of his masculine appeal; how she could ever have been blind enough to think of him as sexless…? A quiver of heat darted through her as her glance rested briefly on the taut outline of his buttocks and then slithered down the length of his legs. Suddenly it hurt to even breathe; she was terrified he would turn round and see what was in her eyes. She reached clumsily for her mug of coffee, her whole body shaking. So this was desire, this fierce, hot need that pushed aside everything that stood in its path; that demanded and aroused. Jon wanted her, he had said so and it ought to be the simplest thing in the world simply to go to him and tell him that she wanted him too, only it wasn't.

'COME AND SHOW me when you've got your dress on.' Alex was in the sitting room with Susan and David, and Sophy smiled and nodded. Jon was already upstairs getting ready but she had only just arrived back with Susan. According to Jon they were supposed to be at his friend's for nine o'clock. She had showered and put on her makeup before going for Susan but she had not changed into her silk dress.

She had decided to drive the BMW tonight—the first time she had taken it out with a passenger, although Jon was the most uncritical of men when it came to being driven.

She almost collided with him at the top of the stairs, his hands coming out to steady her, touching her briefly, making heat sheet through her body.

How on earth had she ever considered him unattractive, she wondered achingly. His hair was still slightly damp and curled into his neck, the white silk shirt he was wearing clinging to his skin. The black pants weren't ones she could ever remember seeing before and then she realised it was part of a dinner suit and that he was carrying the jacket—a new dinner suit, she was sure. He was even wearing a bow tie, and as he moved past her she caught an elusive hint of some masculine cologne, faintly old-fashioned and citrusy.

'I shan't be long,' she told him. 'I've only got to put on my dress and do my hair.'

Once it was on she wasn't sure if the cream silk had been a good idea. She had forgotten that the back was so low that it was impossible to wear a bra under it and the silk, almost perfectly decorous, seemed to hint at the shape of her breasts in a way she found unfamiliar. Her hair she left loose, sliding her feet into cream high-heeled sandals that made her taller than ever. For the first time in her life she was not ashamed or embarrassed by her height. Even in these heels she was nowhere near as tall as Jon. She picked up her bag and went downstairs.

'Wow...you both look smashing!' Alex told her, her admiring eyes going from Jon to Sophy in excited wonder. Susan grinned at her and then blushed bright red as she looked at Jon. A sharp knifing feeling that Sophy recognised as jealousy tore through her. She was jealous! Jealous of an eighteen-year-old...just because that eighteen-year-old had recognised instantly what she herself had been blind to for so long. Jon was an extremely attractive and desirable man!

'We shan't be back late.' Instead of being reassuring her voice sounded slightly brittle. She saw Jon frown as they went outside.

'Are you all right?' he asked her quietly. 'You seem on edge.'

'It's the heat.' It was partially true after all. Surely he knew the reason she was so on edge? He touched her arm as he opened the car door for her and she flinched, red hot darts of sensation destroying her composure.

'For God's sake, Sophy.' His voice was harsh against her ear. 'What the hell do you think I'm going to do? Give in to my animal passions and take you here in full view of the kids?'

He had managed to subdue the harshness to a laconic drawl which infused the words with a certain dry mockery, but they still made her shake with reaction. 'I'm sorry that you find the knowledge that I'm a fully functioning sexual being so distressing, but as I've already told you... you have nothing to fear.'

'I know that.'

'You do?' His mouth twisted in a way she was coming to know. 'Then you've a pretty odd way of showing it.'

He walked round to the passenger door of the car, which she unlocked for him, and got in beside her.

She had lost count of the thousands of times she must have driven him and yet tonight his presence beside her in the close confines of the car disturbed her. She was acutely conscious of the lean sprawl of his legs...of the rise and fall of his chest, and the cool scent of his cologne mingling with a different, more basic scent which her sense responded to on a deeper, primitive level.

She wanted him, she realised despairingly, and she would give anything not to be going to this party tonight but to be alone with him so that they could talk. Instead she forced herself to concentrate on her driving, absently noting the easy way in which the big car responded to her touch. It was a pleasure to drive, but right now she was hardly in a mood to appreciate that fact.

It was ten-past-nine when she pulled up in the drive to Jon's friend's house. A mock Tudor building in an avenue of similar houses, it was an easily recognisable symbol of success.

She walked with Jon to the front door.

A small brunette opened it to them, smiling ravishingly at Jon, and exclaiming, 'Darling, you made it!' She giggled. 'After last night we weren't sure if you'd remember.' She took her time before looking at Sophy.

'So this is your wife? Please come in. You can't know how thrilled we were to bump into Jon last night in Cambridge.' She chattered on as she led them through the house to a long terrace at the back where the rich aromas of barbecued meat mingled with the heat of the evening. 'It's simply ages since we last saw him. Roy, my husband, was so pleased…he's having trouble with this new computer of his and if anyone can help him it will be Jon. How long have you been married?'

She was still talking to Sophy but it was Jon who answered, his expression unreadable as he drawled, 'Not very long…not long enough, in fact.'

Sophy could feel the brown eyes darting speculatively from Jon's face to her own. In time she might quite get to like this petite brunette, but at the moment she was too uncomfortably aware of her speculation and her interest in Jon. My God, she thought despairingly, what was she turning into? A woman who was jealous of every mere look her husband received from other women? She must be going mad, suffering from some sort of sickness brought on by the heat. Or perhaps that frustration Jon had accused her of not so very long ago?

'There's an old friend here of yours that you simply must meet, darling.' Their hostess was talking to Jon now, holding on to his arm in a way that made Sophy's fingers curl into tiny talons.

'Roy, over here a minute, darling,' she called to her husband, and Sophy watched the burly fair-haired man detach himself from a small group.

He looked older than Jon although Sophy recognised that they must be around the same age, clever hazel eyes studying her gravely as he shook her hand.

'So you are Jon's wife? You're a lucky man, Jon, she's lovely.'

'Hey enough of that,' Andrea threatened lightly, punching him on the arm. 'Just remember you are married to me...'

'Ah, you're jealous.' They were simply playing a game... but Jon could have said the same words to her and they would have been all too true.

'I think you'll find you know most of the people here,' Roy was saying to Jon. 'What can I get you to drink?'

'Get him a drink later, love,' Andrea interrupted. 'Jon, there's a very special friend of yours here tonight. An old flame,' she added, winking at Sophy, as though to show it was still a game, but Sophy could feel herself tense. Jon had tensed too, his jaw hardening fractionally, his eyes closing slightly, such minor changes, that she suspected only she was aware of what they portended.

'Oh...?' He wasn't giving anything away in his voice either, Sophy recognised, watching him frown in the hesitant mild manner she had once thought typified the man himself and which she was now coming to know was simply a form of camouflage. What was Jon protecting himself from? Her mouth felt dry, her body tensing almost to the point of pain.

'Yes... Lorraine. You must remember her, Jon. Heavens, you and she were an item for a couple of terms at least. She used to be absolutely crazy about you.'

'But Jon managed to resist all her wiles, didn't you, my friend?' Roy was chuckling, ignoring his wife's frown. 'Just as well too, otherwise Lorraine would have had you neatly trapped in matrimony and then I would never have been able to meet this lovely lady.' He kissed Sophy's fingers gallantly as he spoke.

'We were all a little in love with Jon when he was at university,' Andrea told Sophy with a small smile. 'He was so different from the other under-grads, far more sophisticated and just that little bit withdrawn. It made him seem very exciting and out of reach...challengingly so, I'm afraid. We used to chase after him quite unfairly. All you wanted to do was to be left alone to get on with your work, didn't you, darling?' she added to Jon.

Roy laughed. 'Says you,' he teased his wife. 'How do you think he got that jaded, world-weary air you found so tantalising in the first place? It certainly wasn't by sitting up burning the midnight oil over his books!'

Jon looked distinctly uncomfortable. He tugged at his bow tie as though it were strangling him, but this time Sophy was not deceived. He was not really embarrassed. He was simply pretending he was. If she looked at his eyes, they were cool and faintly aloof, not embarrassed at all.

'Well you must come and say hello to Lorraine or she'll never forgive me,' Andrea insisted, drawing Jon away from Roy and Sophy.

Silently, Sophy watched them go.

'You mustn't mind my wife.' Roy sounded kind and faintly uncomfortable. 'She's right when she said that most of the girls in our crowd had a thing about Jon. Poor guy, he was forced to live like a hermit in the end, just to get rid of them. In those days girls had just discovered sex,' he told Sophy with a grin. 'It was a difficult time for us men, being the pursued instead of the pursuers.'

'I'm sure,' Sophy agreed copying his bantering mood. 'It must have been hell.'

Roy was easy to talk to but that didn't stop her glance following Jon's dark head, watching it bend towards the blonde woman he had stopped beside. Andrea drifted off and left them, Roy was still talking and she must have been making the right responses but inside she was tormented by jealousy. What were they saying? Was this perhaps the one love of Jon's life? She ached to be with them; to hear what was being said, and was given her chance when someone else came up to talk to Roy. She walked unsteadily away, moving towards Jon. He turned as she reached him, surprise and something else—anger perhaps—flickering across his face.

'Lorraine, this is my wife, Sophy.'

There was no mistaking the expression in the other woman's eyes, it was vitriolic. So much so that Sophy found herself taking a step backwards.

'I think I see Peter Lewis over there. I'd like to introduce you to him, Sophy.' Skilfully Jon drew her away from Lorraine, leaving Sophy wondering if what they had been saying before she arrived was something for their own ears alone.

At eleven she began to feel tired. Jon was locked in conversation with Roy in the latter's study, so Andrea had told her. Although everyone seemed friendly, Sophy was disinclined to talk. She wanted to go home. She wanted to be alone with Jon.

'Deserted you already, has he?'

She recognised Lorraine's metallic voice instantly, turning to face the older woman.

'So Jon has finally married! My dear, how on earth did you manage it?' She laughed when she saw Sophy's face tighten. 'Oh come on. I know him, Jon may look like an extraordinarily attractive member of the male species but looks are all there is. Sexually he's a disaster area—I should know, I spent months trying to get him into bed with me when we were at university together and when I did…God, what a non-event!'

Why was Lorraine telling her all this? Sophy wondered, listening to her.

The glossy red lips curled in open mockery. 'Oh, come on…you must know it's true. I know quite well that Jon's been living like a monk since he left Cambridge. He always did have a hang-up about sex, and you *must* be aware of it, unless, of course, you haven't actually been lovers.'

Sophy felt acutely sick. She knew what Lorraine was doing now. The woman hated Jon, Sophy could see that hatred shining in her eyes but she couldn't know the truth, Sophy told herself, she was simply probing, looking for a weak spot in Jon's armour, trying to find a way to humiliate him, as perhaps, Jon had once humiliated her. Illuminatingly she wondered if she had possibly hit on the truth. Could Lorraine, like Louise, have been one of those women who had thought to seduce Jon and found the task impossible? She looked at the blonde, noting the hard eyes and arrogant pose. Lorraine was attractive, there was no denying that. At twenty-one or two she would have been beautiful…and probably even more arrogant, certainly arrogant enough to swear vengeance against any man foolish enough to reject her.

She managed a slight frown. 'I'm sorry,' she began apologetically, 'but—'

'Oh, come on, my dear,' Lorraine interrupted her impatiently. 'Don't give me that, I know Jon hasn't changed. He was sexless at twenty-two and he's sexless now.'

'I'm afraid you're quite wrong.' Suddenly, soaringly she felt gloriously strong, glad to do something for Jon...to protect him from this woman's malice. She even managed to smile freely for the first time that evening. 'I can't speak for Jon's past, of course,' she shrugged delicately, 'but I can certainly tell you that as his wife I have no complaints.'

'But then maybe, darling, you aren't his wife...at least not in the way that really counts.'

Heavens, Lorraine was persistent—and thick skinned—Sophy thought wryly, but she was not going to let her get the better of their exchange.

'You mean you don't think we've made love?' Sophy raised her eyebrows and laughed openly. 'Oh, but we have.' She allowed her voice to become soft and dreamy, watching Lorraine's mouth harden and the colour leave her skin.

'I don't believe you.' Her voice was harsh, and for a moment Sophy felt sorry for her but then she remembered what Lorraine was trying to do to Jon.

'Then I shall have to make you,' she said quietly. 'What is it you want to hear, Lorraine? How Jon makes me feel when he touches me? How I feel when I touch him? Those are very intimate details to discuss with a stranger but what I can tell you is that in his arms I feel more of a woman than I've ever felt before in my life. Under his touch my body burns and aches for his possession. I would have gone willingly to his bed, marriage or no marriage. When his body possesses mine...' She caught the faintly strangled gasp the other woman made as she stepped back, raising her hands as though Sophy's words were blows, retreating to the other side of the patio to glare at her with patent venom.

'Sophy…'

She swung round, going pale as she found Jon standing behind her. How long had he been there? Had he heard? She swallowed tensely and looked at him but he was looking the other way.

'If you don't mind I'd like to leave. This headache…'

Relief flooded through her. Of course he hadn't over-heard! Hot colour scorched her skin as she remembered what she'd said. Now that it was over she felt weak and trembly. There was nothing she wanted more than to leave, and she went mutely with Jon as he sought out their host and hostess.

They drove back in silence, Sophy leaving Jon to go upstairs whilst she took Susan home.

Once she got back she didn't linger downstairs herself. She too was tired, drained of all emotion. She paused outside Jon's room, without knowing why, listening to the floorboard creak beneath her foot.

The door was open and she heard him call her name. She went to the door and stood just inside it. He was sitting on the bed, his head in his hands.

'Why did you do it?'

His voice was a faint thread but she still heard it, the blood freezing down her spine as apprehension gripped her.

'Do what?'

She heard him sigh. 'Come on, Sophy, you know quite well what I mean…that little scene with Lorraine. I heard it all, but both of you were too engrossed in each other to realise I was there. It certainly was a very talented per-formance on your part,' he added tiredly. '*How* did you do it? By calling up memories of how it was with Benson?'

Sophy could feel the blood draining out of her skin.

'No.' She practically choked on the denial. 'No...' she added more quietly, 'I simply used my imagination.'

He wasn't looking at her, but she could feel the tension gripping him. 'What exactly do you mean?'

Suddenly she was tired of fencing...of pretending. 'You're the logician, Jon,' she told him wryly, 'Surely you can analyse what I've said and draw your own conclusions. I didn't enjoy Chris's lovemaking, as a matter of fact. In fact I found it a total turn-off. It was painful...and empty. I can assure you that he found me less than satisfactory as well.'

'Really? So why is he still pursuing you?'

'Because he resents the fact that I appear to be enjoying with another man what I did not enjoy with him,' she told him bluntly, 'and he likes causing trouble.'

'You can say that again.' He looked directly at her for the first time, reaching one hand behind his neck to rub away the tension.

'Headache still bad?'

'Mmm...'

'I'll massage your neck for you if you'd like.'

Now why on earth had she said that? Tensely waiting for his repudiation she was stunned when he turned and stretched out on the bed, muttering, 'Thanks, that would be great.'

He had already removed his jacket, but his shirt was still on. Even so, Sophy dared not suggest that he remove it. Instead she leaned down towards him, flexing her fingers. She had learned the basics of massage after a bad fall in her teens when she had injured her leg and had found relief from the pain of it by massaging the tense muscles and it seemed it was a skill that once learned was never lost, although there was a world of difference in having Jon's hot flesh beneath her hands rather than her own.

Almost by instinct she found the hard lumps of acidic matter that denoted tension and started massaging them. She felt Jon tense slightly and then relax, although he said nothing. Time ceased to exist as she concentrated on her task. Jon was breathing slowly now…so slowly that she felt sure he must be asleep. She eased gently away, flexing her own body.

'Don't stop.' The slurred words stopped her in mid-movement, her eyes widening as Jon sat up, his fingers tearing impatiently at his shirt buttons until he had them all free. Shrugging out of his shirt he threw it on the floor, flopping back down on the bed. 'That feels good, Sophy,' he told her thickly. 'Do it some more.'

She obeyed him mindlessly, smoothing the sleek skin beneath her fingertips, enveloped in the musky male scent of his body as she bent closer to him, trying to tell herself that what she was doing was something she would have done for anyone.

Only he wasn't anyone. He was Jon…and she loved him…*loved him?* She tensed, staring blindly into space, waiting for her heart to catch up on its missed beat. Of course she didn't love him. She wanted him, desired him, yes…but love? She fought hard but it was no use, she *did* love him.

The knowledge was appalling. How long had she hidden it from herself? How long had she loved him? Days, weeks, months…before they were married, even? She shook her head, trying to clear her thoughts, and knowing it was impossible. The shock was too great.

'What's wrong?'

She withdrew as Jon sat up, backing away from him.

He wasn't wearing his glasses but he was looking at her as though he could read every expression on her face.

'I want you.' He said it softly, reaching for her before she could move, fastening his fingers round her wrists and tugging her towards him until her progress was impeded by the edge of the bed. 'Was it true what you told me about Benson?'

'That he was the first man to discover that I was frigid, do you mean?' She was glad that he had reminded her of reality because it gave her something to fight with.

'Is that what you are?' He tugged on her wrists again, not very gently this time, laughing at her as she overbalanced and fell on the bed in an ungainly heap. She tried to roll away from him, her angry protest smothered by the heat of his mouth as it imprisoned her own.

Heat, searing and intense, beat through her in fierce waves, a heat that had nothing to do with the hot summer night outside. This heat was generated within herself, a blazing conflagration that threatened to totally destroy her. She had never, ever felt like this before. It frightened her that she should now.

Every instinct she had told her she must escape before Jon discovered for himself the humiliating truth, but although his grip on her was now only light, somehow it was impossible to drag her mouth from his, to give up the aching pleasure of the way his mouth moved on hers aroused. His tongue touched her lips and they parted, admitting him to the moist sweetness beyond, the breath catching in her throat as the intimacy of his kiss engulfed her and she clung helplessly to his shoulders, aware of the hot sleekness of his skin beneath her fingers; aware of the frantic thudding of her heart against her ribs...of the slow ache coiling through her lower body, the moist heat between her thighs.

Suddenly it was impossible to resist. Her tongue touched his, tentatively at first and then more daringly, her body melting with heat as she heard his fiercely indrawn breath and felt the muscles of his chest compress.

Her whole body was aching with desire for him and he had only kissed her. Only kissed her, that was all. Her lips clung despairingly to his as she felt their pressure ease and she thought she felt him smile as his mouth moved slowly over her skin, exploring the shape of her face, his breath warm against her ear.

'Let me take this off.'

She felt his fingers touch the single fastening that held her dress on and reacted instinctively, her body tensing, as she begged, 'Please don't do this, Jon.'

But it was too late and anyway he wasn't listening to her. His eyes were fastened on the twin peaks of her breasts, fully exposed to him now that their covering of silk had slithered away. Transfixed, she watched as his head bent slowly towards her breasts, remembering on a sudden wave of revulsion how Chris had bitten her tender flesh and how she had recoiled from him in pain and shock. Until now she had forgotten that…but she had not forgotten his anger and contempt.

She reached out protestingly, her fingers digging into Jon's shoulder. Her voice thick with anguish as she pleaded, 'Please…'

The downward movement of his head stilled and he looked at her. 'What is it?' he asked her softly.

Not even the familiar sound of his voice could calm her. 'I don't like it,' she heard herself whimpering. 'It hurts…'

She saw his eyes darken and tensed in expectation of the same angry contempt Chris had shown her but instead he said gratingly, 'Is that what he did, Sophy? Did he hurt you?'

She closed her eyes, not daring to reply in case she burst into tears. What was the matter with her? Not so very long ago she had lain awake at night tormented by her aching need for Jon to touch her but now that he was...

'Well, I promise you I won't.'

She could feel the tension in his body as his hands cupped her breast. Despite herself she shivered slightly. He was looking at her, forcing her to meet his gaze, and then he bent his head and gently kissed each coral nipple with warm lips.

A shuddering sigh was wrenched from deep within her, the fear flooding out of her, pushed by the slow tide of desire coming in its wake. The sensation of Jon's mouth against her breast had been both reassuring and tormenting. She wanted more than the light brush of his lips against her skin, she realised achingly. Much, much more—but Jon was already moving away from her.

Reacting instinctively, she reached towards him curling her fingers into his hair, feeling the unmistakable hardening of her nipples beneath the heat of the sharp breath he expelled.

'Sophy.' He said her name roughly, warningly, but she was past heeding him, her own voice taut with longing as she moaned softly. 'Jon, please...'

'Please what?' His voice was thick and slurred as though the words were unfamiliar to him, one hand cupping her breast, the other drawing her down against his mouth as he muttered against her skin, 'Please this?' and his mouth moved back to her breast.

For long, long moments, the only noise in the room was the tortured sound of her breathing and the moist movement of his mouth caressing her breast, his tongue moving roughly over the aroused peak of it until she was moaning in wild pleasure.

She ached when he released her but not because he had hurt her.

'Don't be afraid, I'm not going to do anything you don't want.'

She closed her eyes as she felt him move. Couldn't he see that what she was afraid of now was that she *would* want it…that in wanting him she would be vulnerable to him and that, like Chris, he would find her lacking and reject her? And that was something she could not endure.

She moved away from him and knew he had registered her withdrawal as he said her name sharply.

'It's late, Jon,' she told him huskily. 'I must go back to my own room.'

For a moment she thought he was going to stop her, and then she heard him sigh.

'Sophy, you know I want you,' he told her tiredly. 'I want you to want me in return, not to be frightened of me. Is it me you're frightened of, or sex in general?'

'A little of both,' she admitted huskily. 'I don't want you to look at me the way Chris looked at me, Jon,' she told him tormentedly. 'Believe me, it's better if I go now. If I stayed I promise you you'd only be disappointed.'

'Is that what he told you?' he asked her roughly. 'That all men would find you disappointing because he did?'

She managed a wry smile. 'I'm not a complete fool, Jon. There have been other men…oh, none of them were ever physically intimate with me because sooner or later our relationship always reached the point where it became obvious that I was disappointing them.'

'Are you sure you're not just saying all this because you find me a turn-off?'

'No!' Her denial rang with truth. She reached out and touched his face hesitantly, trying to smile at him. 'Believe it or not, Jon, I find you extremely desirable. But can't you see that just makes it so much harder? Because of that, I'm frightened of disappointing you.'

She got off the bed before he could say anything and picked up her dress, hurrying out into the corridor and into her own room.

CHAPTER SEVEN

SHE WOKE UP during the night, not knowing what had disturbed her, conscious only of some sound alien to those she normally heard.

Her bedroom door opened inwards and she sat up in bed, her eyes widening as she saw Jon walk into her room.

He was wearing pyjama bottoms, dark silk ones, and she tensed as he came over to the bed, wanting him and yet afraid of what that wanting might lead to when he too discovered how useless she was as a woman.

As he reached for the bedclothes, she wriggled away, smothering a tiny gasp of surprise as he slid into bed beside her.

'Jon!'

Her protest was silenced by the warm brush of his fingers against her mouth. 'I can't sleep without you, Sophy,' she heard him saying huskily, as his arms went round her. 'I only want to sleep with you in my arms, that's all.'

Unbelievably he was already falling asleep as his arm drew her back against the warmth of his body. She knew she ought to wake him up and send him back to his own bed but it was good having him lie beside her, his body against her own. Instinctively she snuggled back against him, sighing faintly as his arm curved round her body just under her breasts.

They were married, after all, she reminded herself as

she fell asleep; and there was nothing immoral in them being here together like this. Apart, of course, from the fact that he did not love her, while she…

He wanted her though, she thought defiantly. He had told her so and there had been no reason for him to lie. What on earth was it that she had that Lorraine and Louise did not seem to possess? Perhaps he just wasn't keen on blondes, she thought wryly, suppressing a self-mocking smile as sleep stole over her.

SHE WOKE UP EARLY conscious that something was different, but not sure what it was until she felt the weight of Jon's arm across her body. It was just gone five in the morning. She really ought to wake him and send him back to his own bed. If Alex should wake early and come in for an early morning cuddle as she sometimes did…

She tried to wriggle out from under his arm so that she could shake him but instantly it tightened around her, threatening to crush her ribs. She heard him mutter something in his sleep and then move slightly taking her with him so that somehow her legs became tangled up in his.

She knew immediately that he had woken up, even before he murmured her name in husky surprise, the tone of his voice subtly changing as he repeated her name.

'Lovely, Sophy,' he murmured against her ear. 'Who would ever have dreamed that I would wake up with you in my arms?' His hand skimmed the shape of her body and she felt him shake slightly as he asked, 'What on earth is this? It feels like something my grandmother might have worn.'

It was in fact a long cotton nightdress which was slightly Victorian in design. Normally she only wore it in winter but last night, for some reason, despite the heat, she had decided to put it on.

'Jon, you really ought to go back to your own bed.' She tried to turn round so that she could look at him, and found she wished she had not as she saw the lazy blue warmth in his eyes as he looked back at her. His jaw was dark and she touched it lightly, her eyes widening at the harsh rasp of his beard against her fingertips.

'You must have to shave twice a day.' Even as she spoke she was conscious of the banality of her comment.

Jon's mouth twitched slightly but his voice was quite grave as he whispered back, 'At least.' His fingers curled round her wrist, transferring hers from his jaw to his mouth. The sensation of his mouth moving against her fingertips was oddly erotic. She could feel herself starting to tremble, a low ache spreading through her stomach as he gently sucked her fingers into his mouth, his free hand stroking down her body to caress her breast.

'Jon…'

He released her fingers and pressed his own against her mouth. 'No, don't speak,' he told her softly. 'Don't say anything, Sophy. Not now.' And because suddenly she seemed to have been transported to a dream world where anything was possible and only Jon existed, she found it easy to acquiesce, to simply let herself follow where he led and give herself over completely to the voluptuosity of his lovemaking.

She had discovered so much she had not known before about him already and here it seemed was something else she had not known, her body recognising instantly that his touch was that of a man who had once learned and never forgotten how to give the utmost pleasure.

Sighing beneath the seductive stroke of his fingers she let him remove her nightdress, crying out softly when the heat of his body touched her own but not with pain, or fear, unless it was the pain of being so close to him and yet not part of him and the fear of losing this pleasure he was giving her almost before it was begun. His pyjamas followed her nightdress on to the floor, his hands drawing her against his body.

'I want you, Sophy.' He murmured the words into her throat, sliding his hands to her hips, holding her bones almost as though he might crush them. She shivered and reached out to touch him, tracing the hard slope of his shoulder, pressing her mouth to his warm skin, gently biting the satin firmness of it until she felt the husky groan move his chest. He had thrown off the duvet and it was light enough for her to see his body. Strong and fully aroused, making her shiver faintly with awareness and desire. It was not the sexual act of possession she feared but her own inability to respond to it; the crushing sense of anticlimax and rejection she knew must surely come when Jon discovered…

'What is it?' His voice was gentle, teasing her slightly as he murmured against her ear. 'Surely you have seen a naked man before?'

She hadn't really—at least not as openly as she was seeing him—but it wasn't that that held her spellbound in some sort of motionless trance. She swallowed and turned to meet his eyes. 'Never one as male as you, Jon,' she told him tremulously…and truthfully, watching his eyes darken and his mouth curl, as his finger traced the shape of her mouth.

'That was a highly inflammatory remark, wouldn't you say?'

She couldn't respond because his mouth was touching hers, caressing her lips with tormenting slowness, until she was forced to wind her arms round his neck and arch her body into his with an impatient moan of need.

She was aware of his fingers biting deeply into her upper arms as he held her against him, just as she was aware of the hard arousal of his body moving against her own, but it was the fiercely draining pressure of his mouth she was aware of the most, the heated movement of his tongue as it sought her own. Desire, sharp and tormenting twisted in her stomach and she pulled her mouth free to whisper his name as she drew painful gasps of air into her lungs.

He was kissing her throat, her shoulders, nibbling at the tender flesh, trailing tormenting kisses down over the upper slopes of her breasts and then the valley between them. Her nipples were stiff, aching for the warmth of his mouth but he seemed determined to ignore them. Stifling a tormented moan, Sophy curled her fingers into his hair, guiding his head to her breast, her body arching up to his mouth in open supplication.

She felt him shudder and for one agonising moment thought she had somehow disgusted him, but even as she tried to pull away his hand cupped her breast, his mouth hot against her skin as he muttered into the creamy flesh, 'Sophy…Sophy…this time I can't be gentle.' And then his mouth was tugging urgently on the coral hardness of her nipple, unleashing a cramping, burning ache low down in her stomach, making her sob his name and drag her nails against his skin as she felt the tiny shudders of pleasure radiate through her body.

There was an odd ringing noise in her head…a distracting sound she did not want to hear, a tormented sound of denial dragged from her throat as Jon abruptly released her.

'The alarm's gone off,' he told her, sitting up slowly. He

was breathing so hard she could see the rise and fall of his chest. Sweat clung to his skin. 'Sophy…?'

Sounds from the next room silenced him. 'Now obviously isn't the time to say all that I want to say to you,' he said wryly. 'I suspect that any minute now you're likely to be invaded.' He reached for his pyjama bottoms pulling them on, his body still openly aroused. 'As soon as we can we're going to have to talk.' He bent briefly and kissed her, just as the door opened and Alex came rushing in.

She stopped abruptly, staring round-eyed at them, demanding curiously, 'What are you doing in here, Uncle Jon?'

'I had a nightmare and your uncle spent the night with me,' Sophy fibbed lightly, giving the little girl a smile.

'Does that mean that you'll always be sleeping together now, like real Mummies and Daddies?' Alex enquired innocently.

Sophy dared not look at Jon. Would he want to sleep with her on a permanent basis…to make their relationship a physical as well as a legal one?

'You're not wearing a nightie.' She had forgotten about that, and blushed guiltily. Jon, standing by the bedroom door was laughing and over Alex's head her eyes met his.

'Mummies don't need them when they sleep with Daddies,' he told Alex with a grin, sauntering out into the landing.

OF COURSE IT WAS too much to hope for that Alex would let the subject drop. She was full of it over breakfast, telling David all about it, and Sophy was conscious of a certain slightly adult awareness in David's expression as he looked at her. 'Married people should sleep together,' he told Alex firmly.

Luckily Sophy was able to change the subject before
Alex could continue it, reminding the children that they
would be having visitors at the weekend.

It was on Friday that Jon's friends arrived from Nassau,
and on Saturday evening they were coming round for
dinner. Sophy still wasn't sure what she was going to serve.
She felt very nervous about meeting them although she told
herself there was no reason why she should.

An emergency call from one of his clients meant that
Jon had to go out immediately after breakfast. His client's
offices were in London and he told Sophy before he left
that he might not be back that night. She felt empty and
very much alone when he had gone, almost as though a
shadow had fallen across her day. If she had doubted that
she loved him before, she didn't do so any longer. It took
a considerable effort to rouse herself enough to take the
children to school and once she had done she found herself
reluctant to go back to the empty house. Instead she drove
into Cambridge and spent what was left of the morning
glancing through cookery books in the library and trying
to plan her dinner party menu.

Something simple, she decided…and something cool.
In the end she decided on salmon and cucumber mousse
followed by chicken and avocado salad with a cheese board
and home-made ice cream to follow. She would have to
consult Jon about the wine. Jon…it was ridiculous how
even the inward sound of his name had the power to arouse
and alarm her. Why should he want *her?* She had no way
of knowing…she could only accept that he did and be
thankful for it.

THE DINING AND DRAWING rooms were not rooms that they
normally used as a family, and Sophy grimaced faintly
over their unappealing appearance. Jon had given her a

completely free hand with the renovation of the house, but the weather had been so hot that she had not been motivated into making any changes. Now, with the dinner party imminent, she wished that she had. There was nothing wrong with the rooms themselves but they were furnished with clumsy, sale-room oddments and badly needed decorating. The only real improvement she could make was to fill them with freshly cut flowers and keep the lighting dim, she decided wryly when she had finished dusting and vacuuming both rooms on Friday morning.

There had been no phone call yet from Jon and while she was missing him dreadfully she was also apprehensive about his return. They needed to talk he had said to her, but what did he intend to say? Now that she had admitted to herself that she loved him, it seemed impossible that she had not known the truth before; that fierce jealousy she had felt when Alex had innocently told her about Louise for instance…she ought to have known then. But she hadn't wanted to know. She had felt safer simply liking him; safer thinking of him as a non-sexual being. She had never even tried to look beyond the façade he presented to the world, because she had been quite content with that façade.

When he still hadn't returned by midnight on Friday evening Sophy went to bed. She knew where he was working and had she wanted to do so she could have put a call through to him at any time during the day, but pride had stopped her. In the past it had always been Jon who rang her to tell her when he was due to return, and she was not going to cause either of them embarrassment by being the one to ring him now. She was painfully aware of what both Roy and Andrea had told her; that in the past Jon had been blatantly pursued by her sex and had apparently not liked it. She had enough intelligence to guess that Lorraine's virulent hatred was more likely to have sprung from Jon's rejection of her than from the lack of skill in bed which she had accused him of—after all hadn't she herself had proof positive that the latter simply was not true?

She shivered slightly beneath the duvet, her bed suddenly far too large and empty without Jon in it but she was not going to be like those others. She was not going to pursue and chase him. That was easy enough to say, she thought tiredly as she gave in to the urge to sleep, but it might be far harder than she envisaged to do.

'WHEN'S UNCLE JON coming back?'

They were having breakfast in the kitchen—a leisurely, late breakfast as it was Saturday morning, and once it was over Sophy intended to devote the rest of the morning to preparing for the evening's dinner party.

'I'm not sure.' She responded to Alex's question as calmly as she could. She had been awake since seven o'clock, her ears straining for the sound of the telephone, but so far there had been no call.

Almost as though she had conjured the sound up by wishful thinking, the kitchen phone suddenly shrilled.

'I'll get it.' Alex was out of her chair first, running to pick up the receiver.

'Uncle Jon...when are you coming back?' She paused and then held out the receiver to Sophy. 'He's leaving now but he wants to speak to you.'

Her hand was shaking slightly as she took the receiver from Alex.

'Hello, Jon.' She hoped her voice sounded calmer to him than it did to her.

'Sorry I couldn't make it back earlier.'

Was she imagining the constraint she thought she heard?

'That's okay. Was the problem more difficult to solve than you expected?'

There was an odd pause and then when Jon did speak his voice was slightly muffled. 'Yes…yes, you could say that. I should be back by midafternoon.'

After asking her if there had been any urgent telephone calls he hung up. Now that he had rung she felt worse than she had done before. She felt as though a wall had suddenly sprung up between them, as though for some reason Jon was deliberately setting a distance between them.

The preparatory work for the dinner party kept her fingers busy but left her with not enough to occupy her mind, and by the time the mousse was chilling in the fridge and the ice cream was in the freezer, she had managed to convince herself that Jon was bitterly regretting ever having touched her. Everything that Chris had said to her was true. Jon found her just as undesirable as Chris had…

She kept herself busy, polishing the old-fashioned silver cutlery she found in one of the sideboard drawers, carefully washing china and crystal that she had also discovered tucked away in the sideboard cupboards.

She had bought an expensive white-linen tablecloth, deeply trimmed with lace, and Alex who had volunteered to help her with the silver polishing and then with the table, stopped to admire the rich gleam of the green and gold banded dinner service and the sparkle of the heavily cut crystal.

Fresh flowers brightened up the heaviness of the room and decorated the centre of the table. All she really had to do now was to prepare the salads and the chicken.

Alex watched round-eyed while she made the mayonnaise, leaving Sophy to reflect that she had after all gained something from her mother, for it was she who had taught Sophy to cook. She recognised now that she had absorbed a good deal of her mother's housewifely skill almost without being aware of it.

At three o'clock Sophy heard a car stop outside. Instantly an explosive mixture of fear and excitement gripped her stomach. Watching Alex's exuberant and totally natural pleasure, she wished for a moment that she too was free to welcome Jon back the way she wanted to but she had to be more circumspect, so she deliberately held back a little washing and then drying her hands, timing her arrival at the front door to coincide with Jon's.

Her first thought was that he looked tired—far more tired than she had seen him looking before, and instinctively she reached out to touch him, withdrawing her hand as though it had been stung as she realised what she was doing.

'You look tired.' The words left her lips before she could stop them.

'I could do with a shower…it's no pleasure travelling at the moment—especially in a taxi without air conditioning.' He bent down and picked up the overnight case he had put on the floor. 'I'll go up and get changed.'

'Would you like a drink or something to eat?'

Jon paused at the foot of the stairs and shook his head. 'No…I ate before I left.' He took off his glasses and rubbed his eyes. Something he normally only did either when he was tired or when something was bothering him. Her love for him tugged at Sophy's heart. She wanted to go up to him and wrap her arms round him but instinctively she was frightened of being rebuffed.

On Saturday afternoon Sophy made her weekly telephone call to her mother, something which was more a duty than a pleasure, especially when her mother still continued to make slightly disparaging references to Jon. For once though, she seemed uninterested in the subject of her son-in-law, rushing to tell Sophy the moment they had exchanged 'hellos'.

'The most shocking thing has happened—I can hardly believe it. Felicity has left Chris. Poor boy, he is absolutely devastated. He adored her, you know…spoilt her really. Of course I've done my best to comfort him. Girls do funny things when they're in her condition but even so…'

Sophy listened while her mother poured out a good deal more in the same vein, inwardly thoroughly bored with the whole subject of Chris.

'He may come over and see you,' she told Sophy just as she was hanging up. 'I told him you'd be delighted to see him. After all it's a time like this that he needs his friends.'

'Mother, I wish you hadn't.' Sophy was really angry but there was nothing she could do other than hope that Chris would have the sense to know that her mother was wrong and that Sophy was not likely to welcome him. She had sensed the last time she saw him that he resented the thought that she had found happiness with someone else and she had no wish to play the sympathetic listener to him. Shrugging in mild irritation she went back to her preparations for the meal.

Jon was outside with the children. Soon it would be time to call them in for their tea. She had got them a Walt Disney video to watch while they were having dinner and both of them had promised to be on their best behaviour. Not that they were ever particularly naughty, she thought fondly. Once everything was done she could go upstairs and get ready. Nervous butterflies fluttered in her stomach. She was dreading meeting Jon's friends and being the object of their curiosity.

AFTER ALL HER apprehension about meeting Jon's friends, Sophy discovered that they were a very pleasant, down to earth couple with whom she instantly felt quite at home. Mary-Beth confided to her over the salmon and cucumber mousse that she sometimes felt she must be the world's worst cook and that even her ten-year-old daughter could make a better sponge cake than she did herself. 'And doesn't she just let me know it,' she groaned with a smile.

Their two children, she explained to Sophy, were staying with her parents in North Carolina.

'Harry has so many meetings organised for this trip that it just wasn't worth bringing the kids with us. I can quite happily waste a few days shopping in London but the kids would hate that.'

She followed Sophy out to the kitchen when she went to get the main course, commenting as she walked in, 'Jon says you haven't had much chance to get to grips with the house yet. Of course, you haven't been married very long.'

'No,' Sophy agreed with a grin. 'And if it hadn't been for the fact that the fault on the Nassau computer was relatively non-urgent, we'd have had to put the ceremony off completely.'

Mary-Beth's eyes widened and she protested. 'Oh, didn't Jon tell you—and I thought it was so romantic too, but poor Harry was practically foaming at the mouth at the time—Jon refused to come out until after the wedding. He told Harry there was simply no question of him postponing it. Not even if it meant that Nassau would have to look for someone else. I must tell you that I was stunned. Jon's a devoted computer man and always has been as long as I've known him. I was, however, delighted to discover that his work means far less to him than you. Fancy him not telling you.'

'I suppose he didn't want to at the time because he knew it would upset me,' Sophy offered, trying to slow down the hurried racing of her heartbeat. Jon had done that. But why? Their wedding could have been put off…and why hadn't he told her?

'He's obviously crazy in love with you,' Mary-Beth continued. 'We could tell that from the way he talked about you when he came to Nassau. Mind you there are some people who can never see a thing.' She lowered her voice slightly. 'One of the women who works on the Nassau project was really smitten with Jon. I told her he was married but she's one of those super-intelligent females who always goes all out for what she wants. You're lucky Jon is the faithful type, I wouldn't be telling you any of this if he weren't,' Mary-Beth assured her frankly. 'To be honest, sometimes Lillian worries me. I don't know what it is…a sort of obsessiveness about her somehow, a facility to blot out everything but what's important to her.'

'Lillian.' Sophy repeated the name lightly. 'Jon mentioned her to me. He used her pool during his rest periods.'

'Yes…I know.' Mary-Beth pulled a wry grimace when she saw Sophy's expression. 'Look, you've got nothing to worry about…Jon's crazy about you. He couldn't wait to rush back home.'

Sophy smiled, sensing that the other woman was regretting ever bringing up the subject of Lillian. It was silly to be jealous of the other woman. After all Jon had married *her;* had told her that he desired her. But not that he loved her, she thought achingly…and that was what she wanted. She wanted Jon to love her in the same total and complete way she loved him. But despite everything that Mary-Beth had said to the contrary Sophy knew that he did not.

It was gone one o'clock when the Silvers left. Leaving Jon in the drawing room Sophy wandered tiredly into the kitchen and started to attack the washing-up.

'Leave that. I'll do it. You've done more than enough.'

Jon had walked into the kitchen so quietly that she hadn't heard him and now he made her jump, almost dropping the plate she was holding.

'You're exhausted, Sophy.' She caught his frown as he reached out and turned her round, taking the plate from her. 'Go on up...I'm still wide-awake. I'll get rid of this lot.'

She wanted to protest that she wanted to stay with him, that they could wash up together, go to bed together but she knew she could not. As she hesitated, still standing within the curve of his arm, she found herself wishing that he would at least kiss her, even if it was only one of the lightly affectionate kisses he gave the children. For a moment she even thought he might. His head bent and then lifted again, and then he was releasing her, gently pushing her in the direction of the door.

She wanted to ask him why he had lied to her about the urgency of the work in Nassau, but she knew she could not.

Even though she tried to stay awake until she heard Jon come upstairs, she fell asleep almost immediately the moment she got into bed, not waking until the alarm went off in the morning.

ON THE FOLLOWING Tuesday Jon got a phone call whilst they were working together in the office. Never a particularly vociferous talker, the brief, monosyllabic curtness of his responses made her lift her head from the correspondence she was studying. It was unlike Jon to sound curt or to look as frowningly involved as he did now.

When he had hung up, she asked automatically, 'Problems?'

For a moment he seemed to hesitate and then he said bleakly, 'Yes...' He paused, and stared out of the window, and Sophy had the distinct impression that his mind was a long, long way away. They had never had that talk he had promised and in fact since the weekend she had been intensely conscious of a barrier between them.

'I'm afraid I've got to go to London again. I'll have to leave this afternoon.'

'Will you be gone long?'

He frowned again, and said curtly, 'I have no idea, Sophy.'

His tone chilled her, it was almost as though she had angered him in some way by asking. Could he sense how she felt about him. Was he already resenting the thought of the demands her love might lead her to make on him?

After that she was careful to keep all her comments to him strictly related to business matters. As soon as they had gone through the post she excused herself, explaining that she wanted to go upstairs and pack for him.

It was strange how being in love with someone could invest even the most mundane of inanimate objects with a special poignancy because they were part of the beloved, Sophy thought, carefully packing Jon's shirts. He was normally very neat in his habits but the shirt he had discarded the previous night lay across a chair and she picked it up, instantly tensing. The scent of Jon's skin clung to the cotton fabric, and she had to fight against a crazy impulse to bury her face in it and absorb that tiny bit of him into herself.

She made them both a light lunch but scarcely touched her own. Jon was not particularly hungry either, she noticed, watching him push his salad round the plate. It struck her then that he had lost weight and even looked faintly gaunt. His expression withdrawn…brooding almost, as though something—or someone—weighed heavily on his mind.

Had he guessed how she felt? Was he, because of that, regretting that he had married her? He wanted her he had said…but that wanting had been a physical need not an emotional one. Perhaps that was what he wanted to talk to her about…to warn her that he could not reciprocate her feelings.

She drove him to the station and waited there until he was on the train. He did not kiss her goodbye, nor did she let him see how much she had wanted him to.

For the children's sake she tried to behave normally, but she missed him intensely and some sixth sense told her that something was wrong…that there was something he was concealing from her.

It was Thursday morning before she heard from him. A brief telephone call merely to tell her what train he would be returning on.

'I'll drive into Cambridge and pick you up,' she offered, but he vetoed her offer, saying, 'No, don't bother. I'll have no trouble getting a taxi.'

Hurt and rebuffed, Sophy said nothing, letting him say 'goodbye' and hoping he wouldn't catch the misery in her own voice as she responded to him. At least he would soon be back…and they could talk. Or at least she hoped they could.

Neither David nor Alex would be home until early evening, as both of them had been invited to a schoolfriend's birthday party and another mother had offered to give them a lift home since she had to pass their house on the way to her own, so if Jon did want to talk to her, today would be an ideal opportunity.

Motivated by an impulse which she told herself she would have been wiser to resist, Sophy spent almost an hour getting ready for Jon's arrival. She put on her yellow sundress and did her face, telling herself as she did so, that all she was likely to achieve was to make Jon feel even more uncomfortable but it was impossible to resist the age-old feminine instinct to make herself as attractive as she could for the man she loved.

When she heard a car coming up the drive, she dropped her mascara wand and brushed her hair feverishly. It was only one o'clock...and Jon had specifically said that the train didn't reach Cambridge until one. It was a half an hour drive from Cambridge to the house...but then of course, it wouldn't be the first time he had got a timetable wrong.

Unable to hide the eagerness in her eyes she rushed downstairs and into the hall, flinging open the front door.

'Well, well, surprise, surprise...so you *are* pleased to see me after all.'

In dumb dismay Sophy watched as Chris climbed out of the car on the drive and staggered towards her. He had been drinking, she realised nervously, and there was a look in his eyes that made her feel slightly apprehensive.

'I thought you were Jon.' The admission was made before she could check herself, and she cursed herself under her breath as she saw the triumph in his eyes.

'So, all alone, are you?'

She made to shut the front door, but it was too late. Chris was inside, breathing heavily as he glowered at her. 'It's all your fault,' he told her thickly, lurching towards her, and grabbing hold of her arm. 'All of it.'

'Chris...you've had too much to drink,' Sophy protested. If only she could get him into the kitchen she might be able to sober him up and send him on his way. 'Look, let me make you some coffee.'

'Don't want coffee.' His voice was becoming slurred. 'Revenge...that's what I want. Ruined my life, that's what you did. Bloody—!' He called her a name that made her wince. 'Frigid bitches like you ought to be destroyed... because that's what you've done to me. It's your fault

Felicity left me. Christ, remembering what it's like touching you is enough to make any man impotent...'

Sophy tried not to listen while he hurled further insults at her. Surreptitiously she tried to free herself from his grasp but he suddenly realised what she was trying to do and grabbed hold of her with both hands, shaking her until she thought her neck would break.

'Are you cold in bed with him?' he demanded thickly, suddenly, his eyes narrowing onto her own, glittering with a hatred that suddenly turned her blood to ice water. 'Are you, Sophy?'

She cried out as he shook her again and her head hit the wall with a sickening thud. For a few seconds she thought she was going to faint but then the pain cleared. 'Let me go, Chris,' she pleaded, regretting the words, the instant she saw the satisfaction gleaming in his eyes. How on earth had she ever imagined herself in love with him... this apology for a man? He was so weak and immature, so ready to blame others for his own failings. Suddenly she was furiously angry with him, her anger overcoming her earlier fear.

'No woman could be cold in bed with Jon,' she told him truthfully, watching the fury twist his face.

'You're lying to me.' He said it thickly, pushing his face against her own so that she was forced to inhale the sour whisky fumes that clung to his breath. 'Don't make me angry, Sophy,' he warned her. 'You won't like it when I get angry. Felicity didn't,' he added, watching her.

Suddenly Sophy knew that he was threatening her with physical violence and she felt acutely sick. This was the man her mother had wanted her to marry; had held up to her as perfect husband material...this...this creature who had just openly boasted to her that he had used violence on his wife.

Suddenly she was so angry that there was no room or fear. 'Is that what you like, Chris,' she sneered, 'hitting women?' She watched his face contort and was horrified by the violence in him but knew that to let him see her shock would be to add to his sense of power over her.

'I think it's time you left, Chris,' she told him coolly. She saw the indecision flicker in his eyes, and knew that her controlled manner had disconcerted him. She could even feel the grip of his hands relaxing slightly. Pressing home her advantage, she added, 'Jon will be home soon.'

She knew instantly that she had made a mistake, the very mention of Jon's name brought forth a torrent of invective and abuse so foul that she had to close her ears to it.

'You made a fool of me by marrying him,' he told her pushing her back against the wall, 'but he won't want you anymore when he sees what I've done to you...'

He must be mentally deranged, Sophy thought as she tried to fight down her own panic, sensing that to show it would only be to inflame Chris even further. Even making allowances for the fact that he was drunk, his behaviour still hinted at an instability of temperament that shocked and frightened her, all the more so for being concealed so carefully in the past. And yet now she remembered that he had always had a streak of cruelty...always enjoyed hurting people.

She was about to make one last plea to him to set her free when she heard a car outside. Chris, still mouthing threats and insults at her, apparently had heard nothing, and Sophy prayed that Jon would find them before Chris did anything to hurt her. She didn't even dare move in case Chris realised...but then she heard a car door slam and saw Chris lift his head.

'Is that him?' he demanded, shaking her. 'Is it...?' He

was starting to drag her towards the kitchen. She had a mental image of the dangerously sharp cooking knives hanging on the wall just by the door and her stomach clenched in mute protest. She mustn't let Chris get in there.

Panic shuddered through her and she reacted instinctively, screaming Jon's name…hoping her scream would penetrate through the thick front door.

For agonising seconds nothing happened…and she was terrified he hadn't heard her. Chris was still dragging her towards the kitchen and then blessedly she heard the kitchen door open, and Jon was calling her name. At the same time the front door opened and a burly taxi driver stood there. Jon had obviously heard her cry for help and had instructed the driver to take the front door whilst he took the back.

'In here, guv!'

She heard the driver call out and then the kitchen door burst open and Jon was standing there. She gave a tiny sob of relief and closed her eyes, only to open them again as Chris was thrust away from her.

'It was her fault,' she heard him telling Jon in a faintly whining tone. 'She asked me to come over here. She told me she wanted to see me…that she wanted me to take her to bed—'

'No! No…that isn't true!' She was sobbing the denial, unable to believe what Chris was saying. She saw Jon raise his fist and Chris cringe away and then the taxi driver was in between them. 'Best not do that, guv,' he told Jon warningly. 'Let the law handle it…it's always the best way.'

'From a legal point of view maybe, but not from an emotional one,' Jon responded rawly but nevertheless his fist unclenched and though he was not particularly gentle as he hauled Chris well away from her, Sophy saw that he had himself well under control.

It was the taxi driver who rang for the police.

After that Sophy lost touch with what was happening. All of them had to go down to the police station, where she had to give a statement. Jon wasn't allowed to stay with her but she knew she had nothing to hide and managed to keep control of herself long enough to answer the questions.

When at last she was reunited with Jon, she was glad of the protective arm he put round her. It was sheer bliss to simply relax against his chest…so solid and safe, after the terror Chris had inflicted upon her.

'Will you be wishing to press charges, sir?'

Jon replied immediately. 'Yes, we will.' He felt Sophy tense and looked down at her. 'I know it won't be very pleasant,' he told her quietly, 'but for the sake of his wife, and any other unfortunate woman who might come in contact with him, I think you should.'

Sophy knew that he was right but more important than that was the recognition that in speaking as he had, he was saying that he completely believed her version of what had happened. She had told him about it in the car on the way to the police station, and he had been so silent that there had been a moment when she had actually wondered if he thought that she was the one who was lying and Chris was telling the truth.

Neither of them spoke about what had happened on the drive back. When they got inside Jon detained her, by placing his hand on her arm.

'I think you ought to go upstairs and try to rest. You're probably still suffering from shock.'

'I can't rest,' she told him honestly, 'I'm far too wrought up. I was so frightened…' she said it under her breath.

She shivered as he said roughly, 'If he had hurt you…'

She stopped him, shaking her head, putting her hand over his in an effort to soothe him. 'But thanks to you he didn't.' She shivered slightly. 'To think I never really realised what he was like.' She paused and then said huskily, dropping her head so that she wouldn't have to look at him. 'Thanks for…for believing me.'

She heard him swear under his breath, something he rarely did and her head jerked up. His mouth was white with strain, his eyes dark with anger. His hand cupped her jaw, his thumb stroking her mouth, the unexpected physical contact making her gulp in air, the raw ache inside her, suddenly mingling with a heady, delirious sense of release. If Chris had managed to deceive her so well about himself, perhaps he had deceived her in other ways as well. Perhaps she was not as sexually inadequate as she had always believed. After all, Chris had never ever made her feel the way Jon did. She had never ached for Chris the way she did for Jon, never melted at his lightest touch the way she did with Jon.

'Sophy…' The husky sound of his voice seemed to come to her from a great distance, almost as great as the distance that lay between them. With a small moan she moved, pressing herself against his body, feeling him tense in surprise and then unbelievably reach for her, taking her in his arms, his mouth hot and urgent on hers. He was kissing her as though he had never touched her before, as though he had starved for the taste and feel of her. She could feel his physical arousal and felt her own body stir in response.

'Sophy…Sophy.' Even when he had stopped kissing her, Jon didn't seem to be able to let her go or stop saying her name. It must be the release of tension which was causing such an intense reaction in him, she thought hazily, shuddering as his hand touched her body, longing suddenly to be free of the constrictions of her clothes.

Almost as though her desire had communicated itself

to him he stepped back from her and then picked her up. She was no tiny little doll but he took the stairs almost effortlessly, shouldering open the door to his bedroom and then turning so that he could use his foot to kick it closed.

'No!' Her protest was an instinctive female denial of the desire she saw glittering in his eyes, but he misinterpreted it, thinking it was him she was denying, and contradicted thickly, 'Yes...' reiterating, 'yes, Sophy. Yes...' as he slowly slid her body back down to the floor, keeping her pressed hard against him, so that she was hopelessly aware of every male inch of him.

Never in a thousand lifetimes had she imaged Jon capable of such intensely sensual behaviour and every pulse in her body quickened in response to it. There was no room for fear that she might somehow disappoint him, that was forgotten in the thick clamouring of her blood.

CHAPTER EIGHT

SECONDS, OR WAS it aeons, passed, Sophy wasn't aware of which…only of the heavy beat of Jon's body into her own, the timeless message of need and desire that passed from flesh to flesh and was returned.

She was dimly conscious of Jon reaching behind her to slide down the zip of her dress, just as she half heard the slithering sound the cotton made as it fell to the floor. All these were peripheral things, barely impinging on what really mattered, on the sensation of Jon's hot flesh pressed against her own as she tugged open his shirt and sighed her pleasure at being able to touch him as he was touching her.

Neither of them spoke. They were too busy touching… kissing. An urgent, aching impatience swept through her commanding her to actions at once both totally familiar and totally necessary so that nothing short of death could have stopped her from reaching down and fumbling impatiently with Jon's zip.

She felt his chest expand as he drew in his breath and for a moment teetered on the brink of her old insecurities but then his hand was on hers, helping her complete her task, his voice raw and thick with pleasure as she touched the maleness of him.

Then he was pushing her back against the door, muttering hoarse words of pleasure and arousal against her mouth, one hand sliding into her hair, the other curling round her waist as she melted into him…greedy for him.

His mouth left hers, long enough for him to groan. 'The bed...Sophy, we can't...' but he was moving away from her and that blotted out the meaning of his words, leaving behind only the sound and her fear that she was going to lose him, so she arched her body into his, winding her arms round him, grinding her hips into his in instinctive incitement.

'Sophy...' She could hear the grating protest in his voice, but could take no need of it. To lose him now would be to die. Her senses clamoured desperately for fulfilment, her body out of her control and obeying a far more primitive command than that of the mind. She wanted him...needed him. Not just against her but within her, deep inside her, at that place where her body pulsed and ached.

Moaning feverishly, she ran her hands over his torso, arching her back until her breasts were flattened against his chest, her hips writhing against him in a sensual rhythm they seemed to know by instinct.

'Dear God, Sophy...'

She felt the shudder run through him and saw the sweat cling to his skin. She could feel his heart racing and knew with a deep thrill of triumph that he had as little control over his response to her as she had of hers to him...less perhaps, she realised as he kissed her fiercely, his tongue eagerly invading her mouth. She could feel the frantic throbbing of his body against her, his weight pressing her back against the door and then suddenly he wrenched his mouth from hers, a harsh, inarticulate sound emerging from his throat. She knew, even without feeling him tug off her briefs that his need could not wait any longer.

She felt him lift her, balancing her weight against him and without having to be told automatically wrapped her legs around him, her hands clinging to his shoulders as she felt the first longed for movement of his body against her own.

Each driving thrust made her shudder with pleasure, her body eager to accommodate him, her muscles supplely responsive to the maleness of him.

Her spine arched her body taut as a bow in mute response to the driving force of him within her, the harsh oddly coordinated sound of their breathing an erotic stimulation she hadn't even realised existed.

It was over far too quickly, their bodies escaping the rationale of their minds, moving frantically together, meeting greedily as though they had starved for this frenetic physical union, Sophy thought, as her body trembled in the aftermath of the convulsive climax that had so recently racked her. She could still hear Jon's harsh breathing. She could feel the tension in his locked muscles as he slowly released her, letting her slide her feet back down to the floor. Neither of them spoke... She didn't honestly think either of them were capable of speaking. Jon arched his back, relieving her of his weight, his arms rigid, his hands against the door either side of her head. He leaned his forehead against his arm, and she could see that his hair at the front was soaked with sweat.

'I shouldn't have done that.' His voice was slow as though he had difficulty in forming the words. He raised his head and looked at her. 'Did I hurt you?'

She ached, it was true...and there had been an edge of violence in their lovemaking but it had been a shared, wanted violence...a need in both of them perhaps to work out physically the tensions Chris had caused.

'Only in the nicest possible way,' she told him honestly, checking as she felt him tense.

'You shouldn't say things like that to me. They have a

disastrous effect on my self-control…' He picked her up, completely surprising her, and carried her over to the bed.

'You lied to me,' he told her pleasantly, watching her eyes.

'I…' She was confused and apprehensive, but he didn't give her time to say anything.

'You told me I wouldn't enjoy possessing you…that I would find you disappointing.'

Incredibly in the fierce urgency of their coming together she had completely forgotten her old fears, and now her mouth fell open slightly. All at once she felt oddly light-headed—free, she realised giddily—for the first time since she reached womanhood, she was truly free of all fear and inhibition.

They were both sitting on the bed, but Jon got up and pulled off his shirt. While she was completely nude he was still almost fully dressed and she blushed to realise she had been so impatient for him she hadn't even paused to consider that fact before…

'What are you doing?'

He paused to smile at her as he pulled off his trousers. 'I'm getting ready to make love to my wife,' he told her with a smile.

Sophy stared indignantly at him. 'I thought you just did…'

The humour died out of his eyes, and suddenly his mouth was grim. 'That wasn't so much making love as satisfying an intense physical need. This is making love.' He turned to her, touching her with gentle fingers, stroking the velvet smoothness of her skin, pushing her down onto the bed and lying beside her, kissing her slowly and thoroughly, until she sighed languorously her body awash with the most deliciously sensual awareness.

Now that the frantic need for haste was gone, she could

touch him as she had been longing to do for so long. With her hands...and with her lips, delighting in his husky moans of pleasure as she discovered how best she could please him.

He had no need to make such discoveries. He already knew how to please her, she thought shiveringly, as his mouth caressed the hard peaks of her breasts, teasing and stimulating them until she cried out and arched against him.

It was only when his mouth touched the moist heart of her femininity that she tensed, trying desperately to wriggle away from him but his hands slid up under her, holding her hips, pinning her to the bed.

He raised his head and demanded rawly, 'Let me, Sophy. I want to pleasure you. I want to give you all that he never did. Trust me...'

She tried to relax, quivering under the slow assault of his tongue, gasping in shock at the sudden surge of pleasure invading her, her restraint completely swept away as Jon took advantage of her involuntary relaxation, his mouth moving delicately against the tender nub of flesh he had so unerringly found, ignoring her frantic protests for him to stop.

Then suddenly she was no longer capable of any form of protests; incapable of anything other than submitting to the waves of pleasure convulsing her body.

Some time later...she wasn't capable of working out how much, she felt him move to take her in his arms and gently lick away her tears of pleasure. He took her hand and placed it on his body and under his guidance she felt the full male power of him.

It seemed impossible that her body should ache for him already but it did, as though simply by feeling his arousal she herself immediately shared it.

'See,' he murmured into her ear. 'That's what loving you does to me, Sophy.'

She shivered, immeasurably affected by the knowledge that he desired her; that she was capable of arousing such desire within him.

This time there was no urgency…no haste…and the slow, almost languorous way he filled her, made her sigh and murmur with delight, her body moving effortlessly to the rhythm he set.

She fell asleep in his arms, conscious of an overwhelming sense of well-being…of inner peace and a joy so intense, she felt it must radiate from her in a physical aura. She loved him…and she was already asleep before she remembered that he did not love her.

'GOOD, I'M GLAD YOU'RE awake. Uncle Jon said we weren't to wake you.' Sophy opened her eyes slowly. What was she doing in Jon's bed? And then she remembered.

To cover her embarrassment she asked Alex, 'What time is it?'

'Supper time,' David told her gloomily. 'I'm starving, and all Uncle Jon can cook is beans on toast.'

'That's a lie,' Alex retorted hotly, immediately defending her idol. 'He can do lots of things.'

'Such as?'

Sophy let them argue, closing her eyes and slowly trying to come to terms with what had happened. She and Jon had made love. She shivered lightly and felt tiny beads of sweat spring up on her skin as she remembered exactly how they had made love.

The children's quarreling suddenly pierced her thoughts and she sat up, clinging to the duvet as she realised that she was still naked.

'Stop it, both of you,' she said firmly. 'I'll get up and come down and make your supper.'

'See what you've done now,' Alex accused her brother, 'Uncle Jon said—'

'What Uncle Jon said was that neither of you were to come in here and wake Sophy up,' that gentleman said drily from the doorway.

None of them had seen him come in. Sophy felt herself flush a brilliant scarlet as he looked at her. Alex, who was looking at her uncle rather guiltily, missed Sophy's reaction but David did not. A little to her surprise he got up off the bed, and taking hold of Alex's hand, said firmly to his sister. 'Come on…we're going downstairs.'

Sophy didn't want them to leave. She didn't want to be alone with Jon… She felt both embarrassed and apprehensive. What must he think of her? Had he guessed that she loved him?

'David, it seems, is growing up,' he murmured lightly as he took the place his nephew had vacated beside her on the bed, elucidating when she looked puzzled. 'He obviously thought we wanted to be alone.'

He bent his head, so that she couldn't see his expression and said slowly, 'Sophy, we have to talk.'

He had said that before but this time the flare of panic inside her was far greater. 'Not now, Jon.' There was a note of pleading in her voice that made him look at her. 'I feel so muzzy,' she told him, fibbing a little. 'Chris, the shock…'

'Of course.' His voice was completely even but she was conscious of a sudden coolness in his manner, a faint withdrawal from her which, because she was so acutely aware of everything about him, she recognised immediately and which defeated her tenuous self-control. This afternoon both of them had been acting out of character. She couldn't blame him if now he was wishing none of it had ever happened, but at least nothing could ever take from her her memories of him as her lover…and as her lover he had been both demanding and tender. She had memories she would cherish for the rest of her life. But memories would not keep her warm at night when Jon was not there…

'We'll talk another time, then.' He was getting up, and soon he would be gone.

She forced a brief smile.

'I'll be down shortly.' She saw that he was about to protest and added, 'I won't sleep if I stay in bed…and besides I'd have to go back to my own room.'

She held her breath as she waited for him to contradict her statement and to tell her that she was sleeping with him from now on, but he didn't, and at last she had to expel it and listen with an aching heart as he said mildly, 'As you wish.'

No doubt he was relieved that she was going back to her own room, she thought bitterly as she showered and then dressed. After all, by making that statement she had saved him the embarrassment of asking her to go back.

WE MUST TALK, Jon had said, but they didn't seem to get the opportunity to do so. It was now almost twenty-four hours since he had returned from London, and he had spent almost all of the morning shut in his study.

Sophy had gone in once with a cup of coffee. Jon had been on the phone, the conversation he was having abruptly cut short as she walked in, almost as though he did not want her to overhear what he was saying. After that she didn't go in again.

What had happened to that easy friendship that once had existed between them? Did love automatically kill friendship, or was it that friendship was quite simply no longer enough?

She was just about to make lunch when Jon walked into the kitchen and announced that he was going out.

'I'm meeting Harry in Cambridge,' he told her, 'I shan't be very long.'

She offered to drive him in, but he shook his head. 'It's okay, I've already booked a taxi.'

Sophy turned away, hoping he would not see the hurt pain she knew was in her eyes, and she thought she had succeeded until she heard him say raggedly, 'Sophy, I...' She turned round and saw the hand he had extended towards her as though he wanted to touch her, fall back to his side, his expression grimly unreadable, as he left his sentence unfinished.

There was such an air of constraint about him that even a complete stranger must have been aware of it, Sophy thought miserably as she watched his taxi drive away. What was causing it? Her? Their relationship?

She had some work to do for Jon—bills to send out and correspondence to attend to, but although her fingers moved deftly enough over the keys of her typewriter, her mind was not really on what she was doing.

When the doorbell rang she started up in surprise, her heart thudding nervously. She was not expecting anyone and after Chris's visit yesterday she felt acutely nervous, her mouth dry and her palms sticky. The bell rang again and she forced herself to get to her feet and walk to the front door.

Keeping the safety catch on, she opened it fractionally.

A tall, dark-haired woman stood there, her back to the door, one high-heeled, sandalled foot tapping imperiously, scarlet nails drumming impatiently against a cream leather shoulder bag.

Water-straight black hair fell to her shoulders in a satin sheet, her arms and legs were deeply tanned and the perfection of her slim body was provocatively revealed in a vibrant red cotton sheath dress that clung to her curves.

As Sophy opened the door she turned her head, slanting faintly almond-shaped, brown eyes surveying Sophy with arrogant disdain. Her face was as beautifully tanned as her body, her mouth painted the same rich scarlet as her dress. The car she had arrived in was parked across the drive, as though it had been stopped in a hurry.

'You are Jon's wife?'

Sophy felt her heart sink as she caught the challenging ring in the American-accented voice.

'Yes. Yes, I am.'

'Good. We have to talk.' She stepped closer to the door, and Sophy automatically released the chain, stepping back.

'I'm afraid I don't know you…' she began, fascinated as well as slightly repelled by the sneering curl of the full mouth as the other woman mocked.

'I cannot believe that. I'm sure Jon must have mentioned me to you. I am Lillian Banks. Jon and I are lovers.'

Sophy recognised the name immediately but distantly, all her powers of concentration focused on her visitor's final statement.

This was the woman whose pool Jon had used when he was in Nassau. The woman Mary-Beth had described to her as rather unbalanced…as almost obsessive about Jon.

'Lovers?' Her tongue felt thick and clumsy, making it difficult for her to form the words. 'I…'

'You are shocked. I can see.' Slim shoulders shrugged. 'I knew how it would be, but I told Jon it was better that you knew. He is a gentle man and would not wish to cause anyone pain.' She shrugged again. 'He has married you because of his responsibilities of course but from the moment we met both of us knew—'

'You're lying.'

The scarlet mouth smiled.

'Why don't we sit down comfortably and discuss this as adults?'

Sophy could not understand how Mary-Beth could ever have thought of this woman as being anything other than completely self-possessed and in control. Like a robot she found herself leading the way to the sitting room, doing what she was instructed to do.

'I know this must be a shock to you but these things do happen. Jon and I knew the moment we met. We have so much in common. His work...our feelings about so many things. You may not believe this—' she looked sideways at Sophy and then smiled secretively, the almond eyes veiled by thick dark lashes as though she were gloating over something very special and private '—but it was several days before Jon and I even went to bed together. We had so much to talk about.' She laughed, and then looked at Sophy again, adding softly, 'Of course when we did go to bed, I knew immediately how it would be.' She moistened her lips with her tongue, and Sophy felt acutely sick, imagining that full mouth clinging to Jon's, touching his body.

'But I love him.' She hadn't realised she had said the painful words out loud until she realised that Lillian was looking directly at her, the almond eyes narrowed and almost feral in their hatred.

'Maybe,' Lillian said flatly, 'but Jon does not love you. He loves me. Oh, yes, it is true,' she continued before Sophy could interrupt. 'Why else would he invite me to come to England? Why else would he meet my plane... book us both into the same hotel?' She smiled again, the cold cruelty in her smile making Sophy feel as though those scarlet nails had just been raked across her heart, inflicting wounds that would never heal.

'Oh, it is quite true,' Lillian said softly. 'You may check if you wish. We were booked into separate rooms of course. Here, I have the number of the hotel.' She opened her bag and gave Sophy a brochure.

'Well…are you going to ring them?'

What was the point? Sophy knew she couldn't be lying. Everything was so clear now. No wonder Jon had been so off-hand with her…so strained before he went to London. But he had come back. He had made love to her…

'Unfortunately we had a quarrel while we were there.' She shrugged again. 'Jon wanted me to come back here with him but I told him he must tell you about us first. We argued and he left. This morning though he telephoned me and we made up…'

Suddenly the reason Jon had made love to her was sickeningly clear to Sophy. He had quarrelled with Lillian and had made love to her out of nothing more than sheer physical frustration. She felt sick to her soul when she thought of how she had responded to him, how she had felt in his arms…but it had not been her he was loving, it had been this woman sitting so triumphantly opposite her, watching her now with hard, cold eyes.

'Why have you come here?' Sophy asked tonelessly.

'Surely that is obvious? To see Jon and to tell you that you no longer have any place in his life. You must understand that Jon and I love one another, that I am the one he wants at his side.'

'But *I* am the one he married,' Sophy persisted, not really knowing why she was fighting or what for; she had already lost it all.

'A piece of paper that means nothing…Jon will divorce you.'

What could she say? Part of her could not believe that any of this was really happening. The Jon that Lillian was talking about was not the Jon she knew…but then what did she really know about the man she had married? She had thought him sexless, remote, totally engrossed in his work and she had discovered for herself that none of those things were true.

'Of course you will be provided for financially.'

Sophy glanced up at that, her mouth hardening, but before she could speak her tormentor continued coolly. 'You will stay here in this house with the children. Jon will come back to Nassau with me.'

She would stay with the children? She blinked and stared at Lillian. 'The children are Jon's responsibility,' she said coldly. 'They are the son and daughter of his dead brother.'

For the first time since Lillian's arrival she felt she was the one with the advantage. Lillian blinked and frowned, her superb composure deserting her briefly, her mouth twisting petulantly.

'Jon does not want them,' she said positively at last. 'All he wants is me.'

Now it was Sophy's turn to frown. That did not sound like the Jon she knew…or at least thought she knew but then she remembered that before they had married Jon had mentioned putting the children in a home. He seemed to love them so much, though. Just as he seemed to want you so much, a bitter little voice mocked her, and look how real that was.

Through the sitting-room window she saw a taxi come down the drive and stop. Motionlessly she watched Jon get out, and pause to pay the driver. He looked tired, she noticed, immediately checking the pain and anguish that welled up inside her.

From her chair Lillian could not see the window. Smiling tightly at her Sophy got up.

'Please excuse me a second,' she muttered moving to open the door. She really could not endure anymore, and certainly not the sight of Jon being reunited with the woman he loved.

She reached the front door at the same time as Jon, opening it for him. He started to smile at her, the smile freezing suddenly, as he demanded, 'What's wrong?'

Sophy was shaking now with a mixture of anger and agony. How could he stand there and pretend a concern for her they both knew he could not possibly feel?

In a voice tight with pain she told him. 'You've got a visitor—in the sitting room. Lillian Banks!' She almost spat the name at him, half of her knowing that she was reacting like someone in a soap melodrama, the other half acknowledging that like any other human being she was conditioned to react to pain so instinctively that her responses were bound to appear trite and theatrical. 'She's just been telling me about your plans for the future—plans which it seems don't include either me or the children... Well, that's fine by me,' she rushed on bitterly. 'In fact it's probably the very best thing that could have happened.' It wasn't what she had intended to say at all, but hurt pride compelled her to make some attempt at self-defence; to at least try to hide from Jon the hurt he was causing her.

His hand shot out gripping her wrist, making her cry out sharply in physical pain.

She had never seen him look so hard or so angry before, and she could not understand why he was doing so now. 'Are you trying to tell me you want our marriage to end, Sophy?' he demanded harshly. 'Is that what you're saying?'

'Yes! Yes!' She practically screamed the word at him, tears flooding down her face as she tried desperately to

pull away from him. The sitting-room door opened and
Lillian exclaimed purringly, 'Jon, darling...' Sophy felt
the pressure round her wrist relax and instinctively made
her escape, fleeing upstairs to the privacy and sanctuary
of her own bedroom.

Once there, oddly enough, her tears stopped. The pain
inside her was too intense for crying. Later she couldn't
recall how long she stayed there...how much time elapsed
after Jon's arrival before he left again, this time with
Lillian.

From her window Sophy saw them both get into Lillian's
car. Lillian was smiling but she couldn't see Jon's face.

So this was how marriages ended, she thought emptily
once they had gone. So this was what it felt like to be the
victim of a broken marriage. Empty...alone...waiting for a
pain so enormous and overwhelming that the very thought
of it made her shiver in dread.

Somehow she managed to go downstairs and through
the motions of making herself a cup of coffee. Somehow
she remembered that the children had to be collected from
school, that life had to go on as normal.

The phone rang. She hesitated before answering it, and
then picked up the receiver.

'Sophy?'

She recognised Harry's American accent straight away.

'Is Jon there?' He sounded anxious and flustered.

'He's just left.' How toneless and light her own voice
was. She replaced the receiver slowly. The phone started
to ring again almost immediately, its summons imperative
and sharp. She stared at it unblinkingly and then took it
off the hook. She had the children to pick up, she must
remember that.

Later Sophy realised that she had had no right to
be driving at all that afternoon, never mind in such a

potentially lethal, powerful car. All her actions were automatic and reflexive, directed by that tiny part of her brain which was not trying desperately to assimilate her pain.

She even managed to smile at David and Alex as they clambered into the car and started chattering to her, although she was conscious of David giving her one or two puzzled looks.

How could Jon not want them? A fierce wave of protective love for them surged over her. Well she would want them and she would fight for the right to love and care for them. Slowly different pieces of information were filtering through her brain. She stared at the house as she parked the car. How could she afford to keep it on? How much of an allowance would Jon give her? He was a comparatively wealthy man but her heart rebelled at the thought of taking so much as a penny from him. If she wanted to keep the children though, she would have to support them. She couldn't work full-time and give them the love and attention they were going to need. Didn't Jon care what he was doing to them, even if he didn't care about her? He owed it to them. She sighed and tried to redirect her thoughts. She had seen this same situation played out so often before…when did adults ever really think about their children, when they were gripped by the intensity of love? People these days weren't brought up to put others before themselves any longer and in many ways that was a good thing. Too many people, mainly of her own sex, had made themselves martyrs to others' demands and needs too often in the past…but the children. Stop thinking about it, she told herself as she went into the house. She knew she had to stop the tormenting thoughts swirling round in her mind or go mad from the agony of them. She tried to submerge them in physical activity, busying herself making the milkshake the children always had when they came back from school.

'When will Uncle Jon be back?' David asked as he and Alex sat down at the table. Instantly Sophy stiffened. What should she tell them? For the first time it struck her that Jon might not come back at all, ever. The knowledge was like a physical blow, so painful that she went white.

'Sophy, what's wrong?' There was anxiety and something else in David's voice. Fear?

Resolutely Sophy pulled herself together and tried to smile. Her facial muscles were so stiff she could barely move them.

'Nothing,' she said as reassuringly as she could. 'I'm not sure when he will be back.'

'Where's he gone?'

That was Alex, frowning slightly, picking up the atmosphere of tension that hung over the kitchen. 'Where is he?'

'He had to go out.' Careful, Sophy, she warned herself, any more of this and you'll be breaking down completely. Walking over to the sink so that she had her back to them, she said as carelessly as she could, 'You know what he's like when he's…working. I don't really know when he'll be back.'

It seemed to satisfy them, but for how long? Surely Jon wouldn't leave her to tell them alone? But no…he wasn't that sort of man. Was he?

CHAPTER NINE

THE PHONE RANG at ten o'clock and she knew it was Jon even before she picked up the receiver. It was the call she had been dreading all evening, ever since she had put the receiver in its place after putting the children to bed.

'Sophy?' He said her name roughly, angrily almost and that hurt. By what right was he angry with her? She was the one who should feel that emotion but her pain was too great to allow her the relief of anger.

'Sophy, we need to talk.' Urgency laced the words closely together making his voice sharper, different. Already he was alien to her...not the Jon she knew but a different Jon.

Jealousy tore at her, making it impossible for her to speak to him without breaking down completely, her 'No!' rough and unsteady.

'Sophy!' He said her name again, and the receiver shook in her damp hand. She knew she did not have the control to go through what had to be gone through right now. She couldn't even listen to the angry cadences of his voice without breaking apart inside, without remembering how he had said her name while they made love...how the reverberations of it had passed from his body to her own.

'Jon, please. Lillian has told me everything.' She was speaking quickly, lightly as though not daring to linger over the words in case that made them too real. She heard him swear and flinched.

'Sophy...please...'

'No...no. I don't want to talk about it, Jon. Let's just go ahead and get a divorce. I'll stay here with the children.' Her voice petered out as she sensed his shock. 'Unless you want us to move out.' She thought she heard him draw in his breath harshly, a sound of painful anguish as though somehow she had hurt him. Or was it that hearing the words was making it real for him too...making him see what he would be doing to David and Alex. The children will stay with you, Lillian had said, we don't want them.

'No! Promise me you won't move out, Sophy. Promise me.'

'Very well...'

She heard him sigh as though her soft acquiescence was not enough and then he was saying thickly, 'Have you thought about what this is going to do to the kids, Sophy?'

Had *she* thought about it? All at once she was angry, so much so that she could not speak to him any more. She put down the receiver with a bang and then wiped her damp palm distastefully on her skirt.

The phone rang again almost immediately and she stared at it wanting to deny its imperative call, but somehow impelled to pick up the receiver.

'Sophy. No, don't hang up...listen to me. If you need to get in touch with me for anything, I'm staying with Harry and Mary-Beth in Cambridge.' As though something in her silence encouraged him he went on raggedly. 'We have to talk, Sophy. We...'

It was that 'we' that did it. There was no 'we' where they were concerned. They were not a single unit but two separate ones.

In a cold precise little voice she barely recognised as her own she asked slowly. 'And Lillian, Jon, is she staying with Harry and Mary-Beth too?'

She heard him swear, and then say curtly. 'Yes, she is, but Sophy—'

She cut him off before he could say any more, telling him quietly, 'Then I don't think we have anything to say to one another really, do you, Jon?'

This time, after she had replaced the receiver, the telephone did not ring again and she did not really expect it to.

Upstairs alone in bed, she tried to clear her mind so that she could force it to accept a truth it did not want to know. It hurt that Jon had not even told her himself about Lillian. She had known something was wrong but she had had no idea what that something was.

She laughed then, a high hysterical sound that shocked her own ears until she controlled it. How ironic that Jon should meet and fall in love with Lillian such a very short time after marrying her.

How doubly ironic when she remembered what Mary-Beth had said about Jon postponing the trip so that they could be married first. How he must have regretted not waiting. She turned uneasily in her bed wondering how long it would take their divorce to go through. She wasn't very well up in the legalities of these things. And then her mind drifted to David and Alex. Both of them adored Jon. How could she tell them what was happening in such a way that neither of them would ever know that their uncle had rejected them?

It was all so out of character somehow and yet wasn't she just telling herself that because she didn't want to believe the truth? She had to hand it to Lillian, coming to see her like that. In her place she doubted that she would have had the courage to do so. And yet Sophy knew that Lillian had enjoyed telling her, hurting her. The thought of Jon deliberately lying to her, so that he could be with

Lillian, was so galling and painful that she could scarcely
endure it. And then to come back and make love to her…
to substitute her for Lillian, because that was surely what
he had done.

He said he wanted you, an inner voice taunted her…
perhaps he had, Sophy acknowledged. Man was a strange
animal and could desire what he did not love…or perhaps
that had simply been his way of trying to fight free of his
love for Lillian. Perhaps he had felt honour bound to at
least try to make a success of their marriage and maybe
he had hoped that in making love to her he could forget
the other woman. Obviously he had not done so.

By the time morning came, she was totally exhausted
and had to drag herself downstairs to get the children's
breakfast.

Both of them commented on her pale face.

'I haven't been feeling very well,' she fibbed to them
and saw David's eyes widen as he asked her curiously,
'Does that mean you and Uncle Jon are going to have a
baby? Ladies sometimes aren't very well when they do.'

A baby? She managed a tight smile and shook her head
negatively. But what if she was wrong? What if she was
carrying Jon's child? It was, after all, perfectly possible.

She would just have to worry about that eventually if it
actually happened, she told herself grimly.

Because it was a Saturday there was no need for her
to take the children to school, but both of them had made
arrangements to see friends and by the time Sophy got
back from ferrying them to their individual destinations
it was gone eleven o'clock.

As she turned into the drive she realised that the day
had become very overcast, the threat of thunder hanging
sullenly on the too still air.

It was time the weather broke; they needed a storm to

clear the air and rain for the over-parched garden. A tension headache gripped her forehead in a vice as she walked inside. She had always been petrified of storms. Not so much the thunder but the lightning—a childhood hang-up from a story someone had once told her about someone being struck by lightning and 'frizzled to death'. Knowing now that her fear was illogical still did not remove it and she shivered slightly as she made herself a cup of coffee, dreading the storm to come.

The house had never seemed more empty. She had loved it when she first came here as Jon's assistant, and what happy plans she had made for it when she had agreed to marry him. She had pictured it as a proper home... Now she was alone with the reality that said a house no matter how pleasant was merely a shell. It was people who made that shell a home.

By one o'clock the sky was a sullen grey; and it was dark enough for her to need to switch the kitchen light on. The sudden ring on the front doorbell jarred her too sensitive nerves.

Jon! She whispered the name, trying to control the crazy leap of her pulses and to deny the sudden mental picture she had of the man. How could there ever have been a time when she had scathingly dismissed him as sexually unattractive? Being married to him had been like discovering a completely different person hidden away behind a protective disguise.

In his touch, in his kiss, was all the maleness any woman could ever want, she acknowledged weakly, knowing, even as she fought to subdue the traitorous leap of hope jerking her heart, that it would not be Jon outside. After all why would he ring the bell when he had a key and why would he come back at all, when he had already taken what he really wanted with him?

Nevertheless she went to open the door, her face losing all colour when she saw Mary-Beth standing outside.

'No. Sophy…please let me in,' the American woman pleaded, guessing from her expression that Sophy did not want to see her.

Good manners prevented Sophy from shutting the door in her face but her back was rigid with withdrawal as she stepped back into the hall.

'Sophy, Jon doesn't know I'm here,' Mary-Beth began, following her into the kitchen, watching as Sophy tensed as she caught the distant noise of thunder—so distant that Sophy had had to strain her ears to catch it. The storm was still a good ways off. She tried to relax. She had no idea what Mary-Beth was doing here, but since she had come… She sighed, and asked her guest if she wanted a cup of coffee.

'What I want is for you to sit down and tell me why you've thrown Jon out,' Mary-Beth told her forthrightly. 'I thought you loved him.'

'I do.' The admission was wrung out of her before she could silence it, her face ashen as she realised her idiocy.

Her ears, tensely alert for the sound, caught the still distant dullness of fresh thunder.

'Do you find storms frightening?'

She gave Mary-Beth a tense grimace, and acknowledged shortly, 'Yes.' Another time she might have wondered at the faintly pleased gleam she saw in the other woman's eyes but not now.

Her defences completely destroyed by losing Jon, the threat of a thunderstorm was just more than she could cope with.

'Sophy, come and sit down.' Very gently Mary-Beth touched her arm, picking up both mugs of coffee and gently shepherding Sophy into the sitting room.

She waited until they were both sitting down before speaking again and then said quietly, 'I can understand why you feel hurt and angry with Jon for deceiving you but why won't you let him talk to you...explain?'

Sophy tried to appear calmer than she felt. 'What is there left to talk about?' she asked emotionlessly. 'I think Lillian has already said it all.' She shrugged and spread her hands, disturbed to see how much they shook. 'She and Jon are lovers...Jon wants to divorce me so that he can be with her. It is all quite plain really...I don't need telling twice.'

Her voice sharpened with anguish over the last words and she got up, pacing over to the window to stare at the yellow tinged greyness of the overcast sky.

'Lillian told you that she and Jon were *lovers?*'

Why was Mary-Beth sounding so shocked? Jon and Lillian were staying with her. She must be perfectly aware of the situation.

'She told me everything,' Sophy reiterated expressionlessly. 'About how Jon asked her to come to London... how they stayed there together in an hotel.' Her mouth twisted bitterly. 'She even suggested I should ring the hotel and check.'

'Sophy?'

She swung round to look at Mary-Beth as she caught the anxiety in her voice, but the frown on Mary-Beth's face suddenly lifted. 'Oh, it's all right. You will be staying here?'

'If Jon lets me. Lillian told me that they don't want the children and even if I didn't love both of them very much myself, I could hardly walk out and leave them.' She saw Mary-Beth look at her watch and then the American was saying hurriedly, 'Look I must run... Are you doing anything during the rest of the day? Going out?'

She must be embarrassed, Sophy realised, and that was

why she was having to take refuge in inane social chit-chat; even so she responded to the questions, shaking her head and explaining that both children were out with friends and would not be back until after supper.

Thunder rolled again, marginally nearer this time and Sophy winced.

'If I were you I'd go upstairs and bury your head under a pillow,' Mary-Beth suggested. 'That way you won't hear it.'

Sophy walked with her to the door and watched until her car had completely disappeared feeling that somehow she had just severed her final link with Jon. The ache in her temples had become a fully fledged pain; pain, in fact, seemed to invade her whole body. She went upstairs on dragging feet, but instead of going into her own room she went into Jon's.

The room was clean and tidy just as she had left it after cleaning it yesterday morning and yet overwhelmingly it reminded her of him. One of his shirts half hung out of the laundry basket by the door and she went automatically to push it in, tensing as her fingers curled round the soft cotton and she was irresistibly aware of how the fabric had clung to his body. Like a sleepwalker she lifted the shirt from the empty basket, pressing its softness to her face. She wanted to cry but the tears had solidified in a lump in her chest—a lump that ached and hurt with every breath she tried to take. A scent that was exclusively Jon's filled her senses with an awareness of him, and almost without realising what she was doing she stumbled over to his bed and flung herself down full length on it, still clutching his shirt. Outside the sky darkened, suddenly split by the first sizzling arc of lightning. Sophy cried out curling up into a tense ball, burying her face in Jon's pillow.

Her fear of the storm seemed to release the tight knot of pain inside her and suddenly she was crying, tearing, ugly sobs that shook her body and soaked the shirt and pillow she was still clinging to. Outside the storm drew nearer and her tears slowly gave way to terror. Logic told her that she should get up and close the curtains but the fear chaining her to the bed was too great.

An hour, maybe more, passed as she lay there too terrified to move and yet oddly comforted by the indefinable presence of Jon that still clung to the room.

Suddenly it started to rain, almost torrentially so, the sound of it drowning out everything else.

Downstairs a door banged and Sophy listened to it, wondering if she had left a window open. If so the floor beneath it would surely be soaked.

Closer now the thunder rolled, lightning arcing brilliant across the sky, illuminating the darkness of the room. She moaned and covered her ears.

'Sophy.'

A hand touched her shoulder. Her eyes opened in stunned disbelief to look into Jon's. He was bending towards the bed. His shirt was soaked through, clinging to his skin and he had brought in with him the cool fresh smell of rain. He opened his mouth to speak, the words drowned out by the ferocity of the storm, the brilliance of the lightning jagging across the sky making Sophy scream out in terror and release her pillow to fling herself against him, burying her face in his shoulder.

She felt him shake and for a moment thought he was laughing at her but then she felt his hand on her hair, his voice roughly concerned in her ear, as his arms came round her, and his voice soothed her fear.

'I'll go and close the curtains.'

She didn't want to let him go but suddenly all that had happened reminded her that she had no right to be in his arms…no place within their security and so she withdrew from him, and watched him walk across the floor.

The curtains were thick, old-fashioned ones, and instantly blotted out the storm, together with what little daylight there was. In the gloom she could barely make out Jon's outline, until he switched on the bedside lamp.

'That's some storm out there,' he told her wryly. 'I'm soaked…I'll have to take this off.' He stripped off his shirt, dropping it into the laundry basket, opening his wardrobe to get another; all simple automatic movements and yet ones that moved her to great joy and pain. He didn't put the shirt on though, pausing to turn and look across the room at her.

'Sophy, why wouldn't you let me talk to you?'

His voice was quiet, and if she hadn't known better she might have said it was quite definitely edged with pain.

She could feel the tight knot returning to her chest and couldn't speak, simply shaking her head. She knew he was coming towards her and that she should get off his bed and move away but something told her that her legs simply would not allow her to stand. As he reached her he stretched out his hand, and gently tugged away the shirt she had been clinging to.

A hot wave of colour flooded her skin as Sophy found herself unable to free herself from his gaze. He had taken off his glasses—to dry them, she supposed, and had not put them back, so that she could quite clearly see the wry amusement darkening his eyes to indigo blue.

'What's this?'

He said it softly, watching her like a hunter stalking his prey…seeing far too much for someone who was supposed to be so short-sighted.

'I was cold.'

She saw his eyebrows lift with pardonable mockery,

shock jolting through her body as he said softly. 'How disappointing... I was hoping it was a love-object substitute...' he sat down beside her and concluded silkily, 'and that that love-object was me.'

How could he do this to her? Her fingers curled into her palms, not even the dying sound of the storm having the power to frighten her now.

'Why are you saying these things to me?' she demanded huskily. 'Isn't Lillian enough for you?'

His prompt 'No,' stunned her. She could only stare silently up at him, her mouth slightly open. All humour had gone from his eyes now and in fact they were almost frighteningly grim.

'I could shake you, Sophy, for being so stupid,' he told her bitingly. 'How on earth could you be so easily deceived?'

'Deceived?'

'I don't care what Lillian might have told you.' He reached out and cupped her face. 'Sophy, Lillian and I were never lovers. Oh, I know what she told you,' he continued before she could speak, 'but only because Mary-Beth told me. I had no idea that Lillian had—' He broke off, his mouth curling in bitter derision. 'That woman astounds me, astounds and frightens...'

'Jon...'

'No...listen to me. Let me tell you the full story,' he paused and when she made no move to speak he started softly, 'I told you that I met Lillian when I went to Nassau, but what I didn't tell you was that she seemed to develop what, for lack of a better description, I can only describe as some sort of fixation about me.' He grimaced faintly. 'It got so bad that I was actually having to find ways to avoid her. When she first invited me to use her apartment and pool I had no idea. In the end I had to appeal to Mary-Beth for help and it was then that I discovered that Lillian has a history of these almost violent fixations. It's a sad story in a way. In many respects she's absolutely brilliant...perhaps almost too much so. Apparently she had some sort of breakdown just after she left university but she's very good at her job and Harry, who's a bit of a softie in many ways, took her on to his staff after he heard about her history of mental problems from his predecessor. Workwise he has no criticism of her at all but emotionally, she doesn't seem to have any conception of reality or self-control.

'When he told me all this I was glad that I was leaving Nassau so soon—and not only for that reason,' he added cryptically. 'I got the shock of my life when I walked into that hotel in London and found her waiting for me there in the foyer. Apparently Harry had had to ring Nassau and he had spoken to her on the telephone—about some problems she was having with her work. She asked him about me and without thinking he mentioned that I was going to London to do some work for Lexicons, which happens to be a company that Nassau deal with.' He shrugged tiredly.

'Harry admits now that that was a mistake, but as he says, it never even crossed his mind that Lillian would ring Lexicons, pretending to be my wife and find out from them which hotel they had booked me into and when I could be expected there.' He saw Sophy's expression and smiled harshly. 'She was quite proud of what she did, believe me. For me it was like the start of a nightmare. Every time I tried to persuade her to go back to Nassau she started threatening to destroy herself. Finally I managed to persuade her to let me ring Harry and he came down to London straight away to talk to her.

'The plan was that Harry would see her safely on to a plane to go home and that she would be met at the other end, but somehow it backfired and she managed to give Harry the slip.

'He rang me yesterday morning to warn me. That was why I went out to see him so that we could try and work out what on earth she was going to do. The last thing I expected was that she would turn up here.

'Lillian is an extremely mentally disturbed young woman, Sophy,' he said quietly. 'If I give you my word that she and I have never been lovers and that I would never want her as my lover, would you believe me?'

'Where is she now?' Her throat was dry with tension.

'With Harry and Mary-Beth. I managed to persuade her to drive me over there yesterday afternoon. I thought you were angry with me because I hadn't told you what was happening. I should have done but our own relationship seemed too tenuous…so fragile that I felt I couldn't risk destroying it by burdening you with problems that weren't really yours. Especially after the shock of Chris's attack.'

'She said you loved her…' Her voice was cracked and uneven. 'She said you wanted to divorce me.'

'She's a very sick person, Sophy, so totally out of touch with reality that I'm afraid she'll never be wholly sane again. Believe me, I did nothing…nothing to encourage her in her fantasies.' He smiled rather grimly. 'There was only one woman on my mind whilst I was in Nassau and that was you. Do you believe me?'

'Yes.' She said it huskily and knew that it was true. Her heart somersaulted as he lifted her hand to his mouth and pressed his lips to her palm, caressing it softly with his tongue.

'How did you know what Lillian had said to me?'

'Mary-Beth told me. She also told me something else.' Sophy tensed and looked at him, remembering her own admission to Mary-Beth that she loved him.

'She said you were frightened of thunder storms,' Jon told her softly, 'and that she'd told you to bury your head under a pillow. I'm glad you chose my pillow, Sophy.'

She could feel the heat coming off his skin, and being in his arms was like coming home to safety having known great pain and fear. His mouth touched hers, lightly, questioningly and she clung to him, abandoning all pride as she was swamped by her own shattering response to him.

She could feel his heart thudding erratically against her, his mouth hot and urgent as it moved over her own. She wanted him to go on kissing her for ever, but already he was releasing her, putting a distance between them.

'I still haven't been entirely honest with you.'

She thought for a moment her heart-beat had stopped. He smiled gravely at her and said quietly, 'When I asked you to marry me I had no intention of it ever being merely a convenient arrangement, devoid of love and physical contact.'

'You hadn't?'

He shook his head, said 'No,' and then laughed at her expression. 'I begin to think you're the one who needs glasses, Mrs Philips,' he teased her softly, 'otherwise you'd surely have seen that I'd been lusting after you ever since you came to work for me. From the very first time we met in fact.'

She stared at him in disbelief, stammering, 'But...but I thought—'

'That I was a sexless, vague, confirmed bachelor, more interested in computers, than human beings,' he said wryly. 'Oh, yes, I do realise that and I had been cursing my far too effective armour plating for quite some considerable time. It was the look on your face when you heard David saying that Louise had wanted to get into bed with me that finally gave me hope.'

'What sort of look?' Sophy asked him suspiciously.

His smile was both innocent and tantalising. 'Oh, the sort that said you were looking at me as a man instead of simply your lame dog boss.'

Sophy shook her head. 'But why pretend to be something you weren't, Jon? Why pretend to be so sexless and…dull?'

He hesitated for a moment and then said slowly, 'I know this will make me sound unattractively vain but when I first went up to Cambridge, like many another before me I wanted to have a good time. My father was comfortably off…those were the days when teenagers didn't have to worry too much about getting a job…when, in fact, our generation thought it was the hub of the whole world. It was my first real time away from home, I had a generous allowance and a small sports car my father had bought me when I passed my 'A' levels. I wasn't short of congenial feminine company. In short I lived a life of hedonistic pleasure rather than scholarly concentration. That all came to an abrupt end just after my third term. My tutors started complaining about the standard of my work…that sobered me up quite a bit, until then I'd never really had to work, you could say that it had all come too easily to me. Then a friend of mine was sent down—drug trafficking; a girl I'd gone out with died—all alone in a filthy squat with her arm all bloated out with septic poisoning from using a dirty needle—she was mainlining on heroin. I had to identify her. It all brought me down to reality.

'When term resumed after the Christmas recess I decided I was going to turn over a new leaf. I'd talked to my brother—Hugh was eight years older than me, already married then, but still enough in touch with his own youth to listen sympathetically to me— but it seemed that my friends or at least some of them didn't want me to change. Then I had to start wearing glasses. I discovered quite quickly that people who didn't know me reacted differently to me…and so gradually I evolved a form of disguise and somehow it stuck with me. There was nothing to make me want to abandon it, until I met you and even then it seemed I wasn't going to be able to reveal myself to you in my true colours, so to speak.'

Sophy looked questioningly at him and he said drolly, 'Ah, well, you see I had observed how you reacted to me…and how you reacted to any male who was even just slightly aggressively masculine and I didn't want to frighten you off. You felt safe with me, that much was obvious and because of that I could get closer to you. Some disguises are used for protection,' he told her, 'some for hunting…' He laughed at her expression. 'Ah, yes, my poor little love, I'm afraid you…'

She didn't let him finish, flushing suddenly as she remembered his bland and extremely irritating indifference to her timid sexual overtures in the early days of their marriage…an indifference which she had naïvely thought sprang from unawareness.

'You knew…' she accused.

'Knew what?' He was smiling dulcetly at her.

She swallowed, and said huskily, 'That I wanted you.'

'After the way you looked at me when I came back from Nassau I hoped you might,' he agreed tenderly, 'but I had to be sure it wasn't merely that I was a challenge to you, Sophy. I had gambled too heavily for that. You see,' he told her quietly, 'as I soon discovered well before I married you, what I once thought was merely lust turned out to be love and that love hasn't diminished for knowing you…quite the contrary. *That* is what I have been trying to talk to you about, Sophy.' He touched her face lightly with his fingers and she trembled wildly, hardly daring to look at him. 'We have been lovers, and you have given yourself to me physically with a generosity that no one else has ever matched or ever could, but have you given yourself to me emotionally, Sophy? *Can* you give yourself to me emotionally or is it still Benson, despite all that he has done to you?'

'Chris?' Sophy stared at him. 'I never loved Chris. Not really, not like...'

'Not like?' His voice was placid, belying the expression in his eyes. It made her heart race and suspended her breath until she realised he was still waiting impatiently for her response.

'Not like I love you,' she told him.

He expelled his breath on a harsh sigh and said roughly, 'God, Sophy, you don't know how you've tormented me.'

She smiled at him, going willingly into his arms as he dragged her against him. 'Oh, I think I've a fair idea,' she told him demurely, 'after all you've done your own fair share of tormenting.'

From the shelter of his arms, she looked up at him, watching the way his eyebrows rose in query.

'All that parading around practically nude,' she elucidated for him, 'making me want you, making me love you...' She looked up at him again and smiled, 'and probably damn well making me pregnant into the bargain.'

'Have I done?' He looked smugly and irritatingly malely pleased at the prospect.

'I don't know,' she admitted, 'but, Jon...' she protested as he turned round with her still in his arms and rolled her onto the bed, following her there, and pinning her down with the superior weight of his body.

'Jon, what are you doing?' she demanded.

He was grinning at her and her heart turned over inside her as she read the purpose in his eyes and he told her softly, 'It would certainly be one sure fire way of keeping you tied to me. Besides…' He paused to kiss her, smothering her mumbled protest until she was forced to give up and respond to him.

'Besides…what?' she asked breathlessly when at last he had released her.

'I love loving you so much,' he told her simply. 'No woman has ever meant to me what you do, Sophy, or ever will. I could have wept when you told me that you weren't fully a woman. I could have killed Benson for what he had done to you. You were too inexperienced to even realise what he *had* done. How he had pushed his own inadequacies off on to you.'

'*You* made me a woman, Jon,' she told him huskily, feeling his body tense against her and thrilling to the vibrant masculinity of it. Only one thing still troubled her, creasing her forehead as she said hesitantly, 'Jon, just now when I said I might be pregnant you seemed pleased but you threatened to put the children into care. You…'

'I gambled that their supposed plight would push you into marrying me far faster than any amount of reasoned argument,' he admitted wryly, 'but believe me I would never have done it. They're my brother's children, Sophy, and I love them very much, just as I shall love our own very much…but never quite as much as I love you.'

Beneath him her body quivered and she reached up to wrap her arms round him, her voice breaking slightly as she murmured, 'Make love to me please, Jon. Show me that this isn't all some impossible dream.'

'No dream, but reality,' he whispered against her mouth. 'The reality of our love.'

* * * * *

THE DEMETRIOS
VIRGIN

CHAPTER ONE

'FOUR FORTY-FIVE.' Saskia grimaced as she hurried across the foyer of the office block where she worked, heading for the exit. She was already running late and didn't have time to pause when the receptionist called out. 'Sneaking off early... Lucky you!'

Andreas frowned as he heard the receptionist's comment. He was standing waiting for the executive lift and the woman who was leaving hadn't seen him, but he had seen her: a stunningly leggy brunette with just that gleam of red-gold in her dark locks that hinted at fieriness. He immediately checked the direction of his thoughts. The complication of a man to woman entanglement was the last thing he needed right now, and besides...

His frown deepened. Since he had managed to persuade his grandfather to semi-retire from the hotel chain which Andreas now ran, the older man had begun a relentless campaign to persuade and even coerce Andreas into marrying a second cousin. Such a marriage, in his grandfather's eyes, would unite not just the two branches of the family but the wealth of the family shipping line—inherited by his cousin—with that of the hotel chain.

Fortunately Andreas knew that at heart his grandfather was far more swayed by emotion than he liked to admit.

After all, he had allowed his daughter, Andreas's mother, to marry an Englishman.

The somewhat clumsy attempts to promote a match between Andreas and his cousin Athena would merely afford Andreas some moments of wry amusement if it were not for one all-important fact—which was that Athena herself was even keener on the match than his grandfather. She had made her intentions, her *desires*, quite plain. Athena was a widow seven years his senior, with two children from her first marriage to another wealthy Greek, and Andreas suspected that it might have been Athena herself who had put the ridiculous idea of a marriage between them in his grandfather's head in the first place.

The lift had reached the penthouse floor and Andreas got out. This wasn't the time for him to be thinking about his personal affairs. *They* could wait. He was due to fly out to the Aegean island his grandfather owned, and where the family holidayed together, in less than a fortnight's time, but first his grandfather wanted a detailed report from him on his proposals to turn the flagging British hotel chain they had recently bought into as successful an enterprise as the rest of the hotels they owned.

Even though Andreas had become the company's chief executive, his grandfather still felt the need to challenge his business decisions. Still, the acquisition would ultimately be a good one—the chain-owned hotels were very run-down and old-fashioned, but had excellent locations.

Although officially he was not due to arrive at the chain's head office until tomorrow, Andreas had opted to do so this afternoon instead, and it looked as though he had just discovered one way at least in which profitability could be improved, he decided grimly, if all the staff were in the habit of 'sneaking off early', like the young woman he had just seen…

SNEAKING OFF EARLY! Saskia grimaced as she managed to hail a cruising taxi. If only! She had been at her desk for seven-thirty this morning, as she had been every morning for the last month, and neither had she had a lunch hour, but they had all been warned that Demetrios Hotels, who had taken over their own small chain, were relentless when it came to pruning costs. Tomorrow morning they were all due to meet their new boss for the first time, and Saskia wasn't exactly looking forward to the occasion. There had been a lot of talk about cutbacks and there had also been grapevine rumours about how very formidable Andreas Latimer was.

'The old man, his grandfather, had a reputation for running a tight ship, and if anything the grandson is even worse.'

'They both favour a "the guest is always right even when wrong" policy, and woe betide any employee who forgets it. Which is, of course, why their hotels are so popular…and so profitable.'

That had been the general gist of the gossip Saskia had heard.

Her taxi was drawing up outside the restaurant she had asked to be taken to. Hastily she delved into her handbag for her purse, paying the driver and then hurrying quickly inside.

'Oh, Saskia—*there* you are. We thought you weren't going to make it.'

'I'm sorry,' Saskia apologised to her best friend as she

slipped into the spare seat at the table for three in the Italian restaurant where they had arranged to meet.

'There's been a panic on at work,' she explained. 'The new boss arrives tomorrow.' She pulled a face, wrinkling the elegant length of her dainty nose and screwing up her thick-lashed aquamarine eyes. She paused as she saw that her friend wasn't really listening, and that her normally happy, gentle face looked strained and unhappy.

'What's wrong?' she asked immediately.

'I was just telling Lorraine how upset I am,' Megan answered, indicating the third member of their trio, Megan's cousin Lorraine, an older woman with a brisk, businesslike expression and a slightly jaded air.

'Upset?' Saskia queried, a small frown marring the elegant oval of her face as she pushed her long hair back and reached hungrily for a bread roll. She was starving!

'It's Mark,' Megan said, her voice shaking a little and her brown eyes full of quiet despair.

'Mark?' Saskia repeated, putting down her roll so that she could concentrate on her friend. 'But I thought the two of you were about to announce your engagement.'

'Yes, we were…we are… At least, Mark wants to…' Megan began, and then stopped when Lorraine took over.

'Megan thinks he's involved with someone else…' she told Saskia grimly. 'Two-timing her.'

Older than Megan and Saskia by almost a decade, and with a broken marriage behind her, Lorraine was inclined to be angrily contemptuous of the male sex.

'Oh, surely not, Megan,' Saskia protested. 'You told me yourself how much Mark loves you.'

'Well, yes, that's what I thought,' Megan agreed, 'Especially when he said that he wanted us to become engaged. But…he keeps getting these phone calls. But when I answer the phone whoever's ringing just hangs up. There've been three this week and when I ask him who it is he says it's just a wrong number.'

'Well, perhaps it is,' Saskia tried to reassure her, but Megan shook her head.

'No, it isn't. Mark keeps on hanging around by the phone, and last night he was talking on his mobile when I walked in and the moment he saw me he ended the call.'

'Have you *asked* him what's going on?' Saskia questioned her in concern.

'Yes. He says I'm just imagining it,' Megan told her unhappily.

'A classic male ploy,' Lorraine announced vigorously with grim satisfaction. 'My ex did everything to convince me that I was becoming paranoid and then what does he do? He moves in with his secretary, if you please!'

'I just wish that Mark would be honest with me,' Megan told Saskia, her eyes starting to fill with tears. 'If there *is* someone else…I… I just can't believe he's doing this… I thought he loved me…'

'I'm sure he does,' Saskia tried to comfort her. She had not as yet met her friend's new partner, but from what Megan had told her about him Saskia felt he sounded perfect for her.

'Well, there's one sure way to find out,' Lorraine announced. 'I read an article about it. There's this agency, and if you've got suspicions about your partner's fidelity you go to them and they send a girl to try to seduce him. That's what you should do,' she told Megan crisply.

'Oh, no, I couldn't,' Megan protested.

'You must,' Lorraine insisted forcefully. 'It's the only

way you'll ever know whether or not you can trust him. I wish I'd been able to do something like that before I got married. You *must* do it,' she repeated. 'It's the only way you'll ever be sure. Mark is struggling to make ends meet since he started up his own business, Megan, and you've got that money you inherited from your great-aunt.'

Saskia's heart sank a little as she listened. Much as she loved her friend, she knew that Megan was inclined to allow herself to be dominated by her older and more worldly cousin. Saskia had nothing against Lorraine, indeed she liked her, but she knew from past experience that once Lorraine got the bit between her teeth there was no stopping her. She was fiercely determined to do things her own way, which Saskia suspected was at least part of the reason for the breakdown of her marriage. But right now, sympathetic though Saskia was to Megan's unhappiness, she was hungry…very hungry… She eyed the menu longingly.

'Well, it does *sound* a sensible idea,' Megan was agreeing. 'But I doubt there's an agency like that in Hilford.'

'Who needs an agency?' Lorraine responded. 'What *you* need is a stunningly gorgeous friend who Mark hasn't met and who can attempt to seduce him. If he responds…'

'A stunningly gorgeous friend?' Megan was musing. 'You mean like Saskia?'

Two pairs of female eyes studied Saskia whilst she gave in to her hunger and bit into her roll.

'Exactly,' Lorraine breathed fervently. 'Saskia would be perfect.'

'What?' Saskia almost choked on her bread. 'You *can't* be serious,' she protested. 'Oh, no, no way…' She objected when she saw the determination in Lorraine's eyes and the pleading in Megan's. 'No way at all.'

'Meg, this is crazy, you must see that,' she coaxed, trying to appeal to her friend's common sense and her conscience as she added winningly, 'How *could* you do something like that to Mark? You love him.'

'How can she risk committing herself to him unless she knows she can trust him?' Lorraine interjected sharply, adding emphatically, 'Good, that's settled. What we need to do now is to decide just where Saskia can accidentally run into Mark and put our plan into action.'

'Well, tonight is his boys' night out,' Megan ventured. 'And last night he said that they were planning to go to that new wine bar that's just opened. A friend of his knows the owner.'

'I can't do it,' Saskia protested. 'It…it's…it's immoral,' she added. She looked apologetically at Megan as she shook her head and told her, 'Meg, I'm sorry, but…'

'I should have thought you would *want* to help Megan, Saskia, to protect her happiness. Especially after all *she's* done for *you*…' Lorraine pointed out sharply.

Saskia worried guiltily at her bottom lip with her pretty white teeth. Lorraine was right. She *did* owe Megan a massive favour.

Six months ago, when they had been trying to fight off the Demetrios takeover bid, she had been working late every evening and at weekends as well. Her grandmother, who had brought her up following the breakdown of her young parents' marriage, had become seriously ill with a viral infection and Megan, who was a nurse, had given up her spare time and some of her holiday entitlement to care for the old lady.

Saskia shuddered to think even now of the potentially dangerous outcome of her grandmother's illness if Megan hadn't been there to nurse her. It had been on Saskia's conscience ever since that she owed her friend a debt she could never repay. Saskia adored her grandmother, who had provided her with a loving and stable home background when she had needed it the most. Her mother, who had given birth to Saskia at seventeen was a distant figure in her life, and her father, her grandmother's son, had become a remote stranger to both of them, living as he now did in China, with his second wife and young family.

'I know you don't approve, Saskia,' Megan was saying quietly to her, 'but I *have* to know that I can trust Mark.' Her soft eyes filled with tears. 'He means *so* much to me. He's everything I've *ever* wanted in a man. But…he dated so many girls before he met me, before he moved here, when he lived in London.' She paused. 'He swears that none of them ever meant anything serious to him and that he loves me.'

Privately Saskia wasn't sure that she could even begin to think about committing herself to a relationship with a man without being able to trust him—and trust him to such an extent that there would be no need for her to use any underhand methods to test his fidelity. But then she acknowledged that she was perhaps a trifle more wary of love than her friend. After all, her parents had believed themselves to be in love when they had run away to get married and conceived her, but within two years of doing so they had parted, leaving her grandmother with the responsibility of bringing her up.

Her grandmother! Now, as she looked at Meg's tear-stained face, she knew she had no option but to go along with Lorraine's scheme.

'All right,' she agreed fatalistically. 'I'll do it.'

After Megan had finished thanking her she told her

wryly, 'You'll have to describe your Mark to me, Megan, otherwise I shan't be able to recognise him.'

'Oh, yes, you will,' Megan said fervently with a small ecstatic sigh. 'He'll be the best-looking man there. He's gorgeous, Saskia…fantastically good-looking, with thick dark hair and the most sexy mouth you've ever seen. Oh, and he'll be wearing a blue shirt—to match his eyes. He always does. I bought them for him.'

'What time is he likely to get there?' Saskia asked Megan practically, instead of voicing her feelings. 'My car's in the garage at the moment, and since Gran's house is quite a way out of town…'

'Don't worry about that. I'll drive you there,' Lorraine volunteered, much to Saskia's surprise. Lorraine wasn't known to be over-generous—with anything!

'Yes, and Lorraine will pick you up later and take you home. Won't you, Lorraine?' Megan insisted with unexpected firmness. 'There's no taxi rank close to the wine bar and you don't want to be waiting for a mini-cab.'

A waiter was hovering, waiting to take their order, but bossily Lorraine shook her head, telling Megan and Saskia firmly, 'There won't be time for us to eat now. Saskia will have to get home and get ready. What time *is* Mark likely to go to the wine bar Megan?' she asked her cousin.

'About eight-thirty, I should think,' Megan answered.

'Right, then you need to get there for nine, Saskia,' Lorraine informed her, 'So I'll pick you up at half-eight.'

TWO HOURS LATER Saskia was just coming downstairs when she heard the front doorbell. Her grandmother was away, spending several weeks with her sister in Bath. A little nervously Saskia smoothed down the skirt of her black suit and went to open the door.

Only Lorraine was standing outside. They had agreed that it would be silly to take the risk of Megan being seen and recognised. Now, as Lorraine studied her, Saskia could see the older woman beginning to frown.

'You'll have to wear something else,' she told Saskia sharply. 'You look far too businesslike and unapproachable in that suit. Mark's got to think you're approachable—remember. And I really think you ought to wear a different lipstick…red, perhaps, and more eye make-up. Look, if you don't believe me then read this.' Lorraine thrust an open magazine beneath Saskia's nose.

Reluctantly Saskia skimmed through the article, a small frown pleating her forehead as she read of the lengths the agency was prepared to have its girls go to in order to test the faithfulness of its clients' men.

'I can't do any of this,' she told Lorraine firmly. 'And as for my suit…'

Stepping into the hall and closing the front door behind her, Lorraine stood squarely in front of Saskia and told her vehemently, 'You have to—for Megan's sake. Can't you see what's happening to her, the danger she's in? She's totally besotted with this man; she's barely known him four months and already she's talking about handing over the whole of her inheritance to him…marrying him…having children with him. Do you know how much her great-aunt left her?' she added grimly.

Silently Saskia shook her head. She knew how surprised and shocked Megan had been when she had learned that she was the sole beneficiary under her great-aunt's will, but tactfully she had not asked her friend just how much money was involved.

Lorraine, it seemed, had not had similar qualms.

'Megan inherited nearly three million pounds,' she told Saskia, nodding her head in grim pleasure as she saw Saskia's expression.

'*Now* do you see how important it is that we do everything we can to protect her? I've tried to warn her umpteen times that her precious Mark might not be all he tries to make out he is, but she just won't listen. Now, thank goodness, she's caught him out and he's showing his true colours. For her sake, Saskia, you just do everything you can to prove how unworthy he is. Just imagine what it would do to her if he not only broke her heart but stole all her money as well. She'd be left with nothing.'

Saskia could imagine it all too well. Her grandmother had only a small pension to live on and Saskia, mindful of the sacrifices her grandmother had made when she was growing up, to make sure she did not go without the treats enjoyed by her peers, contributed as much as she could financially to their small household.

The thought of losing her financial independence and the sense of security that earning money of her own gave her was one that was both abhorrent and frightening to her, and Lorraine's revelations suddenly gave her not just the impetus but a real desire to do everything she could to protect her friend.

Megan, dear sweet trusting Megan, who still worked as a nurse despite her inheritance, deserved to find a man, a partner, who was truly worthy of her. And if this Mark wasn't... Well, perhaps then it would be for the best if her friend found out sooner rather than later.

'Perhaps if you took off the jacket of your suit,' Lorraine was saying now. 'You must have some kind of sexy summer top you could wear...or even just...'

She stopped as she saw Saskia's expression.

'Summer top, yes,' Saskia agreed. 'Sexy...no!'

As she saw the look on Lorraine's face Saskia suppressed a small sigh. It was pointless trying to explain to a woman like Lorraine that when nature had given one the kind of assets it had given Saskia, one learned very young that they could be something of a double-edged sword. To put it more bluntly, men—in Saskia's experience—did not need the double overload of seeing her body clad in 'sexy' clothes to encourage them to look twice at her. And in most cases to want to do much more than merely look!

'You must have *something*,' Lorraine urged, refusing to be defeated. 'A cardigan. You must have a cardigan—you could wear it sort of unbuttoned...'

'A cardigan? Yes, I have a cardigan,' Saskia agreed. She had bought it halfway through their cold spring when they had been on an economy drive at work and the heating had been turned off. But as for wearing it unbuttoned...!

'And red lipstick,' Lorraine was insisting, 'and more eye make-up. You'll have to let him know that you find him attractive...' She paused as Saskia lifted her eyebrows. 'It's for Megan's sake.'

In the end it was almost nine o'clock before they left the house, due to Lorraine's insistence that Saskia had to reapply her make-up with a far heavier hand than she would normally have used.

Uncomfortably Saskia refused to look at her reflection in the hall mirror. All that lipstick! It felt sticky, gooey, and as Lorraine drove her towards Hilford she had to force herself to resist the temptation to wipe it off. As for the unbuttoned cardigan she was wearing beneath her suit jacket—well, the moment she was inside the wine bar and out of Lorraine's sight she was going to refasten every single one of the top three buttons Lorraine had demanded she leave undone. True, they did nothing more than merely hint at a cleavage, but even that was far more of a provocation than Saskia would normally have allowed.

'We're here,' Lorraine announced as she pulled up outside the wine bar. 'I'll pick you up at eleven—that should give you plenty of time. Remember,' Lorraine hissed determinedly as Saskia got out of the car, 'We're doing this for Megan.'

We? But before Saskia could say anything Lorraine was driving off.

A man walking in the opposite direction paused on the pavement to give her an admiring glance. Automatically Saskia distanced herself from him and turned away, mentally squaring her shoulders as she headed for the entrance to the wine bar.

Lorraine had given her a long list of instructions, most of which had made Saskia cringe inwardly, and already her courage was beginning to desert her. There was no way she could go in there and pout and flirt in the enticing way that Lorraine had informed her she had to do. But if she didn't, poor Megan could end up having her heart broken and her inheritance cheated away from her.

Taking a deep breath, Saskia pulled open the wine bar door.

CHAPTER TWO

ANDREAS saw Saskia the moment she walked in. He was seated at the bar, which was now being besieged by a crowd of young men who had come in just ahead of her. He could have stayed in and eaten in the office block's penthouse apartment—or even driven to the closest of their new acquisitions—but he had already endured two lengthy phone calls he would rather not have had this evening: one from his grandfather and another from Athena. So he had decided to go somewhere where neither of them could get in touch with him, having deliberately 'forgotten' to bring his mobile with him.

He hadn't been in a particularly good mood when he had arrived at the wine bar. Such places were not to his taste.

He liked good food served in comfortable surroundings where one could talk and think with ease, and there was also enough Greek in him for him to prefer somewhere more family centred and less of an obvious trawling ground for members of the opposite sex.

Thinking of the opposite sex made his mouth harden. Athena was becoming more and more brazen in her attempts to convince him that they should be together. He had been fifteen the first time he had been exposed to Athena's sexual aggression, and she had been twenty-two and about to be married.

He frowned as he watched Saskia. She was standing just inside the doorway, studying the room as though she was looking for someone. She turned her head and the light fell on her smoothly glossed lips.

Andreas sucked in his breath as he fought to control his unwanted reaction to her. What the hell was he doing? She was so damned obvious with that almost but not quite scarlet lipstick that he ought to be laughing, not... Not what? he asked himself caustically. Not wanting... lusting...

A strong surge of self-disgust lashed him. He had recognised her, of course. It was the girl from this afternoon, the one the receptionist had congratulated on her early departure from work. Then she had been wearing a minimum of make-up. Now... He eyed her lipsticked mouth and kohl-enhanced eyes grimly. She was wearing a suit with a short skirt...a very short skirt, he observed as she moved and he caught sight of the length of her sheer black tights-clad legs. A very, very short skirt!

As the turned-over waistband of her once respectably knee-length skirt made its presence felt, Saskia grimaced. Once she had found Mark she fully intended to make her way to the cloakroom and return her skirt to its normal length. It had been Lorraine, of course, who had insisted on shortening it.

'I can't go out like *that*,' Saskia had yelped.

'Don't be ridiculous,' Lorraine had derided her. 'That's nothing. Haven't you seen pictures from the sixties?'

'That was then,' Saskia had informed her firmly without letting her finish, but Lorraine had refused to give in and in the end Saskia had shrugged her shoulders and comforted herself with the knowledge that once Lorraine was out of sight she could do what she liked with her skirt. The cardigan too was making her feel uncomfortable, and unwittingly she started to toy with the first of its unfastened buttons.

As he watched her Andreas's eyes narrowed. God, but she was obvious, drawing attention to her breasts like that… And what breasts! Andreas discovered that he was starting to grind his teeth and, more importantly, that he was totally unable to take his eyes off Saskia…

Sensing that she was being watched, Saskia turned round and then froze as her searching gaze clashed head-on with Andreas's hard-eyed stare.

For a breath of time Saskia was totally dazed, such was the effect of Andreas's raw masculinity on her. Her heart was pounding, her mouth dry, her body… Helplessly transfixed, she fought desperately against what she was feeling—against what she was not allowed to feel. For this was Megan's Mark—it had to be. She could not really be experiencing what her emotions were telling her she was experiencing, she denied in panic. Not a woman like her, and not for this man, Megan's man!

No other man in the place came anywhere near matching the description Megan had given her as closely as this one did. Mentally she ticked off Megan's euphoric description of him—one Saskia had previously put down to the near ravings of a woman besottedly in love. Gorgeous, fantastically good-looking, sexy… Oh, and he would be wearing a blue shirt, Megan had told her, to match his eyes.

Well, Saskia couldn't make out the colour of his eyes across the dimly lit distance that separated them, but she could certainly see that Megan had been right on every other count and her heart sank. So this was Megan's Mark.

No wonder she was worrying so anxiously that he might be being unfaithful to her... A man who looked like this one did would have women pursuing him in droves.

Funny, but Megan hadn't mentioned the most important thing of all about him, which wasn't just that he was so spectacularly and sexually male but that he emanated a profound and intense air of authority that bordered almost on arrogance; it had struck Saskia the moment she had looked at him. That and the look of discreet male inspection quickly followed by a reactive resultant look of contemptuous disapproval.

That look... How *dare* he look at her like that? Suddenly all the doubts she had been harbouring about what she had agreed to do were vanquished.

Lorraine was right to be suspicious of such a man's motives, especially where a naive, gentle, unworldly girl like Megan was concerned. Saskia didn't trust him one little bit. Megan needed a man who would appreciate her gentleness and treat her correspondingly. This man was powerful, daunting, awesome—and looking at him was, as Saskia was beginning to discover, something of a physical compulsion. She couldn't take her eyes off him. But that was just because she disliked him so much, she assured herself quickly, because she was so intensely aware of how very right Lorraine had been to want to test his loyalty to Megan.

Determinedly quelling the butterflies fluttering in her stomach, Saskia took a deep breath, mentally reminding herself of what she had read in the article Lorraine had thrust under her nose. Then she had been horrified, repulsed by the lengths the girls hired by the agency were prepared to go to in order to entice and entrap their quarry into self-betrayal. It had even crossed her mind that no mere man could possibly find the strength to resist the kind of deliberate temptation those girls offered—everything from the most intense type of verbal flattery right up to outright offers of sex itself, although thankfully offers had been all they were.

A man like this one, though, must be used to women— attractive women—throwing themselves at him. 'He dated so many girls before he met me,' Megan had said innocently.

Saskia would just bet that he had. Megan was a honey, and Saskia loved her with a fierce loyalty, but even she had to admit that her friend did not possess the kind of glamorous instant eye appeal she suspected a man like this one would look for. But perhaps that was what he loved about her—the fact that she was so shy and homely. If he loved her... Well, that was up to Saskia to prove...or disprove...wasn't it?

With the light of battle shining in her eyes, Saskia made her way towards him.

Andreas watched her progress with a mixture of curiosity and disappointment. She was heading for him. He knew that, but the cool hauteur with which she not only ignored the interested looks she was collecting from other men as she did so but almost seemed not to notice them, was every bit as contrived as the unfastened buttons of the top she was wearing. It had to be! Andreas knew the type. He should do. After all, Athena...

'Oh, I'm sorry,' Saskia apologised as she reached Andreas's side and 'accidentally' stumbled against him. Straightening up, she stood next to him at the bar, giving him a winsomely apologetic smile as she moved so close to him that he could smell her scent… Not her perfume, which was light and floral, unexpectedly, but her *scent*— the soft, honey-sweet headily sensual and erotic scent that was her. And like a fool he was actually breathing it in, getting almost drunk on it…letting his senses react to it… to her…

Lorraine had coached her on her best approach and Saskia had memorised it, grimacing with loathing and distaste as she did so.

Andreas forced himself to step back from her and put some distance between them, but the bar was crowded and it was impossible for him to move away altogether, so instead he asked her coldly, 'I'm sorry…do I know you?'

His voice and demeanour were, he knew, cutting enough to make it plain that he knew what she was up to. Although why on earth a woman who looked like this one needed to trawl bars looking for men to pick up he had no idea. Or rather he did, but he preferred not to examine it too closely. There were women, as he already knew to his cost, who would do anything for money…anything…with anyone…

But Saskia was facing him now, her lipstick-glossed mouth parting in a smile he could see was forced as she purred, 'Er, no, actually, you don't…but I'm hoping that soon you will.'

Saskia was relieved that the bar was so dimly lit. She could feel the heat of her burning face. She had *never* in her most private thoughts even contemplated coming on to a man like this, never mind envisaged that she might actually do so. Quickly she hurried on to the next part of her prepared speech, parting her lips in what she hoped was a temptingly provocative smile whilst carefully running her tongue-tip over them.

Yuck! But all that lipstick felt repulsive.

'Aren't you going to ask me if I'd like a drink?' she invited coyly, batting her eyelashes in what she hoped was an appropriately enticing manner. 'I love the colour of your shirt,' she added huskily as she leaned closer. 'It matches your eyes…'

'If you think that you must be colour blind; my eyes are grey,' Andreas told her tersely. She was beginning to make him feel very angry. Her obviousness was nothing short of contemptible. But nothing like as contemptible as his own ridiculous reaction to her. What was he? A boy of eighteen? He was supposed to be a man…a mature, sophisticated, experienced, worldly man of thirty-odd—and yet here he was, reacting, *responding*, to the pathetically tired and jaded sexual tricks she was playing on him as eagerly as though… As though what? As though there was nothing he wanted to do right now more than take her to bed, to feel the hot urgency of her body beneath his, to hear her cry out his name through lips swollen with the mutual passion of their shared kisses whilst he…

'Look,' he told her sharply, cutting off the supply of lifeblood to his unwanted fantasies by the simple act of refusing to allow himself to think about them, 'you're making a big mistake.'

'Oh, no,' Saskia protested anxiously as he started to turn away from her. By rights she should simply accept what he was saying and go back to Megan and tell her that her beloved Mark was everything he was supposed to be. But an instinct she couldn't analyse was telling her that despite all the evidence to the contrary he was tempted. *Any* man could be tempted, she tried to tell herself fairly, but something inside her refused to allow her to listen.

'*You* could never be a mistake,' she purred suggestively. 'To any woman…'

Fatuously Andreas wondered if he had gone completely mad. To even think of desiring a woman who was openly propositioning him was anathema to everything he believed in. How could he possibly be even remotely attracted to her? He wasn't, of course. It was impossible. And as for that sudden inexplicable urge he had had to take her home with him, where she would be safe from the kind of attention her make-up and behaviour were bound to attract. Well, now he knew he *must* be seriously losing it.

If there was one thing he despised it was women like this one. Not that he preferred them to be demure or virginal. No. What he found most attractive was a woman who was proud to be herself and who expected his sex to respect her right to be what she was. The kind of woman who would automatically eschew any act that involved her presenting herself as some kind of sexual plaything and who would just as determinedly turn her back on any man who wanted her to behave that way. This woman…

'I'm sorry,' he told her, making it verbally plain that he was no such thing by the cold tone of his voice, 'but you're wasting your time. And time, as I can see,' he continued in a deceptively gentle voice, 'has to be money for a woman like you. So why don't you go away and find someone else who will be… er…more receptive to what you've got on offer than I am?'

White-faced, Saskia watched as he turned away from her and thrust his way towards the door. He had rejected her…refused her. He had… He had… Painfully she swallowed. He had proved that he was faithful to Megan and he had… He had looked at her as though…as though…

Like a little girl, Saskia wiped the back of her hand across
her lipsticked mouth, grimacing as she saw the stain the
high-coloured gloss had left there.

'Hi there, gorgeous. Can I buy you a drink?'

Numbly she shook her head, ignoring the sour look the
man who had approached was giving her as she stared
at the door. There was no sign of Megan's man. He had
gone—and she was glad. Of course she was. How could
she not be? And she would be delighted to be able to report
to Megan and Lorraine that Mark had not succumbed to
her.

She glanced at her watch, her heart sinking. She still had
over an hour to go before she met Lorraine. There was no
way she could stay here in the bar on her own, attracting
attention. Quickly she headed for the ladies' room. There
was something she had to do.

In the cloakroom she fastened her cardigan and wiped
her face clean of the last of the red lipstick and the kohl
eyeliner, replacing them both with her normal choice of
make-up—a discreet application of taupe eyeshadow and
a soft berry-coloured lipstick—and coiling up her long
hair into a neat chignon. Then she waited in the ladies'
room until an inspection of her watch told her she could
finally leave.

This time as she made her way through the crowded bar
it was a very different type of look that Saskia collected
from the men who watched her admiringly.

To her relief Lorraine was parked outside, waiting for
her.

'Well?' she demanded eagerly as Saskia opened the car
door and got in.

'Nothing,' Saskia told her, shaking her head. 'He turned me down flat.'

'What?'

'Lorraine, careful…' Saskia cried out warningly as the other woman almost backed into the car behind her in shock.

'You mustn't have tried hard enough,' Lorraine told her bossily.

'I can assure you that I tried as hard as anyone could,' Saskia corrected her wryly.

'Did he *mention* Megan…tell you that he was spoken for?' Lorraine questioned her.

'No!' Saskia shook her head. 'But I promise you he made it plain that he wasn't interested. He looked at me…' She stopped and swallowed, unwilling to think about, never mind tell anyone else, just how Megan's beloved had looked at her. For some odd reason she refused to define, just remembering the icy contempt she had seen in his eyes made her tremble between anger and pain.

'Where *is* Megan?' she asked Lorraine.

'She was called in unexpectedly to work an extra shift. She rang to let me know and I said we'd drive straight over to her place and meet up with her there.'

Saskia smiled wanly. By rights she knew she ought to be feeling far happier than she actually was. Though out of the three of them she suspected that Megan would be the only one who would actually be pleased to learn that her Mark had determinedly refused to be tempted.

Her Mark. *Megan's* Mark. There was a bitter taste in Saskia's mouth and her heart felt like a heavy lump of lead inside her chest.

What on earth was the matter with her? She couldn't

possibly be jealous of Megan, could she? No! She couldn't be…she *must* not be!

'Are you sure you tried hard enough?' Lorraine asked again.

'I said everything you told me to say,' Saskia told her truthfully.

'And he didn't make any kind of response?'

Saskia could tell that Lorraine didn't believe her.

'Oh, he made a response,' she admitted grimly. 'It just wasn't the kind…' She stopped and then told her flatly, 'He wasn't interested, Lorraine. He must really love Megan.'

'Yes, if he prefers her to you he must,' Lorraine agreed bluntly. 'She's a dear, and I love her, but there's no way… You don't think he could have *guessed* what you were doing do you? No way he could have known—'

'No, I don't,' Saskia denied. She was beginning to feel tired, almost aching with a sharp, painful need to be on her own. The last thing she wanted right now was to deal with someone like Lorraine, but she owed it to Megan to reassure her that she could trust Mark.

As they pulled up outside Megan's house Saskia saw that her car was parked outside. Her stomach muscles started to clench as she got out of Lorraine's car and walked up the garden path. Megan and Mark. Even their names sounded cosy together, redolent of domesticity… of marital comfort. And yet…if ever she'd met a man who was neither domesticated nor cosy it had been Megan's Mark. There had been an air of primitive raw maleness about him, an aura of power and sexuality, a sense that in his arms a woman could…*would*…touch such sensual heights of delight and pleasure that she would never be quite the same person again.

Saskia tensed. What on earth was she thinking? Mark belonged to Megan—her best friend, the friend to whom she owed her grandmother's life and good health.

Megan had obviously seen them arrive and was opening the door before they reached it, her face wreathed in smiles.

'It's all right,' Saskia told her hollowly. 'Mark didn't…'

'I know…I know…' Megan beamed as she ushered them inside. 'He came to see me at work and explained everything. Oh, I've been such an idiot… Why on earth I didn't guess what he was planning I just don't know. We leave next week. He'd even told them at work what he was planning…that was the reason for all those calls. Plus the girl at the travel agency kept phoning. Oh, Saskia, I can't believe it. I've always longed to go to the Caribbean, and for Mark to have booked us such a wonderful holiday… The place we're going to specialises in holidays for couples. I'm so sorry you had a wasted evening. I tried to ring you but you'd already left. I thought you might have got here sooner. After all, once you'd realised that Mark wasn't at the wine bar…' She stopped as she saw the look on both her cousin's and Saskia's faces.

'What is it?' she asked them uncertainly.

'*You* said that you'd spoken to Mark,' Lorraine was saying tersely to Saskia.

'I did…' Saskia insisted. 'He was just as you described him to us, Megan…'

She stopped as Megan shook her head firmly.

'Mark wasn't there, Sas,' she repeated. 'He was with me at work. He arrived at half past eight and Sister gave me some time off so that we could talk. He'd guessed how upset I was and he'd decided that he would have to tell me what he was planning. He said he knew he couldn't have kept the secret for very much longer anyway,' she added fondly.

'And before you say a word,' she said firmly to her cousin, 'Mark is paying for everything himself.'

Saskia leaned weakly against the wall. If the man she had come on to hadn't been Megan's Mark, then just who on earth had he been? Her face became even paler. She had come on to a man she didn't know…a total and complete stranger…a man who… She swallowed nauseously, remembering the way she had looked, the way she had behaved…the things she had said. Thank God he was a stranger. Thank God she would never have to see him again.

'Sas, you don't look well,' she could hear Megan saying solicitously. 'What is it?'

'Nothing,' she fibbed, but Lorraine had already guessed what she was thinking.

'Well, if the man in the wine bar wasn't Mark then who on earth was he?' she demanded sharply.

'Who indeed?' Saskia echoed hollowly.

CHAPTER THREE

To SASKIA's dismay she heard the town hall clock striking 8:00 a.m. as she hurried to work. She had intended to be in extra early this morning but unfortunately she had overslept—a direct result of the previous evening's events and the fact that initially she had been mentally agonising so much over what she had done that she had been unable to get to sleep.

Officially she might not be due to be at her desk until 9:00 a.m., but in this modern age that was not the way things worked, especially when one's hold on one's job was already dangerously precarious.

'There are bound to be cutbacks...redundancies,' the head of Saskia's department had warned them all, and Saskia, as she'd listened to him, had been sharply conscious that as the newest member of the team she was the one whose job was most in line to be cut back. It would be virtually impossible for her to get another job with the same kind of prospects in Hilford, and if she moved away to London that would mean her grandmother would be left on her own. At sixty-five her grandmother was not precisely old—far from it—and she had a large circle of friends, but the illness had left Saskia feeling afraid for her. Saskia felt she owed her such a huge debt, not only for bringing her up but for giving her so much love.

As she hurried into the foyer she asked Emma, the receptionist, anxiously, 'Has he arrived yet?'

There was no need to qualify who she meant by 'he', and Emma gave her a slightly superior smile as she replied, 'Actually he arrived yesterday. He's upstairs now,' she added smugly, 'interviewing everyone.' Her smugness and superiority gave way to a smile of pure feminine appreciation as she sighed. 'Just wait until you see him. He's gorgeous...with a great big capital G.'

She rolled her eyes expressively whilst Saskia gave her a wan smile.

She now had her own special and private—very private—blueprint of what a gorgeous man looked like, and she doubted that their new Greek boss came anywhere near to matching it.

'Typically, though, mind you,' the receptionist continued, oblivious to Saskia's desire to hurry to her office, 'he's already spoken for. Or at least he soon will be. I was talking to the receptionist at their group's head office and she told me that his grandfather wants him to marry his cousin. She's mega-wealthy and—'

'I'm sorry, Emma, but I must go,' Saskia interrupted her firmly. Office gossip, like office politics, was something Saskia had no wish to involve herself in, and besides... If their new boss was already interviewing people she didn't want to earn herself any black marks by not being at her desk when he sent for her.

Her office was on the third floor, an open plan space where she worked with five other people. Their boss had his own glass-walled section, but right now both it and the general office itself were empty.

Just as she was wondering what to do the outer door

swung open and her boss, followed by the rest of her colleagues, came into the room.

'Ah, Saskia, there you are,' her boss greeted her.

'Yes. I had intended to be here earlier...' Saskia began, but Gordon Jarman was shaking his head.

'Don't explain now,' he told her sharply. 'You'd better get upstairs to the executive suite. Mr Latimer's secretary will be expecting you. Apparently he wants to interview everyone, both individually and with their co-department members, and he wasn't too pleased that you weren't here...'

Without allowing Saskia to say anything, Gordon turned on his heel and went into his office, leaving her with no option but to head for the lift. It was unlike Gordon to be so sharp. He was normally a very laid-back sort of person. Saskia could feel the nervous feeling in her tummy increasing as she contemplated the kind of attitude Andreas Latimer must have adopted towards his new employees to cause such a reaction in her normally unflappable boss.

The executive suite was unfamiliar territory to Saskia. The only previous occasions on which she had entered it had been when she had gone for her initial interview and then, more recently, when the whole staff had been informed of the success of the Demetrios takeover bid.

A little uncertainly she got out of the lift and walked towards the door marked 'Personal Assistant to the Chief Executive'.

Madge Fielding, the previous owner's secretary, had retired when the takeover bid's success had been announced, and when Saskia saw the elegantly groomed dark-haired woman seated behind Madge's desk she assumed that the new owner must have brought his PA with him from Demetrios head office.

Nervously Saskia gave her name, and started to explain that she worked for Gordon Jarman, but the PA waved her explanation aside, consulting a list in front of her instead and then saying coldly, without lifting her head from it, 'Saskia? Yes. You're late. Mr Latimer does not like… In fact I'm not sure…' She stopped and eyed Saskia with a disapproving frown. 'He may not have time to interview you now,' she warned, before picking up the phone and announcing in a very different tone of voice from the one she had used to address Saskia, 'Ms. Rodgers is here now, Andreas. Do you still want to see her?

'You *can* go in,' she informed Saskia. 'It's the door over there…'

Feeling like a naughty child, Saskia forced herself not to react, heading instead for the door the PA had indicated and knocking briefly on it before turning the handle and walking in.

As she stepped into the office the bright sunlight streaming in through the large windows momentarily dazzled her. All she could make out was the hazy outline of a man standing in front of the glass with his back to her, the brilliance of the sunlight making it impossible for her to see any more.

But Andreas could see Saskia. It hadn't surprised him that she should choose to arrive at work later than her colleagues; after all, he knew how she spent her evenings. What had surprised him had been the genuinely high esteem in which he had discovered she was held both by her immediate boss and her co-workers. It seemed that when it came to giving that extra metre, going that extra distance, Saskia was always the first to do so and the first to do whatever she could to help out her colleagues.

'Yes, it is perhaps unusual in a young graduate,' her boss had agreed when Andreas had questioned his praise of Saskia. 'But then she has been brought up by her grandmother and perhaps because of that her values and sense of obligation towards others are those of an older generation. As you can see from my report on her, her work is excellent and so are her qualifications.'

And she's a stunningly attractive young woman who seems to know how to use her undeniable 'assets' to her own advantage, Andreas had reflected inwardly, but Gordon Jarman had continued to enthuse about Saskia's dedication to her work, her kindness to her fellow employees, her ability to integrate herself into a team and work diligently at whatever task she was given, and her popularity with other members of the workforce.

After studying the progress reports her team leader and Gordon himself had made on her, and the photograph in her file, Andreas had been forced to concede that if he hadn't seen for himself last night the way Saskia could look and behave he would probably have accepted Gordon's glowing report at face value.

She was quite plainly a woman who knew how to handle his sex, even if with him she had made an error of judgement.

This morning, for instance, she had completely metamorphosed back into the dedicated young woman forging a career for herself—neatly suited, her hair elegantly sleeked back, her face free of all but the lightest touch of make-up. Andreas started to frown as his body suddenly and very urgently and unwontedly reminded him of the female allure of the body that was today concealed discreetly beneath a prim navy business suit.

Didn't he already have enough problems to contend with? Last night after returning from the wine bar he had received a telephone call from his mother, anxiously warning him that his grandfather was on the warpath.

'He had dinner with some of his old cronies last night and apparently they were all boasting about the deals they had recently pulled off. You know what they're like.' She had sighed. 'And your grandfather was told by one of them that he had high hopes of his son winning Athena's hand...'

'Good luck to him,' Andreas had told his mother uncompromisingly. 'I hope he does. That at least will get her and Grandfather off my back.'

'Well, yes,' his mother had agreed doubtfully. 'But at the moment it seems to have made him even more determined to promote a marriage between the two of you. And, of course, now that he's half retired he's got more time on his hands to plan and fret... It's such a pity that there isn't already someone in your life.' She had sighed again, adding with a chuckle, 'I honestly believe that the hope of a great-grandchild would thrill him so much that he'd quickly forget he'd ever wanted you to marry Athena!'

Someone else in his life? Had it really been exasperation and the headache he knew lay ahead of him with their new acquisition that had prompted him into making the rashest statement of his life in telling his mother, 'What makes you think there *isn't* someone?'

There had been a startled pause, just long enough for him to curse himself mentally but not for him to recall his impetuous words, before his mother had demanded in excitement, 'You mean there *is*? Oh, Andreas! Who? *When* are we going to meet her? Who is she? How did you…? Oh, darling, how wonderful. Your grandfather *will* be thrilled. Olympia, guess what…'

He had then heard her telling his sister.

He had tried to put a brake on their excitement, to warn them that he was only talking in 'ifs' and 'buts', but neither of them had been prepared to listen. Neither had his grandfather this morning, when he had rung at the ungodly hour of five o'clock to demand to know when he was to meet his grandson's fiancée.

Fiancée… How the hell his mother and sister had managed to translate an off-the-cuff remark made in irritation into a real live fiancée Andreas had no idea, but he did know that unless he produced this mythical creature he was going to be in very big trouble.

'You'll be bringing her to the island with you, of course,' his grandfather had announced, and his words had been a command and not a question.

What the hell was he going to do? He had eight days in which to find a prospective fiancée and make it clear to her that their 'engagement' was nothing more than a convenient fiction. Eight days and she would have to be a good enough actress to fool not just his grandfather but his mother and sisters as well.

Irritably he moved out of the sunlight's direct beam, turning round so that Saskia saw him properly for the first time.

There was no opportunity for her to conceal her shock, or the soft-winded gasp of dismay that escaped her discreetly glossed lips as her face paled and then flooded with burning hot colour.

'You!' she choked as she backed instinctively towards

the door, her memories of the previous night flooding her brain and with them the sure knowledge that she was about to lose her job.

She certainly was an excellent actress, Andreas acknowledged as he observed her reaction—and in more ways than one. Her demeanour this morning was totally different from the way she had presented herself last night. But then no doubt she *was* horrified to discover that he was the man she had so blatantly propositioned. Even so, that look of sick dismay darkening her eyes and the way her soft bottom lip was trembling despite her attempts to stop it... Oh, yes, she was a first-rate actress—*a first-rate actress*!

Suddenly Andreas could see a welcome gleam of light at the end of the dark tunnel of his current problem. Oh, yes, indeed, a very definite beam of light.

'So, Ms Rodgers.' Andreas began flaying into Saskia's already shredded self-confidence with all the delicacy of a surgeon expertly slicing through layer after layer of skin, muscle and bone. 'I have read the report Gordon Jarman has written on you and I must congratulate you. It seems that you've persuaded him to think very highly of you. That's quite an accomplishment for an employee so new and young. Especially one who adopts such an unconventional and, shall we say, elastic attitude towards time-keeping...leaving earlier than her colleagues in the evening and arriving later than them in the morning.'

'Leaving *early*?' Saskia stared at him, fighting to recover her composure. How had he known about *that*?

As though he had read her mind, he told her softly, 'I was in the foyer when you left...quite some time before your official finishing time.'

'But that was...' Saskia began indignantly.

However, Andreas did not allow her to finish, shaking his head and telling her coolly, 'No excuses, please. They might work on Gordon Jarman, but unfortunately for you they will not work with me. After all, I have seen how you comport yourself when you are not at work. Unless...' He frowned, his mouth hardening as he studied her with icy derision. 'Unless, of course, *that* is the reason he has given you such an unusually excellent report...'

'No!' Saskia denied straight away. 'No! I don't... Last night was a mistake,' she protested. 'I—'

'Yes, I'm afraid it was,' Andreas agreed, adding smoothly, 'For you at least. I appreciate that the salary you are paid is relatively small, but my grandfather would be extremely unhappy to learn that a member of our staff is having to boost her income in a way that can only reflect extremely badly on our company.' Giving her a thin smile he went on with deceptive amiability, 'How very fortunate for you that it wasn't in one of *our* hotels that you were... er...plying your trade and—'

'How dare you?' Saskia interrupted him furiously, her cheeks bright scarlet and her mouth a mutinous soft bow. Pride burned rebelliously in her eyes.

'How dare I? Rather I should say to you, how dare *you*,' Andreas contradicted her sharply, his earlier air of pleasantness instantly replaced by a hard look of contemptuous anger as he told her grimly, 'Apart from the unedifying moral implications of what you were doing, or rather attempting to do, has it ever occurred to you to consider the physical danger you could be putting yourself in? Women like you...'

He paused and changed tack, catching her off guard as he went on in a much gentler tone, 'I understand from your boss that you are very anxious to maintain your employment with us.'

'Yes. Yes, I am,' Saskia admitted huskily. There was no use denying what he was saying. She had already discussed her feelings and fears about the prospect of being made redundant with Gordon Jarman, and he had obviously recorded them and passed them on to Andreas. To deny them now would only convince him she was a liar—as well as everything else!

'Look… Please, I can explain about last night,' she told him desperately, pride giving way to panic. 'I know how it must have looked, but it wasn't… I didn't…' She stopped as she saw from his expression that he wasn't prepared even to listen to her, never mind believe her.

A part of her was forced to acknowledge that she could hardly blame him…nor convince him either, unless she dragged Lorraine and Megan into his office to support her and she had far too much pride to do that. Besides, Megan wasn't capable of thinking of anything or anyone right now other than Mark and her upcoming Caribbean holiday, and as for Lorraine… Well, Saskia could guess how the older woman would revel in the situation Saskia now found herself in.

'A wise decision,' Andreas told her gently when she stopped speaking. 'You see, I despise a liar even more than I do a woman who…' Now it was his turn to stop, but Saskia knew what he was thinking.

Her face burned even more hotly, which made it disconcerting for her when he suddenly said abruptly, 'I've got a proposition I want to put to you.'

As she made a strangled sound of shock in her throat he steepled his fingers together and looked at her over them, like a sleek, well-fed predator watching a small piece of prey it was enjoying tormenting.

'What kind of proposition?' she asked him warily, but the heavy sledgehammer strokes of her heart against her ribs warned her that she probably already knew the answer—just as she knew why she was filled with such a shocking mixture of excitement and revulsion.

'Oh, not the kind you are probably most familiar with,' Andreas was telling her softly. 'I've read that some professional young women get a kick out of acting the part of harlots...'

'I was doing no such thing,' Saskia began heatedly, but he stopped her.

'I was there—remember?' he said sharply. 'If my grandfather knew how you had behaved he would demand your instant dismissal.' His grandfather might have ceded most of the control of the business to Andreas, but Andreas could see from Saskia's expression that she still believed him.

'You don't *have* to tell him.' He could see the effort it cost her to swallow her pride and add a reluctant tremulous, 'Please...'

'I don't *have* to,' he agreed 'But whether or not I do depends on your response to my proposition.'

'That's blackmail,' Saskia protested.

'Almost as old a profession as the one you were engaging in last night,' Andreas agreed silkily.

Saskia began to panic. Against all the odds there was only one thing he could possibly want from her, unlikely though that was. After all, last night she had given him every reason to assume...to believe... But that had been when she had thought he was Mark, and if he would just allow her to explain…

Fear kicked through her, fuelling a panic that rushed her headlong into telling him aggressively, 'I'm surprised that a man like you needs to blackmail a woman into having sex with him. And there's no way that I…'

'Sex?' he questioned, completely astounding her by throwing back his head and laughing out loud. When he had stopped, he repeated, 'Sex?' adding disparagingly, 'With you? No way! It isn't *sex* I want from you,' he told her coolly.

'Not sex? Then…then what is it?' Saskia demanded shakily.

'What I want from you,' Andreas informed her calmly, 'is your time and your agreement to pose as my fiancée.'

'What?' Saskia stared at him. 'You're mad,' she told him in disbelief.

'No, not mad,' Andreas corrected her sternly. 'But I am very determined not to be coerced into the marriage my grandfather wants to arrange for me. And, as my dear mother has so rightly reminded me, the best way to do that is to convince him that I am in love with someone else. That is the only way I can stop this ridiculous campaign of his.'

'You want *me*…to pose…as *your*…fiancée?' Saskia spaced the words out carefully, as though she wasn't sure she had heard them correctly, and then, when she saw the confirmation in his face, she denied fiercely, 'No. No way. No way at all!'

'No?' Andreas questioned with remarkable amiability. 'Then I'm afraid you leave me with no alternative but to inform you that there is a strong—a very strong possibility that we shall have to let you go as part of our regrettable but necessary cutbacks. I hope I make myself clear.'

'No! You can't do that...' Saskia began, and then stopped as she saw the cynical way he was looking at her.

She was wasting her time. There was no way he was even going to listen to her, never mind believe her. He didn't *want* to believe her. It didn't suit his plans to believe her...she could see that. And if she refused to accede to his commands then she knew that he was fully capable of carrying out his threat against her. Saskia swallowed. She was well and truly trapped, with no way whatsoever of escaping.

'Well?' Andreas mocked her. 'You still haven't given me your reply. Do you agree to my proposition, or...?'

Saskia swallowed the bitter taste of bile and defeat lodged in her throat. Her voice sounded raw, rasping...it hurt her to speak, but she tried to hold up her head as she told him miserably, 'I agree.'

'Excellent. For form's sake I suggest that we invent a previously secret accidental meeting between us—perhaps when I visited Hilford prior to our takeover. Because of the negotiations for the takeover we have kept our relationship...our love for one another...a secret. But now...now there is no need for secrecy any more, and to prove it, and to celebrate our freedom today I shall take you out for lunch.'

He frowned and paused. 'We shall be flying out to the Aegean at the end of next week and there are things we shall be expected to know about one another's background!'

'Flying out to *where*?' Saskia gasped. 'No, I can't. My grandmother...'

Andreas had heard from Gordon Jarman that she

lived with her grandmother, and now one eyebrow rose as he questioned silkily, 'You are engaged to me now, my beloved, surely *I* am of more importance than your grandmother? She will, I know, be surprised about our relationship, but I am sure she will appreciate just why we had to keep our love for one another to ourselves. If you wish I am perfectly prepared to come with you when you explain…everything to her…'

'No!' Saskia denied in panic. 'There's no need anyway. She's in Bath at the moment, staying with her sister. She's going to be there for the next few weeks. You can't do this,' she told him in agitation. 'Your grandfather is bound to guess that we're not…that we don't… And…'

'But he must *not* be *allowed* to guess any such thing,' Andreas told her gently. 'You are an excellent actress, as I have already seen for myself, and I'm sure you will be able to find a way of convincing him that we *are* and we *do*, and should you feel that you do need some assistance to that end…' His eyes darkened and Saskia immediately took a step backwards, her face flaming with embarrassed colour as she saw the way he was looking at her.

'Very nice,' he told her softly, 'But perhaps it might not be wise to overdo the shy, virginal bit. My grandfather is no fool. I doubt that he will expect a man of my age to have fallen passionately in love with a woman who is not equally sexually aware. I am, after all, half-Greek, and passion is very much a factor of the male Greek personality and psyche.'

Saskia wanted to turn and run away. The situation was becoming worse by the minute. What, she wondered fatalistically, would Andreas do if he ever learned that she was not 'sexually aware', as he had termed it, and that in fact her only experience of sex and passion was limited to a few chaste kisses and fumbled embraces? She had her parents to thank for her caution as a teenager where sexual experimentation had been concerned, of course. Their rash behaviour had led to her dreading that she might repeat their foolishness. But there was, of course, no way that Andreas could ever know that!

'It's now almost ten,' Andreas informed her briskly, looking at his watch. 'I suggest you go back to your office and at one o'clock. I'll come down for you and take you out to lunch. The sooner we make our relationship public now, the better.'

As he spoke he was moving towards her. Immediately Saskia started to panic, gasping out loud in shock as the door opened to admit his PA in the same heartbeat as Andreas reached out and manacled Saskia's fragile wrist-bone in the firm grip of his fingers and thumb.

His skin was dark, tanned, but not so much so that one would automatically guess at his Greek blood, Saskia recognised. His eyes *were* grey, she now saw, and not blue as she had so blush-makingly suggested last night, and they added to the confusion as to what nationality he might be, whilst his hair, though very, very dark, was thick and straight. There was, though, some whisper of his ancient lineage in his high cheekbones, classically sculptured jaw and aquiline nose. They definitely belonged to some arrogant, aristocratic ancient Greek nobleman, and he would, she suspected, be very much inclined to dominate those around him, to stamp his authority on everything he did—and everyone he met.

'Oh, Andreas,' the PA was exclaiming, looking in flustered disbelief at the way her boss was drawing Saskia closer to him, 'I'm sorry to interrupt you but your grandfather has been on—twice!'

'I shall ring my grandfather back shortly,' Andreas responded smoothly, adding equally smoothly, 'Oh, and I don't want any appointments or any interruptions from one to two-thirty today. I shall be taking my fiancée to lunch.'

As he spoke he turned to Saskia and gave her such a look of melting tender sensuality, so completely redolent of an impatient lover barely able to control his desire for her, that for a breath of time she was almost taken in herself. She could only stare back at him as though she had been hypnotised. If he had given her a look like that last night... Stop it, she warned herself immediately, shaken by the unexpected thought.

But if his behaviour was shocking her it was shocking his PA even more, she recognised as the other woman gave a small choked gurgle and then shook her head when Andreas asked her urbanely if anything was wrong.

'No. I was just... That is... No...not at all...'

'Good. Oh, and one more thing. I want you to book an extra seat on my flight to Athens next week. Next to mine...for Saskia...' Turning away from his PA he told Saskia huskily, 'I can't wait to introduce you to my family, especially my grandfather. But first...'

Before Saskia could guess what he intended to do he lifted her hand to his mouth, palm facing upwards. As she felt the warmth of his breath skimming her skin Saskia started to tremble, her breath coming in quick, short bursts. She felt dizzy, breathless, filled with a mixture of elation, excitement and shock, a sense of somehow having stepped outside herself and become another person, entered another life—a life that was far more exciting than her own, a life that could lead to the kind of dangerous, magical, awe-inspiring experiences that she had previously thought could never be hers.

Giddily she could hear Andreas telling her huskily, 'First, my darling, we must find something pretty to adorn this bare finger of yours. My grandfather would not approve if I took you home without a ring that states very clearly my intentions.'

Saskia could hear quite plainly the PA's sudden shocked indrawn breath, but once again the other woman could not be any more shocked than she was herself. Andreas had claimed that she was a good actress, but he was no slouch in that department himself. The look that he was giving her right now alone, never mind the things he had said...

After his PA had scuttled out of his office, closing the door behind her, she told him shakily, 'You do realise, don't you, that by lunchtime it will be all over the office?'

'All over the office?' he repeated, giving her a desirous look. 'My dear, I shall be very surprised and even more disappointed if our news has not travelled a good deal further than that.'

When she gave him an uncomprehending look he explained briefly, 'By lunchtime I fully expect it to have travelled at least as far as Athens...'

'To your grandfather,' Saskia guessed.

'Amongst others,' Andreas agreed coolly, without enlightening her as to who such 'others' might be.

Unexpectedly there were suddenly dozens of questions she wanted to ask him: about his family, as well as his grandfather, and the island he intended to take her to, and about the woman his grandfather wanted him to marry. She had a vague idea that Greeks were very interested in protecting family interests and according to Emma his cousin was 'mega wealthy', as was Andreas himself.

Somehow, without knowing quite how it had happened, she discovered that Andreas had released her hand and that she was walking through the door he had opened for her.

'READY, Saskia?'

Saskia felt the embarrassed colour start to seep up under her skin as Andreas approached her desk. Her colleagues were studiously avoiding looking openly at them but Saskia knew perfectly well that they were the cynosure of their attention. How could they not be?

'Gordon, I'm afraid that Saskia is going to be late back from lunch,' Andreas was announcing to her bemused boss as he came out from his office.

'Have you told him our news yet, darling,' Andreas asked her lovingly.

'Er...no...' Saskia couldn't bring herself to look directly at him.

'Saskia,' she could hear her boss saying weakly as he looked on disbelievingly, 'I don't understand...'

He would understand even less if she tried to explain to him what was *really* happening, Saskia acknowledged bleakly. It seemed to her that it was a very unfair thing to do to deceive the man who had been so kind to her but what alternative did she really have.

'You mustn't blame Saskia,' Andreas was saying protectively. 'I'm afraid I'm the one who's at fault. I insisted that our relationship should be kept a secret until the outcome of our takeover bid became public. I didn't want Saskia to be accused of having conflicting loyalties—and I must tell you, Gordon, that she insisted that any kind of

discussion about the takeover was off-limits between us…
Mind you, talking about work was not exactly *my* number
one priority when we were together,' Andreas admitted,
with a sensual look at Saskia that made her face burn even
more hotly and caused more than one audible and envious
gasp from her female co-workers.

'Why did you have to do *that*?' Saskia demanded
fretfully the moment they were alone and out of earshot.

'Do what?' Andreas responded unhelpfully.

'You know perfectly well what I mean,' Saskia protested. 'Why couldn't we just have met somewhere?'

'In secret?' He looked more bored now than amorous,
his eyebrows drawing together as he frowned impatiently
down at her. He was a good deal taller than her, well over
six foot, and it hurt her neck a little, craning to look up at
him. She wished he wouldn't walk so close to her; it made
her feel uncomfortable and on edge and somehow aware
of herself as a woman in a way that wasn't familiar to her.

'Haven't I already made it plain to you that the whole
object of this exercise is to bring our relationship into
the public domain? Which is why—' He smiled grimly
at Saskia as he broke off from what he was saying to
tell her silkily, 'I've booked a table at the wine bar for
lunch. I ate there last night and I have to say that the food
was excellent—even if what happened later was less…
palatable…'

Suddenly Saskia had had enough.

'Look, I keep trying to tell you, last night was a mistake.
I…'

'I completely agree with you,' Andreas assured her. 'It
was a mistake…*your* mistake…and whilst we're on the
subject, let me warn you, Saskia, if you *ever* manifest

anything similar whilst you are engaged to *me*, if you ever even *look* at another man…' He stopped as he saw the shock widening her eyes.

'I'm half-Greek, my dear,' he reminded her softly. 'And when it comes to *my* woman, I'm more Greek than I am British…very much more…'

'I'm *not* your woman,' was the only response Saskia found she could make.

'No,' he agreed cynically. 'You belong to any man who can afford you, don't you, in reality? But…' He stopped again as he heard the sharp sound of protest she made, her face white and then red as her emotions overwhelmed her self-control.

'You have no right to speak to me like that,' Saskia told him thickly.

'No right? But surely as your fiancée I have *every* right,' Andreas taunted her, and then, before she could stop him, he reached out and ran one long finger beneath her lower eyelashes, collecting on it the angry humiliated tears that had just fallen. 'Tears?' he mocked her. 'My dear, you are an even better actress then I thought.'

They had reached the wine bar and Saskia was forced to struggle to control her emotions as he opened the door and drew her inside.

'I don't want anything to eat. I'm not hungry,' she told him flatly once they had been shown to their table.

'Sulking?' he asked her succinctly. 'I can't force you to eat, but I certainly don't intend to deny *myself* the pleasure of enjoying a good meal.'

'There are things we have to discuss,' he added in a cool, businesslike voice as he picked up the menu she had ignored and read it. 'I know most of your personal details from your file, but if we are to convince my family and especially my grandfather that we are lovers, then there are other things I shall need to know…and things you will need to know about me.'

Lovers… Saskia just managed to stop herself from shuddering openly. If she had to accede to his blackmail then she was going to have to learn to play the game by his rules or risk being totally destroyed by him.

'Lovers.' She gave him a bleak smile. 'I thought Greek families didn't approve of sex before marriage.'

'Not for their *own* daughters,' he agreed blandly. 'But since you are *not* Greek, and since *I* am half-British I am sure that my grandfather will be more…tolerant…'

'But he wouldn't be tolerant if you were engaged to your cousin?' Saskia pressed, not sure why she was doing so and even less sure just why the thought of his cousin should arouse such a sensation of pain and hostility within her.

'Athena, my cousin, is a *widow*, a previously married woman, and naturally my grandfather…' He paused and then told her dryly, 'Besides, Athena herself would never accept my grandfather's interference in any aspect of her life. She is a very formidable woman.'

'She's a *widow*?' For some reason Saskia had assumed that this cousin was a young girl. It had never occurred to her that she might already have been married.

'A widow,' Andreas confirmed. 'With two teenage children.'

'Teenage!'

'She married at twenty-two,' Andreas told her with a shrug. 'That was almost twenty years ago.'

Saskia's eyes widened as she did her sums. Athena was obviously older than Andreas. A lonely and no doubt vulnerable woman who was being pressurised into a second marriage she perhaps did not want, Saskia decided sympathetically.

'However, you need not concern yourself too much with Athena, since it is doubtful that you will meet her. She lives a very peripatetic existence. She has homes in Athens, New York and Paris and spends much of her time travelling between them, as well as running the shipping line she inherited.'

A shipping line and a hotel chain. No wonder Andreas's grandfather was so anxious for them to marry. It amazed Saskia that Andreas was not equally keen on the match, especially knowing the hard bargain he had driven over the takeover.

As though he had guessed what she was thinking, he leaned towards her and told her grittily, 'Unlike you, *I* am not prepared to sell myself.'

'I was *not* selling myself,' Saskia denied hotly, and then frowned as the waiter approached their table carrying two plates of delicious-looking food.

'I didn't order a meal,' she began as he set one of them down in front of her and the other in front of Andreas.

'No. I ordered it for you,' Andreas told her. 'I don't like to see my women looking like skinny semi-starved rabbits. A Greek man may be permitted to beat his wife, but he would never stoop to starving her.'

'Beat...' Saskia began rising to the bait and then stopped as she saw the glint in his eyes and realised that he was teasing her.

'I suspect you are the kind of woman, Saskia, who would drive a saint, never mind a mere mortal man, to be driven to subdue you, to master you and then to wish that he had had the strength to master himself instead.'

Saskia shivered as the raw sensuality of what he was saying hit her like a jolt of powerful electricity. What was it about him that made her so acutely aware of him, so nervously on edge?

More to distract herself than anything else she started to eat, unaware of the ruefully amused look Andreas gave her as she did so. If he didn't know better he would have said that she was as inexperienced as a virgin. The merest allusion to anything sexual was enough to have her trembling with reaction, unable to meet his gaze. It was just as well that he knew it was all an act, otherwise... Otherwise what? Otherwise he might be savagely tempted to put his words into actions, to see if she trembled as deliciously when he touched her as she did when he spoke to her.

To counter what he was feeling he began to speak to her in a crisp, businesslike voice.

'There are certain things you will need to know about my family background if you are going to convince my grandfather that we are in love.'

He proceeded to give her a breakdown of his immediate family, adding a few cautionary comments about his grandfather's health.

'Which does not mean that he is not one hundred and fifty per cent on the ball. If anything, the fact that he is now prevented from working so much means that he is even more ferociously determined to interfere in my life than he was before. He tells my mother that he is afraid he will die before I give him any great-grandchildren. If that is not blackmail I don't know what is,' Andreas growled.

'It's obviously a family vice,' Saskia told him mock sweetly, earning herself a look that she refused to allow to make her quake in her shoes.

'Ultimately, of course, our engagement will have to be broken,' Andreas told her unnecessarily. 'No doubt our sojourn on the island will reveal certain aspects of our characters that we shall find mutually unappealing, and on our return to England we shall bring our engagement to an end. But at least I shall have bought myself some time…and hopefully Athena will have decided to accept one of the many suitors my grandfather says are only too willing to become her second husband.'

'And if she doesn't?' Saskia felt impelled to ask.

'*If* she doesn't, we shall just have to delay ending our engagement until either she does or I find an alternative way of convincing my grandfather that one of my sisters can provide him with his great-grandchildren.'

'You don't *ever* want to marry?' Saskia was startled into asking.

'Well, let's just say that since I have reached the age of thirty-five without meeting a woman who has made me feel my life is unliveable without her by my side, I somehow doubt that I am likely to do so now. Falling in love is a young man's extravagance. In a man past thirty it is more of a vain folly.'

'My father fell in love with my mother when he was seventeen,' Saskia couldn't stop herself from telling him. 'They ran away together…' Her eyes clouded. 'It was a mistake. They fell out of love with one another before I was born. An older man would at least have had some sense of responsibility towards the life he had helped to create. My father was still a child himself.'

'He abandoned you?' Andreas asked her, frowning.

'They both did,' Saskia told him tersely. 'If it hadn't been for my grandmother I would have ended up in a children's home.'

Soberly Andreas watched her. Was *that* why she went trawling bars for men? Was she searching for the male love she felt she had been denied by her father? His desire to exonerate her from her behaviour irritated him. *Why* was he trying to make excuses for her? Surely he hadn't actually been taken in by those tears earlier.

'It's time for us to leave,' he told her brusquely.

CHAPTER FOUR

IF SOMEONE had told her two weeks ago that she would be leaving behind her everything that was familiar to fly to an unknown Greek island in the company of an equally unknown man to whom she was supposed to be engaged, Saskia would have shaken her head in denial and amusement—which just went to show!

Which just went to show what a combination of male arrogance, self-belief and determination could do, especially when it was allied to the kind of control that one particular male had over her, Saskia fretted darkly.

In less than fifteen minutes' time Andreas would be picking her up in his Mercedes for the first leg of their journey to Aphrodite, the island Andreas's grandfather had bought for his wife and named after the goddess of love.

'Theirs was a love match but one that had the approval of both families,' Andreas had told Saskia when he had been briefing her about his background.

A love match…unlike *their* bogus engagement. Just being a party to that kind of deceit, even though it was against her will, made Saskia feel uncomfortable, but nowhere near as uncomfortable as she had felt when she had had to telephone her grandmother and lie to her, saying that she was going away on business.

Andreas had tried to insist that she inform her grandmother of their engagement, but Saskia had refused.

'*You* may be happy to lie to your family about our supposed "relationship",' she had told him with a look of smoky-eyed despair. 'But I *can't* lie to my grandmother about something so...' She hadn't been able to go on, unwilling to betray herself by admitting to Andreas that her grandmother would never believe that Saskia had committed herself and her future to a man without loving him.

Once the fall-out from the news of her 'engagement' had subsided at work, her colleagues had treated her with both wary caution and distance. She was now the boss's fiancée and as such no longer really 'one of them'.

All in all Saskia had spent the week feeling increasingly isolated and frightened, but she was too proud to say anything to anyone—a hang-up, she suspected, from the days of her childhood, when the fact that her parents' story was so widely known, coupled with the way she had been dumped on her grandmother, had made her feel different, distanced from her schoolmates, who had all seemed to have proper mummies and daddies.

Not that anyone could have loved her more than her grandmother had done, as Saskia was the first to acknowledge now. Her home background had in reality been just as loving and stable, if not more so, than that of the majority of her peers.

She gave a small surreptitious look at her watch. Less than five minutes to go. Her heart thumped heavily. Her packed suitcase was ready and waiting in the hall. She had agonised over what she ought to take and in the end had compromised with a mixture of the summer holiday clothes she had bought three years previously, when she and Megan had gone to Portugal together, plus some of her lightweight office outfits.

She hadn't seen Andreas since he had taken her out for lunch—not that she had minded *that*! No indeed! He had been attending a gruelling schedule of business meetings—dealing, if the trickles of gossip that had filtered through the grapevine were anything to go by, heroically with the problems posed by the challenging situation the hotels had fallen into prior to the takeover.

'He's visited every single one of our hotels,' Saskia had heard from one admiring source. 'And he's been through every single aspect of the way they're being run—and guess what?'

Saskia, who had been on the edge of the group who'd been listening eagerly to this story, had swallowed uncomfortably, expecting to hear that Andreas had instituted a programme of mass sackings in order to halt the flood of unprofitable expenses, but to her astonishment instead she had heard, 'He's told everyone that their job is safe, provided they can meet the targets he's going to be setting. Everywhere he's been he's given the staff a pep talk, told them how much he values the acquisition his group has made and how he personally is going to be held responsible by the board of directors if he can't turn it into a profit-making asset.'

The gossip was that Andreas had a way with him that had his new employees not only swearing allegiance, but apparently praising him to the skies as well.

Well, they obviously hadn't witnessed the side to his character she had done, was all that Saskia had been able to think as she listened a little bitterly to everyone's almost euphoric praise of him.

It was ten-thirty now, and he wasn't… Saskia tensed as she suddenly saw the large Mercedes pulling up outside her grandmother's house. Right on time! But of course Andreas would not waste a precious second of his time unless he had to, especially not on her!

By the time he had reached the front door she had opened it and was standing waiting for him, her suitcase in one hand and her door key in the other.

'What's that?'

She could see the way he was frowning as he looked down at her inexpensive case and immediately pride flared through her sharpening her own voice as she answered him with a curt, 'My suitcase.'

'Give it to me,' he instructed her briefly.

'I can carry it myself,' Saskia informed him grittily.

'I'm sure you can,' Andreas agreed, equally grimly. 'But…'

'But what?' Saskia challenged him angrily. 'But Greek men do not allow women to carry their own luggage nor to be independent from them in any way?'

Saskia could see from the way Andreas's mouth tightened that he did not like what she had said. For some perverse reason she felt driven to challenge him, even though a part of her shrank from the storm signals she could see flashing in his eyes.

'I'm afraid in this instance you should perhaps blame my English father rather than my Greek mother,' he told her icily. 'The English public school he insisted I was sent to believed in what is now considered to be an outdated code of good manners for its pupils.' He gave her a thin, unfriendly look. 'One word of warning to you. My grandfather is inclined to be old-fashioned about such things. He will not understand your modern insistence on politically correct behaviour, and whilst you are on the island…'

'I have to do as *you* tell me,' Saskia finished bitterly for him.

If this was a taste of what the next few weeks were going to be like she didn't know how she was going to survive them. Still, at least there would be one benefit of their obvious hostility to one another. No one who would be observing them together would be surprised when they decided to end their 'engagement'.

'Our flight leaves Heathrow at nine tomorrow morning, so we will need to leave the apartment early,' Andreas informed Saskia once they were in the car.

'The *apartment*?' Saskia questioned him warily immediately.

'Yes,' Andreas confirmed. 'I have an apartment in London. We shall be staying there tonight. This afternoon we shall spend shopping.'

'Shopping…?' Saskia began to interrupt, but Andreas overruled her.

'Yes, shopping,' he told her cautiously. 'You will need an engagement ring, and…' He paused and gave her a brief skimming look of assessment and dismissal that made her itch to demand that he stop the car immediately. Oh, how she would love to be able to tell him that she had changed her mind…that there was no way she was going to give in to his blackmail. But she knew there was no way she could.

'You will need more suitable clothes.'

'If you mean holiday clothes,' Saskia began, 'they are in my case, and…'

'No, I do not mean "holiday" clothes.' Andreas stopped her grimly. 'I am an independently wealthy man, Saskia; you don't need me to tell you that. Your department's investigations prior to our takeover must have informed you to the nearest hundred thousand pounds what my asset value is. My grandfather is a millionaire many times over, and my mother and my sisters are used to buying their clothes from the world's top designers, even though none of them are what could be considered to be fashion victims or shopaholics. Naturally, as my fiancée…'

Without allowing him to finish Saskia took a deep, angry breath and told him dangerously, 'If you think that I am going to let *you* buy my clothes…'

With only the briefest of pauses Andreas took control of the situation from her by asking smoothly, 'Why not? After all, you were prepared to let me buy your *body*. Me or indeed any other man who was prepared to pay for it.'

'No! That's not true,' Saskia denied with a shocked gasp.

'Very good,' Andreas mocked her. 'But you can save the special effects for my family. I know *exactly* what you are—remember. Think of these clothes as a perk of your job.' He gave her a thin, unkind smile. 'However, having said that, I have to add that I shall want to vet whatever you wish to purchase. The image I want you to convey to my family as my fiancée is one of elegance and good taste.'

'What are you trying to suggest?' Saskia hissed furiously at him. 'That left to my own devices I might choose something more suited to a…?' She stopped, unable to bring herself to voice the words burning a painful brand in her thoughts.

To her bemusement, instead of saying them for her Andreas said coolly, 'You are obviously not used to buying expensive clothes and there is no way I want you indulging in some kind of idiotic unnecessary economy which would negate the whole purpose of the exercise. I don't want you buying clothes more suitable for a young woman on a modest salary than the fiancée of an extremely wealthy man,' he informed her bluntly, in case she had not understood him the first time.

For once Saskia could think of nothing to say, but inside she was a bundle of fury and shame. There was no way she could stop Andreas from carrying out his plans, she knew that, but she fully intended to keep a mental record of everything he spent so that ultimately she could repay him, even if doing so totally depleted the small nest egg she had been carefully saving.

'No more objections?' Andreas enquired smoothly. 'Good, because I promise you, Saskia, I mean to have my way—even if that entails dressing you and undressing you myself to get it. Make no mistake, when we arrive on Aphrodite you will be arriving as my fiancée.'

As he drove down the slipway onto the motorway and the powerful car picked up speed Saskia decided diplomatically that quarrelling with him whilst he was driving at such a speed would be very foolish indeed. It was over half an hour later before she recognised that, in her anxiety to reject Andreas's claimed right to decide what she should wear, she had neglected to deal with the more important issue of her discomfort at the idea of spending the night with him.

But what did she really have to fear? Certainly not any sexual advances from Andreas. He had, after all, made it shamingly plain what he thought of her sexual morals.

She had far too much pride to admit to him that she felt daunted and apprehensive at the thought of sharing the intimacy of an apartment with him. On the island it would be different. There they would be with his family and the staff who ran the large villa complex he said his grandfather had had built on it.

No, she would be wise to grit her teeth and say nothing rather than risk exposing herself to his disbelief and mocking contempt by expressing her anxieties.

As SHE WAITED for the chauffeur to load her luggage into the boot of her hired limousine Athena tapped one slender expensively shod foot impatiently.

The moment she had heard the news that Andreas was engaged and about to bring his fiancée to Aphrodite on an official visit to meet his family she had sprung into action. Fortunately an engagement was not a marriage, and she certainly intended to make sure that *this* engagement never made it as far as a wedding.

She knew why Andreas had done it, of course. He was, after all, Greek to the very marrow of his bones—even if he chose to insist on everyone acknowledging his British blood—and like any Greek man, indeed any *man* he had an inborn need to be the one in control.

His claim to be in love with this other woman was simply his way of showing that control, rejecting the marriage to her which was so very dear to his grandfather's heart and to her own.

As the limousine sped away from the kerb she leaned

forward and gave the driver the address of a prestigious apartment block overlooking the river. She herself did not maintain a home in London; she preferred New York's social life and the Paris shops.

Andreas might think he had outmanoeuvred her by announcing his engagement to this undoubtedly cold and sexless English fiancée. Well, she would soon bring an end to that, and make sure that he knew where his real interests lay. After all, how could he possibly resist *her*? She had everything he could want, and he certainly had everything *she* wanted.

It was a pity he had managed to prevent her from outbidding him for this latest acquisition. Ownership of the hotels themselves meant nothing to her *per se*, but it would have been an excellent bait to dangle in front of him since he obviously set a great deal of store by them. Why, she could not understand. But then in many ways there were a considerable number of things about Andreas that she did not understand. It was one of the things that made him so desirable to her. Athena had always coveted that which seemed to be out of reach.

The first time she had realised she wanted Andreas he had been fifteen and she had been on the verge of marrying her husband. She smiled wantonly to herself, licking her lips. At fifteen Andreas, although a boy, had been as tall as a man and as broad, with a superbly fit young body, and so indescribably good-looking that the sight of him had made her melt with lust.

She had done her best to seduce him but he had managed to resist her and then, within a month of deciding that she wanted him, she had been married.

At twenty-two she had not been a young bride by

Greek standards, and she had been carefully stalking her husband-to-be for some time. Older than her by a decade, and immensely wealthy, he had played a cat and mouse game with her for well over a year before he had finally capitulated. There had certainly been no way she was going to give up the marriage she had worked so hard for for the passion she felt for Andreas, a mere boy.

But then fate had stepped in. Her husband had died unexpectedly and she had been left a widow. A very rich widow…a very rich and sexually hungry widow. And Andreas was now a man—and what a man!

The only thing that was keeping them apart was Andreas's pride. It had to be. What other reason could he possibly have for resisting her advances?

As the limousine pulled up at the address she had given the driver Athena examined her reflection in the neat mirrors fitted into the Rolls's interior. That discreet nip and tuck she had had last year had been well worth the prince's ransom she had paid the American plastic surgeon. She could quite easily pass for a woman in her early thirties now.

Her jet-black hair had been cut and styled by one of the world's top hairdressers, her skin glowed from the expensive creams lavished on it, her make-up was immaculate and emphasised the slanting darkness of her eyes, her toe and fingernails gleamed richly with dark red polish.

A smile of satisfaction curved her mouth. No, there was no way Andreas's dreary little fiancée—an office girl, someone he had supposedly fallen in love with during the negotiations to buy out the hotel chain—could compete with her. Athena's eyes hardened. This girl, whoever she was, would soon learn what a mistake she had made in trying to lay claim on the man *Athena* wanted. What a very, very big mistake!

As she left the limousine the perfume she had especially blended for her in Paris moved with her, a heavy, musky cloud of sexuality.

Her teenage daughters loathed it, and were constantly begging her to change it, but she had no intention of doing so. It was her signature, the essence of herself as a woman. Andreas's English fiancée no doubt wore something dull and insipid such as lavender water!

'I'LL LEAVE THE CAR here,' Andreas told Saskia as he swung the Mercedes into a multi-storey car park right in the centre of the city. Saskia's eyes widened as she saw the tariff pinned up by the barrier. She would never have dreamed of paying so much to park a car, but the rich, as they said, were different.

Just how different she came to realise during the course of the afternoon, as Andreas guided her into a series of shops the like of which Saskia had never imagined existed. And in each one the very aura of his presence seemed to draw from the sales assistants the kind of reverential reaction that made Saskia tighten her lips. She could see the female admiration and speculation in their eyes as a series of outfits was produced for his inspection. For *his* inspection—not *hers*, Saskia recognised and her sense of helpless frustration and resentment grew with each shop they visited.

'I'm not a doll or a child,' she exploded outside one of them, when she had flatly refused to even try on the cream trouser suit the salesgirl had gushingly declared would be perfect for her.

'No? Well, you're certainly giving a wonderful imitation of behaving like one,' Andreas responded grimly. 'That suit was—'

'That suit was over one thousand pounds,' Saskia interrupted him grittily. 'There's no *way* I would ever pay that kind of money for an outfit…not even my wedding dress!'

When Andreas started to laugh she glared furiously at him, demanding, 'What's so funny?'

'You are,' he told her uncompromisingly. 'My dear Saskia, have you really any idea of the kind of wedding dress you would get for under a thousand pounds?'

'No, I haven't,' Saskia admitted. 'But I do know that I'd never feel comfortable wearing clothes the cost of which would feed a small country, and neither is an expensive wedding dress any guarantee of a good marriage.'

'Oh, spare me the right-on lectures,' Andreas broke in in exasperation. 'Have you ever thought of how many people would be without jobs if everyone went around wearing sackcloth and ashes, as you obviously would have them do?'

'That's not fair,' Saskia defended herself. She was, after all, feminine enough to like good clothes and to want to look her best, and in that trouser suit she *would* undeniably have looked good, she admitted inwardly. But she was acutely conscious of the fact that every penny Andreas spent on her she would have to repay.

'I don't know why you're insisting on doing this,' she told Andreas rebelliously. 'I don't *need* any clothes; I've

already told you that. And there's certainly no need for you
to throw your money around to impress me.'

'You or anyone else,' Andreas cut in sharply, dark
bands of colour burning across his cheekbones in a visual
warning to her that she had angered him.

'I am a businessman, Saskia. Throwing money around
for *any* reason is not something I do, least of all in an
attempt to impress a woman who could easily be bought
for less than half the price of that trouser suit. Oh, no, you
don't,' he cautioned her softly, reaching out to catch hold
of the hand she had automatically lifted.

He was holding her wrist in such a tight grip that Saskia
could actually see her fingers going white, but her pride
wouldn't allow her to tell him that he was hurting her.
It also wouldn't allow her to acknowledge that she had
momentarily let her feelings get out of control, and it was
only when she suddenly started to sway, white-faced with
pain and shock, that Andreas realised what was happening.
He released her wrist with a muffled curse and then started
to chafe life back into her hand.

'Why didn't you *tell* me I was hurting you so much?' he
grated. 'You have bones as fragile as a bird's.'

Even now, with his dark head bent over her tingling
hand whilst he massaged it expertly to bring the blood
stinging back into her veins, Saskia couldn't allow herself
to weaken and claim his compassion.

'I didn't want to spoil your fun,' she told him sharply.
'You were obviously *enjoying* hurting me.'

She tensed when she heard the oath he gave as he
released her completely, and tensed again at the sternness
in his voice, one look of grim determination in his eyes as
he said, 'This has gone far enough. You are behaving like

a child. First a harlot and now a child. There is only *one*
role I want to see you play from now on, Saskia, and that
is the one we have already agreed upon. I'll warn you now.
If you do or say *anything* to make my family suspect that
ours is not a true love match I shall make you very sorry
for it. Do you understand me?'

'Yes, I understand you,' Saskia agreed woodenly.

'I mean what I say,' Andreas warned her. 'And it won't
just be the Demetrios chain you won't be able to work for.
If you flout me, Saskia, I'll see to it that you will never be
able to work *anywhere* again. An accountant who can't
be trusted and who has been dismissed on suspicion of
stealing is not one that anyone will want to employ.'

'You can't do that,' Saskia whispered, white-faced, but
she knew all too well that he could.

She hated him now…really hated him, and when in
the next shop he marched her into she saw the salesgirl's
eyes widening in breathless sexual interest, she reflected
mentally that the other girl was welcome to him…more
than welcome!

IT WAS LATE IN THE afternoon before Andreas finally decided that Saskia had a wardrobe suitable for his fiancée.

At their last port of call he had called upon the services
of the store's personal shopper who, with relentless
efficiency, had provided Saskia with the kind of clothes
that she had previously only ever seen in glossy magazines.

She had tried to reject everything the shopper had
produced, but on each occasion apart from one Andreas
had overruled her. The only time they had been in accord
had been when the shopper had brought out a bikini which
she had announced was perfect for Saskia's colouring and

destination. The minuteness of the triangles which were supposed to cover her modesty had made Saskia's eyes widen in disbelief—and they had widened even more when she had discreetly managed to study the price tag.

'I couldn't possibly swim in that,' she had blurt-ed out.

'*Swim* in it?' The other woman had looked stunned. 'Good heavens, no, of course not. This isn't for *swimming* in. And, look, this is the wrap that goes with it. Isn't it divine?' she had purred, producing a length of silky fragile fabric embellished with sequins.

As she'd seen the four-figure price on the wrap Saskia had thought she might actually faint with disbelief, but to her relief and surprise Andreas had also shaken his head.

'That is *not* the kind of outfit I would wish my fiancée to wear,' he had told the shopper bluntly, adding, just in case she had not fully understood him, 'Saskia's body is eye-catching enough without her needing to embellish it with an outfit more suitable for a call girl.'

The shopper diplomatically had not pressed the issue, but instead had gone away, returning with several swimsuits.

Saskia had picked the cheapest of them, unwillingly allowing Andreas to add a matching wrap.

Whilst he'd been settling the bill and making arrangements for everything to be delivered to his riverside apartment Saskia had drunk the coffee the personal shopper had organised for her.

Perhaps it was because she hadn't really eaten anything all day that she was feeling so lightheaded and anxious, she decided. It couldn't surely be because she and Andreas were now going to go to his apartment, where they would be alone—could it?

'There's an excellent restaurant close to the apartment

block,' Andreas informed Saskia, once they were in the car and he was driving her towards the dockland area where his apartment was situated. 'I'll arrange to have a meal sent in and...'

'No,' Saskia protested immediately. 'I'd rather eat out.' She could see that Andreas was frowning.

'I don't think that's a good idea,' he told her flatly. 'A woman on her own, especially a woman like you, is bound to attract attention, and besides, you look tired. I have to go out, and I have no idea what time I will be back.'

Andreas was going out. Saskia could feel her anxiety easing. Her feet ached from the unaccustomed pavement-pounding and her brain was exhausted with the effort of keeping a running tab on just how much money Andreas, and therefore she, had spent.

Far more than she had wanted to spend. So much that just thinking about it was making her feel distinctly ill. Wretchedly she acknowledged that there would be precious little left of her hard-earned little nest egg once she had repaid Andreas what he had spent.

Tiredly Saskia followed Andreas through the underground car park and into the foyer of the apartment block. A special key was needed to use the lift, which glided upwards so smoothly that Saskia's eyes rounded in shock when it came to a standstill. She had not even realised that they were moving.

'It's this way,' Andreas told her, touching her arm and guiding her towards one of the four doorways opening off the entrance lobby. He was carrying her case, which he put down as he unlocked the door, motioning to Saskia to precede him into the elegant space beyond it.

CHAPTER FIVE

THE FIRST THING that struck Saskia about Andreas's apartment was not the very expensive modern art hanging on the hallway's walls but its smell—a musky, throat-closing, shockingly overpowering scent which stung her nostrils and made her tense.

That Andreas was equally aware of it she was in no doubt. Saskia could see him pause and lift his head, like a hunting panther sniffing the air.

'Hell... Hell and damnation,' she heard him mutter ferociously beneath his breath, and then, to her shock, he thrust open the door into the huge-windowed living space that lay beyond the lobby and took hold of her. His fingers bit into the soft flesh of her arms, his breath a warning whisper against her lips as his eyes blazed down into the unguarded shocked softness of hers, dark as obsidian, hard as flint, commanding...warning...

'Alone at last. How you have enjoyed teasing me today, my loved one, but now I have you to myself and I can exact what punishment on you I wish...'

The soft crooning tone of his voice as much as his words scattered what was left of her senses, leaving Saskia clinging weakly to him as the shock ripped through her in a floodtide. Then his mouth was covering hers, silencing the protest she was trying to make, his lips moulding, shaping, coaxing, *seducing* hers with an expertise that flattened her defences as effectively as an atom bomb.

Incoherently Saskia whispered his name, trying to insist on a cessation of what he was doing and an explanation for it. But her lips, her mouth, her senses, unused to so much sensual stimulation, were defying reason and caution and everything else that Saskia's bemused brain was trying to tell them. Her frozen shock melted beneath the heat of the pleasure Andreas's hungry passionate expertise was showing her, and her lips softened and trembled into an unguarded, uninhibited response.

Without being aware of what she was doing Saskia strained to get closer to Andreas, standing on tiptoe so that she could cling ardently to the delicious pleasure of his kiss. Her hands on his arms registered the sheer size and inflexibility of the muscles beneath them whilst her heart pounded in awed inexperienced shock at the intensity of what she was feeling.

Even more than she could smell that musky, over-powering female perfume, she could smell Andreas himself. His heat…his passion…his maleness… And shockingly something in her, something she hadn't known existed, was responding to it just as her lips were responding to him… just as *she* was responding to him, swaying into his arms compliantly, her body urging him to draw her close, to let her feel the rest of his male strength.

Dizzily Saskia opened the eyes she had closed at the first touch of his mouth on hers, shivering as she saw the sparks of raw sensuality darting like lightning from his eyes as he stared down at her. It was like hanging way above the earth in a dizzying, death-defying place where she could feel her danger and yet at the same time know somehow she would be safe.

'You love like an innocent...a virgin...' Andreas was telling her huskily, and as he did so the sparks glittering in his eyes intensified, as though he found something very satisfying about such a notion.

Helplessly Saskia stared back at him. Her heart was thudding frantically fast and her body was filled with an unfamiliar shocking ache that was a physical need to have him touch her, to have his hand run slowly over her skin and reach right through it to that place where her unfamiliar ache began, so that he could surround and soothe it. Somehow just thinking about him doing such a thing *increased* the ache to a pounding throb, a wild, primitive beat that made her moan and sway even closer to him.

'You like that... You want me...'

As he spoke to her she could hear and feel the urgency in his voice, could feel his arousal. Eagerly she pressed closer to him, only to freeze as she suddenly heard a woman's voice demanding sharply, 'Andreas? Aren't you going to introduce me?'

Immediately she realised what she was doing and shame flooded through her, but as she tried to pull away, desperate to conceal her confusion, Andreas held on to her, forcing her to stay where she was, forcing her even more closely into his body so that somehow she was leaning against him, as though...as though...

She trembled as she felt the powerful thrust of his leg between her own, her face burning hotly with embarrassed colour as she realised the sexual connotation that their pose suggested. But it seemed that the woman who was watching them was not similarly self-conscious.

Saskia caught her breath as Andreas allowed her to turn her head and look at the woman.

She was tall and dark-haired, everything about her immaculately groomed, but despite the warmth of her olive skin and the ripe richness of her painted mouth and nails Saskia shivered as she sensed her innate coldness.

'Athena,' Andreas was demanding shortly, 'how did *you* get in here?'

'I have a key. Have you forgotten?' the other woman purred.

The sloe-eyed look she gave Andreas and the way she was managing to totally exclude Saskia both from their conversation and from her line of vision left Saskia ruefully reflecting on her earlier mental picture of a devastated widow being too grief-stricken at the loss of her husband to prevent herself from being bullied into a second marriage.

No one would ever bully *this* woman into anything... and as for her being grief-stricken—there was only one emotion Saskia could see in those dark eyes and it had nothing to do with grief.

She forced down the sudden surge of nausea that burned in her throat as she witnessed the look of pure condensed lust that Athena was giving Andreas. Saskia had never imagined, never mind seen, a woman looking at a man in such a powerfully and openly predatory sexual way.

Now she could understand why Andreas had felt in need of a mock fiancée to protect himself, but what she could not understand was how on earth Andreas could resist the other woman's desire for him.

She was blindingly sensually attractive, and obviously

wanted Andreas. And surely that was what all men fan-
tasised about—a woman whose sexual appetite for them
could never be satiated.

Naively Saskia assumed that only her own sex would
be put off by Athena's intrinsic coldness and by the lack
of any real loving emotion in her make-up.

Andreas had obviously kissed Saskia because he had
guessed that Athena was in the apartment, and now that
the other woman was standing so close to them both Saskia
knew how he had known. That perfume of hers was as
unmistakable as it was unappealing.

'Aren't you going to say how pleased you are to see me?'
Athena was pouting as she moved closer to Andreas. 'Your
grandfather is very upset about your engagement. You
know what he was hoping for,' she added meaningfully,
before turning to Saskia and saying dismissively, 'Oh, I'm
sorry. I didn't mean to hurt your feelings, but I'm sure
Andreas must have warned you how difficult it is going
to be for all his family, especially for his grandfather, to
accept you...'

'Athena,' Andreas was saying warningly, and Saskia
could well imagine how she *would* have felt to be confronted by such a statement, if she and Andreas were
genuinely engaged.

'But it's the truth,' Athena was continuing unrepentantly,
and she shrugged her shoulders, the movement drawing
attention to the fullness of her breasts. Breasts which
Saskia could quite easily see were naked and unfettered
beneath the fine cotton shirt she was wearing.

Quickly she averted her gaze from the sight of Athena's
flauntingly erect nipples, not daring to allow herself to
look at Andreas. Surely no man could resist the demand

that those nipples were making on his attention…his concentration…his admiration for their perfection and sexuality. Her own breasts were well shaped and firm, but her nipples did not have that flamboyant fullness that the other woman's possessed and, even if they had, Saskia knew that she would have felt embarrassed about making such a public display of them.

But then perhaps Athena's display was meant *only* for Andreas…perhaps it was meant to be a reminder to him of intimacies they might already have shared. She did, after all, have the key to his apartment, and she certainly seemed to want to make it plain to Saskia that there was a very special intimacy between the two of them.

As though in confirmation of Saskia's thoughts, Athena suddenly leaned forward, putting one manicured hand against Andreas's face and effectively coming between them. With a sultry suggestiveness she said softly, 'Aren't you going to kiss me? You normally do, and I'm sure your fiancée understands that in Greece family relationships… family *loyalties* are very, very important.'

'What Saskia understands is that I love her and I want her to be my wife,' Andreas informed Athena curtly, stepping back from her and taking Saskia with him. As he held her in front of him and closed his arms around her, tucking her head against his shoulder, Saskia reminded herself just *why* he was doing so and just what her role was supposed to be.

'How sweet!' Athena pronounced, giving Saskia an icy look before turning back to Andreas and telling him insincerely, 'I hate to cast a shadow on your happiness, Andreas, but your grandfather really isn't very pleased with you at all at the moment. He was telling me how concerned he is about the way you're handling this recent takeover. Of course *I* understand how important it must be to you to establish your own mark on the business, to prove yourself, so to speak, but the acquisition of this hotel chain really was quite foolhardy, as is this decision of yours to keep on all the existing staff.

'You'll never make a profit doing that,' she scolded him mock sweetly. 'I must say, though, having had the opportunity to look a little deeper into the finances of the chain, I'm glad I pulled out of putting in my own bid. Although of course I *can* afford to lose the odd million or so. What a pity it is, Andreas, that you didn't accept my offer to run the shipping line for me. That would have given you much more scope than working as your grandfather's errand boy.'

Saskia felt herself tensing as she absorbed the insult Athena had just delivered, but to her astonishment Andreas seemed completely unmoved by it. Yet *she* only had to make the merest observation and he fired up at her with so much anger.

'As you already well know, Athena,' he responded, almost good-humouredly, 'It was my *grandfather's* decision to buy the British hotel chain and it was one I endorsed. As for its future profitability... My research confirms that there is an excellent market for a chain of luxurious hotels in Britain, especially when it can boast first-class leisure facilities and a top-notch chef—which is what I am going to ensure that our chain has.

'And as for the financial implications of keeping on the existing staff—Saskia is an accountant, and I'm sure she'll be able to tell you—as you should know yourself, being a businesswoman—that in the long run it would cost more in redundancy payments to get rid of the staff than it will cost to continue employing them. Natural wastage and pending retirement will reduce their number quite dramatically over the next few years, and, where appropriate, those who wish to stay on will be given the opportunity to relocate and retrain. The leisure clubs we intend to open in each hotel alone will take up virtually all of the slack in our staffing levels.

'However, Saskia and I are leaving for Athens tomorrow. We've had a busy day today and, if you'll excuse us, tonight is going to be a very special night for us.'

As Saskia tensed Andreas tightened his hold on her warningly as he repeated, 'A *very* special night. Which reminds me...'

Still holding on to Saskia with one hand, he reached inside his jacket pocket with the other to remove a small jeweller's box.

'I collected this. It should be small enough for you now.'

Before Saskia could say anything he was slipping the box back into his jacket, telling her softly, 'We'll find out later...'

In the living area beyond the lobby a telephone had started to ring. Releasing her, Andreas went to answer it, leaving Saskia on her own with Athena.

'It won't last,' Athena told her venomously as she walked past Saskia towards the door. 'He won't marry you. He and I were destined to be together. He *knows* that. It's just his pride that makes him fight his destiny. You might as well give him up now, because I promise you *I* shall never do so.'

She meant it, Saskia could see that, and for the first time she actually felt a small shaft of sympathy for Andreas.

Sympathy for a man who was treating her the way Andreas was? For a man who had misjudged her the way he had? She must be crazy, Saskia derided herself grimly.

APPREHENSIVELY SASKIA watched as the new suitcases, which were now carefully packed with her new clothes, were loaded onto the conveyor belt. The airline representative was checking their passports.

On her finger the ring Andreas had given her the previous evening glittered brilliantly.

'It's amazing how good fake diamonds can look these days, isn't it?' she had chattered nervously when Andreas had taken it from its box. She'd tried to disguise from him how edgy and unhappy she felt about wearing a ring on the finger that she had imagined would only ever bear a ring given to her by the man she loved, a ring she would wear forever.

'Is it?' Andreas had responded almost contemptuously. 'I wouldn't know.'

His comment had set all her inner alarm bells ringing and she had demanded anxiously, 'This... It isn't real, is it?'

His expression had given her her answer.

'It *is*!' She had swallowed, unable to drag her gaze away from the fiery sparkle of the magnificent solitaire.

'Athena would have spotted a fake diamond immediately,' Andreas had told her dismissively when she'd tried to protest that she didn't want the responsibility of wearing something of such obvious value.

'If she can spot a fake *diamond* so easily,' she had felt driven to ask him warily, 'then surely she will be able to spot a fake fiancée.'

'Athena deals in hard facts, not emotions,' had been Andreas's answer.

Hard facts, Saskia reflected now, remembering that brief conversation. Like the kiss Andreas had given her last night, knowing Athena would witness it. Andreas himself had made no mention of what he had done, but Saskia had known that her guess as to why he had done it was correct when, immediately after he had ended his telephone call, he had switched on the apartment's air conditioning with the grim comment, 'We need some fresh air in here.'

Later, Andreas had gone out, as promised, and, after picking at the meal he had ordered her, Saskia had gone to bed—alone.

'How long will it take us to reach Aphrodite?' Saskia asked Andreas as they boarded their flight.

'On this occasion it will take longer than normal,' Andreas answered as the stewardess showed them to their seats—first-class seats, Saskia noted with a small frisson of nervous awe. She had never flown first class before, never really done anything that might have equipped her to feel at home in the rarefied stratosphere of the mega-wealthy that Andreas and his family obviously inhabited.

'Once we arrive in Athens I'm afraid I shall have to leave you to occupy yourself for a few hours before we continue with our journey. That was my grandfather who rang last night. He wants to see me.'

'He won't be at the island?' Saskia asked.

'Not immediately. His heart condition means that he has to undergo regular check-ups—a precautionary measure only, thank goodness—and they will keep him in Athens for the next day or so.'

'Athena told me she doesn't believe that our relationship

will last. She believes that the two of you are destined to be together,' Saskia said.

'She's trying to intimidate you,' Andreas responded, the smile he had given the attentive stewardess replaced by a harsh frown.

Impulsively Saskia allowed the sympathy she had unexpectedly felt for him the previous evening to take precedence over her own feelings. Turning towards him, she said softly, 'But surely if you explained to your grandfather how you feel he would understand and accept that you can't be expected to marry a woman you don't... you don't want to marry...'

'My grandfather is as stubborn as a mule. He's also one hell of a lot more vulnerable than he thinks...than any of us want him to think. His heart condition...' He gave a small sigh. 'At the moment it's stable, but it is important that he—and we—keep his stress levels down. If I told him that I didn't want to marry Athena without producing you as a substitute he would immediately become very stressed indeed. It isn't just that by marrying Athena as he wishes I would attach her fortune and assets to our own, my grandfather is also a man to whom male descendants are of paramount importance.

'My elder sister already has two daughters, and Athena also has two. My grandfather is desperate for me, as his direct male descendent, to produce the next male generation...a great-grandson.'

'But even if you did marry Athena there would be no guarantee that you would even have children, never mind sons,' Saskia protested.

'Why are you laughing at me?' she demanded in chagrin as she saw the mirth crinkling Andreas's eyes and a gust of warmly amused male laughter filled the small space between them.

'Saskia, for a woman of your experience you can be very, very naive. You should *never* suggest to any man, and most *especially* not a Greek one, that he may not be able to father a son!'

As the plane suddenly started to lift into the sky Saskia automatically clutched at her armrests, and then tensed in shock as she felt the hard male warmth of Andreas's hand wrapping around her own.

'Scared of flying?' he asked her in amusement. 'You shouldn't be. It's the safest form of transport there is.'

'I know that,' Saskia responded waspishly. 'It's just… well, it's just that flying seems so…so unnatural, and if…'

'If God had intended man to fly he'd have given him wings,' Andreas offered her wryly. 'Well, Icarus tried that option.'

'I always think that's such a sad story.' Saskia shivered, her eyes shadowing. 'Especially for his poor father.'

'Mmm…' Andreas agreed, before asking her, 'Am I to take it from that comment that you're a student of Greek mythology?'

'Well, not precisely a student,' Saskia admitted, 'but my grandmother used to read me stories from a book on Greek mythology when I was little and I always found the stories fascinating…even though they nearly always made me cry.'

Abruptly she stopped speaking as she realised two things. The first was that they were now completely airborne, and the second was…her own bemused awareness of how good it felt actually to have Andreas's large hand clasping her own. It was enough to make her face sting with self-conscious colour and she hastily wriggled her hand free, just as the stewardess came up to offer them a glass of champagne.

'Champagne!' Saskia's eyes widened as she took a sip from the glass Andreas was holding out to her and she gasped as the delicious bubbles exploded against her taste buds.

It had to be the champagne that was making her feel so relaxed and so…so…laid-back, Saskia decided hazily a little later, and when the captain announced that they were coming in to land she was surprised to realise how quickly the time had flown—and how much she had enjoyed the conversation she and Andreas had shared. She was even more surprised to discover how easy it was to slip her hand into the reassuring hold of Andreas's as the plane's wheels hit the tarmac and the pilot applied reverse thrust to slow them down.

'I can either have our driver take you to the family apartment in Athens, where you can rest whilst I see my grandfather, or, if you prefer, I can arrange for him to drive you on a sightseeing tour,' Andreas offered, casually lifting their cases off the luggage carousel.

He was wearing a pair of plain light-coloured trousers and a cool, very fine white cotton short-sleeved shirt, and for some indefinable reason it did odd things to Saskia's normally very sensible female senses to witness the way the muscles hardened in his arms as he swung their cases on to the ground. Very odd things, she acknowledged giddily as the discreet smile of flirtatious invitation she intercepted from a solitary woman traveller caused her instinctively to move possessively closer to him.

What on earth was happening to her? It *must* be the

champagne…or the heat…or perhaps both! Yes, that
was it, she decided feverishly, grateful to have found a
sensible explanation for her unfamiliar behaviour. After
all, there was no reason why she should feel possessive
about Andreas. Yesterday morning she had hated him…
loathed him… In fact she had been dreading her enforced
time as his 'fiancée'—and she still was, of course. Of
course! It was just that…

Well, having met Athena it was only natural that she
should feel *some* sympathy for him. And she had been
fascinated by the stories he had told her during the flight—
stories which had been told to him by older members of
his Greek family and which were a wonderful mix of myth
and folklore. And it was a very pleasant experience not to
have to struggle with heavy luggage. Normally when she
went away she was either with a group of friends or with
her grandmother, and…

'Saskia…?'

Guiltily Saskia realised that Andreas was still waiting
for an answer to his question.

'Oh, I'd much prefer to see something of the city,' she
answered.

'Well, you won't have a lot of time,' Andreas warned
her. 'Our pilot will already have filed his flight plan.'

Saskia already knew that they would be flying out to
the island in a small plane privately owned by Andreas's
grandfather, and what had impressed her far more than
Andreas's casual reference to the plane had been his
mention of the fact that he himself was qualified to fly.

'Unfortunately I had to give it up. I can't spare the
amount of hours now that I believe are needed to keep
myself up to speed and in practice, and besides, my

insurance company were extremely wary about insuring me,' he'd added ruefully.

'It's this way,' he told her now, placing his hand on her shoulder as he turned her in the right direction.

Out of the corner of her eye Saskia caught a glimpse of their reflections in a mirrored column and immediately tensed. What was she *doing* leaning against Andreas like that? As though…as though she *liked* being there… as though she was enjoying playing the helpless fragile female to his strong muscular male.

Immediately she pulled away from him and squared her shoulders.

'Athena would have loved to have seen you do that,' he told her sharply, the disapproval clear in his voice.

'We're supposed to be in love, Saskia…remember?'

'Athena isn't here,' she responded quickly.

'No, thank God,' he agreed. 'But we don't know who might accidentally observe us. We're a *couple*—very much in love—newly engaged…and you're about to fly to my home to meet my family. Don't you think it's natural that—?'

'That I should feel nervous and intimidated…worried about whether or not they'll think I'm good enough for you.' Saskia interrupted him angrily, her pride stung by what he was suggesting. 'And what am I supposed to do? Cling desperately and despairingly to you…afraid of their rejection…afraid of *losing* you…just because—'

She stopped as she saw the blank impatient look Andreas was giving her.

'What I was about to say,' he told her grimly, 'was don't you think it's only natural that I should want to hold you close to me and equally that *you* should want that same intimacy? That as lovers we *should* want always to be physically in touch with one another?' He paused. 'And as for what you have just said, I'm a man of thirty-five, long past the age of needing *anyone's* approval of what I do or who I love.'

'But you don't...' Saskia began, and then stopped as she realised what she had been about to say. Andreas hardly needed *her* to tell him that he didn't love her.

'I don't what?' he prompted her, but she shook her head, refusing to answer him.

'So you want to see the Acropolis first?' Andreas checked with Saskia before getting out of the limousine, having first given the driver some instructions in Greek.

'Yes,' Saskia confirmed.

'I have told Spiros to make sure you are at the airport in time for our flight. He will take care of you. I am sorry to have to leave you to your own devices,' Andreas apologised formally, suddenly making Saskia sharply aware of his mixed cultural heritage.

She recognised how at home he looked here, and yet, at the same time, how much he stood out from the other men she could see. He was taller, for one thing, and his skin, whilst tanned, was not as dark, and of course his eyes would always give away his Northern European blood.

Saskia gave a small emotional sigh as she finally turned her back on the Acropolis and started to walk away. She had managed to persuade the driver that she would be perfectly safe on her own, but only after a good deal of insistence, and she had enjoyed her solitude as she had absorbed the aura of the ancient building in awed appreciation.

Now, though, it was time for her to go. She could see

the limousine waiting where she had expected, but to her
consternation there was no sign of its driver.

There *was* a man standing close to the vehicle, though,
white-haired and elderly. Saskia frowned as she recognised
that he seemed to be in some distress, one hand pressed
against his side as though he was in pain. A brief examination
of the street confirmed that it was empty, apart from the old
man and herself. Saskia automatically hurried towards him,
anxious for his well-being.

'Are you all right?' she asked in concern as she reached
him. 'You don't look well.'

To her relief he answered her in English, assuring her,
'It is nothing...the heat—a small pain. I have perhaps
walked farther than I should...'

Saskia was still anxious. It *was* hot. He did not look
well, and there was certainly no way she could possibly
leave him on his own, but there was still no sign of her
driver or anyone else who might be able to help, and she
had no idea how long it would take them to get to the
airport.

'It's *very* hot,' she told the old man gently, not wanting
to hurt his pride, 'and it can be very tiring to walk in
such heat. I have a car...and...and a driver... Perhaps we
could give you a lift?' As she spoke she was searching the
street anxiously. Where *was* her driver? Andreas would be
furious with her if she was late for their flight, but there
was no way she could leave without first ensuring that the
old man was alright.

'You have a car? This car?' he guessed, gesturing
towards the parked limousine.

'Well, it isn't *mine*,' Saskia found herself feeling obliged to tell him. 'It belongs to…to someone I know. Do you live very far away?'

He had stopped holding his side now and she could see that his colour looked healthier and that his breathing was easier.

'You are very kind,' he told her with a smile, 'But I too have a car…and a driver…' His smile broadened and for some reason Saskia felt almost as though he was laughing a little at her.

'You are a very kind girl to worry yourself so much on behalf of an old man.'

There *was* a car parked farther down the street, Saskia realised, but it was some distance away.

'Is *that* your car?' she asked him. 'Shall I get the driver?'

'No,' he said immediately. 'I can walk.'

Without giving him any opportunity to refuse, Saskia went to his side and said gently, 'Perhaps you will allow me to walk with you to it…' Levelly she met and held the look he was giving her.

'Perhaps I should,' he capitulated.

It took longer to reach the car than Saskia had expected, mainly because the old man was plainly in more distress than he wanted to admit. As they reached the car Saskia was relieved to see the driver's door open and the driver get out, immediately hurrying towards them and addressing some words to her companion in fast Greek. The old man was now starting to look very much better, holding himself upright and speaking sternly to the driver.

'He fusses like an old woman,' he complained testily in English to Saskia, adding warmly, 'Thank you, my dear, I am *very* pleased to have met you. But you should not be walking the streets of Athens on your own,' he told her sternly. 'And I shall—' Abruptly he stopped and said something in Greek to his driver, who started to frown and look anxiously up and down the street.

'Yannis will walk back with you to *your* car and wait there with you until your driver returns.'

'Really, there's no need for that,' Saskia protested, but her new-found friend was determinedly insistent.

'There really is no need for you to come with me,' she told the driver once they were out of earshot of the older man. 'I would much rather you stayed with your employer. He looked quite poorly when I saw him in the street.'

To her relief, as she finished speaking she saw that her own driver was getting out of Andreas's car.

'See, there is no need to come any further,' she smiled in relief, and then frowned a little before saying anxiously to him, 'Your employer… It is none of my business I know… but perhaps a visit to a doctor…' She paused uncertainly.

'It is already taken care of,' the driver assured her. 'But he… What do you say? He does not always take anyone's advice…'

His calmness helped to soothe Saskia's concern and ease her conscience about leaving the older man. He was plainly in good hands now, and her own driver was waiting for her.

CHAPTER SIX

SASKIA DARTED a brief look at Andreas, catching back her
gasp of pleasure as she stared out of their plane and down
at the blue-green of the Aegean Sea beneath them.

He had been frowning and preoccupied when they had
met up at the airport, not even asking her if she had enjoyed
her sightseeing trip, and now with every mile that took
them closer to his home and family Saskia could feel her
tension increasing. It seemed ironic, when she reflected
on how she had dreamed of one day spending a holiday in
this part of the world, that now that she was actually here
she was far too on edge to truly appreciate it.

The starkness of Andreas's expression forced her to
ask, more out of politeness than any real concern, she was
quick to assure herself, 'Is something wrong? You don't
look very happy.'

Immediately Andreas's frown deepened, his gaze
sweeping her sharply as he turned to look at her.

'Getting in some practice at playing the devoted
fiancée?' he asked her cynically. 'If you're looking for a
bonus payment, don't bother.'

Saskia felt a resurgence of her initial hostility towards
him.

'Unlike you, I do not evaluate everything I do by how I

can best benefit from it,' Saskia shot back furiously. 'I was
simply concerned that your meeting hadn't gone very well.'

'*You?* Concerned for *me?* There's only one reason you're
here with me, Saskia, and we both know that isn't it.'

What did he expect? Saskia fumed, forcing herself to
bite back the angry retort she wanted to make. He had,
after all, blackmailed her into being here with him. He
was using her for his own ends. He had formed the lowest
kind of opinion of her, judged her without allowing her
the chance to defend herself or to explain her behaviour,
and yet after all that he still seemed to think he could
occupy the higher moral ground. Why on earth had she
ever felt any sympathy for him? He and Athena deserved
one another.

But even as she formed the stubborn angry thought
Saskia knew that it wasn't true. She had sensed a deep
coldness in Athena, a total lack of regard for any kind of
emotion. Andreas might have done and said many things
she objected to, but there was a warmly passionate side to
him…a *very* passionate side, she acknowledged, trembling
a little as she unwillingly remembered the kiss he had
given her… Even though it had merely been an act, staged
for Athena's benefit he had still made her feel—*connected*
at a very deep and personal level. So much so, in fact, that
even now, if she were to close her eyes and remember,
she could almost feel the hard male pressure of his mouth
against her own.

'As a matter of fact my meeting did *not* go well.'

Saskia's eyes opened in surprise as she heard Andreas's
abrupt and unexpected admission.

'For a start my grandfather was not there. There was
something else he had to do that was more important,

apparently. But unfortunately he did not bother to explain this to me, or to send a message informing me of it until I'd been waiting for him for over half an hour. However, he *had* left instructions that I was to be informed in no uncertain terms that he is not best pleased with me at the moment.'

'Because of me…us?' Saskia hazarded.

'My grandfather knows there is no way I would or could marry a woman I do not love—his own marriage was a love match, as was my parents', even if my mother did have to virtually threaten to elope before she got his approval. When my father died my grandfather admitted how much he admired him. He was a surveyor, and he retained his independence from my grandfather.'

'You must miss him,' Saskia said softly.

'I was fifteen when he died. It was a long time ago. And, unlike you, at least I had the comfort of knowing how much he loved me.'

At first Saskia thought he was being deliberately unkind to her, and instinctively she stiffened in self-defence, but when unexpectedly he covered her folded hands with one of his own she knew that she had misinterpreted his remark.

'The love my grandmother has given me has more than made up for the love I didn't get from my parents,' she told him firmly—and meant it.

His hand was still covering hers…both of hers…and that funny, trembly sensation she had felt inside earlier returned as she looked down at it. Long-fingered, tanned, with well-groomed but not manicured nails, it was very much a man's hand: large enough to cover both of hers, large enough, too, to hold her securely to him without any visible effort. It was the kind of hand that gave a woman the confidence to know that this man could take care of her and their children. Just as he was the kind of man who would always ensure that his woman and his child were safe and secure.

What on earth was she thinking? Agitatedly Saskia wriggled in her seat, snatching her hands from beneath Andreas's.

'Are you sure this is a good idea?' she asked him slightly breathlessly as she tried to concentrate on the reality of why she was sitting here next to him. 'I mean, if your grandfather already doesn't approve of our engagement…'

It was so long before he replied that Saskia began to think that her question had annoyed him but when he did answer her she recognised that the anger she could see darkening his eyes wasn't directed at her but at Athena.

'Unfortunately Athena claims a blood closeness to my grandfather which he finds flattering. His elder brother, Athena's grandfather, died some years ago and whilst there is no way at all that Athena would allow anyone, least of all my grandfather, to interfere in the way she runs her own financial empire, she flatters and encourages him to the point where his judgement is sometimes not all that it should be. My mother claims that the truth will out, so to speak, and that ultimately my grandfather will see through Athena's machinations.'

'But surely she must realise that you don't want to marry her,' Saskia suggested a little bit uncomfortably. It was so foreign to her own way of behaving to even consider trying to force anyone into a relationship with her that it was hard for her to understand why Athena should be driven to do so.

'Oh, she realises it all right,' Andreas agreed grimly. 'But Athena has never been denied anything she wants, and right now...'

'She wants you,' Saskia concluded for him.

'Yes,' Andreas agreed heavily. 'And, much as I would like to tell her that her desires are not reciprocated, I have to think of my grandfather.'

He stopped speaking as their plane started to lose height, a small smile curling his mouth as he saw Saskia's expression when she looked out of the window down at their destination.

'He can't possibly be intending to put this plane down on that tiny piece of land,' she gasped in disbelief.

'Oh, yes, he can, It's much safer than it looks,' Andreas said reassuringly. 'Look,' he added, directing her attention away from the landing strip and to the breathtaking sprawl of his family villa and the grounds enclosing it.

'Everything is so green,' Saskia told him in bemusement, her eyes widening over the almost perfect oval shape of the small island, the rich green of its gardens and foliage perfectly shown off by the whiteness of its sandy beaches and the wonderful turquoise of the Aegean Sea that lapped them.

'That's because the island has its own plentiful supply of water,' Andreas told her. 'It's far too small to be able to sustain either crops or livestock, which is why it was uninhabited—as you can see it is quite some distance from any of the other islands, the furthest out into the Aegean.'

'It looks perfect,' Saskia breathed. 'Like a pearl drop.'

Andreas laughed, but there was an emotion in his eyes that made Saskia's cheeks flush a little as he told her quietly, 'That was how my grandmother used to describe it.'

Saskia gave a small gasp as the plane suddenly bumped down onto the runway, belatedly realising that Andreas had deliberately distracted her attention away from their imminent landing. He could be so entertaining when he wanted to be, so charming and so easy to be with. A little wistfully she wondered how much difference it would have made to his opinion of her had they met under different circumstances. Then she very firmly pulled her thoughts into order, warning herself that her situation was untenable enough already without making it worse by indulging in ridiculous fantasies and daydreams.

There was a bleak look in Andreas's eyes as he guided Saskia towards the aircraft's exit. There was such a vast contradiction in the way he was perceiving Saskia now and the way he had perceived her the first time he had seen her. For his own emotional peace of mind and security he found himself wishing that she had remained true to his first impression of her. That vulnerability she fought so determinedly and with such pride to conceal touched him in all the ways that a woman of Athena's coldness could never possibly do. Saskia possessed a warmth, a humanity, a womanliness, that his maleness reacted and responded to in the most potentially dangerous way.

Grimly Andreas tried not to allow himself to think about how he had felt when he had kissed her. Initially he had done so purely as an instinctive response to his awareness that Athena was in his apartment—that appalling overpowering scent of hers was instantly recognisable. Quite how she had got hold of a key he had no idea, but he suspected she must have somehow cajoled

it from his grandfather. But the kiss he had given Saskia
as a means of reinforcing his unavailability to Athena had
unexpectedly and unwontedly shown him—*forced* him
to acknowledge—something he was still fighting hard
to deny.

He didn't *want* to want Saskia. He didn't want it at all,
and he certainly didn't want to feel his current desire to
protect and reassure her.

Athens had been hot, almost stiflingly so, but here
on the island the air had a silky balminess to it that was
totally blissful, Saskia decided, shading her eyes from the
brilliance of the sun as she reached the ground and looked a
little uncertainly at the trio of people waiting to greet them.

Andreas's husky, 'Here you are, darling, you forgot
these,' as he handed her a pair of sunglasses threw her
into even more confusion, but nowhere near as much as the
warm weight of his arm around her as he drew her closer
to him and whispered quite audibly, 'Our harsh sunlight
is far too strong for those beautiful Celtic eyes of yours.'

Saskia felt her fingers start to tremble as she took the
sunglasses from him. They carried a designer logo, she
noticed, and were certainly far more expensive than any
pair of sunglasses she had ever owned. When Andreas
took them back and gently slipped them on for her she
discovered that they fitted her perfectly.

'I remembered that we didn't get any in London and
I knew you'd need a pair,' he told her quietly, leaning
forward to murmur the words into her ear, one arm still
around her body and his free hand holding her shoulder
as though he would draw her even closer.

To their onlookers they must look very intimate, Saskia

recognised, which was no doubt why Andreas had chosen to give them to her in such a manner.

Well, two could play at that game. Without stopping to think about the implications of what she was doing, or to question why she was doing so, Saskia slid her own arm around *his* neck, turning her face up to his as she murmured back, 'Thank you, darling. You really are so thoughtful.'

She had, she recognised on a small spurt of defiant pleasure, surprised him. She could see it in his eyes—and she could see something else as well, something very male and dangerous which made her disengage herself from him hastily and step back. Not that he allowed her to go very far. Somehow he was holding her hand and refusing to let go of it, drawing her towards the small waiting group.

'Mama. This is Saskia…' he announced, introducing Saskia first to the older of the two women.

Warily Saskia studied her, knowing that if she and Andreas were really in love and engaged her heart would be in her mouth as she waited to see whether or not she and Andreas's mother could build a true bond. Physically she looked very much like Athena, although, of course, older. But the similarity ended once Saskia looked into her eyes and saw the warmth there that had been so markedly lacking from Athena's.

There was also a gentleness and sweetness about Andreas's mother, a timidity almost, and intuitively Saskia sensed that she was a woman who, having loved only one man, would never totally cease mourning his loss.

'It's a pleasure to meet you, Mrs Latimer,' Saskia began, but immediately Andreas's mother shook her head chidingly.

'You are going to be my daughter-in-law, Saskia, you must call me something less formal. Helena is my name, or if you wish you may call me Mama, as 'Reas and my daughters do.' As she spoke she leaned forward and placed her hands gently on Saskia's upper arms.

'She is lovely, 'Reas,' she told her son warmly.

'I certainly think so, Mama,' Andreas agreed with a smile.

'I meant inside as well as out,' his mother told him softly.

'And so did I,' Andreas agreed, equally emotionally.

Heavens, but he was a wonderful actor, Saskia acknowledged shakily. If she hadn't known how he really felt about her that look of tender adoration he had given her just now would have...could have... A man like him should know better than to give a vulnerable woman a look like that, she decided indignantly, forgetting for the moment that so far as Andreas was concerned she was anything *but* vulnerable.

'And this is Olympia, my sister,' Andreas continued, turning Saskia towards the younger of the two women. Although she was as darkly Greek as her mother, she too had light-coloured eyes and a merry open smile that made Saskia warm instantly to her.

'Heavens, but it's hot down here. Poor Saskia must be melting,' Olympia sympathised.

'You could have waited for us at the villa,' Andreas told her. 'It would have been enough just to have sent a driver with the Land Rover.'

'No, it wouldn't,' Olympia told him starkly, shrugging her shoulders as her mother made a faint sound of protest.

She looked anxiously at her, saying, 'Well, he has to know...'

'I have to know what?' Andreas began to frown.

'Athena is here,' his mother told him unhappily. 'She arrived earlier and she...'

'She what?'

'She said that your grandfather had invited her,' his mother continued.

'You know what that means, don't you Andreas?' Olympia interrupted angrily. 'It means that she's bullied Grandfather into saying she could stay. And that's not all...'

'Pia...' her mother began unhappily, but Olympia refused to be silenced.

'She's brought that revolting creep Aristotle with her. She claims that she is right in the middle of an important business deal and that she needs him with her because he's her accountant. If it's so important, how come she had time to be here?' Olympia demanded. 'Oh, but I hate her so. This morning she went on and on about how concerned Grandfather is about the business and how he's been asking her advice because he's worried that you...'

'Pia!' her mother protested again, and this time Andreas's sister did fall silent, but only for a few seconds.

'What I can't understand is why Gramps is so taken in by her,' she burst out, as though unable to contain herself. 'It's obvious what she's doing. She's just trying to get at you, Andreas, because you won't marry her.'

'I'm sorry about this,' Helena Latimer was apologising gently to Saskia. 'It can't be pleasant for you. You haven't met Athena yet, I know—'

'Yes, she has,' Andreas interrupted his mother, explaining when both she and Pia looked at him questioningly, 'Somehow or other she managed to get a key for the London apartment.'

'She's the worst, isn't she?' Pia told Saskia. 'The black widow spider I call her.'

'Pia!' Andreas chided her sharply.

'Mama hasn't told you everything yet,' Pia countered, looking protectively at her mother before continuing, 'Athena has insisted on having the room that Mama had arranged to be prepared for Saskia. It's the one next to your suite—'

'I tried to stop her, Andreas,' Helena interrupted her daughter unhappily. 'But you know what she's like.'

'She said that Saskia could have the room right down at the end of the corridor. You know, the one we only use as an overspill when absolutely everyone is here. It hasn't even got a proper bed.'

'You'll have to say something to Athena, Andreas. Make her understand that she can't...that she can't have that room because Saskia will be using it.'

'No, she won't,' Andreas contradicted his mother flatly, sliding his arm very firmly around Saskia, imprisoningly almost, drawing her right into his body so that her face was concealed from view as he told his mother and sister, 'Saskia will be sharing *my* room...and *my* bed...'

Saskia could sense their shock, even though she could not see their faces. *Now* she knew why he was holding her so tightly, preventing anyone else from seeing her expression or hearing the panicky denial she was trying to make but which was muffled against the fine cotton of his shirt.

There was just no way that she was prepared for anything like this. No way that she could ever be prepared for it. But her attempts to tell Andreas were bringing her into even more intimate contact with him as she tried to look up into his face.

His response to her efforts to attract his attention made the situation even worse, because when he bent his head, as though anxious to listen to what she was saying, her lips inadvertently brushed against his jaw.

It must be a combination of heat and shock that was sending that melting liquid sensation of weakness swooshing through her, Saskia decided dizzily. It certainly couldn't be the feel of Andreas's skin against her lips, nor the dangerous gleam she could see in his narrowed eyes as they glittered down into hers. The arm he had around her moved fractionally, so that the hand that had been resting on her waist was now somehow just beneath the curve of her breast, his fingertips splaying against its soft curve and making her…making her…

'Saskia will be sharing your room!' Pia was breathing, verbalising the shock that Saskia herself felt and that she suspected his mother was too embarrassed to voice.

'We *are* engaged…and soon to be married…' Andreas told his sister smoothly, adding in a much rougher, rawer, spine-tinglingly possessive voice, 'Saskia is mine and I intend to make sure that everyone knows it.'

'Especially Aristotle,' Pia guessed. 'I don't know how Athena can endure him,' she continued shuddering. 'He's like a snake, Saskia. All cold and slimy, with horrid little eyes and clammy hands…'

'Athena endures him because of his skill at "creative" accounting,' Andreas informed his sister dryly.

'You mean he's dishonest,' Pia translated pithily.

'You didn't hear that from me,' Andreas warned her as he started to shepherd all three of them towards the waiting Land Rover.

Whilst they had been talking the driver had loaded their luggage, and as he held the door open for his mother, sister and Saskia to get in Saskia heard Andreas asking him about his family, listening interestedly whilst the driver told him with pride about his son who was at university.

'Grandfather was not very pleased at all when Andreas said that he wanted to use the money our father had left him to help pay for the education of our personal household staff,' Pia told Saskia.

'Pia, you aren't being very fair to your grandfather,' her mother objected.

Andreas had done that? Stubbornly Saskia refused to acknowledge that she was impressed by his philanthropy.

Had he really meant what he had said about them sharing a room? He couldn't have done—could he? Personally she didn't care *where* she slept, even if it was a normally unused bedless room, just so long as she occupied it on her own.

'We have both had a long day and I imagine that Saskia is going to want to have a rest before dinner,' Andreas was saying as the Land Rover pulled up in a cool paved courtyard with a central fountain that sent a musical plume of water up into the air to shower back to earth in millions of tiny teardrops.

'I'll make sure everyone knows that you aren't to be disturbed,' his mother responded. 'But perhaps Saskia would like something light to eat and drink…'

Before Saskia could say anything Andreas was answering for her, telling his mother, 'I'll see to that,' before placing his hand beneath Saskia's elbow and telling her in a soft voice in which she suspected only she could hear the underlying threat, 'This way, Saskia…'

CHAPTER SEVEN

'I CAN'T SLEEP in this room with you!'

Saskia had been able to feel herself trembling as Andreas had whisked her down a confusing maze of corridors. She had known that he must be able to feel her nervousness as well, but somehow she had managed to keep her feelings under control until they were both inside the huge elegant bedroom with the door firmly shut behind them.

Right now, though, she was in no mood to appreciate the cool elegance of her surroundings. Whirling round, she confronted Andreas determinedly. 'No way was *that* part of the deal.'

'The "deal" was that you would act as my fiancée, and that includes doing whatever has to be done to ensure that the act is believable,' he told her angrily.

'I won't sleep here with you,' Saskia protested wildly. 'I don't… I haven't…' She could hardly bear to look at the large king-sized bed as panic filled her, flooding out rationality. She had gone through so much, and now she was hot and tired and very, very afraid. Her emotions threatened to overwhelm her.

Quickly she turned away as she heard Andreas saying, almost mundanely, 'I'm going to have a shower, and if you'll take my advice you'll do the same. Then, when we're both feeling cooler and calmer, we can discuss this whole situation less emotively.'

A shower! With Andreas! Saskia stared at him in mute shocked disbelief. Did he really think that she would… that she could…?

'You can use the bathroom first,' he told her.

First! So he hadn't meant… Relief sagged through her, quickly followed by a furious burst of toxic anger.

'I don't want to use the bathroom at all,' she burst out. 'What I *want* is to be at home. My *own* home, with my own bathroom and my own bedroom. What I want is to be free of this stupid…stupid charade… What I *want*…' She had to stop as her feelings threatened to overwhelm her, but they refused to be contained, spilling out in a furious fierce torrent of angry words. 'How could you let your mother and sister think that you…that we…?' She shook her head, unable to put into words what she wanted to say.

Andreas had no such qualms.

'That we are lovers?' he supplied dramatically for her. 'What else should they think? I'm a man, Saskia, and you and I are supposed to be engaged. And if in reality we were, do you think for one minute that I wouldn't—'

'Want to test the goods before you bought them?' Saskia threw wildly at him. 'Oh, of course, a man like you would be bound to want to do that…to make sure…'

She tensed as she saw the way he was looking at her and the bitter anger in his eyes.

'That kind of comment is typical of a woman like you,' he ground out. 'Reducing everything to terms of money. Well, let me tell you—'

But Saskia wouldn't let him finish, defending herself

sharply instead as she insisted, '*You* were the one who said…'

But Andreas immediately checked her.

'What I said, or rather what I was *trying* to say before you interrupted me,' he told her grittily, 'was that if I genuinely loved you there would be no way I would be able to deny myself—or you—the pleasure of showing that love in the most intimate physical way there is. There would be no way that I could bear to let you out of my sight or my arms, certainly not for the length of a whole night.'

Saskia discovered that she had started to tremble almost violently as his words struck sharply sensitive chords deep within her body that she had not even known existed. Chords that activated a deep core of feminine longing, that brought her dangerously close to the edge of tears she had no idea why she wanted to cry. Panic raced through her veins, flooding out common sense. She could feel her heart thumping frantically with anxiety.

She opened her mouth to tell Andreas that she had changed her mind, that she wanted to go home, that she was not prepared to stay a minute longer, no matter how much he tried to blackmail her into doing so. But her panic didn't stem from any fear of him. No. It was herself she feared now, and the way she was beginning to feel, the thoughts she was beginning to have. She *couldn't* allow herself to feel that way about him. She *couldn't* be attracted to him. He wasn't her type of man at all. She abhorred the way he had treated her, the way he had misjudged her. But the shocking shaft of self-awareness, of longing she had felt as he'd described his desire for the woman he would love wasn't going to be dismissed.

'I can't…' she began, stopping as Andreas held up his

hand warningly, silencing her as someone knocked on the door.

Dry-mouthed, Saskia waited whilst he went to open it, watching as their cases were brought in—not by the driver of the Land Rover but by another smaller, older man to whom Andreas was talking in Greek, smiling warmly at him as he did so, and then laughing good-humouredly as the older man looked past him at Saskia herself, before clapping him on the shoulders with a wide, beaming smile.

'What was that all about?' Saskia demanded curiously once he had gone and they were on their own again.

'Stavros was saying that it is high time I had a wife... and that I must lose no time in getting myself a fine boy child,' he added mercilessly.

Saskia could feel herself colouring to the roots of her hair as she looked everywhere but at the king-sized bed in the centre of the room.

Despite the room's air conditioning she felt stifled, unable to breathe...hunted and desperate to escape.

'I'm going to have that shower,' Andreas told her, mundanely breaking into her thoughts, turning away from her as he did so and heading for one of the three doors that opened off the bedroom.

Once he had disappeared Saskia looked at the door to the corridor, longing to have the courage to walk through it and demand that she be flown back immediately to Athens. But if she did she would lose her job—Andreas would make sure of that!

Fiercely Saskia tried to concentrate on something else, *anything* else but the appalling situation she was in. She hated what Andreas was doing to her...what he was making her do. And she hated Andreas himself too...didn't she?

Unable to answer her own question honestly, Saskia studied the view beyond the large patio doors that opened out onto an enclosed courtyard, which itself surrounded a tantalisingly tempting swimming pool complete with its own bubbling spa pool.

Small oases of green plants broke up the paving and the brilliant harshness of the sunlight. Comfortable-looking sun loungers complete with umbrellas offered a lazy way to enjoy the sunshine. The whole scene looked like something out of an exclusive holiday brochure, the kind Saskia had only been able to glance at enviously, knowing such a holiday was way beyond her means. But right now the only place she wanted to be was safe in her own home.

Andreas couldn't really expect her to share a room— never mind a bed—with him. She couldn't do it. She wouldn't…she was so…

'The bathroom's free…'

Saskia froze. She had been so engrossed in her thoughts she hadn't realised that Andreas was in the bedroom with her…standing right behind her, she recognised as she picked up the clean, warm scent of his newly showered body.

'I'll go and sort out something light for you to eat. Dinner won't be for a few hours yet, and if you'll take my advice you'll try to rest for a while. Greeks eat late and go to bed even later.'

'But I thought that we'd be having separate rooms,' Saskia burst out, unable to control her panic any longer. 'I would never have agreed to come here if I'd thought that I'd— No! Don't you dare touch me,' she protested as she felt him moving closer to her, reaching out to her. She wouldn't be able to bear it if he touched her, if he…

Frantically she turned and ran towards the door, but somehow Andreas managed to get there before her, blocking her access to it, taking hold of her, his fingers biting into the soft flesh of her arms.

'What the hell do you think you're doing?' he ground out savagely. 'What exactly is it you're pretending to be so afraid of? This? A woman like you!'

Saskia gasped and shook from head to foot as his arms closed imprisoningly around her and his mouth came down on hers. He was wearing a robe, but as she struggled to break free it was his bare skin she could feel beneath her flaying hands. Warm, damp...hard, his chest roughened by dark hairs. Her hands skittered wildly over his torso, shocked by the intimate unexpected contact with his bare skin, seeking some kind of purchase to thrust him away and finding none.

He was kissing her with an angry passion that made her feel weak, the blood roaring in her head as her brain recognised her inability to deal with the searing experience of so much furiously male arrogant sensuality.

'Stop acting like a novice, an innocent,' Saskia heard him demanding against her mouth. His tongue forced her lips to part for its entry and the hand that was imprisoning her urged her even deeper into the sensual heat of his parted thighs as he leaned back against the door, taking her with him. His free hand was on her body, arrogantly stroking its way up past her waist to the curve of her breast.

Saskia tensed in shock as it cupped her breast, his thumb-pad circling her nipple and somehow enticing it to peak into a shocking bud of delicious wanton pleasure.

She could feel the aroused heat of him like a brand, and beneath her anger she felt a sharp, spiralling stab of female curiosity and excitement…a dangerous surge to conspire with him, to allow her traitorous body to experience even more of the intimacy of their embrace.

Without knowing she had done so she opened her mouth, hesitantly allowing him access to its sweetness, shyly starting to return his kiss and even more shyly allowing her tongue to mesh seductively with his.

'Andreas? Are you in there? It's me, Athena…I need to talk to you.'

Saskia froze as she heard Athena's voice from the other side of the door, but Andreas showed no sign whatsoever of any confusion or embarrassment. Still holding Saskia against him in a grip she could not break, he opened the door and told Athena flatly, 'Not now, Athena. As you can see, Saskia and I are busy.'

'She is with *you*,' Athena snapped angrily, darting Saskia a look of icy venom. 'Why isn't she in her own room?'

'She is,' Andreas returned coolly. 'My room is Saskia's room. My bed…her bed. My body…her…'

'Your grandfather will never allow you to marry her,' Athena breathed, but Andreas was already closing the door, ignoring her insistence that he listen to her.

'Andreas, let me go,' Saskia demanded. She couldn't bear to look at him. Couldn't bear to do anything, least of all think about the way she had responded to him…the way she had encouraged him…

Derisively Andreas watched her.

'Okay, Saskia, that's enough,' he told her. 'I know I told you I wanted you to act like a faithful fiancée, but that does not mean you have to pretend to be an innocent virgin who has never—' Abruptly he stopped, frowning as he mulled over the unwanted suspicions that were striking him as he looked at Saskia's pale face and hunted eyes.

Even though he had let her go she was still shaking, trembling from head to foot, and he could have sworn just now, when he had held her in his arms and kissed her... touched her, that he was the first man to make her feel so...

For a moment he examined what he was thinking, and feeling, and then firmly dismissed his suspicions. There was no way she could be so inexperienced, no way at all. There was enough Greek in him for him to consider that the gift of her virginity, her purity, was one of the greatest gifts a woman could give to the man she loved, but his cultural heritage from his British father and schooling mocked and even deplored such archaic feelings.

Would a woman expect a man to keep himself pure until he met her? No. So why should it be any different for a woman? As a mature man he accepted and respected a woman's right to choose how she dealt with her own sexuality. But he knew too that as a lover, a husband, there would be a deeply, darkly passionate and possessive part of him that yearned to be his beloved's only partner, an ache within him to teach her, show her the delights of sensual love. And right now something about Saskia's reaction to him was sparking off a reaction he was having to fight to control, a response that was pure primitive Greek male. A need!

'I'm not sleeping in this room with you,' Saskia reiterated numbly. 'I'm...'

If she *was* acting then she deserved an Oscar, Andreas decided grimly. But a fiancée who looked terrified at the very thought of being with him was the last thing he needed. He had to calm her down, to calm them both down.

'Come with me,' he commanded, taking hold of her hand and drawing her towards one of the doors that opened off the bedroom.

When he opened it Saskia could see that the room that lay beyond it was furnished as an office, with all the latest technological equipment.

'Will it make you feel any better if I tell you that I intend to sleep in there?' Andreas demanded.

'In there? But it's an office. There's no bed,' Saskia whispered shakily.

'I can bring in one of the sun loungers and sleep on that,' Andreas told her impatiently.

'You mean it…' Saskia was wary, reluctant to trust or believe him.

Andreas nodded his head grimly, wondering why on earth he was allowing his overactive conscience to force him into such a ridiculous situation. He knew there was no way she could possibly be the naïve, frightened innocent she was behaving as though she was.

'But surely someone would notice if you removed a sun bed?' she was asking him uncertainly.

'Only my room opens out onto this pool area. It's my private territory. The main pool which everyone else uses is round the other side of the villa.'

His own private pool. Saskia fought not to be impressed, but obviously she had not fought hard enough, she recognised ruefully as Andreas gave her an impatient look.

'I'm not trying to make a point, Saskia, one-upmanship of that boastful sort is anathema to me. My grandfather may be a millionaire but I most certainly am not.'

It wasn't entirely true, but something about the look in Saskia's eyes made him want to refute any mental criticism

she might have that he was some kind of idle playboy,
lounging by a swimming pool all day.

'It's just that I happen to like an early-morning swim
when I'm here at the villa; my sisters used to claim that I
woke them up so I had this pool installed for my own use.
Swimming laps helps me to clear my thoughts as well as
allowing me to exercise.'

Saskia knew what he was saying, she felt the same about
walking. Whenever she was worried about something, or
had a problem to mull over, she walked.

As he watched her Andreas asked himself grimly why
he was going to so much trouble to calm and reassure her.
That frightened heartbeat he had felt thudding so anxiously
against his own body just had to have been faked. There
was no way it could not have been. Just like that huge-
eyed watchfulness.

Saskia bit her lip as she looked away from him. It was
obvious that Andreas meant what he said about sleeping in
his office, but right now it wasn't their sleeping arrangements that were at the forefront of her mind so much as
what was happening during their waking hours—and what
she herself had just experienced when he kissed her.

She couldn't have secretly wanted him to kiss her.
Surely it was impossible that that could happen without her
being consciously aware of it. But what other explanation
could there be for the way she had responded to him? her
conscience demanded grittily.

'Right,' she could hear Andreas saying dryly, 'now that
we've got *that* sorted out I've got some work to do, so why
don't you have something to eat and then have a rest?'

'I need to unpack,' Saskia began to protest, but Andreas
shook his head.

'One of the maids will do that for you whilst you're resting.'

When he saw her expression he told her softly, 'They work for us, Saskia. They are servants and they work to earn their living just as you and I work to earn ours.'

'OH, I'M SORRY, I didn't wake you, did I?' Pia said *sotto voce*. 'But it will be dinner time soon and I thought you might appreciate some extra time to get ready.'

As Saskia came fully awake and struggled to sit up in the bed she recognised that her unexpected visitor was Andreas's sister Olympia.

The arcane grin that crossed Pia's face as she added, 'We normally dress down here, not up, but Athena is bound to want to make an impact,' made Saskia warm to her friendliness.

'Where's…?' she began anxiously, but didn't get any further than the first word of her enquiry.

'Where's Andreas?' Pia supplied for her, 'Grandfather telephoned to speak to our mother and then he wanted to have a word with Andreas.' She gave a small shrug. 'He's probably still on the phone, and I have to warn you he isn't in a very good mood.' As she saw the way Saskia's eyes became watchful she hastened to assure her. 'Oh, it isn't you. It's Athena. She's brought her accountant with her and Andreas is furious. He can't stand him. None of us can, but Athena insisted that Grandfather invited Aristotle personally.'

As Pia darted about the room, switching on lamps to illuminate the darkness of the Greek evening, Saskia swung her feet to the floor. She had fallen asleep fully dressed and now she felt grubby and untidy. The thought of having to sit down at a dinner table with Andreas and Athena was not one she was looking forward to, but Pia was right about one thing: she *would* need to make an impact. Andreas would no doubt expect it of her. Still, with her suitcase full of the new clothes he had insisted on buying for her, she had no excuse *not* to do so.

'Maria's already unpacked your cases for you,' Pia informed her. 'I helped her,' she added. 'I love that little black number you've brought with you. It's to die for. Your clothes are gorgeous. Andreas kept coming in and telling me not to make so much noise in case I woke you up.' She pulled another face. 'He's so protective of you.

'Mama and I are so glad that he's met you,' she added more quietly, giving Saskia a look of warm confidence that immediately made her feel horribly guilty. 'We both love him to bits, of course,' she went on, 'and that hardly makes us impartial. But we were beginning to get so afraid that he might just give in to Grandfather and Athena for Grandfather's sake—and we both know he could *never* love her. I suppose he's told you about what she did when he was younger?'

Without waiting for Saskia to say anything Pia continued in a quick burst of flurried words, 'I'm not supposed to know about it really. Lydia, my sister, told me, and swore me to secrecy, but of course it's all right to discuss it with you because Andreas must have told you about it. He was only fifteen at the time—just a boy, really—and she was *so* much older and on the point of getting married. I know the actual age gap in terms of years would be nothing if it had been between two adults, but Andreas wasn't an adult. He was still at school and she… I think it was wonderfully brave and moral of Andreas to refuse to go to bed with her—and do you know something else? I think that although Athena *claims* to love him a part of her really wants to punish him for not letting her—well, you know!'

Athena had tried to *seduce* Andreas when he had still been a schoolboy! Saskia had to fight hard to control both her shock and the distaste Pia's revelations were causing her.

It was true that in terms of years—a mere seven or so— the age gap between them was not large. But for a woman in her twenties to attempt to seduce a boy of fifteen— surely that was almost sexual abuse? A cold shiver touched Saskia's skin, icy fingers spreading a chilling message through her.

Would a woman who was prepared to do something like that allow a mere bogus fiancée to come between her and the man she wanted? And Athena obviously did want Andreas very badly indeed—even if her motivation for doing so was shrouded in secrecy.

Andreas was such a very *male* man it was hard to imagine him in the role of hunted rather than hunter. If ever a man had been designed by nature to be proactive, arrogant and predatory that man was, in Saskia's opinion, Andreas. But there was something so alien to Saskia's own experience in Athena, a coldness, a greed, almost an obsessiveness that Saskia found it hard to relate to her or even think of her in terms of being a member of her own sex.

Her determination to marry Andreas was chillingly formidable.

'Of course, if it wasn't for Grandfather's health there wouldn't be any problem,' Pia was saying ruefully. 'We all know that. Grandfather likes to think that because he works for him Andreas is financially dependent on him, but...' She stopped, shaking her head.

'You are going to wear the black, aren't you? I'm dying to see you in it. You've got the colouring for it. I look so drab in black, although you can bet that Athena will wear it. Whoops!' She grimaced as they both heard male footsteps in the corridor outside the bedroom. 'That will be Andreas, and he'll scalp me if he thinks I'm being a pest.'

Saskia tensed as Andreas came into the room, watching as his glance went from the bed to where she was standing in the corner of the room.

'Pia,' he began ominously, 'I told you...'

'I was awake when she came,' Saskia intervened protectively. She liked Andreas's sister, and if she'd been genuinely in love with him and planning to marry him she knew she would have been delighted to have found a potential friend in this warm-hearted, impulsive woman.

Pia launched herself at Andreas, laughing up into his face as she hugged him and told him triumphantly, 'See? You are wrong, big brother, and you must not be so firm and bossy with me otherwise Saskia will not want to marry you. And now that I have met her I am determined that she will be my sister-in-law. We were just discussing what she is going to wear for dinner,' she added. 'I have warned her that Athena will be dressed to kill!'

'If you don't take yourself off to your own room so that we can *all* get ready, Athena is going to be the only one who is dressed for anything,' Andreas told her dryly.

Kissing his forehead, Pia released him and hurried to the door, pausing as she opened it to give Saskia an impish grin and remind her, 'Wear the black!'

'I'm sorry,' Andreas apologised after the door had closed behind her. 'I asked her not to disturb you.'

So he hadn't been deceived by her fib, Saskia recognised.

'I don't mind. I like her,' Saskia responded, this time telling him the truth.

'Mmm... Pia's likeability is something I'm afraid she tends to trade on on occasion. As the baby of the family she's a past mistress at getting her own way,' he told Saskia in faint exasperation, before glancing at his watch and informing her, 'You've got half an hour to get ready.'

Saskia took a deep steadying breath. Something about the revelations Pia had made had activated the deep core of sympathy for others that was so much a part of her nature. Somewhere deep inside her a switch had been thrown, a sea change made, and without her knowing quite how it had happened Andreas had undergone a transformation, from her oppressor and a dictator whom she loathed and feared to someone who deserved her championship and help. She had a role which she was now determined she was going to play to the very best of her ability.

'Half an hour,' she repeated in as businesslike a manner as she could. 'Then in that case I should like to use the bathroom first.'

CHAPTER EIGHT

'So, Saskia, how do you think you will adjust to being a Greek wife—if you and Andreas *do* actually get married?'

Saskia could hear Pia's indrawn gasp of indignation at the way Athena had framed her question, but she refused to allow herself to be intimidated by the other woman. Ever since they had all taken their places at the dinner table Saskia had recognised that Athena was determined to unnerve and upset her as much as she could. However, before she could say anything Andreas was answering the question for her.

'There is no "if" about it Athena,' he told her implacably. 'Saskia *will* become my wife.'

Now it was Saskia's turn to stifle her own potentially betraying gasp of shock, but she couldn't control her instinctive urge to look anxiously across the table at Andreas. What would he do when he ultimately had to back down and admit to Athena that their engagement was over? That was *his* problem and not hers, she tried to remind herself steadily.

Something odd had happened to her somehow; she was convinced of it. Andreas had walked out of the office adjoining 'their' bedroom earlier this evening and come to a standstill in front of her, saying quietly, 'I doubt that any man looking at you now could do anything other than wish that you were his, Saskia.'

She had certainly never had any desire to go on the stage—far from it—and yet from that moment she had felt as though somehow she had stepped into a new persona. Suddenly she had become Andreas's fiancée and, like any woman in love, not only was she proud to be with the man she loved, she also felt very femalely protective of him. The anxiety in her eyes now was *for* him and *because* of him. How would he feel when Athena tauntingly threw the comment he had just made back in his face? How must he have felt when he had first realised, as a boy, just what she wanted from him?

'Wives. I love wives.' Aristotle, Athena's accountant, grinned salaciously, leaning towards Saskia so that he could put his hand on her arm.

Immediately she turned away from him. Saskia fully shared Pia's view of Athena's accountant. Although he was quite tall, the heavy, weighty structure of his torso made him look almost squat. His thick black hair was heavily oiled and the white suit he was wearing over a black shirt, in Saskia's opinion at least, did him no favours. Andreas, on the other hand, looked sexily cool and relaxed in elegantly tailored trousers with a cool white cotton shirt.

If she had privately thought her black dress might be rather over the top she had swiftly realised how right Pia had been to suggest that she wore it once she had seen Athena's outfit.

Her slinky skintight white dress left nothing to the imagination.

'It was designed especially for me,' Saskia had heard her smirking to Andreas. 'And it is made to be worn exactly the way I most love—next to my skin,' she had added, loudly enough for Saskia to overhear. 'Which reminds me. I hope you have warned your fiancée that I like to share your morning swim so she won't be too shocked…' She had turned to Saskia. 'Andreas is like me, he likes to swim best in his skin,' she had told her purringly.

In his skin. Saskia hadn't been able to prevent herself from giving Andreas a brief shocked look which, fortunately, Athena had put down to Saskia's jealousy at the thought of another woman swimming nude with her fiancée.

Whilst Saskia had been digesting this stomach-churning disclosure she had heard Andreas himself replying brusquely, 'I can only recall one occasion on which you attempted to join me in my morning lap session, Athena, and I recall too that I told you then how little I appreciate having my morning peace interrupted.'

'Oh, dear.' Athena had pouted, unabashed. 'Are you afraid that I have said something you didn't want your fiancée to know? But surely, Andreas,' she had murmured huskily, reaching out to place her hand on his arm, 'she *must* realise that a man as attractive as you…as virile as you…will have had other lovers before her…'

Her brazenness had almost taken Saskia's breath away. She could imagine just how she would be feeling right now if Andreas *had* indeed been her fiancée. How jealous and insecure Athena's words would be making her feel. No woman wanted to be reminded of the other women who had shared an intimate relationship with her beloved before her.

But Andreas, it seemed, was completely unfazed by Athena's revelations. He had simply removed her arm by the expedient of stepping back from her and putting his own arm around Saskia's shoulders. He had drawn her so close to his body that Saskia had known he must be able to feel the fine tremor of reaction she was unable to suppress. A tremor which had increased to a full-flooded convulsion when his lean fingers had started almost absently to caress the smooth ball of her bare shoulder.

'Saskia knows that she is the only woman I have ever loved—the woman I want to spend my life with.'

The more she listened to and watched Athena the more Saskia subscribed to Pia's belief that it wasn't love that was motivating the other woman. Sometimes she looked at Andreas as though she hated him and wanted to totally destroy him.

Aristotle, or 'Ari' as he had told Saskia he preferred to be called, was still trying to engage her attention, but she was deliberately trying to feign a lack of awareness of that fact. There was something about him she found so loathsome that the thought of even the hot damp touch of his hand on her arm made her shudder with distaste. However, good manners forced her to respond to his questions as politely as she could, even when she thought they were intolerable and intrusive. He had already told her that were he Andreas's accountant he would be insisting she sign a prenuptial contract to make sure that if the marriage ended Andreas's money would be safe.

Much to Saskia's surprise Andreas himself had thoroughly confounded her by joining in the conversation and telling Aristotle grimly that he would never ask the woman he loved to sign such an agreement.

'Money is nothing when compared with love,' he had told Aristotle firmly in a deep, implacable voice, his words so obviously genuine that Saskia had found she was holding her breath a little as she listened to him.

Then he had looked at her, and Saskia had remembered just how *they* had met and what he really thought of her, and suddenly she had felt the most bitter taste of despair in her mouth and she had longed to tell him how wrong he was.

At least she had the comfort of knowing that his mother and sister liked her, and Pia had assured her that their elder sister was equally pleased that Andreas had fallen in love, and was looking forward to meeting Saskia when she and her husband and their children came to the island later in the month.

'Lydia's husband is a diplomat, and they are in Brussels at the moment, but she is longing to meet you,' Pia had told her.

She would have hated it if Andreas's close family had *not* liked and welcomed her.

Abruptly Saskia felt her face start to burn. What on earth was she thinking? She was only *playing* the part of Andreas's fiancée. Their engagement was a fiction, a charade…a *lie* created simply to help him escape from the trap that Athena was trying to set for him. What she must not forget was that it was a lie he had tricked and blackmailed her into colluding with.

Aristotle was saying something to her about wanting to show her the villa's gardens. Automatically Saskia shook her head, her face burning with fresh colour as she saw the way Andreas was watching her, a mixture of anger and warning in his eyes. He couldn't seriously think she would actually *accept* Aristotle's invitation?

'Saskia has had a long day. I think it's time we said our goodnights,' she heard him saying abruptly as he stood up.

Saskia looked quickly round the table. It was obvious from the expressions of everyone else just what interpretation they were putting on Andreas's decision, and Saskia knew that the heat washing her face and throat could only confirm their suspicions.

'Andreas…' she started to protest as he came round to her chair and stood behind her. 'I don't…'

'You're wasting your breath, Saskia.' Pia chuckled. 'Because my dear brother obviously *does*! Oh, you needn't put that lordly expression on for me, brother dear.' She laughed again, before adding mischievously, 'And I wouldn't mind betting that you won't be lapping the pool at dawn…'

'Pia!' her mother protested, pink-cheeked, whilst Athena gave Saskia a look of concentrated hatred.

Hastily Saskia stood up, and then froze as Aristotle did the same, insisting in a thick voice, 'I must claim the privilege of family friend and kiss the new addition to the family goodnight.'

Before Saskia could evade him he was reaching for her, but before he could put his words into action Andreas was standing between them, announcing grimly, 'There is only one man *my* fiancée kisses…'

'IF YOU'LL TAKE my advice, you'll keep well away from Aristotle. He has a very unsavoury reputation with women. His ex-wife has accused him of being violent towards her and—'

Saskia turned as she stepped into the bedroom, her anger showing. 'You can't mean what I *think* you mean,' she demanded whilst Andreas closed the door. How could he possibly imagine that she would even contemplate being interested in a man like the accountant? It was an insult she was simply not prepared to tolerate.

'Can't I?' Andreas countered curtly. 'You're here for one reason and one reason only, Saskia. You're here to act as my fiancée. Whilst I can appreciate that, being the woman you are, the temptation to feather your nest a little and do what you so obviously do best must be a strong one, let me warn you now against giving in to it. If you do, in fact...'

If she *did*... Why, she would rather *die* than let a slimeball like Ari come anywhere near her, Saskia reflected furiously. And to think that back there in the dining room she had *actually* felt sympathetic towards Andreas, had actually wanted to *protect* him. Now, though, her anger shocked through her in a fierce, dangerous flood of pride.

'If you want the truth, I find Ari almost as repulsively loathsome as I do you,' she threw bitterly at him.

'You dare to speak of me in the same breath as that reptile? How dare you speak so of me...or to me...?' Andreas demanded, his anger surging to match hers as he reached out to grab hold of her. His eyes smouldered with an intensity of emotion that Saskia could see was threatening to get out of control.

'That man is an animal—worse than an animal. Only last year he narrowly escaped standing on a criminal charge. I cannot understand why Athena tolerates him and I have told her so.'

'Perhaps she wants to make you jealous.'

It was an off-the-cuff remark, full of bravado, but Saskia

wished immediately she had not said it when she saw the way the smoulder suddenly became a savage flare of fury.

'*She* does? Or *you* do…? Oh, yes, I saw the way he was looking at you over dinner…touching you…'

'That was nothing to do with me,' Saskia protested, but she could sense that the words hadn't touched him, that something else was fuelling his anger and feeding it, something that was hidden from her but which Andreas himself obviously found intolerable.

'And as for you finding me *loathsome*,' Andreas said through gritted teeth. 'Perhaps it is unchivalrous, *ungentlemanly* of me to say so, but that wasn't loathing I could see in your eyes earlier on today. It wasn't *loathing* I could hear in your voice, *feel* in your body…was it? *Was it?*' he demanded sharply.

Saskia started to tremble.

'I don't know,' she fibbed wildly. 'I can't remember.'

It was, she recognised a few seconds later, the worst possible thing she could have said. Because immediately Andreas pounced, whispering with soft savagery, 'No? Then perhaps I should help you to remember…'

She heard herself starting to protest, but somehow the words were lost—not because Andreas was refusing to listen, but because her lips were refusing to speak.

'So when exactly *was* it that you found me so loathsome Saskia?' Andreas was demanding as he closed both his arms around her, forming them into a prison from which it was impossible for her to escape. 'When I did this…?' His mouth was feathering over hers, teasing and tantalising it, arousing a hot torrent of sensation she didn't want to experience. 'Or when I did *this*…?'

Now his tongue-tip was probing the lips she was trying

so desperately to keep firmly closed, stroking them, tracing
their soft curves, over and over again, until she could hear
herself moaning helplessly as they parted softly for him.
But still it seemed he hadn't extracted his pound of flesh,
because even this victory wasn't enough for him.

'What? Still no answer…? I wonder why not,' he was
taunting her, before adding bitingly, 'Or do I need to
wonder at all? You are a woman who is used to giving
her body to a man, Saskia, who is used to experiencing
pleasure. And right now you want that pleasure from *me*.'

'No,' Saskia moaned in denial, trying to turn her face
away from his and to break free of him.

'Yes,' he insisted rawly. '*Yes*. Admit it, Saskia… You
want me… Your body wants *mine*. It wants the sexual
satisfaction it's used to…it aches and craves for.'

A shudder of shock ripped through her as Saskia
recognised the truth of what he was saying. She *did* want
him, but not in the way he was suggesting. She wanted him
as a woman wanted the man she loved, she realised shakily.
She wanted him as her lover, not merely as her sexual
partner, someone with whom she could find a release for
a basic physical need, as he was so cruelly saying. But how
could she love him? She *couldn't*… But she *did*.

She had fallen in love with him virtually the moment she
had set eyes on him, Saskia acknowledged despairingly,
but she had told herself that because of her loyalty to her
friend he was out of bounds to her and that she could
not, *must* not allow herself to have such feelings, just as
she could not allow herself to have them now. Although
for very different reasons. Megan was no longer a barrier
to her loving Andreas, but Andreas himself and what he
thought about her certainly was.

'Let me go, Andreas,' she demanded.

'Not until you have admitted that I am right and that you want me,' Andreas refused. 'Or are you trying to goad me into *proving* to you that I am right?'

Saskia flinched as she felt the suffocating, dangerously toxic mix of fear and excitement explode inside her.

She hesitated whilst she tried to formulate the right response, the only sane, sensible response she could give, and then she realised that she had waited too long as Andreas told her rawly, 'You've pushed me too far, Saskia. I want you, but you already know that, don't you? How could a woman like you *not* know it? You can feel it in my body, can't you?' he demanded. 'Here...'

Helplessly Saskia leaned against him whilst she tried to absorb the shock of having her hand taken and placed so explicitly against the hard, intimate throb of his maleness. If only she could find the strength to drag her hand away, to tell him that she didn't want the intimacy he was forcing on her. But despairingly she knew that she was too weak, that there was no way she could stop herself from aching to use the opportunity he had given her to touch and explore him, to know him...to know his maleness...to—

She gave a small moan as her body started to shake with tremors of desire. Andreas's heart was pounding so savagely that she could feel it almost inside her own body. Earlier in the evening, when he had almost absently caressed the ball of her shoulder—the touch of an established lover for his beloved—she had shuddered in mute delight, but that was nothing to what she was feeling now.

She ached for him, hungered for him, and when she closed her eyes she could see him as Athena had so tauntingly described him—proud and naked as his body sliced the water. She moaned again, a high, sharp sound this time that had Andreas covering her mouth with the hard, hot, demanding pressure of his, the words he was groaning against her lost as his passion sent a kick of shocking voluptuous pleasure searing through her.

Her mouth was properly open beneath his now, her tongue hungry for the sensual melding stroke of his, and the intensity of her own feelings was dizzying and dazzling her.

'You want me… You need me…'

She could feel him mouthing the words and she couldn't deny them, her body, her emotions were saturated with the intensity of a response to him so new to her that she had no defences against it.

Everything else was suddenly forgotten, unimportant. Everything else and everyone else. All she needed… All she wanted… All she could ever want was here within her reach.

She moaned and trembled as she felt Andreas's hands on her body and over her dress, their touch hard, hungry… excitingly, *dangerously* male. The unfamiliar intimacy of his body against hers was depriving her of the ability to think or to reason properly. There was no place for reason to exist in this new world she was inhabiting anyway.

'I want to see you…watch you whilst I make love to you,' Andreas was saying thickly to her. 'I want *you* to see me… My God, but I can understand *now* just why all those other men fell victim to you. There's something about you, some witchery, some— What's wrong?' he demanded as he felt the abrupt way Saskia had tensed against him in rejection.

Saskia could not bear to look at him.

With those few contemptuous words he had destroyed everything, totally obliterated her wonderful new world and brought her crashing back to her old one. She felt sick to her soul from her own behaviour, her own folly.

'No, no, I don't want *this*,' she protested frantically, pushing Andreas away.

'What the...?' She could hear the anger in his voice, feel it almost, but still he released her.

'If this is some kind of game—' he began to warn her, and then stopped, shaking his head in disbelief. 'My God, I must have been out of my mind anyway, to even contemplate... I suppose that's what too many years of celibacy does for a man,' he threw at her unkindly. 'I never thought I'd be idiotic enough...'

He turned back to her, stopping when Saskia froze.

'You're quite safe,' he told her grimly. 'I'm not going to touch you. There's no way—' He broke off and shook his head again, and then walked abruptly away from her, telling her brusquely, 'I've got some work to do.'

THE BEDROOM WAS in darkness when Saskia woke up, and at first she didn't know what had woken her. Then she heard it again, the rhythmic sound of someone swimming. The patio doors to the pool area were open, and as she turned her head to look towards them she could see the discreet lights which were illuminating it.

Andreas was swimming... She looked at her watch. It was three o'clock in the morning and Andreas was swimming...tirelessly up and down the pool. Warily she sat up in bed to get a closer look as his powerful crawl took him to the far side of the pool. As he executed his turn Saskia lay down again. She didn't want him to see her watching him.

Beneath the bedclothes she was naked, apart from a tiny pair of briefs. The one thing Andreas had apparently forgotten to buy for her had turned out to be any kind of nightwear. *That* discovery had caused her to remain for nearly fifteen minutes in the locked privacy of the bathroom, agonising over what she should do until she had finally found the courage to open the door and make an undignified bolt for the bed, her body hidden from view by the towel she had wrapped around it. Not that she need have been so concerned. Andreas had remained out of sight in his office.

But he wasn't in his office now. Now he was swimming in the pool.

Beneath the protective cover of the bedclothes Saskia's brain worked feverishly. Should he be swimming alone at night? Was it safe? What if…? Almost the very second that fear formed her ears registered the fact that she could no longer hear the sound of Andreas swimming. Quickly she lowered the bedclothes and looked anxiously towards the pool area. The water was still, calm—and empty of its sole swimmer.

Andreas! Where—? She gripped hold of the bedclothes as she saw him climbing out of the water—totally naked—totally! She tried to drag her recalcitrant gaze away from his body but it was no use; it was refusing to listen to her, refusing to obey her, remaining fixed in hungry female appreciation on the pagan male beauty of Andreas's nakedness.

Surely any woman would have found the sight of Andreas breathtaking, Saskia thought fervently, her gaze devouring the pure sensuality of his back view as he walked across the tiles. His skin shone sleekly, still damp from his swim, and beneath it the muscles moved in a way that had a shockingly disconcerting effect on her *own* body.

Naively Saskia had always previously assumed that there could be little difference in seeing a statue or a painting of a naked man and viewing the real thing, but now she knew how wrong she had been. Perhaps it was her love for him that made the difference, perhaps it was… She gasped as he suddenly turned round. He seemed to be looking right into the bedroom. Could he see her? Did he *know* that she was watching him? She lay perfectly still, praying that he could not do so, unable to bear the humiliation of his mockery if he were to come in to her now. If he were to…

She just managed to suppress the audible sound of her own longing. If he came to her now and held her, touched her, kissed her…*took* her as she was so aching for him to do, it wouldn't be in love but in lust. Was that really what she wanted? she asked herself sternly. No, of course it wasn't, was her helpless response. What she wanted was for Andreas to love her the way she did him.

He was turning away from her now, his body silhouetted by the light. Saskia sucked in her breath sharply, every feminine instinct and desire she possessed flagrantly ignoring her attempts to control them. He looked… He was… He was *perfect* she acknowledged, silently whispering the soft accolade beneath her breath as her eyes rounded and she saw that the male reality of him far, far outreached anything she had ever thought of in her innocent virginal imaginings.

Once again he looked towards the bedroom and

Saskia held her breath, praying…hoping…*waiting*… She expelled it on a small rush of sound as he reached down and retrieved his robe, shrugging it on before walking not back to the bedroom and to her but away from it. Where was he going? she wondered. Back to his office?

For what felt like a long time after he had gone Saskia lay where she was, afraid to move, unable to sleep and even more afraid to think. What was the matter with her? How could she possibly love a man who had treated her as Andreas had done, who had blackmailed her, threatened her, refused to allow her to tell him the truth about herself? A man who had the lowest possible opinion of her and yet who, despite that, had still kissed her. How could she? Saskia closed her eyes. She didn't know the answer to that question. All she knew was that her emotions, her heart, her deepest self were crying out—how could she *not* love him?

'SUNBATHING? I NEVER thought I'd see the day when you would just laze around,' Pia teased Andreas as she came hurrying out of the villa in the tiniest little bikini Saskia had ever seen and curled up on the vacant sun bed next to where Saskia was lying.

'Saskia didn't have a good night. She needs to rest and I didn't want her overdoing things or lying too long in our strong sun,' Andreas lied unblushingly to his sister.

'Oh, poor you,' Pia immediately sympathised with Saskia as she studied her pale face.

Guiltily Saskia said nothing. After all, she could hardly admit that the reason she was so jaded was because she had spent so many of the night hours when she should have been sleeping thinking about, *fantasising* about the man lying right next to her. In daylight Saskia dared not recall the very personal and intimate nature of her fantasies. She knew that if she did so her face would be as brightly coloured as it was now pale. Mercifully Andreas had put her huge eyes and pale face down to travel tiredness.

'Well, that's one improvement you've made on my brother's lifestyle already, Saskia,' Pia approved with a grin. 'Normally when he comes to the villa we can't get him out of the office. When did Grandfather say he is going to arrive?' she asked Andreas.

'I must say I'm surprised that your grandfather intends to come to the island at all at the moment,' Athena answered for Andreas as she and her accountant came out of the villa to join them.

Saskia's heart sank a little as she saw them. Over breakfast Ari had been so over-fulsome in his praise of her, and so obviously sexually motivated, that she had been glad to escape from him.

As Pia started to frown Athena added maliciously, 'He isn't very happy with you right now, Andreas...'

'My grandfather is never happy with anyone who takes a different view from his,' Andreas told her dryly. 'He has a quick temper and a short fuse and thankfully an even shorter memory—'

Andreas had insisted that Saskia was to lie beneath the protection of a sun umbrella because of her fair skin, but as she watched Athena untying the wrap she was wearing to reveal an even smaller bikini than Pia's, Saskia felt envious of her rich golden tan.

'How uncomfortable you must be lying in the shade,' Athena said, adding bitchily, 'I would *hate* to have such a pale skin. It always looks so...'

'Saskia's skin reminds *me* of the purest alabaster,' Andreas interrupted Athena smoothly.

'Alabaster—oh, but that is so cold.' Athena smiled, giving Saskia an assessing look. 'Oh, now you are frowning and looking grumpy,' she told Andreas softly, 'and I know *just* the cure for that. Let me put some oil on for you, Andreas, and then...'

Saskia could hardly believe it when she heard herself saying firmly, 'I'll do that for you, darling.' Turning to look at Athena, she added boldly, 'A fiancée's privilege.' And then, ignoring both the frowning look Andreas was giving her and her own shaking hands, she got up off her sun lounger, took the bottle of oil Pia was offering her with an approving smile and walked over to where Andreas was lying.

Very carefully Saskia poured a little of the oil into her cupped hand and then, even more carefully, leaned over Andreas's prone body, making sure as she did so that she stood between his sun bed and the one Athena was reclining on in a pose carefully designed to flaunt to full effect her generous breasts.

Saskia's hair swung over her face as she nervously started to smooth the oil over Andreas shoulders. His skin felt warm and sleek beneath her touch. As sleek as it had looked last night. She paused as her hands began to tremble. Last night! She must *not* think about *that* now. But somehow she found herself doing so; somehow, too, her hands were moving sensually against his skin, stroking, smoothing, even kneading instinctively when she found that his muscles were bunching beneath her touch.

He had been lying on his stomach with his eyes closed,

but suddenly they opened and he told her abruptly, 'That's enough. I was about to go for a swim anyway.'

Even so it was still several seconds before he actually got up and walked away from her to the end of the pool, diving in cleanly and then swimming virtually a full length beneath the water before resurfacing and starting to lap the pool with a hard, fast-paced crawl.

Andreas tried to concentrate on what he was doing, to empty his head of any thoughts as he always did when he was swimming. It was his favourite way of relaxing— or at least it had been. Right now the *last* thing he felt was relaxed. Even without closing his eyes he could still remember exactly how it had felt to have Saskia's hands moving over his body, soft, caressing…knowing…

He slid beneath the water, swimming under it as he tried to control his aching body. God, but he wanted her; ached for her; lusted for her. He had *never* felt like this about anyone before, never needed anyone with such an intensity, never been in a situation where he simply could not control himself either physically or emotionally. She *must* know what she was doing to him, a woman of *her* experience…a woman who prowled bars at night looking for a man. Of *course* she must; of course she *did*. And yet…

And yet he couldn't stop himself from contrasting what he knew cerebrally about her with the way she had felt in his arms, the soft, hot sweetness of her kiss, the desire hazing her eyes and the shock which had later replaced it. She had caught him off guard just now, when she had refused to allow Athena to touch him—caught him off guard and filled him with a certain hot male triumph and pride that she should feel so possessive about him. But of course she didn't—did she? She was simply acting, playing out the role he had forced her into.

Andreas frowned. His own mental use of the word 'forced' and the admission which it brought rasped against his conscience like sandpaper. It was wholly out of character for him, against his strongest held beliefs to force anyone to do anything, but he had begun to fear he could find no way out of the present situation without endangering his grandfather's health. What he was offering was an explanation, not an excuse, he warned himself sternly and if he had now discovered that he had merely exchanged one hazard for another which was even more potentially dangerous then he had no one but himself to blame.

Had Saskia seen that betraying surge of his body before he had turned away from her? Athena had. Athena... Andreas's mouth hardened.

At fifteen, and still a schoolboy, he had tried to convince himself that he was mature enough to take over his father's role, strong enough to support and protect his mother and his sisters. But a part of him had still been childish and he had often ended up crying alone at night in his bed, confused and angry and missing his father, wondering furiously why he had had to die.

That period had surely been the worst of his life: the loss of his father and then Athena's attempt to seduce him. Two events which together had propelled him into an adulthood and maturity he had in no way been prepared for.

Athena's desire for him had held none of the classic 'Mrs Robinson' allure. She had been coming on to him for weeks, ever since he had returned home from school for the summer holidays, but he had never dreamed that she was doing anything other than playing some mysterious adult female game that was beyond his ability to comprehend—until the day he had found her in his room—naked!

When she had handed him the vibrator she was stroking herself with, commanding him to use it on her, it had been all he could do not to turn on his heels and run. But boys ran, and he hadn't wanted to be a boy, but a man…the man his father would have wanted him to be, the man his mother and sisters needed him to be.

'I don't think you should be in here, do you?' he had asked her woodenly, avoiding looking at her naked body. 'You are engaged to be married.'

She had laughed at him then, but she hadn't been laughing later, when he had held open his bedroom door and commanded her to leave, warning her that if she didn't he would have no compunction in getting a couple of members of staff to physically remove her.

She had gone, but not immediately, not until she had tried to change his mind.

'You have a man's body,' she had told him angrily. 'But like a fool you have no knowledge of what to do with it. Why won't you let me show you?' she had coaxed. 'What is it you are so afraid of?'

'I'm not afraid,' he had responded stoically, and truthfully. It hadn't been fear that had stopped him from taking advantage of what she was offering but anger and loathing.

But Athena was a woman who couldn't endure to accept that he didn't want her. Tough! Her feelings, if she genuinely had any—which he personally doubted—were her problem. His grandfather was a very different matter, though, and even without the cloud currently hanging over his health, Andreas would have been reluctant to quarrel with him—though he felt that the old man was being both stubborn and difficult. How much of the blame for that lay with Athena and how much with his grandfather's fiercely guarded fear of growing old and the future Andreas could only hazard a guess at.

It was ironic, really, that the means he had adopted to help him overcome his problems should have resulted in causing him even more. An example, perhaps, of the modern-day ethos behind the ancient Greek mythology Saskia had expressed a love of. She might love Greek mythology but she most certainly did not love him. Andreas frowned, not wanting to pursue such a line of thought.

'THAT IS A VERY pretty little ring you are wearing,' Athena commented disparagingly as she got up off the lounger and came to stand next to Saskia.

They were alone at the poolside, Athena's accountant having gone to make some telephone calls and Pia having left to help her mother, who was preparing for the arrival of her father.

'But an engagement ring is no guarantee of marriage,' Athena continued. 'You look like a sensible girl to me, Saskia. Andreas is a very wealthy and experienced man. Men like him get so easily bored. You must know that yourself. I suspect that the chances of you actually walking down the aisle and marrying Andreas are very limited indeed, and they will become even more slender once Andreas's grandfather arrives. He doesn't want Andreas to marry you. He is very old-fashioned and very Greek.

He has other plans for his only grandson and for the future of the business he has built up.'

She paused, watching Saskia calculatingly, and Saskia knew what she was thinking. Athena too had other plans for Andreas's future.

'If you really loved Andreas then surely *he* would be far more important to you than your own feelings. Andreas is devoted to his grandfather. Oh, I know he may not show it, but I can promise you that he is. Think what it would do to him emotionally, not to mention financially, if there were to be a rift between them. Andreas's mother and his sisters are both financially dependent on their grandfather... If he were to banish Andreas from his life then Andreas would be banished from *their* lives as well.'

Athena gave a deep, theatrical sigh and then asked pseudo-gently, 'How long do you think he would continue to want *you* once that had happened? And I can *make* it happen, Saskia...you know that, don't you. His grandfather listens to me. It is because he wants my business to be joined to his, of course. That is the Greek way of doing things.' She bared her teeth and gave Saskia an unkind smile. 'It is *not* the Greek way of doing things for a millionaire to allow his heir to marry a penniless foreigner.

'But let's talk of something more pleasant. There is no reason why we shouldn't come to a mutually happy arrangement—you and I. I *could* sit back and wait for Andreas to leave you, but I will be honest with you. I am approaching the age when it may become less easy for me to give Andreas the sons he will want. So, to make it easy for us both, I have a proposition to put to you. I am willing to pay you *one million pounds* to remove you from Andreas's life—permanently.'

Saskia could feel the blood draining out of her face as shock hit her. Somehow she managed to drag herself into a sitting position on the sun lounger and then to stand up, so that she and Athena were face to face.

'Money can't buy love,' she told her fiercely. 'And it can't buy me. Not one million pounds, not one hundred million pounds! *No* amount.' Tears stung her eyes and she told herself that shock had put them there. 'If at any time Andreas wants to end our engagement then that is his prerogative, but—'

'You're a fool—do you know that?' Athena breathed, her whole face contorted with fury and malice. 'Do you really think Andreas meant what he said about not insisting on a prenuptial agreement? Ha! His grandfather will *make* him have you sign one, and when Andreas grows tired of you, as he undoubtedly will, you will get *nothing*... not even any child he may have given you. Greek men do not give up their children. Greek *families* do not give up their heirs.'

Saskia didn't want to hear any more. Without even bothering to pick up her wrap she started to walk towards the house, only just managing to prevent herself from breaking into a run.

As Saskia reached the house Pia was coming out of it through the open patio door.

'Saskia...' she began in concern, but Saskia shook her head, knowing she was in no fit state to talk to her—to her or indeed to anyone. She felt degraded by what Athena had said to her, degraded and angry. How dared Athena believe that her love was for sale...that *money* mattered more to her than Andreas...that she would *ever*...? Abruptly Saskia stopped. What was she *thinking*? She turned round and went back outside, heading not for the pool area but beyond it…to the island and the pathway along the cliffs. She needed to be on her own.

The full irony of what had happened was only just beginning to sink in. She had agreed to come to the island only because Andreas had blackmailed her into doing so and because she couldn't afford to lose the income from her job. Yet when she was offered what amounted to financial security for life, not just for herself but more importantly for her beloved grandmother, as well as an immediate escape from her intolerable situation, she turned both down.

ANGRILY PIA started to hurry towards where Athena was lying sunning herself. After what she had just overheard there was no way she was not going to tell Athena what she thought of her. How dared she treat Saskia like that, trying to bribe her into leaving Andreas?

Andreas!

Pia came to an abrupt halt. Perhaps she ought to tell her brother what Athena had been up to and let him deal with her. Saskia had looked so dreadfully upset, and no wonder. Reluctantly Pia listened to the inner voice warning her that Andreas would not thank her for pre-empting his right to be the one to confront Athena. Turning on her heel, she walked back inside the villa in search of Andreas.

CHAPTER NINE

LESS THAN A third of the way along the path that circum-navigated the island Saskia stopped walking and turned round. She couldn't go on; she had had enough. Loving Andreas—being so close to him every day in one sense and yet with such an unbridgeable gap between them in all the senses that really mattered—was more than she could cope with. Her love for him, her longing for him, was tearing her apart.

Slowly she started to walk back to the villa. She had no idea what she was going to do—throw herself on Andreas's mercy and beg him to release her from their 'agreement'? There was no point in trying to tell him what Athena had done. He was hardly likely to believe her, not with his opinion of her, and besides, she didn't want him to know. If he did…once he did… Andreas was no fool, he was an astute, sharp-minded businessman, it wouldn't take him long to guess what had happened, how she felt, and that was something she could not endure.

Once she reached the villa Saskia went straight to 'her' room which, thankfully, was empty. The maid had been in and the bed was freshly made. Quickly removing her swimsuit, she went to have a shower.

'ANDREAS,' ATHENA purred seductively as she saw him coming out of his grandfather's office.

'Not now, Athena.' Andreas cut her short. He had spent the best part of the last couple of hours trying to come to terms with feelings he had never expected to have, never mind *wanted* to have, and now that he had come to a decision he was anxious to act on it without any delay, especially from Athena.

It was no use trying to hide the truth from himself any longer.

He had fallen in love with Saskia. How? Why? When? To his exasperation no amount of analytical self-probing on his part had been able to produce any kind of logical answers to such questions. All his heart, his body, his emotions, his very soul kept insisting over and over again was they wanted her; loved her; craved and needed her. If the logical-thinking part of him that was already fighting a desperate rearguard action should dare to argue, then his emotions would see to it that his life was no longer worth living.

But look at what she *is* he had tried to remind himself. But his emotions had refused to listen. He loved her as she was, past errors of judgement and all. Errors of *judgement*? Picking up men in bars…coming as near as dammit to selling herself to them—if not for money then certainly for the pseudo-love they had offered her.

It wasn't her fault, his heart had protested in loving defence. She had been deprived of her father's love as a child. She was simply trying to compensate for that. With love, *his* love, she could be made whole again. She would forget her past and so would he. What mattered was the here and now and the future they would share…a future which meant nothing to him without her in it.

And so it had continued, on and on, when he was

supposed to be working. In the end he had had no option other than to give in, and now he was on his way to find Saskia to tell her…ask her…to beg her if necessary.

'Is Saskia still outside?' he asked Athena, impatient to tell Saskia how he felt.

Athena's eyes narrowed. She knew that look in a man's eyes, and to see it now, in the eyes of the only man she wanted, was not to be tolerated. If Saskia couldn't be induced to leave Andreas then *he* must reject her, and Athena knew exactly how to make *that* happen.

'Oh…' Immediately she faked a look of concern, 'Didn't you know? She's gone for a walk…with Ari. I know you won't like me saying this, Andreas, but—well, we all know how much Ari likes women, and Saskia *has* been making it rather obvious that she reciprocates… Not whilst you're around, of course…'

'Andreas—' Pia tried to stop him several minutes later but he refused to stop or listen.

'Not now, Pia, whatever it is…' he said brusquely, before striding down the corridor towards his suite.

Goodness, but he looked angry, Pia reflected as she watched his departing back. Well, what she had to tell him wasn't going to lighten his bad mood, but he would have to be told. She knew that.

Andreas could hear the sound of the shower running as he walked into the bedroom and slammed the door behind him.

'Saskia?' he demanded, striding towards the bathroom and pulling open the door.

Saskia blanched as she saw him. She had just that second stepped out of the shower and wrapped a towel around her damp body—thank goodness.

'Why are you having a shower?' Andreas demanded suspiciously.

Saskia stared at him nonplussed.

'I've just been for a walk and it was hot and…'

Andreas could feel the shock of his jealousy jolt right through his body, exploding inside him, almost a physical pain. It furnished him with some very vivid and very sexual images of just why Saskia might want to cool down. Like any man in love, he couldn't bear the thought of his beloved in the arms of someone else, and he reacted predictably.

Taking hold of her, his fingers gripping painfully into the delicate flesh of her upper arms, he gritted jealously, 'You just couldn't wait, could you? Where did he take you?'

'He…?' Saskia started to protest, confused by both his words and his actions. 'What on earth…?'

But Andreas wasn't listening.

'Was it out in the open, where anyone could have seen you? Is *that* what you like, Saskia…demeaning yourself so completely that…? But of course you do. I already know that, don't I? You *want* to be treated badly, to be used and then discarded like a… Well, then, if that's the way you like it then let's see if *I* can come up to your expectations, shall we? If I can give you what you so obviously want.'

He was a man no longer in control of what he was doing, wanting passionately to stamp his possession on her—body and soul—to make her his and wipe from her memory all thoughts of any other man!

What on earth had happened to turn Andreas from the cool, remote man she was familiar with into the raw explosion of male fury and passion she was facing now?

Saskia wondered in bemusement. It was passion she could sense most strongly, she recognised dizzily. It emanated from him like a heat haze, drawing her into its danger and excitement, melting, burning away her own protective caution.

Wasn't this secretly what a part of her had *wanted* to happen? For him to look at her as he was doing now, with the fierce, elemental need of a man no longer able to fight off his own desire.

Somehow, seeing Andreas so close to losing control allowed her to give full reign to her own feelings and longings.

'You're mine,' Andreas was telling her rawly as he pulled her hard against his body. 'Mine, Saskia… And what is mine I mean to have full measure of,' he added thickly.

Saskia could feel her skin starting to quiver responsively where he was touching it. He slid his hands oh, so deliberately up her bare arm and over her shoulder, his fingertips caressing the nape of her neck. Blissfully she arched her spine, offering herself up to his touch, feeling the quiver-raising goosebumps on her skin moving deeper, growing stronger, as they became a pulse that echoed and then drove her heartbeat.

'Kiss me, Andreas…'

Had she actually said that? Demanded it in that unfamiliar husky little voice that sounded so sexy and made Andreas's eyes glitter even more hotly?

'Oh, I can promise you that I'm going to do far more than just kiss you,' Andreas assured her as his hands very deliberately removed the towel from her body. 'Far, far more,' he repeated sensually, before adding, 'But if a kiss is what you want…'

His hands were spread against her collarbone and her throat, his thumbs massaging her fragile bones, his lips brushing just the merest tantalising breath of heat against the pulse that raced so frantically beneath her skin.

'Where exactly is it you want me to kiss you, Saskia?' he was asking her. 'Here…? Here…? Here..?'

As his mouth moved tantalisingly over her throat and then her jaw, covering every inch of her face but her lips, Saskia heard herself start to moan softly with longing until, unable to endure any more of his delicious torment, she put her hand against his face and turned his mouth to hers, exhaling in a soft swoon of relief as she finally tasted the hard warmth she had been aching for.

'Andreas… Andreas…' She could hear herself whispering his name as she slid her fingers into his hair and clasped his head, probing the hard outline of his lips with small, frantic thrusts of her tongue-tip.

Over her shoulder Andreas caught sight of their entwined reflections in the mirror. Saskia's naked back view was as perfectly sculpted as that of any classical statue, but her body was composed of living, breathing flesh, and just the feel of her sweetly firm breasts pressing against him, never mind what the dedicated assault of her honey tongue was doing to him, totally obliterated everything but the way he felt about her.

Against the delicate pallor of her Celtic skin his hands looked shockingly male and dark as he caressed her, held her, moulded her so close to his body that he could taste her small gasp of sensual pleasure as she felt his arousal. His clothes were a hindrance he no longer wanted, but he couldn't make the time to remove them until he had punished that sexily tormenting tongue of hers for the way it was destroying his self-control.

He felt the deep, racking shudder of pleasure that ran right through her body as he opened his mouth on hers, taking into his domain full control of their kiss and of her.

Saskia gasped and trembled, yielding the sweet intimacy of her mouth and the soft-fleshed nakedness of her body to Andreas's dominance. What was happening between them was surely the pinnacle of her whole life, the reason she had been born. Here, in Andreas's arms, love and desire were coming together for her in the most perfect way possible.

Saskia had forgotten what she had been going to tell him, why it was so imperative for her to leave. *This* was what she had wanted to happen from the very first second she had set eyes on him.

Unable to bring himself to break the intoxicating sensuality of their shared kiss, Andreas picked Saskia up and carried her over to the bed. Whatever she had been before no longer mattered. From now on she would be his.

The heavy natural linen curtains Saskia had closed over the large windows before taking her shower diffused the strong sunlight outside, bathing the room in a softly muted glow that turned her fair skin almost ethereally translucent. As he laid her on the bed Andreas gave in to the temptation to caress the taut quivering peak of one breast with his lips, savouring it in a slow, careful exploration which made Saskia's whole body shake with sharply intense arousal.

'No, I don't want to rush this,' Andreas denied to her, his voice thick, almost cracking over the words as he refused the frantic pleas of her writhing body. 'I want to take my time and savour everything!' he emphasised as his hand caressed the breast he had just been suckling, his thumb tip etching unbearably erotic circles around the sensitively receptive nub of flesh.

'I want you so much,' Saskia whispered achingly. 'I want you...' She stopped, her eyes clouding with a mixture of anxiety and uncertainty as she heard her own voice and briefly recognised her own danger.

It was too late. Andreas had heard her. Pausing in the act of removing his clothes, he leaned over her, bracing himself so that the muscles in his arms corded tautly, capturing her awed gaze whilst he asked her rawly, 'Where do you want me, Saskia? Tell me... Show me...'

But he already knew the answer to his question because he had already lifted his hand from the bed and brushed his knuckles in the gentlest of touches the full length of the centre of her body, letting it come to rest palm-down against the soft swelling of her most intimate heart.

'You haven't answered my question, Saskia,' he reminded her softly, as his fingertips drew delicate circles of pleasure against her, so jaw-clenching desirable that Saskia thought she might actually faint from the heat and intensity of the longing they were arousing.

'Tell me...tell me what you want,' Andreas was insisting, spacing each word between kisses so ravishingly tender that Saskia felt as though she was melting.

In the cocoon of her own private world he had become for Saskia the lodestone that drew her, the focus of everything she was experiencing, of everything she was and ever wanted to be, the centre of her world.

'I want you,' she responded feverishly to him. 'I want you, Andreas. I...' She shuddered, unable to say any more because Andreas was kissing her, sealing her mouth with a kiss that was a hot, passionate brand of possession. As he wrapped his arms around her Saskia clung to him shyly, stroking the side of his face.

'Look at me,' he demanded.

Hesitatingly she did so, the melting, soft, languorous longing of her gaze entrapped by the hot, fierce glitter of his.

Very slowly and tenderly he began to caress her. Saskia felt as though her whole body was going to dissolve with her longing for him, her need of him.

She reached out to touch his bare shoulder, his arm, and made a helpless little sound of taut female need against his throat as she pressed her lips to it.

Beneath his hands her body softened and responded magically, welcomingly, as though his touch was a special key. But *he* was the key to what she was feeling, Saskia acknowledged hazily, lost fathoms—oceans—deep in her love for him.

'There isn't going to be much time...I want you too much,' he told her almost bluntly, softening the words with another hotly passionate kiss that made her hips lift achingly against him whilst her whole body writhed in longing for him.

'Next time we can take things more slowly,' Andreas gasped harshly against her breast, his voice and actions revealing his increasing need.

Next time... Saskia felt as though she might die from happiness. 'Next time' meant that he shared her feelings, that he felt the same way as she did.

It seemed to Saskia almost as though the air between them throbbed with the intensity of their shared passion, with the way their bodies synchronised together with a perfection surely only given to true lovers.

Each sigh, each gasp, each heartbeat served only to bind her closer to him, emotionally as well as physically, until she was captive to him and her desire, her love, was laid as bare to him as her quivering body.

When he finally whispered to her, 'Now, Saskia... Oh, God, now!' she knew her body had given him its most eager assent before her lips could even begin to frame the words she wanted to say. Automatically she was already wrapping the slim length of her legs around his waist, raising up to meet him, to feel him. She heard him cry out as he entered her, a sound of both torment and triumph, and then he was filling her with his own unique intimate, heavy warmth, and her body, pausing only to tense briefly in sweetly virginal shock, welcomed each ever deepening thrust of him within her.

Andreas felt her body's unexpected resistance, his brain and his emotions even registered their shock at what it meant, but his body refused to react to that knowledge. It loved the hot snug fit of her around him, holding and caressing him, urging him to forget what he had just experienced and to satisfy the age-old demand her femaleness was making on his maleness. Deeper, harder, stronger, until you reach the deepest heart of me, each delicately soft contraction of her flesh around his urged him. Deeper, stronger, surer, until you are *there*. Yes, there...*there*...

Andreas felt as though his heart and lungs might burst as he drove them both to the place where they could finally fly free.

Saskia cried out in softly sweet awe and relish as she experienced for herself what true completion was...what it truly meant to be a woman, completely fulfilled, elevated to a place, a state...an emotion so piercingly intense that it filled her eyes with hot, happy exhausted tears.

Someone was trembling... Was it her...or was it both of them? She had heard Andreas groan in those final unbelievable seconds before he had wrapped his arms securely around her and then sent them both hurtling into infinity, calling out her name in a way that had made her tingle with raw emotion.

As he fought to regain control of his breathing, and himself, Andreas looked down at Saskia.

She was crying, huge silent tears. Of pain? Because of *him*...because he had...?

Even now his thoughts skidded away from the reality, the truth that his brain was trying to impose on him. She couldn't have been a virgin... It was impossible.

But his self-anger and guilt told him that it wasn't, and she had been. Unforgivably, he had hurt her and made her cry, selfishly taking his pleasure from her at the price of her innocence, so unable to control what he felt for her that he had not been able to stop when he knew that he should have done.

Sickened by his own behaviour, he pulled away from her.

'Andreas...' Saskia reached out towards him uncertainly. Why was he withdrawing from her? Why wasn't he holding her, caressing her...*loving* and reassuring her?

'What is it...what is wrong?' she begged him.

'Do you really need to ask?' Andreas responded tersely. 'Why didn't you tell me...*stop* me...?'

The anger in his voice was driving away the sweet mist

of her joy and replacing it with anxiety and despair. It was obvious to her now that what had been so wonderful, so perfect, so *unique* for her had been nowhere near the same kind of experience for Andreas.

Andreas was furious with himself for not somehow having had the insight to know. She had been a virgin, and he, damn him, had practically forced himself on her... He was disgusted with himself, his pride scorched not just by his actions but his complete misreading of her.

'You *should* have stopped me,' he repeated as he got off the bed and went into the bathroom, returning with a towel wrapped around his naked body and his robe, which he handed to Saskia, and sitting down on the bed, turning away from her as she tried to put it on.

What would he say if she were to tell him that the last thing she had wanted was for him to stop? Saskia wondered wretchedly. Her hands were shaking so much she could hardly pull the robe on, never mind fasten it, and when Andreas turned to look at her he gave an impatient, irritated sigh and pushed her hands out of the way, pulling it on properly for her.

'You aren't safe to be let out alone. You realise that, don't you?' he exploded savagely. 'Even if *I* hadn't, Aristotle—'

'Aristotle!' Saskia picked his name up with loathing in her voice and in her eyes. She shuddered, and told him fiercely, 'No—never... He's loathsome and...'

'But you went for a walk with him...'

'No, I didn't,' Saskia protested.

'Athena said you'd gone for a walk,' Andreas insisted, but Saskia wouldn't let him finish.

'Yes, I did...on my own. There were things I wanted...' She stopped, lowering her head and looking away from him. Then she told him in a tear-filled voice, 'I want to go home, Andreas. I can't...'

He knew what she was saying; of course he did, Andreas acknowledged—and why! Of *course* she wanted to get away from him after what he had done...the way he had...

'You should have told me.' He stopped her sharply. 'If I'd known that you were a virgin...'

He might be concerned about taking her virginity but he obviously had no compunction at all about breaking her heart, Saskia decided angrily. For her the loss of her emotional virginity was something that hurt far more— and would continue to hurt.

How could she have been stupid enough to think he felt the same way about her as she did about him? She must have been crazy...*had* been crazy, she recognised grimly. Crazy with love for him!

'I thought...' she heard him saying, but now it was her turn not to allow him to finish.

'I know what you thought,' she cut in with sharp asperity. 'You've already made it very plain *what* you thought of me, Andreas. You thought I was some cheap, silly woman throwing herself at you because of your money. And when I tried to explain you wouldn't let me. You *wanted* to believe the worst of me. I suppose that Greek male pride of yours wouldn't allow you to acknowledge that you might just possibly be wrong...'

Andreas looked at her. His jealousy had led to this... had led to his unforgivably appalling treatment of her. He ached to be able to take her in his arms, to kiss away the traces of tears still on her face, to hold her and whisper to her how much he loved her, how much he wanted to protect her and care for her...how much he wished he could wipe away the wrong he had done her, the pain he had caused her... He ached too, if he was honest, to lie her down on the bed beside him, to remove the robe she was wearing and to kiss every silky inch of her adorable body, to tell her how he felt about her, to show her too. But of course he could do no such thing...not now...

To keep his mind off what he was feeling...off the way he wanted her, he told her gruffly, 'Explain to me now.'

For a moment Saskia was tempted to refuse, but what was the point? She *would* tell him, and then she would tell him that she intended to leave—but she certainly wouldn't tell him why.

Just for an irrational silly female heartbeat of time she ached for him to reach for her, to stop hurting her with words she did not want to hear and to caress and kiss her until her poor deluded heart believed once again that he loved her as she did him.

But thankfully she had enough instinct for self-preservation left to stop herself from telling him so. Instead she began to explain about Megan and Mark and Lorraine.

'She made you do *what*?' Andreas demanded angrily.

She was hesitantly explaining about Lorraine, and her insistence that Saskia make herself look more sexy, when, after a brief rap on the door, Pia burst in and told them, 'Grandfather has arrived. He wants to see both of you.'

'I'd better get dressed,' Saskia mumbled self-consciously.

Pia seemed oblivious to her embarrassment, adding urgently, 'Oh, and Andreas, there's something I want to talk to you about...before you see Grandfather.'

'If you're going to ask for an advance on your allowance,' Saskia heard Andreas saying hardily to Pia as he walked with her to the door, allowing Saskia to make her own escape to the bathroom, 'you haven't picked a very good time.'

CHAPTER TEN

SASKIA GLARED reprovingly at the reflection glowing back at her from the bedroom mirror. Her own reflection. The reflection of a woman whose body had enjoyed in full measure every nuance of sensual satisfaction and was proud to proclaim that fact to the world.

That was *not* how she wanted to look when she confronted Andreas's grandfather—the man who was ultimately responsible for her being here…the man who did not think she was good enough for his grandson…the man who preferred to see him marry Athena. Neither did she want *Andreas* to see her like this.

Why on earth couldn't her idiotic body see beyond the delicious fulfilment it was currently basking in and instead think ahead to the loneliness and pain her emotions already knew were lying in store?

Andreas had returned to their room very briefly after Pia's interruption, showering and dressing quickly and then informing her that, although his grandfather was insisting that he wanted to meet her as soon as possible, there were certain matters he needed to discuss with him in private first.

'It won't take very long,' he had told her grimly, before striding out of the room without giving her a chance to tell him that right now, for her own sanity and safety, she wanted to get as far away from him as fast as she could.

Soon, now, he would be coming back for her, to take her and introduce her formally to his grandfather.

Saskia pulled an angry face at her still glowing reflection. She looked, she admitted angrily, the perfect picture of a woman in love. Even her eyes had a new sparkle, a certain glint that said she was hugging to herself a wonderful, special secret.

She had tried over and over again to tell her love-crazed body just what the real situation was, but it simply refused to listen. And so now... She gave a nervous start as she heard the bedroom door opening...

Andreas took a deep breath before reaching out for the bedroom door handle and grasping it firmly.

Pia had been so incensed, so protective and angry on Saskia's behalf, that it had taken her several minutes to become calm enough to spill out, in a way that made sense, the conversation she had overheard between Athena and Saskia.

'Athena actually tried to bribe Saskia to leave you. She promised her a million pounds if she did. Of course Saskia refused, but I don't see why Athena should be allowed to get away with such insulting and...and offensive behaviour. Grandfather should be told what she's really like—and if you aren't prepared to tell him...' she had threatened darkly.

'Andreas?' she had demanded when he made no response, obviously puzzled at his lack of reaction, but Andreas had still been trying to come to terms with the 'insulting' and 'offensive' behaviour *he* had already inflicted on Saskia. Now, to learn what Athena had done and how nobly Saskia had behaved made him feel… How *could* he have been so wrong about her, so judgemental and…and biased?

A tiny inner voice told him that he already knew the answer. Right from the first second he had set eyes on her there had been something—a sharp warning thrill of sensation and, even more dangerously, of emotion— which he had instantly tried to suppress. His infernal pride had resented the fact that he could fall in love with a woman who was so obvious, and because he had listened to his pride, and not his heart, he had witlessly destroyed something that could have been the most wonderful, the most *precious* part of his life. Unless… Unless Saskia could be persuaded to give him a second chance…

But, whether or not she would allow him the chance to prove his love for her, there was something that *had* to be done, a reparation that *had* to be made. He was Greek enough to think that Saskia should bear his name well before there was any chance of the world knowing that she might bear his child. She had given him her innocence and in exchange he would give her his protection, whether or not she wanted it.

He had told his grandfather exactly what he planned to do, adding truthfully that Saskia was far more important to him than wealth and position and even the love and respect of his grandfather himself.

He had even been tempted to refuse to allow his grandfather to meet her, rather than subject Saskia to any possible hurt or upset, but there was no way he wanted his grandfather to think that he was hiding Saskia from him because he feared she would not be good enough for him.

Not good enough! She was *too* good, *too* wonderful...*too* precious...

His final act before heading back to the bedroom had been to tell Athena to leave the island immediately.

'Don't bother to try and persuade my grandfather to allow you to stay. He won't,' he had warned her truthfully.

Now he hesitated before going into the bedroom. He could see Saskia standing waiting for him, and his heart rocked on a huge surge of longing and love for her.

She looked as radiant as a bride, her eyes sparkling, her mouth curved in a smile that was a cross between pure joy and a certain secret, newly discovered womanliness. She looked...

She looked like a woman who had just left the arms and the bed of the man she loved.

But the moment she saw him her expression changed; her eyes became shadowed, her body tense and wary.

Helplessly Andreas closed his eyes, swamped by a wave of love and guilt. He longed more than anything right now to close the door on the rest of the world, to take her in his arms and hold her there for ever whilst he begged for her forgiveness and for the opportunity to spend the rest of his life showing her how much he loved her.

But he had his responsibilities, and primarily, right now, he had to fulfil the promise he had just made to his grandfather that he would introduce Saskia to him.

For his grandfather's sake he trusted that the older man would remember the promise *he* had made that he would treat Saskia gently.

As Andreas crossed the room and took hold of her hand Saskia shrank back from him, terrified of betraying her feelings, knowing that she was trembling from head to foot simply because of the warmth of his hand clasping hers.

She knew that he was bound to make some irritated, impatient comment about the role she was supposed to be playing, but instead he simply released her hand and told her in a low voice, 'I'm sorry to have put you through this my…Saskia…'

'It's what you brought me here for,' Saskia reminded him brutally, not daring to look at him. Surely she must be imagining that raw note of remorse in his voice.

As they left the room the pretty little maid who looked after it came in, and Andreas paused to say something to her in Greek before following Saskia into the corridor.

It was only natural in the circumstances, Saskia knew, that Andreas should take hold of her hand again and close the distance between them, so that when they walked into the cool, simply furnished room that gave out onto the main patio area they did so with every outward appearance of a couple deeply in love. But what was surely less natural, and almost certainly unwise, was the sense of warmth and security that she got from being so close to him.

To try and distract herself from the effect Andreas's proximity was having on her, Saskia looked to where his sister and mother were standing talking to an elderly white-haired man Saskia knew must be Andreas's grandfather.

As they walked towards him he started to turn round, and Saskia could hear Andreas saying formally, 'Grandfather, I'd like to introduce Saskia to you.'

But Saskia had stopped listening, her attention focused instead on the familiar features of the man now facing her. He was the same man she had seen in the street in Athens, the man who had seemed so unwell and whom she had been so concerned about. He didn't look ill now though. He was smiling broadly at them both, coming forward to clasp Saskia's free hand in both of his in a grip heart-rockingly similar to that of his grandson.

'There is no need to introduce her to me, 'Reas.' He laughed. 'Your beautiful fiancée and I have already met.'

Saskia could see how much he was enjoying the shocking effect of his announcement on his family. He was obviously a man who liked to feel he was in control of things…people…who liked to challenge and surprise them. But where that trait in Andreas had angered her, in his grandfather she found it almost endearing.

'You and Saskia have already met?' Andreas was repeating, frowning heavily as he looked from his grandfather to Saskia.

'Yes. In Athens,' his grandfather confirmed before Saskia could say anything. 'She was very kind to an old man, and very concerned for him too. My driver told me that you had expressed your concern for my health to him,' he told Saskia in a broadly smiling aside. 'And I have to confess I did find that walk in the heat plus the wait I had for you to return from the Acropolis a trifle… uncomfortable. But not, I suspect, as uncomfortable as Andreas was, arriving at my office to discover that I had cancelled our meeting,' he added with a chuckle.

'You didn't really think I'd allow my only grandson to marry a woman I knew nothing about, did you?' he asked Andreas with a little swagger that made her hide a small smile. He was so very Greek, so very macho. She knew she should be annoyed, but he was so pleased with himself that she didn't have the heart to be cross.

Andreas, though, as it soon became obvious, was not so easily appeased.

'You decided to check up on Saskia—?' he thundered, giving his grandfather a hard look.

'You have definitely made a good choice, Andreas,' his grandfather interrupted him. 'She is charming…and kind. Not many young women would have taken the time to look after an old man who was a stranger to them. I had to meet her for myself, Andreas. I know you, and—'

'What you have done is an insult to her,' Andreas cut him off coldly, whilst Saskia stared at him in astonishment. Andreas defending and protecting *her*? What was this? And then, abruptly, she remembered that he was simply acting out a role…the role of a loving protective fiancé.

'And let me tell you this, Grandfather,' Andreas was continuing. 'Whether you approve of Saskia or not makes no difference to me. I *love* her, and I always will, and there are no threats, no bribes, no blandishments you can offer that could in any way change that.'

There was a brief pause before the older man nodded his head.

'Good,' he announced. 'I'm glad to hear it. A woman like Saskia deserves to be the focus of her husband's heart and life. She reminds me very much of my Elisabeth,' he added, his eyes suddenly misty. 'She had that same kindness, that same concern for others.' Suddenly he started to frown as he caught sight of Saskia's ring.

'What is *that* she is wearing?' he demanded. 'It is not fit for a Demetrios bride. I'm surprised at you, Andreas…a paltry plain solitaire. She shall have my Elisabeth's ring, and—'

'No.' The harshness in Andreas's voice made Saskia

tense. Was he going to tell his grandfather that it was all a lie? Was the thought of Saskia wearing something as sacred to their family as his dead grandmother's ring too much for him to endure?

'No,' he continued. 'If Saskia wants a different ring then she shall choose one herself. For now I want her to wear the one *I* chose for her. A diamond as pure and shiningly beautiful as she is herself.'

Saskia could see Andreas's mother's and sister's jaws dropping, as was her own at such an unexpectedly tender and almost poetic declaration.

Ridiculously tears blurred her eyes as she looked down at the solitaire. It *was* beautiful. She thought so every time she put it on. But for her to treasure such a ring it would have to be given with love. It was the commitment it was given with that made it of such value to a woman in love, not its financial worth.

But Andreas's grandfather was brushing aside such irrelevancies, and demanding jovially, 'Very well, but what I want to know now is when you plan to get married. I can't live for ever, Andreas, and if I am to see your sons…'

'Grandfather…' Andreas began warningly.

LATER, AFTER A celebratory lunch and rather more vintage champagne than had perhaps been wise, Saskia made her way with solemn concentration back to her room. Andreas was with her, as befitted a loving and protective fiancé.

Outside the room Andreas touched her lightly on her arm, so that she was forced to stop and look at him.

'I'm sorry about what happened in Athens,' he told her, his brusqueness giving way to anger as he added, 'My grandfather had no right to subject you to—'

'In his shoes you would have done exactly the same thing,' Saskia interrupted him quietly, immediately leaping to his grandfather's defence. 'It's a perfectly natural reaction. I can remember still the way my grandmother reacted the first time I went out on a date.' She laughed, and then stopped as she saw that Andreas was shaking his head.

'Of course she would be protective of you,' he agreed flatly. 'But didn't my grandfather realise the danger you could have been in? What if he had mistimed his "accidental" meeting with you? You were alone in an unfamiliar city. He had countermanded my instructions to your driver by telling him to keep out of sight until he saw him return to his own car.'

'It was broad daylight, Andreas,' Saskia pointed out calmly. But she could see that Andreas wasn't going to be appeased. 'Well, at least your grandfather won't be trying to convince you that you should marry Athena anymore,' she offered placatingly as they walked into the bedroom. She came to an abrupt halt as she saw the new cases Andreas had bought her for their trip in the middle of the bedroom floor. 'What…?' she began unsteadily but Andreas didn't let her finish.

'I told Maria to pack for both of us. We're booked onto the first flight in the morning for Heathrow.'

'We're leaving?'

Even as she spoke Saskia knew that showing her shock was a giveaway piece of folly. Of course they were leaving. After all, there was no need for Andreas to keep her here any more. His grandfather had made it very plain during lunch that Athena would no longer be welcome beneath his roof.

'We don't have any option,' Andreas replied flatly. 'You

heard my grandfather. Now that he's been given a clean bill of health he's itching to find something to occupy him. Organising our wedding and turning it into something between a lavish extravaganza worthy of a glossy magazine and a chance to gather as many of his business cronies under one roof as he can isn't going to be an opportunity he'll want to miss out on. And my mother and sister will be just as bad.' He started to scowl. 'Designer outfits, a wedding dress that could take months to make, plans to extend the villa so that it can accommodate the children my mother and my grandfather are so determined we're going to have...'

Greedily Saskia drank in every word. The mental image he was creating for her, the blissful pictures he was painting were becoming more alluring with every word he said. Mistily she allowed herself to dream about what she knew to be impossible—and then Andreas's next words sent her into shocked freefall.

'We need to get married immediately. We just don't have the time for that kind of delay. Not after... If you are already carrying my child then...'

'What are you saying?' Saskia protested, white-faced. 'You can't be serious. We *can't* get married just because...'

'Just because what?' Andreas challenged her bitterly. 'Because you were a virgin, an innocent who had never known a man before? I...I am Greek, Saskia, and there is no way I would *ever* abandon any child I had fathered. Under the circumstances there is nothing else we *can* do.'

'You're only half-Greek,' Saskia heard herself reminding him dizzily, before adding, 'And anyway I may not even be pregnant. In fact I'm sure I'm not.'

Andreas gave her a dry, almost withering look.

'And you're an expert on such things, of course. You, a woman who hasn't even...'

'They say you don't always...not the first time...' Saskia told him lamely, but she could see from his face that he had as little faith in that particular old wives' tale as she did herself.

'I don't want this, Andreas,' she insisted, trying another tack. Her voice and her body had both begun to shake with shock at what Andreas intended.

'Even if I am to...to have a child...these days that doesn't mean... I could bring it up by myself...'

'What on?' he challenged her. 'Not the one million pounds you turned down from Athena, obviously.'

Saskia's eyes looked bewildered at the way he'd slipped the thrust up under her guard.

'A child needs more than money. Much, much more,' she defended herself quickly. How did he know about Athena's offer to her? Athena herself wouldn't have told him. 'A child needs love,' she continued.

'Do you think *I* don't know that?' Andreas shot back. 'After all, surely I am far better placed to know it than you, Saskia. I had the love of both my parents as a child, and I can promise you I would *never* allow a child of mine to grow up without my love.'

He stopped abruptly as he heard the quick indrawn gasp of pain she had given, his eyes darkening with remorse.

'Saskia, my beloved heart, I am so sorry. I didn't mean to hurt you, just to make you understand that I could no more walk away from our child than I can from you.'

Saskia stared at him, unable to speak, to move, to breathe as she listened to the raw fervency of his declaration. He was acting. He had to be. He *didn't* love her. She *knew* that. And somehow hearing him say to her the words she so much ached to hear whilst knowing they were lies filled her with more anguish than she could bear.

Tugging frantically at the ring he had given her, she started to pull it off, her eyes dark with anger, sparkling with tears of pride and pain whilst Andreas watched her as he had been watching her all through lunch, and then afterwards when the wine she had drunk had relaxed her.

'I felt so angry when Athena offered Saskia that money,' Pia had told him passionately. 'And so proud of her. She loves you so much. I used to think that no one could ever be good enough for you, my wonderful brother, but now I know I was wrong. She loves you every bit as much as you deserve to be loved, as I one day want to love the man I marry...'

'She is perfect for you, darling,' his mother had whispered to him.

'She is a beautiful young woman with an even more beautiful heart,' his grandfather had said emotionally.

There had been one unguarded moment after lunch, when his grandfather had been teasing her about something and she had turned to him, as though seeking his protection. The look in her eyes had made him ache to snatch her up and carry her away somewhere he could have her all to himself and create that look over and over again.

Finally she managed to pull the ring off, holding it out to him she told him, head held high, 'There is no way I would ever marry a man who does not love me.'

Andreas closed his eyes, replayed the words to make sure he hadn't misheard them, and then opened his eyes again and walked purposefully towards her. He was about to take the biggest gamble he had ever taken in his entire life. If he lost he would lose everything. If he won...

He took a deep breath and asked Saskia softly, 'Shouldn't that be you wouldn't ever marry a man you did not love?'

Saskia froze, her face going white and then a soft, deepening shade of pink.

'I…that was what I meant,' she began, and then stopped as panic overwhelmed her. 'I can't marry you, Andreas,' she protested as he closed the distance between them, masterfully sweeping her up into his arms.

'And I won't let you go, Saskia,' he told her in a low, throbbing voice.

'Because of what happened…because there might be a baby?' she guessed, but the words had to be mumbled because Andreas was holding her so tightly, his lips brushing irresistibly tender kisses against her throat and then her jaw, moving closer and closer to her mouth.

'Because of that,' he agreed, whispering the words against her lips. 'And this…and you…'

'Me?' Saskia started to squeak, but Andreas wouldn't let her.

Cupping her face instead, he looked down into her eyes, his own grave with pain, heavy with remorse, hot with love and desire, as he begged her, 'Please give me a chance to show you how things could be between us, Saskia. To show you how good it could be, how good it *will* be…'

'What are you trying to say?' Saskia demanded dizzily.

Still cupping her face, Andreas told her, 'I'm trying to say with words what my emotions, my heart, my soul and my body have already told you, my beloved heart, my adored, precious love. Surely you must have guessed, felt how it was for me when we made love?'

Lifting her head so that she could look into his eyes, search them to see if she actually dared believe what she was hearing, Saskia felt her heart starting to thud in a heady mixture of joy and excitement. No man could possibly fake the way Andreas was looking at her, and if that wasn't enough his body was giving her a very distinct and intimate message of its own. Unable to help herself Saskia started to blush a little as she felt her own body respond to Andreas's arousal.

'I...I thought that must just be sex,' she told him bravely.

'What have I said?' she demanded in bewilderment when Andreas started to laugh.

'My dearest love,' he told her, still laughing, 'if I hadn't already had incontrovertible proof of your innocence, that remark would have furnished me with it. *Any* woman who had experienced "just sex" would have known immediately that—' He stopped and smiled down at her, tenderly kissing her before telling her gruffly.

'No. Why should I bother to explain? After all, there's never going to be any way that you will know what it is to have "just sex". You and I, Saskia, will be making love, sharing love, giving one another love for all our lives.'

'Oh, Andreas,' Saskia whispered deliriously as he pulled her firmly into his arms.

'No, Andreas, we can't,' she protested five minutes later as he carried her towards the bed and started to undress her.

'All my clean clothes are packed...I won't have anything to wear...and...'

'Good,' Andreas informed her without the remotest hint of remorse. 'I can't think of anything I want more right now than to have you naked in my bed with no means of escape.'

'Mmm... That's funny,' Saskia told him impishly. 'I was thinking exactly the same thing myself!'

Epilogue

'WELL, YOUR GRANDFATHER may not have got his own way over our wedding, but he certainly wasn't going to allow us to have a quiet family christening!' Saskia laughed with Andreas as they both surveyed the huge crowd of people filling the recently completed and refurbished 'special occasions' suite at the group's flagship British hotel.

'Mmm... Are you sure that Robert will be okay with him?' Andreas asked anxiously as he focused with fatherly concern on the other side of the room, where his grandfather was proudly showing off his three-month-old great-grandson to his friends and business cronies.

'Well, as your grandfather keeps on reminding us, he's held far more babies than you or I in his time,' Saskia said, laughing.

'Maybe, but none of them has been *our* son,' Andreas returned promptly, adding, 'I think I'd better go and retrieve him, Sas. He looks as though he might be starting to get fretful, and he never finished that last feed...'

'Talk about doting fathers,' Pia murmured to Saskia as they both watched Andreas hurrying proprietorially towards his son. 'I always knew that Andreas would be a good father, mind you...'

Saskia smiled at her as she watched her husband expertly holding their son—born nine months and one day exactly after their quiet wedding, tactfully arriving three weeks after his predicted birth date. But of course only she and Andreas knew *that*…just as only they knew as yet that by the time he reached his first birthday he would have a brother or a sister.

'Isn't that a bit too soon?' Andreas had protested when she had first told him her suspicions, and Saskia had blushed and then laughed, remembering, as she was sure Andreas was as well, that *she* had been the one to initiate their first lovemaking after Robert's birth.

Andreas was the most wonderful father, and an even more wonderful husband and lover. Saskia gave a small sigh, a look darkening her eyes that Andreas immediately recognised.

If his mother was surprised to be suddenly handed her grandson whilst Andreas insisted that there was something he needed to discuss with his wife in private, she gave no sign of it, going instead to join Saskia's grandmother, with whom she had already formed a close bond.

'Andreas! No, we *can't*,' Saskia protested as Andreas led her to the most luxurious of the hotel's refurbished bedrooms and locked the door.

'Why not?' he teased her. 'We own the hotel and we are married—and right now I want you so much.'

'Mmm… Andreas…' Saskia sighed as his lips found the exquisitely tender cord in her throat that always and unfailingly responded to the sweet torment of his lips.

'Mmm… Andreas…what?' he mouthed against her skin.

But Saskia didn't make any verbal response, instead

pulling his head down towards her own, her mouth opening sweetly beneath his.

'I knew the first moment I set eyes on you that you were a wanton woman.' Andreas laughed tenderly. '*My wanton woman...*'

* * * * *